CRIME S

Maurice Gee is one of New Zealand's best-known writers. He has won the James Tait Black Memorial Prize in Britain and numerous awards and prizes in New Zealand. He is the author of both adult and children's novels, including the award-winning trilogy *Plumb*. He lives in Wellington with his wife and has two daughters and a son.

by the same author

PLUMB

MEG

SOLE SURVIVOR

PROWLERS

THE BURNING BOY

GOING WEST

MAURICE GEE

Crime Story

faber and faber

LONDON · BOSTON

First published in New Zealand and Australia in 1994
by Penguin Books New Zealand Ltd
First published in Great Britain in 1995
by Faber and Faber Limited
3 Queen Square London WC1N 3AU
This UK paperback edition first published in 1996

Printed in England by Clays Ltd, St Ives plc

A CIP record for this book is
available from the British Library

ISBN 0–571–17331–4

2 4 6 8 10 9 7 5 3 1

For Abi

Acknowledgements

'The Dead One', from *Evening Land: aftonland*, by
Pär Lagerkvist, translated by W. H. Auden and
Leif Sjöberg, Souvenir Press, 1977

I would like to thank the Katherine Mansfield
Memorial Trust for awarding me its ECNZ
Katherine Mansfield Memorial Fellowship, 1992.
My thanks also go to the Electricity Corporation
of New Zealand for sponsoring the fellowship,
and to the Queen Elizabeth II Arts Council of
New Zealand.

I would also like to thank the many people who
helped me with advice – medical, financial and
criminal – for this novel.

The characters in *Crime Story* are imaginary. No
likeness is intended to any person living or dead.

1

One

He looked like them and moved like them but knew he must not open his mouth. Walk fast so no one's got the time to ask any questions, but not too fast or they'll notice you. Up past the bookshop, up the path by the graveyard. Look like you're going to a lecture, is that what they call the bloody things?

His clothes were dead right, they couldn't be better. Jeans like his were coming down the hill, sneakers like his, though half of them were Reeboks and his were only Lasers. He'd look in shoe cupboards and get himself a pair of Reeboks soon. And get a sweatshirt with a university name. Uppsala. Where was that? Texas State. Or maybe he should look for one that said Cubs or Bears, although he could not wear a name when he was out working.

He crossed the quad. That was what they called it, because he'd heard a girl say, 'Meet you back here in the quad' when he'd passed through last week, sussing out Kelburn. He strode under the glass roof, with the library on his left. How did you get in there and get out again? And why would you want to anyway? Books made him suspicious. He felt that they were a part of some big con.

Smokers were sitting on the steps. They had the sour look of people kicked out and he went amongst them, turning left and right, knowing he was okay, he could sit down and light up and no one would think he didn't belong. But he had come without his cigarettes. Most students didn't smoke, he'd noticed last week, and he wasn't going to do a thing to make himself stand out. He wanted a smoke to calm his nerves and he inhaled secretly in the grey air.

9

He joined the students dodging cars on Kelburn Parade, then slowed down on the footpath. Out here he knew what to do. He felt like a shark in the streets, swimming round, waiting for something to swallow. When he worked in the Hutt or out in Miramar it was like the mudflats, but here it was like nosing up the side of a reef, coming from deep down towards the houses in the trees. Rosser grinned. He felt his teeth shining and air like water moving in his mouth.

'Got the time?' a student asked – neat and clean she was, pale jeans and shirt, shoes as white as milk, blue ribbon banded on her forehead. She should have her own watch, a gold Tissot, a present from Daddy. Easy to snatch her bag and run – be up those steps and out of sight, flick of his tail – but he didn't do bag-snatching any more. Showed his teeth at her instead, hooked his sleeve back with his little finger, bared his watch; made her turn her head on one side, and then walked on.

'Thanks,' she called. He didn't look back, kept walking round the curve, and the university showed itself again, twin towers, red and grey, with people in offices eight storeys high, working on a level with him as he went by. He wondered what they did in there, what was so important. All of it was a con and the way he got his own money just as honest to him. He crossed the road and went into a street that doubled back on a higher level. Swam into it, half pace. Nothing fast and nothing slow. He had to look as if he knew where he was going. See the chance and take it, then vanish down a hole. They've seen a student in the street, that's all. He'll sink into the quad, past the graveyard, and then into the city, where he's lost.

If this street gave him nothing, the next one would or the one after that. Sometimes he felt drunk with it – the hundreds of houses waiting for him, all in a row.

The dog came first, with its belly naked and its legs like a dwarf. It pulled the woman into the road but she jerked it back while she slammed her gate, then let it lift its leg on the agapanthus by the fence.

'That'll do,' Rosser told himself. The woman looked about fifty, which probably meant her old man wasn't retired but the kids were gone. The house would be empty with any luck. She crossed the road, then stopped to let the dog shit, fair in the middle of the footpath, and rolled the turds over the kerb with her shoe. They made a pile in the gutter, shining like cheerios. A dachshund. They didn't go for rottweilers round here.

He turned his eyes left as he passed her, and she the same – cancelled out the shitting, cancelled each other out – but he'd had a look at her while it was going on. Watch and shoes, and even the dog-lead, showed that she only bought the best. Her dog was probably pedigree and mated with its own kind. It wheezed like it had asthma, dragging her along. Rosser grinned. She was taking it for its daily walk, or maybe to the butcher for a piece of fillet steak, but on the way back she'd have to carry the bloody thing. He could give himself a clear ten minutes in her house.

Opposite the gate he looked back and saw her dragged from sight around the bend, her skinny legs, her skinny butt – she probably went to jazzercise. He put his foot on a brick fence and pulled his shoelace undone and tied it again, getting the lines of sight worked out. No one could see him from the downside, the houses were below street level there. Up top they were hidden by trees. One leaned its second storey over the branches but the windows angled southwards towards Pencarrow Head. The risk came from people in the street or in their gardens.

He took his chance, crossed over, and went into the cutting by the gate. It was like a cave, with agapanthus growing up each side and oozing gluey sap from butchered leaves. 'Dog on Duty' the gate said. 'Bloody liars,' Rosser grinned. That wheezing dachshund wasn't a dog. A good drop kick would lift it clean over the neighbour's fence. He opened the gate and stepped inside; stood motionless, listening; then walked up the path as if he belonged, switching on a smile as the windows came in sight. 'Is Clyde at home?' he would ask if anyone was there. People didn't think you could make up Clyde.

A car went by down in the road, close enough to jump on the roof. Volvo. Volvo country. The flying brick. He wouldn't have one even if he won it as a prize. The car he would get one day was a Porsche, wait and see. A Porsche for driving and a Mercedes for the garage. A Volvo didn't have any class.

He went on to the front porch and knocked at the door,

loud enough for someone inside but too soft for the neighbours. Waited for the grandma to climb out of her chair, though they didn't keep grandmas much in this sort of place. He felt easy on the porch. He was going to have a house like this one day, though not in Kelburn, with dog shit on the footpath and Volvos all over the place – on a hill out the Hutt, next door to the millionaires, and another one in Sydney, by the harbour. 'I'm King of Crime,' he whispered to himself, and knocked again. No one came.

He went around the back, deep in a path between the side wall and a hedge. They looked as if they might have a gardener, some old pensioner growing radishes, he needed to see. Hi, I'm looking for Clyde: he had it ready. But an empty glasshouse, growing ferns, a birdbath with a sparrow, a flymo on the half-cut lawn – that was all. A padlocked shed. A seagrass chair unravelling underneath a plum tree. I'm in, he thought, and tried the back door, and Christ the bloody thing opened, just like that. He almost stepped back. Someone had to be at home. But he waited, one foot in, one foot out, breathing soft. 'Clyde, you at home?' The woman had looked too sharp and mean to leave her door open, she looked the sort for deadbolts and alarms.

After a moment Rosser stepped inside. He wiped the handle with his handkerchief and closed the door softly. All right. He took his rubber gloves out, a size too small, and felt like a surgeon as he worked them on. His eyes were darting. Kitchen and dining room on the right, staircase left, living room ahead, with a view, probably, over the harbour. The bedrooms would be upstairs. That was where he'd find the money and jewels that he was after, and maybe a small camera – anything small. Leave the videos and computers and sound systems for the boys who came round in the vans.

He went up quickly, two at a time – not a creak or whisper from his feet. Doors all wide – fresh air freaks: he wasn't going to open one and find some kid with the measles staring at him from a bed. 'Shit!' A cat. It was by him like a weasel and down the stairs. He heard a cat-door rattle in the kitchen and stood still for a moment, calming down. But he liked that sort of cat, not the ones that slimed around your legs. He couldn't work

12

with cats watching him. There was a guy in England who strung them up with pantyhose from the wardrobe door. Trademark. It disgusted Rosser. He wasn't a nutter, he was a pro. No sign at all was his mark.

He looked in two rooms and found them empty, with the beds stripped; so he was right, her kids were gone. And in the big front bedroom there was only a single bed, centred on the wall, with the paper bright on each side where a double bed had been. She was widowed or her old man had taken off. It disappointed Rosser, his chances would be halved. But he wasted no time thinking: went to the windows, moving sideways along the wall, and looked out round the curtain; saw the road with a car, another bloody Volvo, going down. Further off, on a strip curving out of hedges and curving in, he saw her and her dog crossing over, the dog still pulling along in front. They climbed the steps over the hump leading to Upland Road. So she was heading for the shops. It gave him time – but he didn't need time. Whatever the conditions he worked fast, cutting risks to the minimum. It was a test he put himself to: get in and out fast, no matter how much he wanted to enjoy a house – eat the food, lie on the beds, piss in the fancy toilets. He never did that. Never trashed a place – hated the bastards who did. He liked the people he stole from. The richer they were the better he liked them.

He didn't like this woman though. What was she, some female hermit? She had *nothing*. A stack of ten cent coins tipped on its side on the dressing table. A two dollar note with a scrap of paper clipped to it – 'library fines'. No jewel box. A wedding ring lying in the dust by the coins. That was all. Rosser couldn't believe his bad luck. All the time he needed and a house with nothing in it. He dropped the ring and the two dollar note in his bag and felt he was cheapening himself. No one lived like this in a half-million dollar house.

He pulled out the drawers and felt underneath the clothes. He opened the cabinet by her bed and found her nightie and bedjacket stuffed inside. It made him curl his lip as he felt under them. Clothes should be folded, you didn't just bunch them up and shove them away. He shook the books, each one, in the stack by her water glass, he even felt in her slippers and

13

went through the clothes in the wardrobe. She was fooling him in some way, he was sure. There had to be something in the room.

He went into the bathroom – en bloody suite – which didn't look as if she used it much. A toothbrush, child-size, dangled from a holder, with an uncapped tube of Colgate underneath. Nothing in the shower, not even shampoo, although she'd been in today because the curtain was wet. He took off a glove and felt in the lavatory cistern, but found only a brick to save on water. Rosser felt a surge of rage. The bitch was cheating him. He lifted out the brick, meaning to slam it in the toilet bowl, but controlled himself and pressed it on the toothpaste tube instead. A worm of paste wriggled out and made a cock and balls. Rosser didn't like that and he squashed it with the brick. He dried his hand on a towel and worked his rubber glove on, then went back to the bedroom and hunted some more. How could people live like this? It was immoral.

He looked in the main bathroom. The bath was furred with dust around the plughole. A dead blowfly lay on its back beside a dried-out cake of soap cemented to the enamel. Downstairs was no better. The dining-room looked as if she never ate in it. There were books all over the table and leaning in stacks against the wall.

'Two fucking dollars,' Rosser said. You got that sort of place but it shouldn't happen in Kelburn.

There was nothing to do but get out now, leaving no mark. Then he remembered the brick and was offended with himself. Lack of discipline, that's what it was. He went upstairs again to make everything tidy. They had to wait until they found their jewellery gone before they knew Brent Rosser had been around.

He put the brick back in the cistern. He wiped the bench top clean with toilet paper and stopped himself from flushing it away. Some flushes were so loud you could hear them next door. He crushed the paper into a ball to chuck into a rubbish tin down town.

'Drat the girl,' a voice whispered harshly in his ear. Rosser almost dropped the wadded paper. He thought someone was in the bathroom with him, then found the range of the words

14

and realised they came from outside. He stepped to the window and looked down between the louvre blades on to the side porch of the house next door. A woman with silver-yellow hair and bare shoulders and bony knees was bending over a potted fern on a wooden stand, fiddling with the moss around the roots. Rosser watched with pity and approval. They all thought their hiding place was original.

She stood up and stepped out of sight, clattered in wooden sandals down the steps and down the path. He heard a gate open and close and a garage door rattle. He put the toilet paper into his bag, stepped neatly out of the bathroom and slid along the wall to the front windows. Half an eye was enough. A car backed out of a garage dug underneath the lawn. It went away with a jump and Rosser watched until it appeared on the stretch of road further down. He felt he had been made a gift, and he took the two dollar note from his bag and put it back on the dressing table. Next door would make it up to him.

He went downstairs, let himself out, closed the door softly. The cat was by the birdbath and it shot off behind the garden shed. He liked cats because they were loners – and where you found cats you didn't often find big dogs. All the same he stopped at the gap in the hedge and looked for a kennel, looked for bones. It was dangerous coming at a house from the back.

Clyde. He got it ready. A trampoline with a sweatshirt lying on it arms spread out, stood on the lawn, on blocks of wood. So there were kids – but school wasn't out. Sheets and towels and tea towels hung on the line: the hot wash, no panties. Rosser put the thought out of his mind. He wasn't a perv. Once he'd nicked an envelope filled with dirty photos but had felt sick having them in his bag and got rid of them in a rubbish tin back in town. Ponder would have given him something, maybe quite a lot, but that wouldn't make up for carting them around. He didn't do porn and he didn't do drugs.

A lawnmower was growling two or three houses away and through a gap between trees, on the next hillside, a man was painting a roof from silver to green. Close by there was nothing. The section was still and the house was empty. Even the wind seemed to turn away.

Rosser went along the path to the side porch. He found the

15

key in the moss, first try; opened the door a body-width, slipped inside. This was better. This was going to be the place. Okay, it was untidy: vacuum cleaner sitting in the middle of the floor, phone book open, whiteboard full of messages half smeared out, a pile of old *Dominion*s spilling off a chair. But he knew that untidy didn't mean you were short of loot. Sometimes it meant the opposite: you were so rich you didn't have to care. It made him contemptuous all the same, made him draw himself in a little. Keeping tidy was part of keeping clean. Two houses in a row with dust and blowflies. He felt he deserved to take everything they had.

He closed the door, looked in the kitchen; and saw a plastic dish of dog biscuits by the pantry. He would have gone back to the door and out of the house if he hadn't seen a basket by the window, lined with torn blankets and old towels. A chewed golf ball lay on the floor beside it. Small dog. Maybe another dachshund.

'Hey dog, come here.'

Everything was quality though. A big round table with six chairs filled the dining room. The pictures – he didn't know about pictures but he'd bet the one of women in a garden drinking tea was worth a bit. And leather sofas in the lounge, and leather chairs, not two but four, and books, not library books, everywhere. The whole thing was spoiled by a bucket of water that smelled of disinfectant, with a rag torn off a sheet hanging over the side, and a wet patch on the carpet with the pile rubbed the wrong way. The dog had probably puked his caviare.

'Hey dog,' Rosser said. Then he ran upstairs. The woman had left the job half done, which meant she was coming back. Two bedrooms opened off the hall, with a third, the big one, at the front, running the whole width of the house. A waterbed, king size, took up half a wall. A scotch chest that would take a crane to lift filled the other. Bulging windows looked at the view. 'Dressing table,' Rosser breathed, and struck it rich at once. The thing was antique and carved with leaves and bunches of grapes, with hankie drawers beside the mirror – drawers that locked. But a key was fitted in the left hand one and in there, all alone, was a satin box embroidered with a

16

dragon on the lid. He opened it and found a tangle of bracelets and necklaces and rings. 'Gotcha,' Rosser said. He had been around long enough to know that they weren't fakes. Coloured stones. White stones. Some pearls down there, gleaming away. He only hoped the bitch hadn't damaged them. He didn't untangle them but lifted the box and checked the catch, then put it in his bag. He tried the right-hand drawer, which slid open without a key, and found some lacy handkerchiefs and shoelaces in a knot and nail files and clippers, and sitting neatly on its side a bundle of twenty dollar notes. Rosser felt its thickness. 'Five hundred bucks.' He grinned at himself in the mirror. Money was the best thing; Ponder never got a cent. He put it in his bag, then opened the rest of the drawers and felt in the clothes. Nothing. He liked the rub of cloth on his gloves. If he had more time he'd choose a blouse for Leeanne, although good clothes never looked right on her. But he had to hurry, and he went to the scotch chest and hunted through the drawers. Athol Peet, a passport said, lying in the top one. Old Athol had enough clothes to fit out a basketball team – sweatshirts, tracksuits, a drawer full of underpants, some still in their wrappings. But nothing Rosser wanted, nothing to go with the jewels. Quick and clean he put things back in place.

He went to the wardrobe, felt along the suits – seven suits – and at the end struck it rich again. A wallet in the inside pocket held ten one hundred dollar notes. Athol's emergency cash. Rosser dropped it in his bag. His head was light. Already he had seen the Reeboks lined up on the rack with the other shoes. He knew that they would be his size because everything in this house was his. He sat on the edge of the bed and slipped off his Lasers; the Reeboks were made for him. He walked across the room and looked in the mirror. 'Rosser,' he said, baring his teeth. He wanted to spread himself through the house, use the beds, eat the food, fuck the wife and daughters; but in the colder part of his mind he knew that he should get out now, while his luck was holding. He knew he shouldn't let himself think about women.

He took the Reeboks off and put them in his bag. It held enough, it weighed like groceries. 'Get out,' he said. Then time shifted back a step and he knew that he had stayed too long.

The noise he hadn't heard while grinning in the mirror became the rattle of a roller door. Sandals clattered on the porch.

'Athol, is that you?' the woman called.

Okay, Rosser thought. He was calm. Speed became his weapon. He could move five metres to her one. He stripped his gloves off to be ready for the street. The door was open so he did not need his hands again. He got his Lasers tied with a flick. Out through the hall while she looked in the lounge, up the path, across the lawn – he'd vanish next door and she wouldn't know she'd lost her jewels until she looked in her drawer. He picked up his bag and moved along the passage to the corner. He should hear her voice again and hear her moving about.

Wrong, Rosser thought, something's wrong. There was only silence.

He looked around the corner. She was standing in bare feet on the landing. He saw her sandals just inside the door.

'Who are you?' she said, with her blue eyes wide.

Rosser moved fast. 'Out of my way, lady.' But she turned, fast herself, and went ahead of him down the steps, crying, 'Liv.' She filled the stairway, blocking his escape. Fear made Rosser agile. He found himself doing what he did. Later he would recall the moment by a memory in his muscles and his joints. 'I didn't mean to do that,' he said.

His sole was on her back and his knee opened out. She flew down the steps; and if he slowed her movement down, put her in slow motion, he saw her leaning flatter as she fell. She touched the floor as lightly as a dancer but her upper body had the weight of lead. She struck the door edge with her face. It was rigid at the impact but swung against the wall as she slid down.

Rosser jumped and ran at her. Blood was springing from her slanted mouth. He stepped across her middle part, high like a dancer, not to touch. Her eyes seemed to open wide at his moving shape. He told her, saying nothing, that she shouldn't have come back. Then he saw a girl half risen on the porch steps. Her green school uniform made her look swollen. She watched him coming at her, dropped her bag and turned side on. He ran by without touching her, although his own bag thumped her on the arm. He went up the path, found the gap in the hedge, ran back parallel, not more than two metres from her, invisible; and heard her say 'Mum', in a rising voice. The woman wasn't hurt too bad, he thought. She'd need some stitches in her face. It would take them ten minutes to get themselves organised. By then he would be gone down The Terrace, in town. He was pleased at how quickly he was calm. Walk out the gate, don't run, he said.

The street was quiet. One or two cars were parked in the Residents Only zone. He walked down at what his mother would call a medium pace. Everything should be medium – except that now and then you had to move fast. He had been fast. He smiled at that, but pulled a face at the blood. She'd bled a lot, real quick, so the door, maybe the tongue in the lock, must have cut her deep. It served her right for coming back and breaking the rules. And she should have gone into the lounge and taken the girl with her so he could get out of the house without being seen. That was how he would have arranged it. It spoiled his perfect record, being seen. But what was he – a nose, a mouth, some eyes? Identikits were a joke, kids could draw better.

He wasn't pleased about it all the same. He wasn't pleased about kicking her. It counted as assault with the cops, and that made them just a bit more keen. Okay, he thought, from now on no one sees me.

He turned down steps to the lower road. Trees leaned over, making a cave. Wellington was perfect for dropping out of sight. You came out on a new road, on a different level of the world. He crossed among cars and felt their wind on his face. A bus went by with people looking down. Their eyes stopped short of him or moved on past. The bag, weighing heavy in his hand, seemed to pull him out of sight.

He walked among students on the footpath. A lecture had come out, maybe. Rosser felt he'd like to stay and swim around amongst them. His heart was going easily, at its normal pace.

On the far side of Kelburn Parade he stopped and looked back. The hill stepped up sharply, with houses lit on one side by the sun and trees frothing out and insulators shining on telegraph poles. A stretch of white railing showed like a lookout platform. He saw the first woman walking by, trailing her dog chain. She had wrapped it round her fist and left half a metre free. The dog must be loafing along behind. She turned and waited for it, resting her elbow on the rail. Go home, Rosser thought, your neighbour needs you.

He went through the bicycle barrier into the university. The girl in the school uniform would be phoning for the cops. By the time they got a car out he would be in the James Smith carpark, in his own. He grasped the bar to lever himself round. Then a memory came up through his palm. His heart gave a kick. He felt a pressure in his head, as though part of his brain was sucked away from the skull. The stair rail! Fucking stair rail! He had put his hand on it. When he shoved his foot in the woman's back his hand had come down, whole grip, for balance on the rail.

'Shift it, mate,' someone said, banging with his hip.

'Sorry.' Rosser felt his palm burning, his forehead prickling with shame.

He went through the quad. He walked like any student. But he knew that people could see him now. He'd marked himself and must go home and lock himself in.

Everything was turned around to face the other way.

Two

The dog was half dachshund and half pug, a mix that denied it both intelligence and charm. Gwen Peet, who liked birds – free birds – lizards, weasels, possums, mice, and cats when independent, in descending order, and dogs hardly at all, was not able to be kind to the animal. Smelly, overfed, useless – tugging it along. She dragged it away from fences and hurried it up and down kerbs with her shoe. If it were left to her she would ban dogs from the streets or make special neigh-bourhoods where they and their owners must live, and mark the boundaries with some dull dog-turdy colour or dog-turd sign and fine anyone who stepped outside.

Would Olivia go there, with her Butch, or would she choose people?

Gwen walked the dog each day as a favour to Olivia. Now and then she called it a contribution. Grandma did this for me, she imagined the girl saying, and saw her slip each favour like a coin into her purse. She did not think of it as buying love. A contribution, a necessary chore, like spooning Farex into her not so long ago. She did not want love from Olivia, liking would do – for the reason, she agreed, that she did not love the girl herself, but merely liked, and liking was much to be preferred. It was nourishing and steady, while love was always too much or too little and made one overcertain or uncertain, never sure.

So, the dog was a mongrel. And Gwen was a divorcée, not a wife. Although she could look younger, she was sixty-four. She lived in the Kelburn house (not worth half a million, but $300,000 perhaps) which her husband had left her when he left.

21

It was all she had apart from a small investment that earned enough for food and electricity and the rates. She had no car but rented her garage to a neighbour for forty dollars a week. She bought, when she had to, good clothes and shoes, because they lasted longer and worked out cheaper in the end. Carefulness was something she had learned, it did not come naturally to her and she committed extravagances that did not reveal themselves at once but drove her to arithmetic when she could not sleep in the night. Four a.m. was her bad time. The house creaked and the walls found new alignments and sets of figures moved like draughts about the room. Curtains stirred and lifted in her mind. There was darkness outside, no bright day, and past and future were alike, without significance. It sometimes helped her then to think that people she was attached to were next door, sleeping on a level with her – even if the filthy dog had left his basket for a place on Olivia's bed. 'Smelly thing,' she muttered, and touched its hind parts with her toe, making it scuttle out of range.

Gwen walked to the top of the cable car and round the bus roundabout and back to Central Terrace and so home every weekday, wet or fine, but did not go into the gardens because the dog spoiled them. She walked there in the mornings and on cool late afternoons. She thought about many things – money, food, the mountains, being alone, being further south, down where it snowed, with nothing but grey oceans between her and Antarctica; and of a little house in the bush, up from Karamea perhaps, and no one there with her, not even a dog, just the birds and the river and the weather and the sky – lovely, she imagined, knowing it would suit her for a day or two; and she thought of people she had known, and still knew but did not see for this reason or that, and those she did see and still enjoyed, and those she could not get out of her life without causing pain. How many friends could a person have – half a dozen perhaps? And what could be done with the others, who knocked against one, claiming, importuning?

She thought of the future often, and of what Ulla called her 'lot in life'. The two would not come apart. Her lot in life determined all the things that she would do. Oh no, she said, not everything, not all. There were so many freedoms she could claim – freedoms of the mind. There was nowhere she could not travel in there – except, she conceded, those places put off limits by race and gender, by language and by temperament, by prejudice, belief. Oh dear, dark continents, she thought, but was not distressed because it was the same, or much the same, for everyone. It was still huge, was limitless, the world outside her 'lot in life'.

All the same, she thought of that and of how it constrained her. Boundaries had been changed by her divorce, but boundaries were not done away with. A huge natural feature was removed. The sun shone longer; at night more stars were in the sky, and she could stride on paths closed off before; but in the end day and night remained much as they were, just more of them, or less, and hotter, brighter, colder than before. Eating, sleeping, ageing still went on, and the house still creaked and the garden grew and prices rose and shoes wore out and Gwen Peet was altered here and there but was recognisably the same. There were boundaries she still couldn't cross.

Howie had said, 'Take it. You've earned it,' and meant no criticism of himself. It was, of course, already in her name, and she would have had it anyway. Her house. 'My house.' But let him think it lay within his gift. Too much energy would be spent in making him understand that he had never lived in it. And pleasure outweighed her bitterness. She made him a cup of coffee and put a little Scotch in – the last of his Scotch – and waited for him to become sentimental, and thought that his face was redder and fatter, all in a month, while his body was leaner, perhaps to facilitate new pleasures of the bed. Be careful Howie, she thought of saying, don't overdo things; but her own happiness wouldn't allow it and she found herself thinking, Go for it, old boy, get in there.

He would, of course. All her men were greedy, Howard, Athol, Gordon: grabbers and getters. But Howie was a natural, born with a money scoop for a hand and a reach like a praying mantis, while his sons, her sons – it amazed her, men from her body – paused too often and thought too much. She was afraid for them. She did not like them. Against her mature judgement, she still liked Howie. Being divorced from him was better than

23

being married, though. ('Take your maiden name again,' some of her friends had insisted. But no, she would stay Peet because it took her life in. Let Howie take a new name, he was the one who wanted to put those years aside.)

She turned in the roundabout, let the dog pee, then walked back towards Upland Road, past the doctors' rooms and the reassuringly scruffy seven-day dairy. The gallery – another station on her dutiful way – came next, with new paintings in place, ugly and bright. Deliberately ugly? There was a lot of that about, and now and then she saw the point. Deliberately beautiful never had anything to say, or even show, when you got down to it. She did not tie the dog up and go in, had not sufficient strength of mind for glum women with shopping bags and jowly Roundtablers – were they? – even in paint. She did not want to know about hunger and poverty, either of the body or the mind, not just now. There were times for being angry and times for fear, and the air was fresh this afternoon, the wind lifting petrol fumes into the upper air. She did not want her easiness disturbed.

'Come on, mongrel,' she said, and crossed the road against the flow of students; climbed up, climbed down, into Central Terrace, and paused for the distant mirror glass and the soaring cranes. The tallest of them stood on the site Howie had failed to secure; but he was busy down the Quay with another deal, a better site. There was always better, and there was great. 'Good' never described a project – it was too tame. 'Best', too, had little use. It suggested an end, and Howie and his mates meant to go on for ever. One more time was built into them like a sense, and no more than an animal – no more than this dog snuffling in the puha, and surely within a year or two of pegging out – did they seem to have any sense of death. Or was that to assume too much? Did they, did Howie, have bad times at 4 a.m.? Did the swinging cranes rust in their moving parts, the foundations fill with water and grow weeds, the mirror glass crack? It had all run down for Gordon, it had finished for the players who had failed to – what was it? – dictate each event of the day to a secretary, and notarise it and put it in the lawyer's safe? Cover themselves. Howie had, Gordy hadn't. So the father was busy on the Quay, putting a

24

new deal together, while the son sat in Auckland in a courtroom and heard the prosecution lawyers call him 'a man greedy to the very marrow of his bones'. It wasn't true; Gordy was a dupe and not greedy in that way. He wanted simply to play with the big boys and was not bright enough or quick enough – and nowhere near long enough in the arm for it.

Not true, not fair, she said, but with no strength, for anger was educated out of her now, and pity for Gordon was as much as she could feel. Pity for him; admiration for Howie, with some contempt. But for Athol – anger, yes, anger and dislike. If she loved him a little more she would also hate him. If she loved him as she had when he was a child . . .

Gwen unfastened the lead from Butch's collar. He was tired and would waddle along without leaving the footpath. She could go at her own pace and seem not to know him, and if the chain hanging from her fist gave her away she was far enough ahead to make it seem she was not aware of his comfort stops. One day she would come down with a bucket of hot water and Sunlight soap and a scrubbing brush and scrub the path clean – had not ruled it out as an eccentricity for her old age. Her seventies perhaps. Sixty-four could not get away with it; her mind still sharp, some few expectations still in place, rules to obey. Sons to nudge along and raise her voice against; Ulla to watch, Ulla to be eyes and ears for, and home and nation; Olivia; Damon: all these a consequence of Gwen and Howie meeting and marrying. They were now her lot in life, or a part of it. Not a part of Howie's, of course. Howie did not have a lot in life. He simply had opportunities. Down there a city block emptied out, and down there a shining tower rose in Howie's mind, to take its place.

Yes, he dreamed. Yes, he had a vision of beauty. Athol did not have one. Gordy had some poor lopped-off thing. And she, Gwen? What she saw would not hold its shape; what she desired was multifarious.

The university emptied out its children. They hopped and sidestepped, danced and angled on Kelburn Parade and behaved no differently from the boys and girls of her day; then, fresh from Nelson, she had read Livy and Tacitus and Molière and Racine. Now they studied commerce, most of

25

them, didn't they, and business management and marketing, and probably only two or three were left in French and Latin. She had heard Bob Jones would sooner take them on than new young property lawyers and cost accountants, but who else would? No one she could think of. Not Howie or any of his mates. Not Hopkins of Lupercal, who had liked the sound of it when she had suggested that name for his company. 'Latin, eh? That'll do me', and they drank to it. A grotto sacred to a Roman god? It had some class. He had not asked her which god.

So she did a nasty secret thing. And now Lupercal was in deep shit, as Howie would say, and in the papers daily, in the courts, and Hopkins and those men who had raised their glasses in her living room, with the city shining at their feet, were waiting judgment, waiting prison almost certainly, and her son Gordon, who had tried so hard to be big with them, was heading that way too and would not escape for all that he remained incurably small. Her clever little jab at them was punished in that way. It was rather Greek (she had done Greek too) and she had no energy to quarrel with it.

Gwen turned away from the city and watched a police car go by, squealing its tyres on the winding road. Macho men were everywhere, in uniforms, in business suits and black nylon socks as much as in jeans and studs and leather. Those wretched nylon socks, she thought, how nice it was not to have to wash them any more; and a pair for his briefcase so he could change at midday and not run the risk of feet that might compromise a deal.

'Butch, come on.'

Honeysuckle, dog turds, cool breeze, police car – and what was it doing at Athol's gate? She walked fast, and ran a step or two, and hurried back and chained the dog and dragged him along. Inside the gate she freed him and threw the chain on the lawn.

'What's wrong?' she called at the policeman talking into his radio on the porch. He frowned at her and motioned her away.

'My son lives here. Is someone hurt?'

'You're a relation?'

'Yes. My name's Mrs Peet. I live next door. What's wrong, please?'

He spoke again into his radio and clicked it off. 'Did you see anything, madam? An intruder?'

'I've been out. You passed me in the street. Please, is Ulla . . . ?'

She stepped on to the porch and saw Olivia kneeling in the hall in her Marsden blazer, with her tie thrown over her shoulder; and bare feet, yellow soles, Ulla's long feet, her longboat feet, with big toes crossed; and Ulla lying there; and blood on the towel in Olivia's hand.

'Ulla,' she said, and made the vowels perfectly – perfect at last.

'There's an ambulance on its way. I wouldn't go in.' The policeman put his arm across the door. Olivia looked up and did not see and shifted the towel a little on Ulla's face, and the other policeman, squatting at her side, said, 'Not too hard. Easy goes.'

Butch clicked past Gwen on the porch and climbed the doorstep. He paused to look at Ulla, then waddled out of sight into the lounge. She heard him lapping water from his bowl and heard his basket creak as he climbed in.

She ran past the constable, dipping under his arm. She knelt by Ulla and looked at her, then looked at Olivia, and knew from each face equally that all their lives were changed. Ulla did not see. She did not hear and did not feel. Ulla was alive but was out of the world. Gwen bent closer and saw her face, her northern face, which had become for ever different. Ulla gone. And Olivia, although she said, 'Grandma' – a raw sound from the back of her throat – had shifted away and could no longer be herself.

'Is it her neck?' she asked the policeman.

'Can't be sure, lady. Can't be sure how bad it is.'

There was another towel, made into a pad, under Ulla's neck.

'Who put that there?'

'She did. Fixed her mum up. Then phoned the ambulance and us. She's a good kid. Aren't you, love?'

'Yes,' Olivia whispered.

27

'Stay with it.'

There was blood on the cuffs of her pale-blue shirt. There was blood on her cheek where she had wiped her hand. Gwen leaned across and touched her on the side of her throat and felt it throb. She wanted to kiss Ulla and hold her hand, but stood up and went out to the porch.

'Have you phoned Athol? My son?'

'That'd be her husband? Mr Peet?'

'Yes.'

'Not yet.'

'Damon won't be home till after three. Damon's her son. Get her to the hospital first. Get the ambulance first.'

'That's it now.'

She heard a wail, which faded and rose on the hill.

'Who did it?'

'Haven't had time to ask any questions yet.'

'A burglar?'

'Intruder. The girl saw him.'

Olivia's bag lay where it had fallen, with a science textbook half slipped out.

'Did she know him?'

The policeman looked at her sharply, a blue-eyed boy, simple and suspicious and too quick. 'Should she?'

'I don't know. Why would he . . . ?' She meant attack Ulla, and made a movement of her hand at the tableau in the hall, knowing there was no answer he could give.

'They hit first and run. All they've got to do is get away. Ah, here's our boys.'

Two men were on the path, one middle-aged, one young. They were detectives, she understood, and was angry to see them here ahead of the ambulance. She went back inside and knelt by Ulla and touched Olivia again, and was aware of one of the new men looking over the top of her head but did not move to make it easy for him. She took Ulla's hand and almost cried at its conflicting looseness and warmth. The man went into the lounge. Butch yapped at him but then stayed quiet.

'Ulla,' she said; and now horror and grief began to work, in a lurching way that meant they were too great to be contained.

28

'She can't hear,' Olivia said.

'Has she said anything?'

'No.'

'Her eyes are open.'

'I don't even know if she's breathing.'

'Yeah, she's breathing,' the policeman said. 'I'd've done mouth to mouth, but I think it's best . . .' He meant that nothing should be done that put a strain on her neck.

'Ulla, can you hear?' Gwen said.

'She can't, I told you.'

'Ulla.'

'She's dying.'

'I don't think you can say that,' the policeman said.

'No,' Gwen said. She was trying to remember the first aid she had known, and where the spinal cord must be cut for a person's breathing to be stopped. The third or fourth or fifth vertebra, somewhere there. 'Shouldn't she have a blanket?'

'Yeah, she should.'

'Hypothermia starts almost straight away.' Gwen stood up and headed for the stairs.

The young detective stopped her. 'Hold on, lady.'

'She's got to have a blanket. I need a blanket.'

'These boys'll do it. They're the experts.'

Two ambulance men came in: white shirts with shoulder flashes, brightly polished shoes. She put all her hope in them and stood breathless as their eyes moved along Ulla, taking her in. One squatted by Olivia and lifted her hand but kept the towel in place, then had a look at the wound, which was an open cut running from below her eye to the angle of her jaw. It seemed to be full of thick cool blood. He touched her cheek-bone and Gwen saw the fracture from the way the ridge was pushed out of line: that ugly/beautiful line that often seemed more Slavic than Nordic. Depressed fracture, that was the name.

'There's a lump as big as your fist on the back of her neck,' the policeman said.

'Yeah.' He had seen it. He was clearing the smaller injury away. 'What's her name, love?' – to Olivia.

'Mrs Peet. It's Ulla.'

29

'Right.' He gave her the towel and knelt down close. 'Can you hear me, Ulla?'

She could not. Gwen remembered another term: spinal shock. She said to herself, She's in shock.

'Ulla,' the ambulance man repeated, managing the vowels surprisingly well. He took her hand and pinched her wrist. 'Can you feel that, Ulla?'

'Shall I bring it all?' the other man said.

'Yeah, the works. Oxygen too. Can you give him a hand?' – to the policeman.

'She should be kept warm,' Gwen said.

'There's some blankets coming. Do you know which way her head went? Backwards? Forwards?'

'I wasn't here.'

'Back,' Olivia said. She stood by Ulla's feet with the bloody towel in her hand. 'She came down the stairs and hit the door and her head went back.'

'Yeah, hyperextensive' – and Gwen thought, You don't know, you're only a zambuck. She wanted him to do things, not say: cover Ulla, make her warm, make her talk and breathe again and make her eyes see.

'Can't you put something on her face?'

'In a minute.' His eyes went past her to the detective on the stairs. 'Can I have two of your boys to help with the lifting?'

'Sure. Say when. You're the one who saw it, eh?' – to Olivia.

'Yes.'

'Olivia?'

'Yes.'

'You feel up to talking about it, Olivia?'

A technique, Gwen thought. Say the name as often as you can. She went out to the porch and saw the men on the path, festooned with gear. She did not want to watch Ulla being masked, braced, lifted, in ways meant to preserve the little life that remained in her. How much life? Not enough for consciousness, which, they were agreed, was at the centre of being human, and at the cutting edge as well. So what was Ulla now? Some simple thing, single-celled, hanging on by automatic response? There was all her self at the back of that, waiting for the decision – to come out or quietly go away.

30

Gwen peered back inside. The ambulance man was looking closely into Ulla's eyes and feeling at her temples as if he too wanted to locate her.

Gwen went down the steps and round to the back of the house. She sat in a canvas chair by the trampoline, where Ulla would pretend to read as Damon practised his crazy flips. Swedish Ulla. Ulla with no country any more – and now with nothing left except a pulse, with nothing but a movement in her blood, which might be enough to bring her back. I do love you Ulla, I love you more than any of the others.

Gwen cried, sitting in the chair. Then she wiped her eyes. Be practical, she thought. Get ready for Athol and Damon. Get ready for Olivia; and to find out how bad Ulla is. Broken necks don't always mean you die. They don't even mean paralysis, not every time. She wanted to run back inside and watch for signs of feeling. She should have pinched Ulla's hand herself. Surely then Ulla would have moaned and moved her eyes. That was what you did for your best friend.

The young detective came out and looked at the back of the house. He looked at the gap in the hedge, then asked Gwen her name and wrote it down.

'You live through there?'

'Yes.'

'And you were out when it happened?'

'I was out walking. Ulla was at home. When I came back . . .'

'Did you see anything, Mrs Peet? Any strangers or people who didn't belong?'

'No one. I go out each day. I walk the dog.' She heard how pathetic it sounded. 'It's Olivia's dog. It was sick on the carpet.' She tried a new start. 'I only saw students. Why don't they get her to hospital?'

'What students? Were they in this street?'

'Only going up and down the steps. They come up all the time, going to Kelburn. What does the ambulance man say? Isn't he just for broken legs and things?'

'He's a paramedic, Mrs Peet. She's in good hands. Was anyone at the top of Central Terrace when you walked down?'

'One person. I didn't look very hard.'

'What time was that?'

'Ten to two. A quarter to. Why is Olivia home? It's far too early.'

'What did he look like?'

'I don't know. A student. Young.'

'Tall or short?'

'Medium. Lightly built.'

'What colour hair?'

'I didn't take any notice. The dog – it made a mess on the footpath and that embarrassed me so I looked the other way.'

'Dark or fair you'd notice though.'

'Yes. Fair. A Pakeha.'

'Did you see what he was wearing?'

'Jeans, I think. And a sweatshirt. It was black or else navy blue.'

'Anything written on it?'

'I can't remember.'

'What sort of shoes?'

'Sneakers probably. They all wear those.'

'Bag?'

'He had one. Slung on his shoulder. That's just an impression. I can't say what sort.'

'Had you seen him before? Does he live around here?'

'I've never seen him. I don't take much notice of the students. Shouldn't they have a doctor before they shift her?'

'One more question, Mrs Peet. Did you see him when you were coming back?'

'All I saw was the police car.' She did not like his jaw. It was almost deformed. His upper teeth closed inside the lower. Eating must be impossible.

'Is he the man Olivia saw?'

'We can't say yet, Mrs Peet. It might be best if you phone her husband. Can you do it from your own place?'

She went through the hedge and into her house and rang Athol's office. She did not know what she would say but it must be straight because that was Athol's style and he would not thank her for trying to soften things.

'Jacquie,' she said to his secretary, 'it's Athol's mother. Can I speak to him please?'

But Athol was not in his office and the woman would not let her have the number of his car phone. 'I can ring him for you but it has to be urgent.'

'Oh, it is. Tell him his wife's been hurt and he should go home.'

'Is it serious? Mr Peet's very particular – '

'Just say her neck is broken. They're taking her to the hospital. Say there was a burglar in the house.' She hung up. Say, she thought, you might have lost some of your property.

Gwen sat down. She held her hands between her knees to stop them trembling. Her eyes were dry and hot and felt as if thumbs were pressed in them. She got up in a moment and bathed them at the sink, then went upstairs to the bathroom and ran water in the basin. She washed her hands and face. Athol, you are nothing, she thought. I won't let you make any difference to me.

Then she saw that someone had been in the house. There was no shock in it – the knowledge affected her casually. She should call the policeman over and point to the tube and say, 'It was almost full,' and let him worry why a burglar would squeeze it. But the man who broke Ulla's neck would not take shape alongside Ulla there.

Gwen went into the toilet and found she could not use it, but flushed it and lowered the lid and opened the louvres wide. That got intruders out. Intruder, what a word. It had a legal use, didn't it, as well as a common, something cut and dried to do with usurpation of rights? But for the police it was a term to blur focus with, for people outside, until they had assembled everything and could be sure. And while that was going on Ulla lay there dying. It was like two radios in the same room, playing different voices. One spoke softly, urgently, while the other kept a patter up. She looked across at Ulla's house and saw the boss detective at an upstairs window, watching her.

I won't explain, I'm in my own house. Get out of Ulla's bedroom, she thought.

The man turned away.

She looked down over the top of the hedge and saw Olivia come on to the porch. She had put the towel down somewhere

33

but still had her tie thrown over her shoulder. Her pale hair, sleek with washing, had worked free at the back and was belled above the ribbon, which any moment would drop off, and then her hair would spread like water over her back. Gwen had seen it happen a dozen times. The girl had trouble keeping herself trimmed up in the Marsden way. She came out sideways, then backed into the potted fern, making way for the stretcher where Ulla lay strapped down with her face framed in a collar like an Elizabethan ruff. Her eyes were open. They had taped a dressing to her cheek. The front man backed with care and felt for the top step with his foot.

I should go down; but no, she did not want to, she wanted to stay at the window and preserve what she and Ulla had. I'll send to you, you send to me, through the ether. She smiled at their joke. Stay alive for me, I'm your best friend.

A car door slammed and the gate crashed open. Athol. He must have been in Kelburn when the call came. Now he stopped the stretcher and wanted everything explained. But the men took no notice and he ran back and forth – Ulla, Olivia, the constable at the door – with his forehead shining and his glasses making little squared-off screens on his eyes. He tried to take Ulla's hand. 'I'm coming in the ambulance.' Then he saw Gwen at the window.

'For God's sake Mum, come and look after your grand-daughter. Try and get something right.'

Gwen found it a reasonable request. The girl was standing at the top of the steps. She had nowhere to go and must not be allowed to turn back and commune with her dog. That would be to lose Olivia. Gwen walked through the bathroom and along the hall. She hurried down the stairs and past the open door, which stood as Ulla's had, immoveable, with its tongue shining like a knife. The burglar should have pushed her, she would not have minded. Her face would have split open and her bones cracked like glass and she would have died instantly, and that would have been all right if Ulla could have been left alive.

'Olivia,' she said, climbing to the porch, 'come inside.'

'I don't want to.'

More men had come: one dusted with a little brush and

34

one was on his knees as though hunting for moth eggs in the carpet.

'I wanted to go in the ambulance but Dad wouldn't let me.'

'There's nothing he can do there, even himself. He'll ring us up as soon as he knows.' She freed Olivia's hands from the porch rail. 'We'll go to my house. I'll make us something to drink.'

'No.'

'We'll have to get ready for Damon soon.'

'He won't care.'

'He'll care more than you think, dear. Damon only plays tough.' She plucked the ribbon to save it from being lost, and smoothed the girl's hair on her back. 'Take your tie off. Take your blazer off.' Olivia obeyed. Gwen hung them on the porch rail. She slid the science book into the bag and leaned it on the fern pot. 'Come and wait on the lawn', taking Olivia down the steps. 'They'll call us if there's any news.'

'I didn't know if she was hurting or not. I couldn't tell,' Olivia said. She held the springs fringing the bed of the trampoline, then climbed on it and lay on her back, staring at the sky.

Gwen told her about spinal shock, and how, for the moment, all feeling was cut off. She said to herself, I'm making it up. She told Olivia that very often people with neck injuries recovered completely and soon learned to walk again, the spinal cord was simply bruised and was taking a rest.

Olivia said, 'I heard it. A crack like a stick when she hit the door.' Her hands lay spread on the trampoline as though she was holding them for someone to trace.

'What was he like, the man? What was he doing?'

'Taking stuff, I suppose. He kicked her. She came down the stairs and hit the door.'

'What did he look like?'

'A student. That's all.'

'The police will make an identikit picture. They'll catch him.'

'I don't care about that.' She rolled on to her side, away from Gwen, and curled up. She was like that diagram, Gwen thought, the ball on the rubber sheet, used in physics books to

35

show how gravity curved light. I mustn't let her go away, how can I keep her here?

'What brought you home so early, anyway?'

'I felt sick at school.'

'Did they ring Ulla?'

'I didn't tell them. I walked down to Boundary Road and rang from Tricia's place. If I hadn't . . . '

That was better. A little bit of guilt, easy enough, and back she came. She uncurled into her earlier position.

'You can't blame yourself,' Gwen said, and that was easy too. She heard a seagull screaming from high in the air. 'We'd go crazy if we went back and tried to change every little thing that caused something else.'

'Who said I wanted to?'

'No.'

'Dad should have let me go. I'm better than him.'

'There's nothing anyone can do. Except the doctors . . . '

'Everyone knows how they feel. But he's got to pretend he's upset now.'

Such terrible ease, without knowledge of time, and multiplicity, and the vertiginous turning over of things, and the subtleties and accommodations. Gwen wanted to shield herself; and wanted to shield herself from Athol too, for although he was subject to far more than he knew, all of it would be denied. He kept a kind of innocence; achieved a terrible simplicity. Yet now, she agreed, he would pretend, for it made a part of his straight road.

'Come over to my house. I'll make a cup of tea.' And who was pretending now? Pretend grandmother.

Olivia said, 'She'll never get to Sweden, that's for sure.'

'Who knows? We mustn't . . . ' Sentence her? Yet Ulla was a fact, lying there barely alive and cut off from herself. She was incontrovertible and she became her future. Unless . . . but what unless was there, *unless* an alteration down all the branchings of our consciousness and we emerge somewhere else, Ulla and I? Though not in Sweden.

The gate, crashing open, could only be Damon. All the marvellous energy that turned to assault. All the quickness that in the end only made him sudden.

'Damon,' she called, and he came around the side of the porch, thumping the weatherboards with his bag.

'What are all these cops doing here?' He saw Olivia. 'Who said you could get on my trampoline?'

'Damon – '

'She's still wearing her shoes. Hey, that's my sweatshirt you've got your feet on.'

'Damon, listen please.' She told him and his stillness surprised her. Only the bag moved, twisting and untwisting its cord.

'How bad is she?'

'We won't know until your father calls.'

'I want to see her.'

'You will. We'll all go in, but right now they'll be – doing things.'

'What things?'

'There's x-rays, and traction I think it is. And getting all sorts of things settled down. Damon, there's every chance she'll be all right.'

The boy put his bag on the ground. He sat down and took off his shoes and socks. 'Get off, Liv.' He moved in a way soft for him. His voice was polite. Olivia climbed down and lay on the grass.

The springs squeaked and sang and the canvas made a hollow boom. Gwen watched Damon somersault in the air. The turns were slow and easy and inevitable, but she had never seen before how tightly the body must be held.

Three

There's my view, he thought, there's all the sea and sky a man can ask for, and islands out there in the gulf, and I can go round the back and see the parts people never see, in my launch. She was down there at Westhaven, tied to a pole – forty feet of her and lines like a girl. And up here on the cliff was his house – Greek, or maybe Roman, with what Gwen would call an atrium. Out the back, which was of course the front to face the view, was a swimming pool and a barbecue pit and a tennis court as green as grass. White carpets spread into the house, with chairs as fat as wool bales angled on them and multi-coloured throwmats like bed quilts. The fireplace was big enough to hold a wattle log. The chandeliers, red and blue, fell like coloured rain, and the cabinet, of kauri he had scavenged for himself, opened on to every drink a man could ever wish for. He wouldn't go past Johnny Walker Black, not for all the malt snobs in the world, but if a malt snob came it was in there, take your pick. Choose a cigar. There, in the humidor. Havana?

Pictures and porcelain led upstairs to bed. Up the split levels, past the dens and bathrooms and live gardens, potted trees, to face the corrugated water and the islands again – the water in the sunlight or the moonlight, diamonds and gold. And there in the big bed – big big bed – Darlene his naked lady lay. Naked sleeper, Darlene, who woke and slid at him and repaid him and repaid . . . All this for the sawmill boy; the kapok mattress, outside dunny, broken sofa, broken lino boy; Henderson boy. Iron stove, wooden tub, barefoot through the hoar frost, holes in his teeth, torn pants, no underpants, rags

38

for a hankie – that sort of boy. Standard one, standard six, leather strap, England and the king, Depression boy, swimming at Falls Park, dog paddle and overarm, and diving from willow trees that swayed in the wind and climbing the skinny kanuka, agile as a monkey and monkey-screaming at the girls in their changing shed. Hooligan boy. Apprentice boy. Canvas apron, hammer in his belt. Howard Peet. Howie Powie! The toughest thing that ever came out of Henderson school.

Now, tonight, he was sixty-six and two-thirds, he was two-thirds there, and he still felt like a boy. When he said that, and he often did after a few – 'I feel like a boy tonight' – people supposed he meant in energy and appetites; but no, he meant that he was waiting for the best part of his life to start. That did not mean he was dissatisfied with what he had had. Not for a moment. He was more than satisfied. Sometimes he was astonished at how well he had done. But yesterday was only for today, and now, when you finished it, was only for tomorrow. He didn't stop here, he started there. His skin, his fingertips, his spine, the shiver and the tingle told him that. When Howie looked back he had no sense of travelling great distances, even though times were far away. The creek, his mother's kitchen, the islands and the launch, the bloomered girls in the roofless shed, and Gwen, Darlene – there was no break; it was not even linked like a chain. 'This is me, by God, and it goes on tomorrow.' That was why he said, 'I feel like a boy.'

He ambled on the patio. He put his foot on the rail and leaned his forearm on his knee – no hands behind the back for him, no cigar upthrust. He was no King Howie. On nights like this he rolled his own. He flicked his butt across the lawn and tried to hit the birdbath naked lady on the bum, and took another paper and stuck it on his lip while he shaped tobacco in his palm. He made the rules on his bit of land and no one told him not to drop his ash on the carpet or not to take a leak off the cliff if he was inclined. Out in the world he knew what to do, and what to wear, and what to say – food, drink, manners, the right word; it was easy. He had known since he'd put his first half-crown in the bank, since he stood up on the bus in his schoolboy shorts to offer his seat to a lady. Call it rules, he thought, but it's mostly common sense; and all the rest, the poncy stuff, that was just a joke he could enjoy behind a straight face and a steady eye. But here, this is my place, he said, and I tell people what to do and if they don't like it they needn't come.

He walked across the lawn and followed the shell path to the end of the tennis court where if your lob was too heavy it floated over the cliff and dropped two hundred feet on to the rocks and took a crooked bounce into the sea. A kid fishing down there retrieved a ball once and tucked it in the front of his togs and climbed the cliff, came up grinning over the lip, and Howie was so pleased with him he gave him ten dollars. It was the sort of thing he would have done himself, in Henderson, or the sort of thing Damon might do. He smoked his cigarette and flicked the butt away and watched it like a falling star until it went out, then watched the lights on the harbour bridge, way up past the wharves, making a lovely female curve. The North Shore glowed and flickered. Ponsonby and downtown Auckland prickled and swam with lights. Out west, a long way out, the Waitakere Ranges made a crooked line on the sky. The Henderson valley lay somewhere below, wet and green. That was where he'd started from and this was where he'd got to. Howie was pleased, not with his life but with himself.

He turned back to the house and saw Gordon watching him from the living room. It spoiled his mood. The living room was like a goldfish bowl – and Gordon was a grey fish there, hugging the bottom. Gordon had no lift in him, no fight; he would never rise. And Howie thought, I can't be bothered with you, son. Gordon was too round and soft, and spongy with all the things he could not decide; a sick man, somehow, with his disappointments. Howie had no advice for him, not any longer. He had given him advice and told him, do this, don't do that, and Gordon had taken it or not; but when he had taken it, had somehow made it wrong. Gordon was a loser. Gordon won small; and when he tried to go big he lost everything. He wanted it too much and that was what turned it bad for him. He didn't care about doing it; he just wanted to be there with

40

his hands full of cash at the end. That was not the way it worked or what it was about. Gordon did not know, and Athol did not know. You've got to move, you've got to play, by God you've got to *flash*, there's got to be light.

Gordon pulled the door back and leaned out, trying to see. 'Dad.'

Howie did not answer. He went past the birdbath, caressed the naiad's flank, stepped up to the pool and watched Darlene's bedroom light undulate on the glossy surface. He slipped off his espadrilles, rolled up his trousers and sat with his feet in the pool. The water came half way up his shins, cold as ice. He felt it burning between his toes and tightening his Achilles tendons. A shiver took his scrotum and ran up his spine. Great. Alive. He leaned down and dipped in his hands as far as the wrists, and felt the skin tighten and stand the hairs up on his finger backs. He was on the point of balance; if he went another inch he would slip in. Too cold for that, with his clothes or not. The pool was only scrubbed and filled with water yesterday. He liked the smell of chlorine – impolite, like a lot of things you couldn't get by without in life. He washed between his toes. Dried his feet with his handkerchief. Barefooted, he walked on the lawn and felt the mown grass prick his soles. I used to walk on road metal once, in my bare feet; and he remembered stone-bruises and stubbed toes, and skating on ice puddles with feet that had no feeling left in them.

'It's getting late, Dad,' Gordon called.

'Sure. Okay.'

'I've got to be in court in the morning.'

Darlene's light went out, which meant that she had finished another ten pages of *Crimson* or *Damson* or whatever it was, and would go to sleep and snore sweetly like a virgin until she woke. Now the only light was round Gordon in the glass wall, frightened to come into the dark. He held an empty glass in his hand – frightened even to pour himself a drink. Howie pushed past him and walked across the carpet, collapsing the pile with his feet, which buoyed him up. He lobbed his espadrilles into a chair.

'Drink, son?'

41

'No, I've got to drive. Dad – '

'Yeah, I know. They're making you look like a nana.'

'I wouldn't mind, but it's simply not true. Dad, I didn't do all those things.'

'You did them but you didn't know.'

'Yes – '

'That's just as bad.' He sat down. 'You've got to know.' He could say, I told you not to go in with Hopkins. He liked the old term 'wide boy' for that one. Hopkins was as wide as they came and crunched up little players, Gordy and his kind, as easily as salted cashew nuts. But now Hopkins was getting crunched himself, along with Gordon and the rest of them; and good bloody riddance too, for playing outside the rules which said you didn't stuff full every damn sock you could find, every pie bag. All the same he would help Gordon if he could, the way he had helped him all his life. Long division at the kitchen table? Sure, if he could. The boy, the poor dumb softy, was his son.

'Anyway, when you went in they had six million going round already. With put and call options from here to kingdom come. You know enough to stay away from round robinning.'

'It wasn't like that.'

'What was it then? You tell me.' Tell me again. It was like patting him on the back after his bottle to bring up his wind. Howie needed Gwen for that sort of thing. And he thought at once, Gwennie, and was automatically sentimental. Clever wee bitch, giving them Lupercal for a name; he wished he had someone as clever as that with him now, even if she did button her jamas up to the neck. His eyes stung and he brushed them, and gulped his drink and crossed to the cabinet for more, while Gordon lilted up and down the scale of his grievances.

'You didn't have a right to know you had an obligation,' Howie said. 'It's no defence to say they kept you in the dark. They keep office girls in the dark. You're supposed to find things out, that's your bloody job.'

'I know, but listen . . . '

Gordy would get off lighter than the rest, but still they would put him away for a year or two, for jumping in without looking round. For keeping his blinkers on as long as the money rolled in. For his damned stupidity and greed, which made him just as crooked as Hopkins and Dingle and Rope. The difference was only in scale. Gordon didn't go around every corner blind.

They had taken him, Hopkins and Dingle, because they'd hoped to get Howie too. Gordy was a favour; or maybe he was bait. But nothing would have drawn Howie in with that pack of sharks. Yeah, sharks, in a feeding frenzy soon enough, and Gordon in there with them, snapping up stray bits. Howie felt ashamed. I warned him, I told him. And Gwen warned him too – 'Be your own man, son,' in her bloody moralistic way. But too late, the water had turned red . . .

'Don't say you didn't know. Don't say it in court. Because they're not going to believe you. Say you're sorry if you like. Say you made a mistake. But never ever that you didn't know.'

Gordon swallowed. He worked his throat. 'What I didn't know is it had got so big. I wasn't in on the Boniface stuff, and going round through Hong Kong, God knows where. That was Hopkins and Dingle, only them. The lawyers had these bloody Chinese walls. All I did was – I don't know – '

'Hang up the hats.'

'All right.'

'Sharpen the pencils.'

'Yes, all right.'

'The office boy. So how come you end up with two million bucks that isn't yours?'

'That was legitimate. Okay, it was pushing it, maybe it bent things a bit too far. But it was still inside the law, I thought.'

'And the Serious Fraud Office didn't think.'

'It's Hopkins and Dingle they're after.'

'And they'll get you on the way. You and Carmichael and Broadhead and Rope. A nice little clutch of office boys. You can't expect them to turn it down.'

'So what do I do, Dad? What do I do?'

'You listen to your lawyer. You don't come to me.'

'My lawyer can't get me off.'

'No, he can't. But what he can do is get you maybe eighteen months instead of two years. You'll be out inside twelve months. Good behaviour, Gordy, you'll be good at that. And lots of weekend leave. They're giving it to all the boys with nice clean fingernails. They'll park your Audi by the prison gates.'

'Jesus, you're a mean old prick.'

'That's better' – and it was – 'call me names.'

'Dad – '

'Don't start to whine.' Forty what? Forty-two and he hadn't learned to take his lumps.

'Dad, I can't go to prison. It'll . . . ' Was he going to say 'kill me'? He hadn't got the guts to use big words. 'Ruin me' was what he would say. 'It'll stuff me up. It'll be the end. I won't survive.'

In what way? Howie thought. Suddenly he was moved by Gordon. Won't survive in what way, son? What was the part that was going to die? Was it something Gwen had put in him? Or something Gordon reckoned he, his father, had done? Some bad dad thing? He could not tell whether Gordon had found some hardness in himself or had simply uncovered a new layer of softness. (Soft in the mouth, soft around the middle, soft ear lobes that bent like supplicating hands, and soft small feet and soft toes – Howie remembered counting them, this little piggy – cramped up white and tight in black shoes and nylon socks. He had told Gordon several times, 'Don't come here in uniform,' but Gordon wouldn't get out of his suit and tie because he seemed to lose himself and get even softer. He was loose in colours, loose in loose shirts; his throat, even his throat, seemed to collapse.)

'Listen, Gordy.' He didn't want money. He didn't want advice. He wanted Howie to go round there and punch the prosecutor on the jaw. 'There's nothing I can do. They've got you and there's no way they're going to let you go. I can't even stand close to you – because I've got my own deal and I can't let your thing rub off on mine. You shouldn't even be round here tonight. But stuff that, eh, no one tells us we can't talk to each other, because I'm your dad. But as far as the rest of it goes, listen' – wisdom now – 'you've got to take it, you've got to go in and take your lumps, and come out smiling on the other side, because if you don't,' yeah, wisdom from Dad, 'you're no good any more. You're no good to yourself any

44

more. You're finished, boy. And you don't finish yet, not at forty. You keep on. Because there's nothing else you can bloody do.' And there wasn't. He had said everything Gordon needed to know. 'And when you come out, you pick yourself up and get on with it.' Yes, that was something, that was something else. 'Now have a drink and get out of here and let me get upstairs to my wife. And, Gordy, don't come back. Don't come back again, unless it's just to say, "Gidday, Dad".'

He poured his son a Scotch and meant him to knock it back in a single gulp. But Gordon only turned himself side on. 'It's easy for you,' darting a look that caught a gleam of red from the chandeliers. He had turned away so he would not seem responsible.

'Easy?' Howie answered. He was in a sudden rage but would not twist and vanish in the way his son did. 'Do you want to know how I started out?' Told it straight – the ravelled jersey and bare feet and bed with holes rusted in the wire, and two of them in it, top and tail, his brother's feet digging under his chin all night long. And no sheets. No underpants. Dripping instead of butter on the bread . . . until Gordon said, 'That's not what I'm talking about.'

Howie would not stop. 'I dragged you and Athol and your mother on my back. No one helped me. I did it by myself. And I kept my nose clean. I could have taken short cuts, short cuts is easy – you think I didn't see them doing it. Half of them from King's College, in their poncy voices. I'm just the chippy from out west, I'm just good for banging in the nails. Well, I showed them, and I kept it straight, I kept it honest, and in the end they were coming to me. Hopkins and his mob.' He had cooled down. Because they were not the enemy; they were only men he moved amongst, whose rules he obeyed when he had to, men he climbed over, doing things in his way while doing it in theirs. There was no enemy, there was just yourself in a contest with yourself – and Gordon would never understand.

'Ah what the hell, you've heard it all before, drink up your whisky and go home.'

The phone had been ringing and he held it at his side while he gulped his own drink. 'Yeah, who is it?'

'Dad? It's Athol. Bad news, Dad.'

45

'You too?'

'A burglar got in this afternoon and he pushed Ulla down the steps. She's in hospital with a broken neck. It looks as if she might be paralysed.'

'From a broken neck. Can they say paralysed as quick as that?'

'They think it's . . . They're talking about, I don't know, complete lesion maybe, whatever that is. But it means she might be a quadriplegic. They've got a whole lot more tests to do.'

'How are the kids? How's Damon?'

'They're okay. They haven't been allowed to see her yet. It's in the fourth vertebra and that means she might lose everything.'

'Stuck in a bed, you mean, for the rest of her life?'

'It might be that.'

'But Jesus, she's only thirty-six.'

'At the moment they're trying just to keep her alive. It's her breathing up there, the fourth vertebra. Everything just cuts off. I got in to see her and she looks as if she's dead.'

Tell them to let her die, Howie wanted to say.

Gordon was at his shoulder, listening. 'Gordon's here, you'd better tell him.' He thrust the phone at Gordon and went across to pour another drink. But it was air not whisky he wanted. Nothing could be worse, stuck on a bed. Your body lying there like a sack, full of what? Full of nothing. And alive only in your head and no way to touch it, no way to touch your eyes and mouth.

He went outside and felt the tiles sting his feet with cold. Poor bloody Ulla, poor little bitch. But he had no sense of her, only of himself. There was a rolling, a dislocation, in his hips, like a socket loose. Shit, he said, don't go soft on me.

He straightened himself up. He walked straight on the grass. The naiad glimmered at him. He put his fingers on her spine but she was made without vertebrae, her neck covered by a loop of hair. He turned away. Ulla, who rhymed with fuller: it was a name he could not say and he had blamed her for having it. Her voice came to him, more English than the English, as though she had been asked to read the news. 'Oh,' removing her tanned arm, which he had laid his palm on, 'that is because of the pigment in my skin.' Where did a Swede get a word like that? And why couldn't he touch his son's new girlfriend on the arm? But she had always drawn away. He had never known her, never liked her, and had thought Athol a fool to marry a woman who looked round to the other side of the world, looked back home. You can't be happy, Howie thought, except in your own land.

His eyes filled with tears for Ulla. He was pleased by that.

'Dad.' Gordon advanced over the lawn. 'That's awful, bloody awful, isn't it?'

Howie grunted.

'My God, we have bad luck in this family.'

Yours isn't bad luck, yours is greed, Howie thought. 'Go home, son. Phone me up tomorrow.'

'I'd string up the bastard who did that.'

'Yeah, yeah. Go home.'

He took him through the house and put him out the door, closed it and locked it and turned out the yard lights, the gate lights, the porch. He switched on the alarms – stupid bloody things, always going off when they didn't need to, it would be better to have a dog – and used the bathroom, cleaned his teeth. Ulla, he thought, six-foot Swede, cold as ice – except that she was not cold to anyone else. Gwen and she talking, talking, mixing bread together and going out on walks and going out to movies where you had to read the screen; and Gwen telling him, Oh go and see James Bond then; and in James Bond you saw girls who looked like Ulla looked, but who behaved like a woman should. He felt his neck, he traced the vertebrae down his back, then reversed his arm and tried to come from below but felt a stab in his shoulder where the doctor said bursitis and wanted to pump it full of muck . . . He could feel things, feel his shoulder, feel his legs. Ulla could not. She wouldn't go long-striding down the road or leap up the front steps three at a time. He tried to get her, tried to make her more than just a picture, but she wouldn't come, and he realised that she had never smiled at him.

'Hollo, Howard,' Ulla said from across the room.

So now she was helpless, now she would know . . . But

Howie put that aside almost with disgust. He wanted to do something – cure her, lift her up – and get past her coldness at last. He saw Ulla look at him and smile. That was all he wanted. He wanted to help.

Women were people you helped. That was why, with most of them, he never had any trouble.

Howie washed his feet in the handbasin. He could still lift his leg up, even though it made a grating in his hip. He changed the water and rinsed the flannel, making it as hot as in an aeroplane, and washed his anus and private parts. Darlene had asked him to do that, for hygiene she said, and he played along. Usually it started to get him ready. Not tonight. He wouldn't tonight. Not after news like that. He wouldn't for Ulla.

Howie went into the bedroom, where the bed was like a raft floating on the sea, and like the sea itself with its duvets all in waves. Darlene's was peach – she called it peach – and blue and brown (which was chocolate), and his was green and purple, which he did not feel were colours for a man, but Darlene said yes they were, all that had changed. So okay, it was the bedroom, she could run things there – and sleep curled up, hugging herself, and snore like a rustling in dry leaves, which was female enough, and with the bit of coarseness that he liked. He put his clothes on a chair and was proud of himself for sleeping naked. Not many men my age – but cancelled age from that, and got under his duvet and waited for her to slide at him with a long puff of warm air, knowing he would tell her, Not tonight, even though he knew that now he wanted her after all.

'Howie – mmm,' she murmured, and here it came, the sweet and sweaty air and her body heating him down his side. Her damp cheek and mouth filled the curve of his neck. Darlene was Ulla's age. Exactly.

He thought, We'll have Damon up. I'll buy a trampoline.

'Howie Powie,' Darlene said as her hand grew full, 'you're a real phenomena.'

He did not correct her – had not known himself until Gwen had used it once, in the singular, about some flash of lightning or cloud in the sky, some Gwen bloody thing.

Howie groaned. 'You get on top' – although he did not let her as often as she'd like.

'Sure, Howie, you bet. All right?'

'That's good.' He kept his hands on her back, wanting to feel her spine.

'I'm going to buy a trampoline,' he said, which made her laugh.

What he liked most about Darlene, he made her laugh.

Gordon lived in Herne Bay. He leased an apartment with a view across the harbour to the Chelsea Sugar Works. Soon he would have to give it up and live somewhere cheaper. He would have to sell his car, and then what would it be, a second-hand Toyota? Nobody knew how broke he was. He would have to sack his lawyer and apply for legal aid. He would have to get a flat in Grey Lynn. He sometimes saw himself as one of those men who rented one-room sheds at the back of gardens and cooked on an electric ring and came up the yard and across the porch to use the toilet and came in once a week for a bath. It struck him with terror when he thought of it and he went blind for a moment and did not know where he was. They washed their underpants in a plastic basin and laid them out to dry on the window sill. They dug in the garden to save a few dollars on the rent.

Gordon couldn't work out how he had arrived where he was. He knew where he was, knew exactly, although he turned away and turned away. He remembered a time when he was doing nicely. But from Lupercal onwards nothing held still for him to see. What he couldn't remember was 'why'. He knew 'what' and 'how' all right but 'why' escaped in a way that tipped him sideways and left him feeling seasick, like on his father's damn launch in a swell.

Had he been in this condition, sick air-bubble in his chest, eyes seeing blurred, all that time? Was it what his mother might call a moral displacement, hanging there with feet not touching the ground, never quite finding anything solid under them?

He felt light-headed in the car. He felt as if the car was floating too.

Why didn't I see that it was going to fall apart? Dad, fuck him, told me. Why didn't I see they were all crooks? I'm not a crook but I'm going to jail anyway.

It never got more complicated than that. Gordon was a simple man. He was not a bad man. He was kind to people, he was generous, and when he had heard of Ulla lying in hospital with a broken neck he had been filled with horror at what he took to be the evil of the burglar's attack. He knew that with Lupercal he had been stupid; he had been greedy. But nothing he had done could ever be called evil. Moral corruption, the lawyer said. Men who are greedy to the marrow of their bones. It was wrong to allow people to get up there in public and say that – about me, Gordon thought, about *me*. He made it sound as though I'm going rotten; Jesus, he made it sound as though I smell.

The Audi swerved softly, floated off line, and Gordon could not understand the arrow pointing at him; then he pulled left and was safe. He had better park the car and sit still. Or take it down the harbour and drive in.

No, he thought. No. No! That was an idea to punish people with and make them grieve. Now he saw dark water and felt it closing over his head. 'No,' he said.

He stopped the car. Where was he? Everything was suddenly tipped on an angle. He felt sick in a different way. He was terrified.

Get out of here, he thought, and wrenched the Audi into gear and butted his way among cars released from a traffic light. He went at their pace and did not like it when they opened out. He got in close behind one and saw a fluffy dice suspended in the rear window, and a fisted hand with a smoke in it, burning above kissing heads. A sticker said: Plumbers do it with a wrench. The driver reached up and angled his mirror to kill the light. Gordon dropped back. He turned away and crawled in suburban streets and thought, They're all in their houses and I'm out here; and had another vision of dark water. Where can I go?

He drove into Broadway and up Khyber Pass Road and had no place ahead except his flat. Trees and gravestones. Roads that fell away, down out of bright lights into the dark.

He stopped around a corner and backed up; beckoned a woman smoking by a wall.

'Do you want to go for a drive?'

She sneered at him. 'You bloody mad or something? I don't go for drives.'

'How much?'

'Depends what for.'

She might be Indian, she might be Lebanese. Her lipstick was black in the dead light and her eyes were black.

'I don't know, I'll have to think.'

'My friend's seen your face, Mac, and she's got your number.'

'Yes, okay.' He saw her friend standing in a doorway. 'As long as she forgets it later on.'

'Sure, we can forget.' The woman got in the passenger seat. 'Where to?'

'Just down the street. We'll park somewhere.'

'You're fucking mad, mister. I don't do cars.'

'Just a hand. A hand job. Fifty dollars.'

Hand, he thought, driving where she showed him; as long as it was somebody else's, not his own. His own was wrong, his own was solitary and corrupt.

A dark place between trees that grew out of asphalt in the street. Strong scents in the car. This is a person, he thought, and this is something happening to me.

'What's your name?'

'Jilly. What's yours?'

'Nev.' Which was not a lie.

'Okay, Nev. A hand is what you get. Money up front.'

'Yes,' he said.

She had borstal tats on her finger backs and a triangle of dots in the web between her finger and thumb. He saw her work, half clumsy, not very good, but it didn't matter. Someone called Jilly, in a place between trees, in a street.

He gave her his handkerchief.

'That's an easy fifty bucks,' meaning to be friendly.

'You don't like it, too bad. You don't get any more.'

'I don't want any more. Okay, thanks.'

'You better drive me back. Here's dangerous.'

51

'It's only five minutes to K Road. Here, take a taxi.' He gave her another five dollars. 'Hey,' when she was out of the car, 'drop this in a rubbish tin.' He held out his handkerchief.

'Get rid of your own mess.'

He dropped it in the gutter beside the car, where some woman would find it and wash it, he supposed. Silk handkerchief, embroidered G.N.P. – which used to make him happy once, before Lupercal.

Four

Gwen found four nails and a hammer in the shed and a square
of brown board as hard as iron in the glasshouse. The cat had
abused his privileges for the last time. She had found him on
the bench chewing her steak, and had screeched at him and
chased him out, then hurled the ruined steak at the tunnel in
the hedge where he had vanished. Now she would hammer
his private entrance up, and leave the glasshouse open – let
him sleep there; and if he howled in the night she would turn
the hose on him. He knew the rules. She told herself that she
was growing tough.

She held the board in place with her foot and hit the first
nail, but it snapped a corner off like a malt biscuit and she
thought, What would Howie do? He'd drill a hole. Back in the
shed she put the piece of board in the clamp and drilled four
holes, shifting it round; then, getting clever, chose smaller
nails, the sort called brads, and went back to the cat-door for a
second try. Howie improved my vocabulary, she thought with
surprise; and she wondered who would win if each made
a list of words they had taught the other. 'Brads': one to him.
'Say peetza, Howie, you can't say pizzer': one to her. And
'moderation' and 'common decency' for her. 'Self-interest' for
Howie. She'd show the cat what self-interest was, with brads
and hammer and hardboard – thank you, Howie. Say thank
you Howie, don't just grunt.

She closed the cat door, nailed it up, and that was that,
another relationship adjusted. Another relationship mini-
mised; which from her point of view, in the present case, meant
improved. Now she'd have a slice of toast and packet-soup for

53

tea. She hadn't wanted steak anyway.

'What was all that hammering?' Athol appeared in the room, making her start.

'I nailed up the cat-door. If you frighten me like that I'll do the back door as well.'

'Sorry.' He went outside; inspected; came back. 'That's a rough job. Why didn't you get a man to do it?'

'I like to do my own repairs.'

'Yeah, but things nailed up like that, it starts to take the value off a house. Isn't there a catch you can lock a cat-door with?'

'Yes,' Gwen said, surprised, 'there's a pin inside. I forgot.' She gave a single mirthless caw at her stupidity.

'God,' Athol said, 'I give up.'

'Yes, do. What is it, Athol? What do you want?' Which was her welcome nowadays, where once she had pulled them in and kissed them and tried to make a difference in their lives.

'I can't go tonight,' he said. 'There's something I can't get out of.'

'Do you want me to?'

'Yes. I know you and Olivia were there this afternoon, but she doesn't want me. She looks at me once and that's that.'

'Moving her eyes is all she can do.'

'She talks to you. They told me.'

'You'd hardly call it talking. I do the talking.' I say, Hello, Ulla, I'm here, I'm holding your hand, I'll kiss you now. And what do you say? she wanted to ask Athol, but did not because it was unfair. One could only be careful with Ulla now. Be alert but hold oneself in abeyance too. She was good at it, while Athol wanted to alter things by an act of denial, for his own benefit and – she must be fair – for Ulla's too.

'Yes, I'll go. Does Damon . . . ?'

'I don't think it's good for him to see her like that. I talked to Dad today. He wants Damon to go up.'

'To Auckland, you mean?'

'Yes. After his school year. He could be there for his holidays. And then maybe, next year . . . '

'Ulla will be in Auckland. At the spinal unit.'

'I know, but by then it won't be so . . . '

54

'Harrowing for him?' Gwen said.

'Yes. She'll be . . . '

'Better adjusted?'

'Jesus, Mum.'

'What about Olivia?'

'We thought – '

'You and Howie?'

'Yes, we thought you and her, you could stay together. And Damon and Dad. That way . . . '

'The boys with the boys and the girls with the girls. What does Damon say?'

'He's all right. He knows Ulla will be going up.'

'And you want Olivia and me – ? Was it Howie's idea?'

'No, both of us.'

'You know he doesn't have any say in my life?'

'It's not you we're thinking about, it's Olivia.' She could only push Athol so far, then he showed his teeth.

'I'll have a talk with her and if I think it's what she wants . . . but don't you talk about me with Howie, I won't have it. What was he down here for anyway?'

'He's got this deal, PDQ, the old Kitchener block.'

'On Lambton Quay? Is that still on?'

'It's starting again. They thought they'd lost out to the Framework mob – you're not interested in this, Mum.'

So Howie Powie wins again, with Dorio and Quested, PDQ. She had hoped he would be finished with Wellington and would keep himself to Auckland where he belonged.

'How long does he spend here?'

'Two or three days.'

'At the Glencoul?'

'It's nothing flash. Just a room.'

'And this time he thought he'd fit Ulla in? Did he visit her?'

'It was a courtesy. He won't be going back.'

Courtesy, she'd taught him. It was a word, a function, he had learned fairly well and that he put to good use now and then. But Gwen did not believe in it here. Involving himself with Ulla was likelier to be an act of imperialism. She was angry. But she could not entirely subtract good feeling from his visit. It came with his sentimentality.

'Did he say anything about Gordon?'

'Not much.'

'How is Gordon?'

'God, Mum, anyone would think he wasn't your son.'

'Well, how is he?'

'Read the papers.'

'Gordon's just a little fish, isn't he?'

'That's his best chance. He's talking about a cheaper flat. And going on legal aid. Dad and I are going to have to pay for his lawyer.'

'But you won't pay his rent for him.' Gwen knew exactly how far their charity would go. They would keep Gordon just afloat for as long as they could, and try to keep him clean, or the Peet name clean; then they'd let him sink. And perhaps would find a job for him when he came out, an office without windows at the end of the corridor.

'He shouldn't have played on the money-go-round,' Athol said.

'Isn't that what Howie does?'

'Dad's in development. He's doing a job.'

'What about you? Are you doing a job?'

'Lay off, Mum.'

'You're in the papers.'

'My job is rental property.'

Fifty houses, Gwen thought. How many houses does a man need? Newtown, Mt Cook, Island Bay, Miramar: bits of Athol scattered all over Wellington. If you brought them together they'd make a suburb: Atholtown. And the people there all worried about their drains and their rent, and the rent flowing steadily into Athol's pocket. But he would say, I'm giving people houses, I'm putting a roof over their heads. It's simple business, supply and demand – which was true, but it had a flaw in it that she couldn't see. You'd have to go right back to Athol for the flaw, and there it became too difficult.

'This other thing is on the side,' he said. 'The *Post* will make a fuss but it was legitimate. My part was, anyway. All I did was make an investment.'

'Is that what Mr Fox did, make an investment?'

'Yes.'

56

'But wasn't he involved, as an engineer?'

'It's ancient history, Mum. He hasn't done anything wrong.'

'The opposition wants him to resign.'

'They always want that. You've only got to – hiccup.'

He had almost used a coarser illustration. All her men were good at being coarse. What did Howie say about Neil Hopkins – he's got a ten-foot flame shooting out his arse? Gordon and Athol had their little flames, propelling them all over the place like Christmas balloons shooting out their air. But Gordon hadn't managed to 'keep his nose clean'. She hated that, more than all the faecal and sex ones, because she had wiped too many infant noses and at times had seemed, as Howie said (leaving for work), up to her ankles in snot – which came from Gordon, there in court, and Athol here, lean and bald and brown, with a rat-trap mouth. His pink mouth was gone now, and his soft nose, from which everything that came, no matter how messy, had somehow seemed natural and clean.

She put the kettle on. She took a packet of chicken soup from the cupboard. 'Well,' she said, 'I'll talk to Olivia. She won't be as comfortable here, you know.'

'She would if you'd look after the place.'

'I look after it my way. She can't have the dog. He'll have to stay over there with you.'

'That won't work.'

'Why not?'

'He sleeps on her bed. She's soppy about him. You can't ask her to stop now, not with Ulla . . . '

'I've just got rid of the cat, Athol. I don't want a dog.'

He heard something weak in her voice. 'We'll see. What did you think of the identikit picture?'

'It looked like James Dean. Didn't they see the poster in her room?'

'She told them that was what he was like. They seemed to think it was pretty useful.'

'He had a more closed-in look than that.'

'Well, you tell them. They don't catch loners much, that's what I heard.'

'Even when they've got fingerprints?'

'Fingerprints are no good if he hasn't got a record. Dad wants to offer a reward.'

Gwen gave her mirthless caw again. Where had it come from, in a few days? Was it a response to Ulla, a statement that escaped? There was no amusement left even though funny things kept on happening. Howie would catch the burglar, catch James Dean. Funny, funny! He would buy Ulla a new spine if he could, and so would Athol – and at least they'd buy a special bed for when she came home, if she came, and turning and lifting devices, and an implanted receiver for her sacral nerve so she could pee, if that's what she needed. Howie could visit her and use the transmitter, he would love that, the next best thing to catching the man who had crippled her. She made the sound again, and again; and Athol had her by the shoulders, holding her.

'Come on, Mum, come on, it's all right, it's a shock for us all.'

'Let me go, Athol.'

'It's all right.'

'Let me go.' He obeyed. 'And it's not all right. Nothing is going to be all right. Do you understand what's happened to Ulla?'

'You'd better not go tonight. No one needs to go.'

'Do you understand?'

'No, I don't. How can anyone? It's one thing that leads on to another. We can't stop just because she's stopped – if she has.'

'Oh, she hasn't, that's the point. She goes on.'

Gwen sent Athol home. She made soup and toast and ate it at the kitchen table, then rinsed the dishes and left them in the sink. She drank a glass of water, Wellington water tasting of chemicals and rot, and remembered Athol's scheme for buying the rights to a South Westland stream and shipping tanker loads of water – 'Find a name for us, Mum' – to Europe and the Middle East; and how it had shocked her so profoundly – water was like sunlight and air – that she had found herself stepping back from him and putting up her hands to ward him off. Well, he had dropped that idea, though not for her reasons, and not before he had cried at her, 'I notice you don't mind drinking that stuff of Ulla's' – by which he meant Ramlösa, which Ulla bought for its name and the bottle's shape.

It all comes back to Ulla, Gwen thought.

Does that mean I'm not allowed to die?

Dial-a-Dinner arrived with steak and vegetables and chips, which Athol and Olivia ate off their knees in the livingroom. Damon was having a night out with Howie at the Glencoul: a swim in the pool there, then dinner in the Magic Isles restaurant – a name the boy had screwed up his nose at, showing good judgement in Athol's view. Fancy naming meant fancy pricing. He didn't believe in being on the receiving end of that. But he wished that Howie had asked Olivia too. It was natural that he should favour the boy but it left Athol feeling that he had to make it up to her. Getting dinner sent in didn't seem enough. He felt they should be talking and laughing.

Olivia turned off the game show on TV. 'I hate her, she's so skinny.'

'Isn't that what models are supposed to be?'

'She's not a model, she's a presenter. She looks as if she's going to snap all the time.'

'Ha, crack!' Athol said, but that seemed to be the end of it. Then he thought of Ulla's spine and he glanced at Olivia. She hadn't picked it up. She fed Butch a piece of steak, which he gulped noisily then stood looking up with bulging eyes, wanting more. That's the best thing, Athol thought, I'll have that bloody dog out of the house. He thought of Damon gone and was surprised to find that his life would be much easier. Olivia next door with his mother – he would see her. But Damon's never liked me. He likes Ulla better, they both like her.

'It's good not having dishes, eh?'

'I don't mind dishes.'

He saw her think of Ulla then; Ulla washing them.

'Have you got much homework?'

'A bit.'

'What?'

'Maths.'

One word conversations. Silences around single words.

'Make a cup of coffee, Liv.'

'Sure.'

'We should have got a pudding.'

'I'm still dieting.' She made the coffee and put it on the table by his knee. 'I'll be upstairs.'

'Yes, okay. I've got to go out. Your grandma's going in to see your mum. She's coming over soon to talk to you.'

'What about?'

'Just an idea she's had. She'll say what it is.'

'All right.'

Olivia went upstairs with the dog paddling behind her. So that's that, Athol thought. He took his glasses off and polished them. He felt a little sick and greasy round his mouth, and he pushed the cup of coffee away and got a can of beer from the fridge. He would have liked to stay home. Ulla was bossing him still, in the silent way she had perfected. Where would he go? He could go to the office. He could go and see Fox. Fox wanted to see him, but only to worry and complain. He drank some beer and looked at the movie ads in the *Evening Post*, but none of the names meant anything. The actors and actresses, who were they? And were the pictures meant to be funny or serious? He turned away from them, rattled pages over, and looked at the identikit picture again. He could not tell whether the burglar was a boy or a man. He had a nose too sharp and long – no one had a nose like that – and brows too clean. He should be a thug, he should be a Maori, not someone who looked as if he was walking home from school. Caucasian, Athol read. That meant white, although, of course, it pointed to a place where someone, some scientist, had said we started off; us white people, Athol thought. He did not know if the theory stood up. Had it been superseded, as scientific theories always were? His mother would know, it was her sort of thing. He wished there were only white people in the world. That would be a damn sight easier even if it still left things like this. Okay, Athol thought, he's Pakeha, but the inside of his mind has gone way back, he's primitive.

His mother came in but went past the living room and

climbed the stairs to Olivia. He heard their voices sound, one, two, and cut off as the bedroom door clicked shut. The house seemed built in cubes like building blocks. He shifted Olivia's room to his mother's house; saw his own with an empty space and frowned at it. But he could bring her back whenever he chose; bring Damon too. Ulla, he knew, was never coming back.

She wouldn't even look at me, he thought. It was good having her out of the house – except, of course, she wasn't out. She was everywhere, with her words going up and down in the way he had grown used to and not heard for years, and then had started hearing again, and felt the wrongness of and had wanted to stop.

'I didn't push her,' he said.

Fox, he thought, I'll go and see Fox. He left the beer half drunk and went upstairs. What he would like most was to go jogging in the botanical gardens, but he had said to both of them that he was going out. And his new running shoes were gone. Athol straightened, with his hands soapy, and thought of the rat-faced boy wearing his shoes. It made all his clothes, and the house, seem polluted. It hollowed him out with revulsion and fright. He washed the soap off and dried himself. Pull yourself together, he said. He hated having his mind go out of control; he wanted all the ways it went to lie in his command and no places, either dark or light, to be reached unexpectedly. Since Ulla, since the burglar, things kept arriving to disturb him. The house is the same, he thought, nothing's changed at all; just some jewellery gone, and a bit of money, and my shoes. I'll buy new shoes.

He changed into a paler suit and put on a tie with colour in it. He brushed his hair around the sides – the burglar should have taken the brushes, they would fetch a bit – and polished his forehead and took a fresh handkerchief from the drawer. The pile was getting low and he'd have to make arrangements for the washing soon. What he would do was hire a woman for two or maybe three days a week. He had been at Ulla for years to get some help. The way she had let the house run down made him furious. He saw that now he could change all that.

Athol cleaned his ears and dropped the tissue in the lavatory pan. He knocked at Olivia's door and put his head in.

'I'm off.'

'You can give me a ride down town,' his mother said. She stood up and touched Olivia on the crown of her head. 'All right?'

'Yes.'

Gwen kissed her. 'You're not nervous alone?' Olivia shrugged. 'Keep all the doors locked.'

'He's not coming back,' Athol said.

'Wait downstairs, Athol. I won't be long.'

He waited in the hall. Except by pushing her out and closing the door he couldn't see any way of stopping her from talking to him as though he were a child. He stood on the porch when he heard her coming.

'She shouldn't be left alone.'

'She's all right. She's fifteen now.'

'She's fourteen. Are you sure you know what form she's in at school?'

'You don't let up, do you?'

'I'm trying to civilise you, Athol. Why didn't you tell me Damon was having dinner with Howard?'

'Was it any of your business?'

They got in the car.

'Who are you going to see? Mr Fox?'

'That's not your business either.'

'Foxy-Loxy.'

'What?'

'The gentleman who smiles with his teeth and strokes his nice red whiskers.'

'You always have to be smart, don't you, Mum?'

They drove down Central Terrace, down Kelburn Parade, into town. The traffic lights, and footpaths going up and going down, and people on the crossings, were familiar to Athol; they made him feel he'd stepped across into the world that made sense after the one where meanings turned away. He blew his horn at the car in front to make it move.

'Here will do. I'll take a bus,' his mother said.

Athol pulled alongside the kerb.

'Is there anything you'd like me to tell Ulla?' she said.

'No.'

'Ring Olivia, Athol. Make sure she's all right.'

'You coddle them too much.'

She stopped with the door half open. Her hands closed like bird claws on the bamboo handles of her bag. 'Are you sure you know what's happened, Athol? Your wife's in hospital with a broken neck. Her spinal cord is cut in two and it can't be put back together again.'

'Get out of the car, Mum.'

'She can't feel anything below her neck and she never will. Her body is alive but there's no way it can let her know, and no way she can tell it that it belongs to her. They're worried about her breathing. And spasms. And bed sores. And how to empty her bladder and how to stop her kidneys being infected. That's how it's going to be for the rest of her life. Did you know?'

'Get out.'

'Olivia knows.'

'You're all words, Mum. You're in some fancy world and you haven't got a clue what the real one's about.'

'I think perhaps she could use some coddling. Think about it.'

She got out and closed the door with a three-inch slam. She left him with the smile – slanted, skewed – that seemed to say she knew, she knew, and he must learn one day. He hated it. He'd seen it all his life and hated it. He could not understand how Ulla's accident had somehow put him in his mother's power. That was something he must not allow – and going his own way, being alone, getting on with his work, were things that he must do now, no matter who got hurt.

He drove into Lambton Quay and turned off at the Kitchener block, half of it dead buildings and the rest barely alive, where one day his father's glass tower would rise. His father knew. Howie knew, better than his mother, and made no fuss about fine feelings and mystery. He knew that Kitchener was inside the line where a building would work, where tenants would come, he knew to a metre where the line ended, and why the Glencoul stayed full while the Plaza went broke. He knew when all the leases ran out everywhere in town and how much the tenants paid and when they would want better space. He knew how long to bed down a deal. He thought ahead. Research. Know-how. Acceptable risk. No mysteries. No smiles that said I know, you don't. Learn the system, work it, think ahead, take your chance, and go, go, go – make a difference that way, with new buildings and new jobs, and don't stop to wring your hands like poor fucking Gordon when the thing doesn't end up right. Cut your losses, try again. That was the lesson, and no stuck-up smile that said feelings were the main thing. That was for girls. He wanted Howie to have Damon.

I'm better off alone, that's my way, Athol thought.

He parked the car and went up dark steps into a lobby where broken tiles clanked under his feet, and found a lift waiting and pushed the button for the penthouse floor. On my way to see a minister of the crown, he thought, even if he is just a little one. The ease amazed him. You walked in, up you went, no security, and Fox would answer his own door. What was it Howie said? A man could make a fortune here in the assassination business if only someone wanted the silly buggers shot.

Red whiskers. A fringe along his jaw from ear to ear to emphasise the line of it and make him seem strong, make him seem his own man, who lived by his own rules, while in fact he was a wimp, with no opinions of his own, in and out of the shadows, grinning in the light with his strong teeth, and smirking in the corner, waiting for the main chance, which he wouldn't know when it came, and licking arse. That was Fox. A gift for words, in quantity not quality, and a gift for obedience, and a raging unfocused greed.

'Hello, Gilbert.'

'Athol. Come in, boy. I was just thinking about you.'

'Yes?'

'How's the lady wife? How's she getting on?'

'It's a broken neck, Gilbert. They don't mend.'

'Medical science is full of miracles. Don't give up hope. That's an order. I was reading in *Newsweek* the other day about a Korean boy, all sheared off at the hips he was and they've kept him alive, they've got him working again down there, built him a whole bag of works, new bladder, little plastic bag for his shit to go in. Can't give him a new donger though so I guess he hasn't got full privileges, ha ha, but what I mean, Athol, if they can do that for some kid, in some slant-eye place, no offence, then there's something they can do for your wife. Keep smiling, boy. Fox has spoken. What will you have? Scotch?'

'Thanks. With water. Half and half.'

'Water is a capital offence. It's the ruination of good Scotch.'

'It's the way I like it,' Athol said mildly. He sat on the sofa. 'How's it going, Peter?' – to the man there.

'So so.'

'Teaching him his steps?'

'You could say that.'

Okay, Athol thought, clam up. I don't want to know anyway, I just want to see how the pair of you perform.

'There is, of course, the other side of it,' Fox said, handing Athol his drink, 'and that is law and order, that's what concerns me most. Your wife's is a private tragedy, and I feel for you, Athol, I feel it here,' putting his hand wide-splayed on his chest, 'because I lost a lady wife too, before her time, in different circumstances – there was no lower life came off the streets, she was called Home you might say. I know you boys aren't of my persuasion, but a happening of that sort – enough! What concerns me here, a decent woman coming home to her own house, in the middle of the day, sun shining outside, birds in the sky, and she finds some creature, animal, in there, and he strikes her down. I want stronger laws to cage – they're sub-human, Athol, Peter. They lack a faculty, and in my opinion – put them down! That's our duty. We're human, they are not. Up from the drains. Half a brain. Fox has spoken. Drink up. That's an order.'

He should leave it to the minister of police, he does it better, Athol thought. 'What are you going to do about Shearwater, Gilbert?'

'Shearwater? Shearwater? Some sort of seagull, is it? Ha ha!'

'I don't like the way my name keeps getting dragged in. I bought something and sold something, a simple piece of business, years ago. I don't like being in the political stuff. So don't try and play me, Peter,' turning to him, 'or I'll say what really happened and that won't make Gilbert look very good.'

'It's on the record, Athol,' Peter Kleber said. 'You owned some property, that's all. We're not saying anything else.'

'There seems to be a suggestion that I persuaded him.'

'No.'

'Twisted his arm. Maybe you don't know it, Peter, he came to me.'

'Hey,' Fox cried, 'I'm here.'

'He said we should form a company and buy Shearwater farm because when the stormwater dam went in – you know all that.'

'Gilbert wasn't in politics then,' Peter Kleber said.

'He was in planning. He knew where the houses were likely to go – '

'Hey – '

'But the information didn't come to me in a privileged way. I'm a businessman. I invest. I don't know how it is for him, of course.'

'I'm buggered if I'll be talked about – '

'Why did you sell so quick?'

'Because I thought it wouldn't go. I told Gilbert that. And it didn't go. It's still sitting there.'

'And he still owns it,' Peter Kleber said.

'Not my fault. He could have got out when I got out.'

'It wouldn't have made any difference. As soon as he bought that land, knowing what he knew – '

'I won't tolerate this,' Gilbert Fox cried. 'I'm here, in this room, and I'm a minister of the crown and I won't be talked about as if I can't add two and two. Shearwater was a mistake. I wrote it off years ago. And I would have quit that property if I could have done it without taking a loss – '

'Wouldn't have helped,' Peter Kleber said.

'I know it wouldn't have helped. I know all I can do is damage control. But I'm an honest man, I didn't do anything wrong. Buying that land wasn't dishonest to me. I knew there was a chance the scheme would be shelved. I took a risk. But what I won't tolerate, in my own house, is to be patronised by some jewboy moneygrubber who counts his takings into a jam jar every night.'

'Jewboy?' Athol said, amazed.

'You act like a jewboy. Your brother's a crook. Your old man skates just inside the law. Peet's a dirty word. Athol, you told me Shearwater was all right, there was nothing I needed to worry about. Finished. Done. You sold at a profit. And you left the rest of us holding the can.'

'I told you to make your own minds up. Anyway, I'm off.' He had not touched his drink. 'I came by to say what I've just said – leave me out or I'll tell the *Post* how it started and I don't think there'll be much of you left after that, Gilbert.' He grinned at Peter Kleber. Grinning was hard. 'You're the one who should be in politics.'

Going down in the lift he thought, Jewboy! And Peet a dirty word. Gordon had made it that, with his chase after money. Work was not about money, money was a by-product and had to be respected, it was a way of measuring things; but work was about itself and for itself. If you did it properly you grew not in wealth, not in power, which was for people like Fox, but in busyness and accumulated pleasure in yourself. He came smiling from the lift – and thought of Kleber's stillness up there, at the end, and the instant pinkness in his cheeks. Kleber was, of course, a Jew, which Fox would be remembering. But Kleber wouldn't stay, he wouldn't take it, you took so much and then you got out. And Fox, without his right-hand man, was done for. Athol laughed. It was the first time he had laughed since Ulla had been attacked.

He drove to his office and let himself in. The Shearwater story was in his safe – all the records, with clippings from the *Dominion* and the *Post* – and he spent an hour turning pages. Not that there was any need; he had it in his head: his part, the purchase, 406 hectares, with Fox and Baster and Smythe – and there he was, Athol Peet, there was his name, but it did no harm, for he had sold his share and gone in the early days when he had seen that nothing would move, and that was the end of it for him – and Fox's part, the four-dollar companies with the inverted names, Treblig, Retsab, and the interest never declared. A stupid man, Fox, a greedy man, and not the smiling schemer his mother thought. There was nothing criminal in what Fox had done, but he would come tumbling down because he was in politics and someone had found out his secrets and his greed.

Athol was pleased. Stupidity should be punished and quick ways not succeed. Steak and oysters, French wine, fruity words, and all that slapping on the back and fat jokiness: for amateurs. Athol was a pro. He saw his way as monkish, simple, strait. He felt his sharp nose and polished head. The office was his place; he squeaked his chair, he rapped his desk.

I could put a bed behind the door. I could live in here, Athol thought.

Gwen sat at Ulla's bedside, by her head, which, she thought, was the whole of her. Torso, legs, stretching away, arms arranged, fingers spaced, they were nothing now, they were bone and tissue fastened on with latching that was merely mechanical and Ulla was up here in the dry melon of her head. How could it be, how could Ulla survive? Mind and body were linked, sacramentally one might say, if nature were allowed its sacraments, and now that this divorce had taken place did the partner here at home have a way of making herself seem whole?

She slept. Who slept? Could she any longer signal sleep to the parts down there? Perhaps they were awake, independently. Gwen shivered – and thought, Stop. She was not the one it was all about. She had to think of Ulla as a person on a bed even if hideous things were going on. She held Ulla's hand – it *is* her hand, although I could stick pins in her and she wouldn't know – and traced Ulla's mouth with her fingertips. That would be felt, perhaps, in her fractured sleep. But her own hands seemed divorced from each other, and her left to betray her right. No, stop, she thought, I musn't imagine or I'll go mad and I'll be no use to her then.

The stitches exposed in Ulla's cheek were comforting. They closed a wound that she must feel. Her lips, swollen and dry, and her eyelids, swollen too, and moist, seemed filled with the excess of life stored in her head. It was all up there in that round shell held in the halo brace. Could Ulla be seen as larger now? In spite of the screws fixed in her skull? In spite of the shrinking that her clipped hair seemed to show – the desiccation on the surfaces?

Gwen dipped her finger in the water glass and wet Ulla's lips. 'Ulla,' she whispered. Did she have night and day or was she simply intersecting planes of consciousness, and lights, and spaces, and faces that leaned and receded? Did she have memories, and did she have now? And understanding, did she have that? Ulla, she thought, I don't want you to understand. Then: Ulla, you've got to know it all. She too seemed broken into parts, and did not know which one she must stay with.

'I'll sit with you for ever, love, if it will help,' she said. And blushed a little at the falseness of it. I want to help her live, she thought; but how much life is left, and does all that body down there count?

Meanwhile Ulla slept, and half woke, and slept again, receding, advancing, on slopes that tipped her sideways and made her hold on. From time to time – although there was no time – she found a land where she could be still. It stretched to far horizons in a dark blue night and glowed from deep within itself. Lakes looked through to empty other worlds and the sun lay invisible below the smooth outline of the hills. A mountain gleamed like a dog's tooth and two or three yellow stars blinked in the sky. She tried to stay there . . .

2

Five

The money was safe but not the jewellery. He did not look at it again but put it in two handfuls in a sock and tied the top with string and drove up the Ngaio gorge and down Old Porirua Road, where he threw it from his car window into the bush. He followed it, a harder throw, with the satin box. The other sock, knotted to give it weight, he lobbed over the car roof as he drove back to town on the Hutt Road. For a few moments he was free. He felt as if he'd drunk too much and gone outside and spewed and now felt good. Or as if he'd washed his hands and face. The ballsed-up day was over; he had fixed up his mistake.

At the start he had locked his door and sat on his bed, doubled up as though his guts were aching; he had looked out the window, and lain down, and heard noises, and waited for something to happen. Up the hill the cops were in the house. The space between there and here was gone. They could grab him by reaching out an arm. Everything stood hard up against him.

He saw the woman touch the floor lightly. Her head rushed at the edge of the door. A crack like kindling wood. The door swung with her weight as she slid down. 'The stupid bitch.' But mostly he remembered his hand on the stair rail and every time he thought of it an itching started in his palm.

He turned on the radio and heard the ZB news at six o'clock. It was there. A thirty-six-year-old woman hurt in an attack by an intruder in her Kelburn home. The police were looking for a slightly built male with fair hair, in his early twenties, wearing a navy sweatshirt and carrying a dark-coloured bag. Some money and jewellery were missing from the house. .

It made him feel better. That could be anyone. Fair hair, jeans, a bag. Anyone. If you didn't have dark hair it was fair. If you weren't tall or fat it was slightly built; and jeans and a sweatshirt, anyone. Then all his details of face and body – mouth, nose, knees that bent, eyes that looked out – crowded in and the man was him. He recognised himself. He felt that he must not let anyone see him any more.

He drank some Coca-Cola from the fridge. When it was dark he drove out to Ngaio and dumped the jewellery, remembering not to keep the odd sock. He bought some fish and chips from a Chinese in Courtenay Place. A burger was what he wanted but McDonald's was too bright; he thought it sensible not to go in there. And sensible to go home and get off the streets. He ate his fish and chips sitting on the bed and drank another can of Coke and counted the money again. Fourteen hundred and forty dollars. With what he had in the bank it brought him to over five thousand. He felt that he should celebrate. Go somewhere. Listen to some rock and have a beer. And not think of his hand and fingerprints. Stop thinking about the woman and wondering if she would die. The woman was no business of his.

He put his jacket on and walked three streets down to the Hermitage. Went in from the alley, past a car with an insane rottweiler inside, bought himself a beer, sat in the dark listening to the band: Karori kids with a name like that, Killing Bambi. The place started to fill up – guys wearing bandannas and torn-off sleeves and leather vests, girls with nose studs and shaved hair. Too many nigs though, too many tats, it made him nervous. He edged to the bar – rub of leather smooth as soap, with smells sucked up in it. Bought another beer, slid back. Kept himself alone against the wall.

More people came in. The lead singer started a death-metal roar. Lights bulged and shrank like jellyfish. They turned from red to green, going faster; faces and biceps were printed on the dark. Eyes that shone like oil turned at him. Rosser put his beer on the floor, where it spilled and coiled between his feet. He held his hands over his face until the roaring stopped.

'You okay, mate?'

'Gotta go.'

He ran out almost doubled up. The rotty clawed and slobbered on the glass. Eyes gone mad. Rosser ran the three streets home; locked the door again; curled up in the dark on his bed. 'I've got to stop this' – but could not think of any way he might. He knew that what was perfect had been broken. He knew that now he could not act in his own way but must watch what other people did and then do something in return. It seemed that he would never be alone. People were around him everywhere.

So what do they see? And what do I do? The jeans, the sweatshirt. He stood up and took them off. He picked his bag up in the dark, heard something fall and roll away, but did not switch the light on until he had stuffed his clothes in and zipped the bag. He stood in the room in the light. Opened the bag again, put in the sneakers and socks he had worn that day. 'Yeah,' he said, and took his underpants off and put them in too and stood naked on the mat. He looked at his new Reeboks down against the wall. They glittered there like ice. 'Shit,' he said. 'Jesus,' he said. He wanted those. But made himself put them in the bag. He zipped it up and flattened the bulges in its sides.

He took clothes from the cupboard and put them on. He put his old sneakers on and went out with the bag into the night. Cars were parked on both sides of the street, some dark, some coloured where the street lamps hit them. He walked along to his Escort, but it was under a lamp, green although it was blue in the day. He did not want to go into the light and open the door where anyone could see him, and did not want to leave his prints on the car. Shit, his prints were everywhere, all over Wellington; wherever he touched things there they were. Rosser felt his hands were diseased.

He turned back at the edge of the light and went out the other end of the street. It climbed left and climbed right, losing its footpath, and levelled out between walls covered with graffiti. The concrete was broken back to reveal the clay, and the lower holes were stuffed with beer cans and old sacks. He could push his bag in there; but it was too close to home. Light

75

shone down in this gully too from houses high on the banks and people could look at him from the windows there. He put his head down and walked fast and turned into a narrow street, keeping away from a seven-day dairy on the corner. The Indian was leaning on the counter, adding up, but his eyes kept looking out after each sum. He seemed frightened of the night outside his shop. Rosser went away, showing his back, down and left and right and up again. His idea had been to drive out to the Ngaio gorge and put the bag in the charity bins by the auction yard. Now he did not know where he was going. He was looking for a rubbish skip. He was looking for a hole. Brooklyn was above him and Mt Cook behind, and Newtown lay spread across the flat. Brent wasn't sure where he was. The streets ran below a row of trees.

He came to a place that showed Adelaide Road. A red light stopped cars one by one, banking them up. An ambulance went through, using its siren, and a police car nosed out and followed it, flashing the light on its roof. They only had to stop him and look in his bag and he was gone. It felt like a hump. Eyes were looking at him everywhere.

He went into a park where children's swings hung over worn grey patches in the grass. They squeaked in a breeze, iron squeaks almost too soft to be heard. Over against the black trees, cigarettes: someone there. He sat on a bench and put his bag beside him. He wanted a cigarette himself but did not want to light up his face. He sat still; kept very still. Tried to make the voices out. Kids. Islanders? Maoris? Now and then a laugh. Now and then a mask, a gleam, as one of them sucked on his cigarette.

Rosser thought, I'll leave it here, they've got to come out. They would find the bag and share what was inside. It would go all ways and none of it would ever be found. Better than the clothing bin. Nothing would be given to the cops. He felt a lightness as he stood up. He felt as if something had been scooped out of him and a hollow left. He crossed the grass and stepped outside and clanged the gate. That would bring them. He felt that he could show his teeth again.

Feet padded on the grass. 'Hey, man.'

So they had found it. In the still night he heard the zip.

76

'Mine. Hey, I found 'em. Give 'em back.'

Let them fight as long as they took the stuff away. He walked back the way he'd come and lit a cigarette and went into the dairy for a new pack. The Indian took his money, gave him change, without a word.

'Cheer up, mate.'

He went out and stood on the corner. I've got five thousand dollars, he thought. He wanted to see someone, knowing what he knew. Leeanne, he thought. She was down there somewhere, in the hollow. He'd know the street as soon as he saw it; it had a panel beater on the corner. He went past narrow houses and tiny front yards. Leaves brushed his face and a scent of flowers came and went in a single breath. He reached a corner, saw the panel beater's leaning shed, and turned right into a street of houses more hunched up and closed in than before. It made his own place look like Kelburn. Leeanne should find somewhere better to live. He walked along by windows he could have leaned across the fence and touched – opened, climbed in, taken what they had, if anything worth taking was in there. Rosser curled his lip. No money. No jewels. Just TV sets and beat-up heaps parked in the gutter and kids' broken toys on the path.

Leeanne was at the end. Her house was dark. He pushed the gate open and stepped on to a wooden porch as closed in as a wardrobe. He knocked on the door, one, one two. She shouldn't be in bed yet; it was only eleven o'clock. He heard someone swear, and feet bang on the floor. A window squealed up beside his head. He saw a torso gleaming and tattoos on huge arms.

'What the fuck you want?'

'Leeanne. I want Leeanne.'

'This fucken late?' The man turned his head into the room. 'Leeanne,' he shouted. He vanished and a door opened inside the house. 'Leeanne. Some joker for you.' Feet came back, the window slammed, a bed creaked, a man's and a woman's voice rumbled and breathed in the dark.

Rosser waited. He heard another door and heard bare feet. The front door opened a narrow crack and Leeanne said, 'Who's there?'

77

'It's me, Brent. Let me in, Leeanne.'

'What's the matter? What do you want?'

'I just thought I'd call in. I haven't been round lately.'

'This late? Jesus, Brent.'

'It's only eleven. What's everyone in bed for?'

'They have to work. Keep your voice down.'

'Who is he?'

'Jody's boyfriend. Go down in the kitchen. I don't want Sam to wake up.'

He went half a dozen steps down the hall, found an open door, turned on the light. A sink, a sideboard, a table and two chairs. He sat in one. A smell of fish and chips and sour milk and old rags. His mother should see this, she'd have a fit. Leeanne came in. She sat down and shivered in her nightie.

'What do you want?'

'Nothing. I was passing. I dropped in.'

'No one passes here.'

'I do. Make us a cup of tea, eh? I'm thirsty.'

'Listen, Brent, I need my sleep. Sam wakes for a feed at two o'clock.'

'Who's Sam? Ah, the baby.'

'Yeah, your nephew. Don't pretend you're bloody interested.'

'Sure I am. It's hard to get used to. How old is he now?'

'Ah, shut up.' She closed the door and put the kettle on. Skinny, skinny. Stringy legs. Big boobs, from feeding he supposed. And stains on her nightie from her milk. He looked away. He felt ashamed of her. She had been good-looking once and everyone had been after her.

'You got a job yet?' she said.

'There's no jobs. Have you?'

'With Sam? Grow up. How do you live, Brent? You can't run a car on your benefit.'

'Who says?'

'You're in some racket, aren't you? Pinching or something.'

'Bullshit,' he said.

'Don't get caught. I'm enough for Mum and Dad.'

'Do you go and see them?'

'A couple of times. You should too.'

78

'So the old lady can tell me off? No way.'

'She's not so bad now. She's giving up.'

'Not before time. How does she like . . . ?' He hooked his thumb at the wall.

'Sam? Not much. Dad's good with him though.'

'A coconut grandson.' He grinned to take the sting out of it.

'Yeah, he is. He's real brown, Brent. I love his brown.' She smiled at him, which made her pretty again. He wondered what she would say if she knew how much money he had.

The kettle boiled and she made tea, using the same tea bag in each cup. She gave him the strong one.

'Who's Jody?' he said.

'A friend of mine. We share the rent.'

'What about the boyfriend? Jeez he's big.'

'Yeah. You be careful if you're coming round here. He's got a temper. He whacks her round.'

'Does he touch you?'

'Ssh. No. The walls are thin.'

'Do you have to share with them?'

'How else am I going to pay the rent? Wait on. Jesus!' She stood up. Little wet patches showed on her nightie. She opened the door and went up the hall and he heard a whimpering from the baby, quickly cut off. She came back in a moment, carrying him. Already he was latched on her breast. His snuffling and grunting put Rosser off his tea.

'There,' Leeanne said, 'your nephew. What do you think?'

'He's brown all right. He's browner than before.'

'He loves his mum. He can't get enough of his mum.'

'Is his father ever coming back?'

'No. He's not.'

'I thought the Islanders didn't like to let their babies go.'

'Yeah, well, Sione doesn't know. And that's the way I like it. Okay?'

'Sure. Okay.'

'You going now?'

He wanted to stay and talk, but not with the baby making sounds that turned him in his stomach. The brown of him against her skin was wrong. Leeanne was blonde and white. It

79

was like one of those pictures you saw in the paper, one animal being sucked at by the babies of another.

'Yeah, I think I will.'

'Come around sometimes, Brent. Not so late though, eh.'

'Okay.' But he would not, unless she sent the baby back, got rid of it somewhere. He put his hand in his hip pocket; a five and a ten there, he didn't know which would come out. 'Hey, Leeanne. Can you use . . . ?' It was the five. He was relieved and put it on the table.

'Sure I can. I can always use money. Thanks.'

'See you.'

'Don't bang the door, eh. Danny gets stroppy.'

'I treat big fellers real careful.'

He left her and went up the hall and out of the house. Closed the door with care. Left her happy. She was happy. Rosser couldn't understand it. As long as it was sucking she was happy, he supposed. He shivered and turned away in the dark street.

Leeanne was the only person he had ever liked.

Rosser stayed at home the next day. He heard the people in the flats on either side of him: heard their radios and heard them cooking and shitting, and Mrs Casey crying after her husband left for work, and heard her smash something, a cup or plate, on the wall. He hadn't heard them screwing the night before, which was unusual. He lay on his bed and listened to the radio, and went down to Adelaide Road and bought a *Dominion* at ten o'clock. He carried it home before reading it. There wasn't much there, and hadn't been much on the radio. The woman was serious, that was all. Her name was Mrs Ulla Peet, which was German he supposed, a name like a joke. It shouldn't worry anyone if she died. He hoped she would because she'd seen his face. So had the girl. If this was a movie he would go after the girl. The killer always had to get the ones who saw his face. Killer, he thought. He liked it, and it scared him. But serious meant she'd live; they hadn't said she was critical.

The same description of him, and nothing about fingerprints. Maybe they hadn't found them. Maybe they just did doorhandles and stuff like that. Rosser felt his confidence come back. He bought two pies for lunch and threw a half he couldn't eat to the Laverys' doberman in the yard. In the afternoon he swept his floor and wiped the lavatory seat with disinfectant and squirted Harpic in the bowl. He always thought of his mother when he did that. He thought of her cleaning the fridge and the hand basin and the bath – wiping away at things already white. His mother was, he knew, a little mad. 'She's disinfectant crazy,' Leeanne used to say. He would like her to see how clean he was keeping his place. He would like to tell his father that he had five thousand dollars.

Later on he watched the tennis on TV. Tennis didn't interest him, but the running and the sweating and the serious way they took it, he liked that. He liked to see them swearing under their breath and banging their rackets on the ground. The names were good too – Andrea Stradnova, Sabine Hack; names like that just up the road and round the corner, in the wind. You could find a name like Ulla Peet there. He watched their shirts get sweaty and stick to them and their legs scissoring and their ankles straining and teeth flashing and he admired the way they kept on hitting and did not stop, each one closed up in herself. He wanted both of them to win. Stradnova did. That was okay. She was a big good-looking girl, not trying to be sexy.

Mrs Lavery came home and fed her dog. She kept it, Lavery said, because she was scared of getting raped. Casey came in, and laughing sounded through the wall. Rosser cooked potatoes and peas and lamb chops, and was eating when Lavery came in from the pub. Silence on that side. She'd freeze him until they started shouting later on. Both lots would have kids soon, with names like that and Jesus on the wall, but they'd shout and laugh and break things and creak the bedsprings until they did. When kids started crying Rosser thought he would get out. He could afford a better flat than this. He drank some Coke and washed his dishes. He walked out for a *Post* and found nothing new. And nothing new on the radio or on TV. He had a sense of all the streets and houses in Wellington. How could they find one person there?

He slept well. The house groaned and shifted in the wind but he felt the walls around him hard and firm, and no cars, no dog barks in the night had anything to do with him. There were sirens at a quarter to two – he read his watch glowing in the dark – but they were fire not police, and he imagined the house in Kelburn burning, with flames like sheets wrapping round the walls and the girl screaming in a window, and maybe he would rescue her and maybe not. The next thing he knew Mrs Casey was busy with her pots beside his ear.

He would shift soon, he thought, lying in bed. He didn't have to get woken up by women in the kitchen, that was something he had heard all his life – and it meant get up, get washed, get dressed, do something with yourself son, the world wasn't made for lying in bed. A pity he couldn't show her his five thousand. The biggest thing she'd ever seen was probably a tenner. Tenner, said his dad in his old slang, I wish I had a tenner on me now, that nag will bolt in. Rosser slept. He woke with his cock hard and he held it and stroked it for a while, thinking of the tennis players, then stopped because he'd promised himself only once a week. After a while it went down. I'll shift, he thought, I'll go to Auckland. I might even go to Oz. The Laverys were quiet, and so were the Caseys, and soon she went and he went to work, and Lavery sloped off to do whatever he did in his no-work day, and Mrs Casey started the wash. Stuck in here between two lots of Catholics, he thought. His mother would get thin in her mouth if she knew. Romans, she would say. 'The tykes,' said his dad, 'the biggest boozers of the lot. It's okay for them, son, they can go and tell the priest and start all over again.' Sometimes Rosser felt in danger, caught at the arse end of the house, with Romans on two sides and the dobie chewing his bones in the yard. I'll go, he thought, I'll go to Oz. I've got five thousand dollars. I'll sell the car and take off. He thought of himself doing houses along Sydney harbour where the millionaires lived. They didn't have his fingerprints over there.

He got up, he washed, he had his breakfast. He counted his money again. I should have given Leeanne more than five. I'll give her a hundred when I go.

At lunch time he was at Oriental Bay, parked under the

Norfolk pines, watching swimmers in the choppy se
didn't stay long. A cruise ship was tied up at the o
terminal, as big as half a city, shining white, an
Americans were probably all over town. He smoke
dropped his butts out the window. If I could get on the
thought, and get in some of those cabins. He felt like a shark
again, cruising underwater; and coming up the sides in black,
with suckers on his palms, and through the open hatch and
down the corridors, and no one sees. Rosser laughed. He'd fill
his bag with dollars and watches and rings until it wouldn't
hold any more. 'Yeah,' he said.

He drove around the bays and saw the hill road to
Wainuiomata, and thought of his mother there pegging out the
clothes, and his father thinning carrots in the garden. He
wouldn't tell them when he left, they didn't need to know. A
letter from Oz, that was what they'd get. He saw the prison on
the hill and a Qantas jet taking off over Lyall Bay, leaving its
exhaust in the sky, and swinging right as it climbed over the
strait. Okay, he thought, I'm going. I'll get my money out, I'll
buy a ticket. He could be on that plane tomorrow.

Rosser drove back to town through the tunnel. He drew
three thousand six hundred dollars from his account, and left
a few dollars to keep it open. He might come back some time,
you never knew, and it saved messing round to have an
account. The teller didn't say anything about the amount, just
asked him for ID and how he wanted it. She didn't put it in an
envelope. He thought they always did that when you took out
a lot. He frowned and looked the other way when she told him
have a nice day.

Rosser stopped at a car yard and asked for a price on his
car.

'It's not much use to us, mate, not in that condition. I can
let you have two-fifty, that's top price.'

'Hey, come on.'

'No one wants these things any more.'

Stuff you, Rosser said under his breath. He went away. The
pleasure had gone from his afternoon. The Escort was worth a
thousand. Had to be. He didn't drive it hard, he kept it tuned,
the warrant was up to date, the rubber was good. All cars that

age had a bit of rust. He would ask Ponder about it. Ponder knew the price of everything. She might even buy it herself. There was nothing you could name that Ponder didn't buy if the price was right.

There was no need to tell her he was leaving for Oz.

He found a park off Tory Street – 'Don't you put your car in front of my place, young Brent' – and walked across to the top of Cuba. Up the hill the houses in Central Terrace made a jagged edge on the sky. He could not pick out the two he had been in, and if he stopped to work it out people would notice him. Anyway, that was gone, ancient history. He crossed the street, heading towards the big crane over the new foundations in Ghuznee. Sunlight reflected from the driver's box, blinding him. That was what he'd always wanted to be – not a pilot, not a truck driver: he had wanted a crane. Wanted to climb up high, on the iron ladder, and sit in the glass box, leaning forward, with the city spread out below, the men in hard hats, the concrete trucks, and turn the whole circle with his load and drop it neat. Seeing everything. He watched the arm swing slowly and the counterweight come round. The glass made the driver invisible. I could still do that, Rosser thought, there's got to be a way of getting that.

But he had stood too long in one place and he moved, found the iron door to Ponder's yard and side-stepped in among her rotting junk. She didn't like him coming in the front way, he had to wind among the old lawn mowers that never got covered from the rain and would never sell, the stacks of timber spiked with rusty nails, the window frames and warped doors and fire places with the tiles dropped off; and the canoe with the rotten canvas, the piebald horse from a circus roundabout, the park bench, the bike frames and bike wheels, the chain harrow, the basketball goal, the stacks of rusty corrugated iron, the ship's propeller. What did she keep these things for? They'd been lying in the yard for as long as he'd been coming. Under a lean-to the whiteware stood, black with grime around the foot and furry with dust. Handprints in it. Faces. Half a sum someone had not found the answer to. Washing machines further along, fridges and stoves out of the Ark. Freezers that would hold a horse, if anyone could lift them out of here. Rosser slipped amongst them and looked in at the door. Kapok mattresses roped up or flopping out like tongues. Bed wires, beds, ends of carpet, chests of drawers, wardrobes, bookshelves, books – and nothing ever changed and nothing sold. He saw her in her office, half way down, with what she called 'my antiques, dear, my really good stuff' between her and the street door. She wiped it with a rag sometimes but none of it sold either.

Rosser went towards her, rubber-soled. Shark, he thought. But when he was still five metres away she said, 'Don't come creeping up like that, young Brent.' She must have mirrors; she couldn't have heard, not with traffic passing in the street.

'How are you, Mrs Ponder?' he said, and stood at her door the way she liked.

'You can come in. You can sit down.'

You had to wait until she asked. He sat on the hard chair, almost touching knees with her as she squeaked around to face him in her secretary chair, and he shivered at her scent as strong as Harpic and the purple lipstick that leaked into the wrinkles round her mouth. She was fifty, sixty, seventy, you couldn't tell, with her hair red from a bottle and her eyes coloured up and her eyebrows shaved off and painted on and her nails dark red. 'No decent woman paints her nails,' his mother used to say. No decent woman, Rosser said, uses scent like that. He wondered what other smells it hid and what she might be like under her dress. Outside in the street she had a Volvo, bloody Volvo, and out in the Hutt somewhere a house crammed to the doors with stolen property, so he'd heard. She sat in here and played at junk and old furniture and all the time she was the biggest fence around. With millions in the bank probably. And never caught. Rosser had been passed on to her by Leon Briggs, who had let him play the Game City machines as payment for nicked stuff. He had got too big for Leon. And now he was too big for Mrs Ponder – moving on. He smiled at her.

'Did you want me for something, dear?' she said.

'Yeah, I wondered' – he swallowed and was angry with himself – 'I wondered if maybe you'd like to buy my car.'

She watched him for a moment, then she smiled. Little

brown quick eyes, she had. 'You need your car, don't you, Brent, you travel around so much?'

'Yeah, well, I thought I might get a better one.'

'So what you're saying is, you want to sell me one that's not very good?'

'I didn't say that. It runs okay. I've never had any trouble with it.'

'Keep it then, dear. Never sell a car that's running well.'

'Sure, if you say so.' She did this to him, tied him up, every time. He knew that he had made a mistake in coming to her.

'Is there something else, Brent? Something you wanted to tell me?'

'No, nothing.'

'You haven't been leaving it somewhere you shouldn't?'

'Course not.'

'Well, that's good.' She put on a pair of glasses and looked at him over the top. 'So many people bungle things. But you're always such a careful boy.'

He understood at once that she knew something. And then believed that she knew everything. Ponder had a way of swelling out and wrapping herself round you so that you couldn't move and couldn't speak. His mother was the same. Knew everything.

He managed to say, 'What do you mean?' And saw from her smile that he had told her even more.

'That horrible business in Kelburn, where the poor woman had her neck broken,' Ponder said. 'That's an unlucky family, Brent.'

'How? Unlucky?'

'You should read the paper, dear.' She tapped an *Evening Post* folded on her desk. 'Her husband's brother is in court for stealing millions of dollars. Gordon Peet. And talk about coincidences, Brent, her husband is your landlord. He owns the house where you live.'

'No he doesn't.' He could not move his arms from his sides. 'I pay the rent to something called Athco Properties.'

'Oh yes, that's him. Athco. Athol Peet. He owns more than forty houses, would you believe? But now his wife has got a broken neck. And her jewellery is stolen too.'

86

It was like a dream where you had to run but your legs were dead.

'I daresay whoever took it has thrown it in the harbour. That would be the sensible thing.'

'Yeah. I s'pose,' Rosser croaked.

'And of course he should never work again. Not anywhere.'

'Why's that?'

'They've got his fingerprints. Don't ask me how I know, I just hear things. Have you seen the paper, Brent? No, of course, it's just come out.' She unfolded the *Post* and opened it at page three. 'They've made an identikit picture.'

He looked at it. It wasn't him. It couldn't be him.

'Now let's drop this silly nonsense, Brent,' Ponder said. 'You're a good boy, you're a nice boy, but you're finished in Wellington and I never want to see you or hear your name again.' She took off her glasses and laid them down. 'What you do is, you go away. And you never do your kind of work again, you do something straight, and you never say boo to a policeman. And most of all you never mention me. To anyone. Never ever, Brent, do you hear what I say?'

'Yes, all right.'

'Say it then.'

'I never talk about you.'

'And I go away.'

'I go away.'

'Because I can drop a word, in the right ear. Any time, Brent. Australia would be best. You go there.'

'Australia. Yes.'

'So that's all. Except one thing.'

He waited, dry-eyed. He felt as if his face had withered up.

'You took some money too. I want that.'

'No, Mrs Ponder.'

'Yes, Brent.'

'I need it, I need it for Oz.'

'You've got more. I know you've got more. I'm feeling generous so I'll let you keep that. But I know how much you took from up in Kelburn. You bring it here tomorrow night. It's my late night.'

He turned about, and turned, in his mind, but there was nowhere he could go. 'Yes. All right.'

'Come in the back way. And then, Brent, remember, Ponder never sees you again.'

He nodded his head. He could not speak.

'Don't look so sad. It's a lesson in life, dear. Off you go now.'

He stood up. He went out through the old furniture and mattresses and through the junk-filled yard into the street. He did not know whether he should turn left or right. The weeds flowering in the gutter burned like fire. Lights in the sky shone down on him and there was nowhere he could hide.

Six

Leeanne had breakfast with Jody in the kitchen. She supplied the cornflakes and Jody opened a can of peaches. Leeanne fed peach syrup to Sam as he stood holding her leg. She liked to feel his nails, paper thin, cutting her. It hurt, but it didn't matter; Sam was standing up and holding on. She loved each new thing that he did, like his first tooth, even if it made her nipples sore. Soon he would walk. That was when she would have to watch him. Sam was going to be lightning quick, like his old man. He'd go down the sideline and dive in at the corner and they'd be left sprawling on the ground, the beergut forwards and the skinny fullbacks, Auckland ones or Aussie ones, it made no difference. Sione's patch, that was what they'd called the corner where he had dived in; and now he was in Sydney, trying to make it, and maybe he'd get a run for Souths next season and play in the grand final on TV. She would show Sam his father scoring in the corner and say, 'That's him, that's your old man, you be like him, you play for Souths, no you play for Manly or Balmain, and you be famous and make us a million bucks.'

Sione wasn't coming back, Leeanne knew that. The truth was she didn't want him back. Sione was beautiful and Sione overflowed, and when you were with him you felt full yourself and were happy like him. But who was Sione? He shifted round so much in his head, and he was gone, nobody there, or someone else was there and you had no place with him even when you had his baby inside. Sione no-name. He'd left her sprawling on the grass like a slow forward. Okay, he's gone, he's doing something else; she was not going to get in his way.

She didn't love him, she'd just had fun with him, but fun always ended and she had come out of it with Sam and he had crossed the Tassie and got himself a Souths girl. Good luck, Sione. Show them, Sione. Get in the Kiwis, Sione, and I'll tell Sam who you are.

She had left home at sixteen and gone to Auckland and fluked a job and followed a team and had been Sione's girl, and now she was back home with a baby, in Wellington, and that was okay, but she wished to God they'd give her more in her benefit. Even the twenty-two bucks they took off because she wouldn't say who Sam's father was, that would help. She could maybe get rid of Jody then – not that Jody was a problem, but getting rid of her would get rid of Danny too and she hated him; it was like having an animal in the house, a pig, or a wild boar, yeah, grunting and farting and knocking things around and showing his muscles and his gut and his stupid tats and guzzling cans and squashing them and chucking them under his leg at the rubbish tin and always missing and Jody had to pick them up; and eating stew, that she had to pay a third share of, piled up like horse turds on his plate; and screwing Jody all night long until you thought there was a whole herd of pigs in there.

She wanted Danny out, but had to have someone to help with the rent. Another solo, that would be the story, and they could share on all sorts of things, split the washing and cooking and mind each other's kids so they could have a night out now and then, just go to the flicks – she hadn't seen a picture since before Sam was born. Danny had taken Jody's TV into the bedroom so she didn't even get to see that now.

'Give us a smoke, Jody.'

'Can't. I've only got one left.'

Cigarettes were something else she had to do without. She only smoked when Jody was feeling generous.

'He do anything to you last night?'

'Nothing he hasn't done before.'

'You should boot him out, Jody.' She had bruises on top of bruises. It didn't matter whether he was angry or excited, the horse bites on her thighs hurt as much as the punches. 'He'll hurt you real bad one day.'

90

'I know.' Jody took her last cigarette and lit it. 'How do I get some money if he goes?'

'The benefit.'

'I still got three months stand-down. I shoulda stayed with Norman.'

'Boot Danny out and get Norman in.' Whoever he was.

'How do you boot out someone like Danny?'

'Just tell him. I'll do it. You want me to do it?'

'No.' Jody looked frightened.

'I don't want him here, Jody. You don't want him either. Get him out.'

Leeanne did her washing. The wash-house was a lean-to shed at the back of the house. She took the nappies out of soak and rinsed them and put them in the old beater machine with her towels and sheet and nightie and blouses. Knickers too. All in together. Save on electricity. Stop the machine and take the delicates out so they don't get beaten to death. Sam stood with his hands on the bowl to feel it churn – all through the wash, feeling it. 'If you didn't piddle so much, Sam, I wouldn't have so much washing to do.' She pegged it out, and there he was, quick as a flash, just as quick as Sione, across the yard on his hands and knees, and hauling himself with dirty hands half way up the sheet. She put him in the back door in his bouncer.

'I'm going out,' Jody said.

'Where?'

'Dunno. Down town. You going out?'

'I might go and see Mum and Dad out Wainui.' She needed to sit in a place Danny hadn't stunk out, in a clean kitchen, and talk to someone she knew, even if her mum still wore her mouth like a zipper and gave Sam back as quick as she could. Her dad would cuddle him. She could talk to her dad in the garden, where the veges ran in rows, and bring home silverbeet and radishes. The five dollars Brent had given her would just about pay for the fare. 'Your turn for tea, eh?'

'Fish and chips.'

'No way, Jody, you did that last time. I'll bring some vegetables. You get some meat.'

'I can't cook it the way Danny likes.'

'For Christ's sake, put it in the pot and make a stew. Get

91

some mince if you like and thicken it with flour. Okay? Okay?'

'Yeah, okay.' Jody left.

'Bloody no-hoper,' Leeanne said. The truth is she wanted Jody out as well as Danny, and a solo like herself to share the house, no complications. Women together, and their babies, three maybe, even if the place was too small, and boyfriends out by eleven o'clock. She didn't need a boyfriend now, not after Sione. She drank a cup of tea at the table and dreamed of him – Sione kissing. Kissing was just about the best part with him; he seemed to suck her life out and draw it into him, she almost died. Hours they'd spend; not like all those other useless buggers her girlfriends had, in out and let's go down the pub and have a beer.

She caught a unit after lunch and changed to the bus at Waterloo. Up the hill they crawled and over the top, and suddenly it was a different world: the town in the valley, with bush all around. She had grown up here and when people said, 'You come from Wellington, eh?' she always answered, 'No I don't, I come from Wainuiomata, different place.' She had it in her mind, the streets and houses and shops and schools, like a map; and the park where she had watched the league from the time her father took her when she was four and sat her on his shoulders to see over the heads. Wellington, okay, sparkled when you got to the top of the hill; it shone in the night and the road leading to it was like a string of beads. But coming back was better – down the hill, top speed, screaming on the corners, coming home. Wainui was best. That was what she had believed all the time she was growing up.

Even now it made her mad when people ran it down. State houses eh, working class, and all those Islanders and all those Maoris, and gang fights eh, and murders eh, and no jobs and half the people unemployed? But that wasn't Wainui; that was everywhere, except a few suburbs up on hills where they didn't have to know what went on because they were rich up there and didn't have to see. Here in Wainui you had to see, and in Petone, and in Porirua up the line. All the league places. Her loyalty flared up and she thought of Sione running for the corner flag.

She passed the street where the fight had been – Islanders

and Maoris and two people dead. So what? Up in Khandallah the doctors poisoned their wives and the lawyers bolted to Oz with other people's money, millions of it. Here at least you hit with lumps of wood and robbed the corner dairy and got caught down the pub.

She stopped at the end of her parents' street and looked at the house where she had grown up. State house, yeah, but her dad was buying it. The best-kept house in the street, best lawn, best garden – because he enjoyed it, not to show the neighbours up. That's where he would be. Potatoes hoed and mounded, and the pea shoots breaking through, with bamboo stakes criss-crossed down the line. And the compost heap working in the corner, hot when you stuck in your arm, if you had the nerve, and the worms in there pinker than the worms you dug outside. Her father wasn't useless any more when he got a spade or fork or hoe in his hands, when he got seeds in his palm and squinted at them, picked a dud one out and flicked it away. She went along in front of him, poking her finger in the soil, and he walked patiently behind, dropping a wrinkled pea down each hole. 'This one is the queen pea, she'll grow extra pods', and she believed him. It came up first and had fatter peas, she was sure.

Sam squirmed in the pushchair. He wanted out. 'You'll have the whole lawn soon,' she said, and walked along to the gate. There it was, like a bowling green. With borders of impatiens, and freesias scenting the air. 'Smell it, Sam.' She went in and stopped on the path and picked a flower for him, but of course he wanted to eat it. She unbuckled him and left the pushchair at the side of the path and rang the bell. 'Keep your fingers crossed, Sam.'

Her mother came; a shadow behind glass. 'Oh, it's you,' and stepped away.

'Hi, Mum. Long time no see.'

'Wipe your feet. Is that baby dirty?'

'Sam's his name. No, he's clean. Kiss him, you don't have to touch. Kiss Granny, Sam.'

'I'll call your father. He's in the garden.'

'We came to see you too, Mum. Where do we go, in the kitchen? Hey, you're looking well. Is that biscuits in the oven?

93

They smell good.' She kept a patter up so she would not put the baby under one arm and hit her mother. One day she would hit her, nothing surer. 'Well, what's new?' She sat down at the table and held Sam on her knee.

'Ask your father.'

'I'm asking you.'

'Why doesn't Brent come and see me?'

Always the same, always Brent. 'I'm here instead. Say "Nice to see you, Leeanne." Say "Welcome, dear."' The same worn puffed-up face. How could it be worn and puffed up at the same time? The same kitchen heaviness and greyness. Once she had been pretty, in a round-faced way, and that was what her father had gone for, she supposed, and ignored the rest. Words came out of her like stones. And yet she kept on loving Brent. It was no wonder he kept away.

'I suppose you want tea?'

'Sure, a cuppa, that's good. And a biscuit, eh. Sam's got a new tooth, Mum. Open up, show Granny your tooth.'

Her mother turned her back and filled the kettle, then stood waiting for it to boil. Back to Leeanne, hands on the bench. Eyes looking where? Nowhere. That was how Leeanne remembered her, standing still at the kitchen bench. Half of her life must have been spent there, switched off from things she disapproved of. Except, today, she seemed further away. She'd held Sam last time, for a minute, and kissed Leeanne on the cheek. Now her disapproval was set fast and somehow didn't need to be shown. It frightened Leeanne.

'You're sure you're okay, Mum? You're not sick?'

Her mother turned as though something had gone click in her mind and took the tray of biscuits from the oven. She put it on the bench and gave each one a tap to set it free. The kettle boiled. She warmed the pot. Warmed the cups. Made tea. Everything perfect. Everything dead.

'Has Brent got a job yet?' That was alive.

'I think he must have. I don't see him much. He's got some money.'

'Tell him to come and see me. I need to know what state he's in.'

'How do you mean?' But she knew that her mother meant

94

Brent's soul. What about my soul? she thought. Why don't you save me, Ma? Save my little Sambo bastard here. You bloody try!

She heard her father taking off his boots at the back door. He washed his hands in the wash-house and came in wearing his socks.

'Hi, Dad,' she said.

'Leeanne. Hey, my grandson, give 'im here.' He kissed Leeanne and took Sam and sat him on his arm and looked at him: all done somehow with a pause, a space in his behaviour where his wife must be looked at. 'He's grown, Leeanne. Well, you're a big boy now, aren't you?'

'We've got a new tooth,' Leeanne said. She wanted to cry.

Her mother poured the tea. She put warm biscuits on a plate. Then she took her cup away and closed the bedroom door.

'What's wrong with her?'

'She's under a strain. Take it easy on her, Leeanne.'

'She should take it easy on me. She hasn't even touched Sam. It's like we've got bloody Aids or something.'

'Come outside and drink it on the lawn.'

She was glad to. The garden shone. All the leaves were polished and the earth like chocolate. She put Sam on the lawn and let him go. Eat what you like, she felt like saying.

'You haven't lost your touch, Dad.'

'No.'

'But what's wrong with her?'

'She's going to some place over in the Hutt.'

'What? A church? What happened to the Presbies?'

'Not far enough out, I guess. This lot dunks you in a big bath. They want me too, Leeanne. There's a guy comes round, a skinny little bloke, looks like a crab, he grins at me and says there isn't much time left for getting saved.'

'Jesus, kick 'im out.'

'I can't. Your mother. They do, tongues they call it. They talk a kind of gabble and fall over on the floor. I had to get out of there, that's not the place for me. She can have them.'

'Sure, she's welcome. Don't you do what you don't want to, Dad.'

'I won't. Leeanne, I don't know, the worst thing is – she's got no love, it's all dried up, her love is gone.'

She never had any in the first place, Leeanne thought. Almost said. Instead she said, 'She's got some left for Brent.'

'No she hasn't. She'd burn him at the stake, I reckon, if she thought it would save his soul. There's something called Last Days, I think, is coming. You're a goner, Leeanne. There's no hope for you.'

'Three cheers.'

'She reads this stuff about, beasts it is, and signs and so on. It's all crazy.'

'Brent couldn't stop it.'

'No one can. I don't know what to do. I guess I just have to keep on going. I'd have you here, Leeanne, you know, I'd have you like a shot, but I can't, with her.'

'It's okay, Dad. I'm okay.'

'Tell Brent to keep away.'

'I will if I see him. Don't worry about him, Dad. He's got a job. He gave me five dollars to get out here.'

'How are you off for money?'

'I'm okay.' Lies all in a row, coming out. She wanted to pat her father and comfort him. 'Anyway, the garden's looking good. The peas are up.'

'There's still time for a frost.'

'We'll leave out something for the Frost King, eh?' They had done that, the pair of them, when she was a child – a lolly, a biscuit, half a banana, and it was always gone in the morning. But her father would not smile at her. He lay on his back and gave a sigh. His cup tipped over and the tea ran into the grass.

'What is it, Dad? Is something else wrong?'

'Yeah, I guess.'

'What?'

'I got made redundant last week.'

Jesus, she thought, one thing after another. We've got all the bad luck in the world. But it wasn't luck, not only luck. The Rossers didn't know how to work the system, they got stuck at the bottom because they didn't know. When you were down there you turned into rubbish and they swept you out the back door with a broom. Sam was at the garden, tipping

96

off the lawn on to his nose and grabbing dirt. She rescued him and let him start again.

'So what happens now?'

'I don't know.'

'Did they give you some money?'

'A bit.'

'How much?'

'Fifteen hundred. I'm using it to pay off the house.'

'They've got to give you more than that. Jesus, Dad, you were there twelve years.' Driving on the vans and then as a storeman.

'I know. But Bostons is a small firm. They can't afford proper redundancies.'

'That's what they say. Does the union know?'

'They don't care. Only me got laid off, they're not going to worry about one man. Anyway . . . '

Yeah, anyway. He did not want to make a fuss. Too decent, that was his trouble. He'd creep away and lie on the lawn and not know what to do. And in the end he'd get up and look for another job, and never find one. Who wanted a man of forty-six who could drive a van and put things on the shelf? There wasn't a place for him any more. And he had thought he had it made, house and family and job and garden.

'Is everything paid off, Dad? It paid the mortgage?'

'Just about.'

'Well then. When do you go on the benefit?'

'There's some sort of stand-down. I've got a bit saved up. We'll just about get through.'

'So you're okay. Nothing to get your knickers in a twist about, eh? Why don't you work in other people's gardens? Advertise yourself, why not? Let Clyde Rosser turn your section into a radish farm. Hey, worms for sale, worms for sale, eh?' She fetched Sam and sat him on her father's stomach. She went into the kitchen for more tea.

I'll end up carrying this family on my back, Leeanne thought.

She went to the bedroom and knocked once on the door. 'More tea, Mum?' She was sitting at a little desk, almost like a student – her mother who had never read a book in her life, reading now something with a golden cross on it, and marking things in pencil; and the double bed gone, which meant that her father was kicked out to another room. But it's not my business, Leeanne thought. 'Would you like a biscuit?'

'No thank you. Nothing for me.'

'Okay, Mum.' She closed the door. She felt as if she was saying goodbye for the last time.

She played with Sam, her father played. They changed him when he was dirty, wiped him with newspaper and burned it in the garden incinerator. The sun shone, her father laughed. He fetched a supermarket bag from the wash-house and together they pulled carrots and radishes and little white turnips, half grown, and cut silverbeet leaves that were not ready yet, but so tender Leeanne ate one raw – and when she left he picked a bunch of freesias by the gate. Their scent filled the bus going home.

She felt she was taking her childhood over the hill with her to Wellington.

Almost six o'clock and no one in the house. No tea ready, nothing on the stove. It meant that Jody had got stuck with Danny in the pub – and fish and chips for tea again, nothing surer than that. She left Sam in his pushchair and brought her washing in: bone dry, that was something. She took it to her bedroom and threw it on the bed. A piece of paper lay on the pillow.

Hey Leeanne I'm shooting through. Can't say where or Danny will find out. Good luck mate. See ya! Jody.

'Shit!'

She looked in Jody's bedroom. Everything was gone. The TV gone. The bed stripped. But Danny's stuff was still there: his clothes on nails, his stack of six-packs down behind the door.

She went to the kitchen and fed Sam mashed vegetables and topped him up with milk. He had slept on the bus so she let him amuse himself on the floor while she cooked some silverbeet for herself and fried an egg. She would have to move fast, get Danny out tonight and look for someone tomorrow.

Jody still owed rent and getting it from Danny was a no-no. She thought of what she might say to him. Telling Jody she would get him out had been easy, but now, faced with it, did she have the nerve to say, Sorry mate, you don't live here any more.

She put Sam in his cot. She washed the dishes and listened to the radio, holding it on an angle to get it clear. New batteries soon – another expense. She should hit Danny up for Jody's rent. But maybe he had come in and found a note of his own and gone hunting for her, and maybe he was never coming back. Lazy sod, even his six-packs wouldn't bring him: plenty more six-packs down the pub.

Just stay calm, Leeanne told herself. Off you go, Danny. Close the door behind you. Don't come back.

At half past ten she locked the house and went to bed. She listened to the cars at the end of the street, and Sam breathing like an old man, and she told herself, okay he's gone, I'm okay now, and she was asleep when he came.

She heard the gate bang and heard him on the porch and at the door. 'Come on, fucken Jody, open up.'

Oh God, she thought, oh shit, what do I do? She got out of bed and went to the window, took the dowelling peg out, ran it up.

'Jody's not here, she's gone. You'd better go away.'

'Fucken hell she's gone.'

'She has. She left a note. You'll have to find somewhere else to live. I'm sorry, Danny.'

'Fucken hell she's gone.' He pushed the door.

'It's locked, Danny. Go away. You can get your stuff tomorrow.'

'I fucken live here.' He put his hip on the door and heaved. It burst open.

Sam, she thought, and ran out to the hall and shut the door. Danny heaved her away and she went running backwards and fell on her behind and smacked her head on the bathroom door. He turned on the light in Jody's bedroom.

'Fucken bitch, she took the TV.' He came out and stood Leeanne up against the door. He put his hand on her face, the web of his thumb and fingers under her nose, and lifted, pushed her up until she thought her nose was tearing off. 'Where'd she go?'

'Don't know,' Leeanne managed to say, half scream.

'Where?'

'Note. She lef' . . . '

'Where?'

'Kitchen.'

He let her go. 'Show me.'

She squeezed by him, cringing, and turned the kitchen light on. Her mouth was bleeding and her nose felt broken. She took the note from the kitchen drawer. Danny read it. He looked up red-eyed; he was breasted, bellied, huge. 'Fucken bitch. Good fucken riddance.' Even with her damaged nose she smelled him filling the kitchen.

'So now you want me out, eh? Get rid of the fucken boyfriend?'

'No . . . but I can't – '

'Who you think pays the fucken rent?'

'I don't want . . . '

He put his hand in his pocket and pulled out a wad of notes, took some off. 'Here, the rent.'

'No – '

'Take it, bitch. You fucken take it.' He pulled the top of her nightie out and rammed the notes in. They scratched her breasts. She turned round and took them out, and knew that if she tried to give them back he would twist her or break her in some way, so she put them on the bench.

'Okay. So now you're my landlady. So where's the fucken tea?'

'There's nothing. Nothing here to cook.'

'What about beans? She leave some beans?' He pulled the cupboard open and took out a can. 'Cook those. We got any eggs?'

'There's two.'

'So fry them. Go on, landlady, cook some tea.'

'I want – '

'Where you going?'

'I want to put something on.'

'Nah, stay like that.' He took the last can of beer from the

100

fridge. 'You think I want a skinny bitch like you? I like my sheilas with some meat on them. Go on, cook.'

But she knew that he would want her. Half a dozen beers on, a feed on, she would be the next thing, he'd want her.

She opened the beans and put them in a pot. She put the frying pan on the stove.

'Fry 'em in butter. Plenty of butter,' Danny said. He went to the bedroom and came back with a six-pack. 'Next time you keep it in the fridge. I don't like my piss warm.'

I could get out, she thought, the front door's open. I could beat him into the street. But that left Sam. There was no way she could get Sam out. Scream, she thought, scream in the street. But he'd only drag her in. Screams round here happened all the time. No one ever called the police.

She served his meal, beans with eggs on top.

'That's a fucken useless feed. Where's the rest of it?'

'It's all there is, Danny. It wasn't a big tin. I'm sorry.'

He liked her apology. 'Buy big tins, okay? An' pork chops tomorrow. With plenty of spuds. And some pudding. No fucken pears or shit like that. Peaches is what I like. We got some now?'

She looked in the cupboard. 'There's a tin.'

'So open it. Make like a landlady. And wipe your fucken nose, eh. I don't want no blood falling in.'

She washed her face at the kitchen sink. She opened the can.

'Forget the fucken plate. Come on.' He ate the peaches with his fork and drank the syrup from the can.

'Listen, Danny, you can stay,' she said. 'I'll do the cooking and your washing and stuff like that. But that's all.'

'Sure it's all. I told you, I like my sheilas so I can get hold.'

And tomorrow when he was at work she'd do what Jody had done and go . . . where, for God's sake, where? Not Wainui. Maybe Brent's, she could go to Brent's and stay with him until she found a new place. Getting through tonight though, how did she get through tonight?

He lobbed the peach can at the rubbish tin. It bounced off the door jamb and rolled into the hall. 'Fucken missed.'

She picked it up. The front door was open and she saw the

gate beyond, open too, and the street, with a gleam of cars.

'You got a skinny arse,' Danny said. 'Nah, give it here. 'Nother shot.'

She brought the can to him and he missed again. 'Not my night. Gizz a look at you, Leeanne. Jeez, you're a dirty bitch.' He flicked his fingers at her breasts, where the nightie was stained from Sam's feed. 'It's enough to put a man off his tucker.' He raised the front of her nightie with his toe. 'I'd never get in there, eh, too fucken small. Jody, you bitch, where'd you go . . .'

Leeanne took his plate and rinsed it at the sink. Her mouth was dry. Her hands did not tremble but gave jerks and she put them on the taps and held on hard to keep them still.

'Jody,' Danny said. She risked a look. Tears were rolling down his face. She took a can of beer from the fridge and put it in front of him.

'I've got to go to bed,' she managed to say.

'Yeah, piss off. Get outa my fucken sight. And don't try running out, because I'm fast. I'll tear your fucken head off if you try.'

She went up the hall and into her room and closed the door; leaned against it, listening for sounds. Sam was breathing softly. A radio was talking, and was suddenly switched off, over the street. She heard the hiss of Danny opening the can. Now, she thought, get Sam and run. But her arms and legs felt weak, she did not believe she could do it. If he chased her and caught her with Sam . . .

She closed the window and put the peg in. There was no key for the door and nothing she could use to jam it shut. She lay on her bed and held a napkin over her mouth, tasting blood. All she could hope for was he'd drink himself blind and flake out and go to work in the morning and she would have the whole day to get out. She could go to one of those refuges, they would take her, she had a bruised mouth and nose to prove it. She stood up and crept at Sam and felt his forehead and cheeks. Warm, warm. He breathed and sighed and made sucking noises and slept again. Lucky Sam. She would kill Danny if he tried to come into her room.

She lay down again. She heard him throw the empty can

at the rubbish tin and heard it bounce and roll on the kitchen floor. She heard him open one, two, drinking through the wall, and talk to himself, and heard him belch. If he drinks enough, and goes to sleep . . .

He walked up the hall and fetched another six-pack and went back to the kitchen and started those. She counted, then she dozed, a little safer, and heard him pissing at the middle of the bowl, emptying himself, five minutes long. He finished, zipped, did not pull the chain. Walked in the hall . . .

'Hey, Leeanne.'

Oh Christ no, oh please no.

'Can I see the baby, Leeanne?'

She ran to the door. 'Go away, Danny.'

'I want to see the baby. I like babies.'

'He's asleep. Go away.'

He turned the knob and pushed; slid her back.

'No, Danny.'

'Won't hurt 'im. Just want to hold 'im for a minute.'

'No – '

'Hey, Leeanne, that stuff about skinny, eh, that was kidding, eh.'

She slipped by him into the hall, yanked him back, closed the door. 'Not in there. You're not going there.'

'Don't you push me round, Leeanne. I don't like fucken people pushing me round.'

'Stay out of my room. Okay? Okay?'

'Sure okay. Don' wake the baby, okay?'

'Go in there. In your room. Go and sleep in there.'

'Sure I will. That's my room. You come too.'

'No, Danny.'

'You're not so skinny. You got nice tits.'

'Stop that.'

'Shouldn' waste good tits on the baby. Hey, Leeanne, lemme see you feed him, okay?'

'In here, Danny. There's your bed. Lie down now. Go to sleep.'

But it was, she knew, no good. Danny would not sleep. There was knowledge in him. He need not be as drunk as he was letting himself be. She would fuck him to stop him waking

103

Sam. No way out. She must try to keep him friendly. She must try to get away and feed Sam by herself.

And somewhere in the night Danny would hurt her. She wondered how badly he would hurt.

Seven

Like tiddlywinks, Howie thought, flying into Wellington. Up into the air and down into the bowl. He didn't like this city, cramped up in an arse-end place and full of hot-air merchants, full of wankers, who thought that the important thing was a set of rules they'd just made up. Seventeen meetings over seven months, and still they were inventing objections.

He looked at the buildings cluttered on the edge of the sea. Without the reclamation there would be no city there. Great harbour but the land was second rate. It should have been left to the seals. A little fishing port maybe, that should be Wellington, with a wooden wharf sticking into the sea. Auckland was the proper place for the capital. He felt that he was dropping down conferring benefits and he looked forward to the time when he would climb back into the sky and fly north to the town where he belonged. He felt, too, like a Viking coming out of the mist, standing in the prow ready to leap on to the beach and loot the churches, sling the women over his shoulder and sail off.

It would please the newspaper hacks if they knew he felt like that; it would make them yabber with delight, for that was how they liked to portray him: a raider. Even the cartoonists had fastened on to him, without of course bothering to look: shark teeth, top hat, popping champagne corks. The pot belly they drew on him offended him most. If they bothered to look they'd see that he was muscle and bone. And if they ever talked to him they'd know he was more than that.

It amazed Howie that no one had ever asked him what he thought – what the mental and imaginative components might be. They believed that he had nothing in his head. They believed he was a pair of grasping hands and an open mouth and a belly popping buttons off its shirt. They drew him as though he was never quiet and never alone. He saw and grabbed, they seemed to say; but they could not begin to understand all the things that made up 'seeing', or that 'grabbing' was part of a process and not instinctive at all, not greedy at all, but a reasoned step. The instinctive bit came earlier. Howie had worked it out, the three parts: imagination, purpose, action. Money had a place all right. Money had to be got, like men and materials, to make the project – whatever it was – move. It was part of the content in a plan or scheme, a part of design. Due proportion, Howie thought – money comes in there. And if I make some cash at the end, why shouldn't I be paid for my time? It was wages. The cowboys, the quick-flick boys, went out in '87 and now it was five per cent stuff, and okay too, okay with him. He didn't want more than he could earn.

Ron Quested did. Ronnie had to be watched. He was one of the arse-flame boys who had come through clean, by accident; and now he believed he was – who was that bloke of Gwen's whose mother dipped him in a creek so spears wouldn't touch him? Ronnie believed he was like that. He wanted more than he could earn, and he would probably get it. He could always add up quicker than the next guy and grab the bits that got left lying round. Watch him, Howie thought, don't let the bugger screw the scrum. Keep him out of the way when you say, This is the deal. Howie always did that part as open as a book, no matter what the lawyers were computing.

Tony Dorio drove him into town. They came out of the tunnel on to the Basin and Howie began to like Wellington more. Its cramped spaces made him feel that he could knock down and put up endlessly. It got his adrenalin flowing, which was good for a meeting that might be filled with quick and sudden stuff. Tony would do the talking and Lonnie Baldwin keep score, but they knew, everyone knew, that he was the one who said, This is it, let's go.

'How's Ronnie? Sulking?'

'Not too much. I think he'd be sorry if we screwed up.'

'We won't screw up. If we play it right we'll go through on the casting vote. You keeping him busy?'

'When he's in. He's out most times.'

'Doing what?'

'He wants to build a restaurant. He's out with Peter Kleber looking at sites.'

'Why Kleber?'

'He's split with Gilbert Fox, that's the word. He and Ronnie went to school together.'

'The old boys, eh? Wanking in the dormitory. And now they want a restaurant so they can be Hudson and Halls.'

'It's not like that,' Tony said mildly.

'Maybe not. Tell him to put something together and we'll look at it. Just keep him out of Kitchener.'

'Sure, Howie,' Tony said. He drove in his non-Italian way, changing down, changing up, everything smooth. Tony never went off line and never took a risk. He's perfect for what I need him for, Howie thought. He's the other part of me. Without his steadiness and his attention, PDQ would have missed getting Kitchener. The client liked him, AMP; the planners liked him too, that's why Howie let him do the talking. But I'm the life in him, Howie thought; behind it all there's me. I'm the one who sees it, no one else. It was like being up the willow tree, swaying in the wind, with the whole of Falls Park, the changing sheds, the diving board, the picnics and sprat-jaggers and canoes spread out below. No one but Howie Powie had the whole view.

What we need now is the demolition, he thought. Until that building's down they'll keep on trying to change the rules. Today was just one more attempt. Seven months ago Council had voted fifteen-five in favour of an underground carpark on Kitchener, jointly funded, twenty per cent to eighty per cent, by PDQ and themselves. That twenty was the PDQ sweetener – parking spaces to keep the shopkeepers happy, and Council, or the Citizens amongst them, happy too. What Howie was after was the airspace above. That was where his tower would go. The tower was the reason for it all. He had known that the greenies and their mates, the sandal-wearers and lentil-eaters, and the usual claque of old-building freaks and car-haters, would get busy and swing a few, but he had not foreseen how many, or that they would force another vote. It was ten-all now and everything depended on the mayor.

A bloody professional wobbler, Mrs Dunwoodie, the mayor. She was ending her first term and was up for re-election in November and so was trying to please everyone. Who was the politician who said, I must follow them, I am the leader? That could be Mrs Dunwoodie's motto. The only way to firm her up was to wave the big stick.

'Get me Lonnie Baldwin on the phone,' he said in the office. 'Lonnie,' he said, 'Howie here. Have you got that letter ready to go?'

'Hey, no,' Tony Dorio said from the door.

'Hang on a minute, Lonnie. Yeah, what?'

'It'll backfire.'

'No it won't. You point the gun, you pull the trigger. She's not going to go to court and lose the Council more than a million bucks.'

'You could push some of the others offside.' Tony, with palms lifted, was Italian suddenly. 'I hope you know what you're doing, Howie.'

'I do. Lonnie? Send it so they get it early in the afternoon. And I'll want you there tonight, so come round here and you and me can work out a strategy.' He put down the phone.

'I think we've blown it,' Dorio said.

'Ah Tony, if we blew it we blew it a long time ago. Now I want to talk to our lady friend before she gets the squitters too damn bad. Get me the mayor,' he said to his secretary.

'Mrs Dunwoodie. Cora. I know you're going to stand firm on this. I've checked with our lawyers and the precedent says you vote for the status quo. That means the decision of March 10, approving the project.'

'I'm not sure I know what you mean.'

'The March 10 decision is the status quo, that's what I mean. You're bound by it.'

'No, I'm not. I've taken legal advice as well. The status quo is that we do nothing, because nothing has been started yet. There's no contract.'

'I think you're wrong there, Cora. The agreement consti-

108

tutes a binding contract. That's what my lawyer says. You decided fifteen-five. You voted for it yourself.'

'But I can't go against my own advice. I can't do that.'

'You're getting bad advice, Cora. It's going to be a tied vote so the decision's yours. And you have to vote for the way things are. That's the rule.'

'I'm not going to be pressured, Mr Peet.'

'Hey, call me Howie. Look, get some independent advice. Get someone from outside Council.'

'I can't do that. You don't understand, there's great opposition to this carpark. I must be seen to do the right thing.'

'You must be seen not to wobble, Cora. That's the right thing for you, politically. And you can't go costing Council big sums of money. There's been too much of that, the ratepayers don't like it at all.'

'I think we might have to discuss all this in public – '

'You can't do that. It's confidential stuff. You'll be in breach of contract.'

'Well – what did you mean, costing Council big sums of money?'

'For the work we've put into Kitchener already. There's a letter from our lawyer on its way round right now. All the details are there. We don't want to go to court over this.'

'I haven't seen any letter.'

'It's on its way. They'll send a copy straight through to you.'

'I think you're making a big mistake.'

'Well, we don't want to do it this way. But you've backed us into a corner so there's not much we can do. The only one who can make a mistake now is you. I think you should go for the status quo in there tonight. In fact it's what you've got to do. We'll see you, Cora, in, what, nine hours time? I hope it all works out okay. Bye for now.' He hung up. 'Shit, bye for now' – to Dorio – 'I never thought I'd hear myself say that.'

He felt as if he'd been in bed with Cora Dunwoodie and left her flattened out on the mattress. It sustained him through an afternoon of phone calls and discussions with consultants and councillors friendly to PDQ, and Dorio and Baldwin as well, and when they went into the Council Chambers that night he felt a burning in his blood and a fullness in his chest – adrenalin working – and he was ready for another bout. If he won here the next step would follow; he could get the Kitchener building down, and once that was done there would be no turning back: games were over and the real thing was under way.

He kept himself remote, but secretly, behind a still face, conducted the meeting like an orchestra. Tony and Lonnie Baldwin talked for him – Tony neatly, going over the negotiations between PDQ and Council step by step, keeping it simple, turning everything into a fact; Lonnie in his singsong voice, a bit like a nervous schoolboy, but effective all the same, pointing out that Council's decision had established a binding contract, which might lead to court action if an attempt to rescind were made. PDQ – and Lonnie made Tony read the figures – had clocked up seven thousand professional staff hours and costs exceeding a million dollars in preparing the proposal.

Beasley, the Council chief executive, replied that no contract existed because he had refused to sign one. Unlawful, Lonnie said, but never mind; the contract was legal without his signature because PDQ had met Council's requirements at every point in negotiations.

That was thin, Howie knew, but he kept his eye on Cora Dunwoodie – advanced into her and knew her again. She was the one who counted, the vote was hers. And he knew that he had her – felt her reading things politically, felt her cross the boundary into choice, into risk, with a jolting in his own heart and with a rushing in his blood that for a moment dizzied him. Good girl, he said.

She interrupted Waterhouse, the greenie: 'I feel I must warn councillors at this point, I must ask them to remember that anything they say can be used in court if legal action follows tonight's decision.'

Good girl. He did not object – though Lonnie objected – when Council moved into closed session to talk to their lawyers.

'Don't worry,' he said as they waited, 'we've got her.' There's only two people here, he wanted to say, and it's her and me, and I've got her tied up and delivered; she's only a girl after all.

The vote, when it came, was a nice little production; it satisfied him. Cora used her casting vote with a manly resolution. He felt Tony's hand on his arm, restraining him, but he did not need it. He was not going to jump up and down with delight. They voted a second time, and again Cora Dunwoodie made it eleven-ten, instructing Beasley to move ahead with the contract and get it signed.

He nodded at her, smiled, but did not approach; left her to the journalists, avoided them himself. Back in the office he let his pleasure open quietly. It was too soon for the big celebration; that would come when they said, Rip it down, put it up. All he could do was done and he was satisfied and pleased to have a time for being still. Tony and Lonnie could handle the next two weeks – the contract, the resource consent application, the demolition permit. Then he would come in again, getting the builders on the job. That was the part he liked best. He opened a Black Label and called Tony and Lonnie in.

'Good stuff, Tony. Fucking good work, Lonnie.'

I'm going to put a building up, with mirror glass all the way, she'll be a diamond in the sky, and higher than anyone has gone. He felt himself open like a flower. Yeah, a rose. He wanted to say it to see how Tony and Lonnie would react. But only Gwen would know what he meant – and he thought of her, scruffy, dried up, sharp, with places in her mind that unfolded and unfolded just when you thought she'd reached the end. Gwen would know what he meant by rose. Howie Powie, you're no dope, standing on her toes to kiss his cheek. She would hate his building though. She would say, A monstrosity. He closed up sharp.

Ron Quested came in. 'So?' he said, grinning.

'Have one, Ronnie. Here's to us.'

'You got her?'

'She rolled over and put her legs in the air.'

He drank with them for half an hour, then left them with the bottle. He walked to the Glencoul and stopped on the corner for a better view of it, bronzed and sheathed, stepping

111

into the sky. Beautiful, he thought. And full of people doing things. It's there for a reason and it works. Stuff Gwen, she doesn't know a thing.

He stopped in the bar for another drink – sat alone, enjoying himself. He would never be rid of Gwen; she was a mozzy in the night, you slapped and thought you'd got her, but she kept coming back. And you kept on itching because the bitch could bite. Okay, Howie thought, she's part of my life, like bursitis, eh; she's something I've done and you don't get rid of what you've done, no way, but I make the big rules, so bite away, Gwennie, there's nothing else you can do. He toasted her with a final drink.

Back in his room he rang Darlene and heard her wake. 'Howie, ah Howie' – yawn – 'I thought you'd never ring. Do you know what I did today, I mowed some of the lawn.' He liked her to do that.

'You clean the mower?'

'Yes.'

'Oily rag?'

'Yes, Howie. I had a swim. I did four lengths.'

'Good on you. Overarm?'

'A little bit of dog-paddle. I get sore arms, Howie.'

'You dive for the stone?'

'Yes. I nearly got it. I'll get it tomorrow. Did you wow them, Howie? At the meeting, I mean.'

'Sure I wowed them. They didn't know their arse from their elbow.'

'I knew you would. Do you want me to talk some stuff to you?'

'Nah, save it, honey. Tomorrow night. We'll do it then and stuff the talking, eh?'

Darlene laughed. 'I'm touching myself.'

'Well, cut it out. I've had enough excitement for one day. Anyone call?'

'Gordon did.'

'What did he want?'

'I don't know. He's creepy, Howie. I know he's your son but I wish he didn't kind of creep all the time. It's like he's always coming out of the dunny.'

112

Howie was startled. Darlene was like that, talked silly for hours on end and then said something exactly right.

'Give him a drink and send him home. You don't have to listen to his stuff.'

'That's what I did.'

'Okay, love. Now keep after that stone. I know you can do it.'

'Yes, I will. And don't you go ringing up for one of those hotel girls.' She said it to please him and he was pleased.

'There's no such thing, love. Not at the Glen.'

'You could find one if you wanted.' That was to please him too. 'I'll think about you, Howie.'

'I'll think about you.'

'Kisses.'

'Kisses.'

He put down the phone, smiling widely, feeling warm. Darlene was his luck. Darlene was his lucky find. He hadn't thought he could be continuous again, with anyone. He had thought, with women, it would be what he could get and moving on. And hotel girls. Gwen had left him soured and unready. Then Darlene, in the shop, selling shoes, had smiled and knelt and measured his foot and laced the new shoes tightly and made him walk and clapped her hands and said, 'They really suit you, you look great,' and he was sweet and ready again, no other words; he was sweet and ready for Darlene. A New Lynn lady, out his way, who pleased him and laughed at him and thought he was 'a phenomena'. Darlene up front, even when she played the little girl. Darlene in delight, with money and clothes and swimming pool, hardly believing her luck. And wanting to be wanted, and not needing to be told that he loved her all the time. Ease, that was Darlene, and knowing where you were, and no pretence. She left him free. Love wasn't in it; fun and pleasure and liking, that was what they had, and better than the 'communion' Gwen had gone on about. He had never known what she meant by it. You had to make your hard-on seem like something pure.

Gwen again. He shook his head to get her out, and thought of Darlene in the pool, dog-paddling like a six-year-old, neck stretched, head high, and that bit of fear that he liked in her

113

eyes. He thought of her getting ready to dive, with her hands like a child praying. He slapped her butt, said, 'Go', and she obeyed, but popped up like a cork and he had to go in and pull her out. The river stone was there still, on the bottom, white as a pearl – a paperweight, stuff it, from Gwen – but Darlene would get it before long.

He stood at his window and looked over the harbour, which glimmered close in and then was dark across to the eastern beaches and the string of lights along the bottom of the hills. I could build over there. Eastbourne needs a good hotel. You'd see it standing up against the hills. Ten storeys, that would be enough, with the windows glittering with light. It would hang there like a painting on a wall. He was warm still with the pleasure of the day, and he thought that Darlene knew a thing or two – hotel girls. No way, he said. I'll be faithful. Anyway, he had had Cora Dunwoodie already today.

Howie laughed and went to bed and slept without dreaming.

The next day he was busy again – consultants, journalists, Tony and Lonnie – but had had enough by five o'clock. He went to the hotel and swam in the pool, then had a drink or two in the bar. At seven o'clock he went to the restaurant – beat the crowd. He would come at six if he wanted to and say to the waiters, 'Where's my tea?' It had been six and tea, the Henderson way, until he married Gwen, who tried her poncy shift to eight o'clock and 'dinner time'. She hadn't got real till the babies came.

'The wine list, sir?'

'Bring me a beer.'

The steak was good, the pudding good. He enjoyed himself. Back in his room he switched on the TV set, then switched it off. Smart-arse blondes wisecracking: too damn pushy. He read the *Post* and there was Cora Dunwoodie getting stick – but she would survive. He came out of it sensibly. The way he came out bored him tonight. He found the name Lupercal flea-jumping down a column, and Neil Hopkins, happy and big, white knight in those days, '86, showing his back-slanted teeth. They should print a photo of him the way he was today, with half the weight gone from his face and his eyeballs yellow. Gordon wasn't mentioned. Gordon would be heard another time. They'd better not do him until I get Kitchener pulled down, Howie thought.

He telephoned Darlene and talked with her for half an hour, then sent her to bed – but wasn't going to end up there himself at nine o'clock. He would go and see Athol. He would get Damon's shift to Auckland sorted out; it was time. I'll buy a trampoline, he thought. He saw the boy turning in the air while the gulf sparkled behind.

The taxi dropped him at the gate and he looked first at Gwen's house, nervously. She sat at darkened windows, looking out – and said that she was happy. Just thinking, she said. It had seemed to leave him nowhere in the house to go.

A light shone in an upstairs window. Not her bedroom, one of the spares. He wondered if Olivia had shifted across and if that meant Damon would be ready for his move. Darlene would be good for Damon, she would make him laugh. He needed to get that frozen look off his face. He needed, by God, to climb and wrestle, and piss up the wall and fart with his mates, not just do his fancy tricks on his bit of rubber. Sport was rugby and boxing not bouncing in the air. I'll teach him to play tennis, Howie thought, even though the game was full of pansies, in their whites.

He went up Athol's path, went in without knocking, and stood in the hall where Ulla had broken her neck. The carpet was soft enough but she had fallen wrong, with the burglar's foot in her back. He opened the door again and found the angle she had left it at: no give either way, as rigid as the end of a wall. He felt his spine shrink as though it felt a terror of its own.

'Jesus, Dad, don't you ever knock?' Athol stood in the kitchen door, with a carving knife in his hand.

Howie laughed. 'Are you going to stick me with that?'

'I would have. By God. If it had been . . . '

'Your little burglar? Hold the thing pointing up, don't hold it like a girl.' He looked like Bette Davis in a movie. 'Any news? The police told you anything yet?'

'No.' Athol went past him and closed the door. He walked into the kitchen and laid the knife on the bench. 'They've got a lot of men on it. They're up here all the time. Bloody Mum.'

'What's she done?'

'He was in her place before he came here. They think he saw Ulla hide the key from the bathroom window. She wasn't going to tell them but I made her. You should have heard the cops getting into her.'

'Is it going to catch him? Did she lose anything?'

'Her wedding ring.'

'What?'

'Her wedding ring, that's all. He squeezed the toothpaste tube, she says. It doesn't make any sense.'

'Leave fingerprints?'

'No.'

'They found some here though?'

'They can't match them. He hasn't got a record. Loners always get away, that's what I've heard.'

'You tell them about my reward?' Wedding ring, he thought. It robbed him and made him want to cry.

'They don't want it yet. They'll let you know. Do you want a drink? Come into the lounge.'

Howie sat down with a whisky. 'He wouldn't get more than a couple of dollars for that ring.' It had cost him five pounds, and was worn thin with their years as man and wife. 'Anyway,' he said, 'what about Ulla? I like Ulla. How is she?'

'People with broken necks don't get better.'

'Yes they do.'

'People with their spinal column cut right through. That's what she's got. Complete lesion. Mum tells me, she's been talking to the doctors and reading it up.'

'So she's on her back for the rest of her life, is that what you're saying?'

'Yes. Most of them don't live more than ten years, about.'

'Have you talked to her? Does she know?'

'She knows. According to Mum. I don't go and see her any more.'

'Why not?'

'She doesn't want me. We were finished, Dad. We were finished before this happened. I'm not going to pretend now, just because . . . '

'Okay. Sure. Where does she go? What happens to her?'

116

Athol shrugged. It was a tired movement, although his face was smooth and his eyes were bright. He was tired only of Ulla, not of his life.

'To Auckland. There's a spinal unit where they do rehabilitation. For what it's worth. But I don't know whether she'll agree to go.'

'Where to after that?'

'Here. I'll fix it up. I'll pay.' He gave a grin. 'She's my wife. We'll hire a full-time nurse. You can get special beds and all that stuff. I'll live somewhere else.'

'What about the kids?'

'Olivia's next door already. Damon, well . . . '

'He can come to me. We talked about that.'

'It's up to him.'

His carelessness in giving things up made Howie draw back. Yet there was a stillness under it, as though Athol had found some other place to go. Maybe he had found another woman.

'It'll be hard to divorce her when she's paralysed. No one's going to like you for that.'

Athol smiled. 'I don't want a divorce. Damon's in his room if you want to see him.'

'Does he see Ulla?'

'If you're going to say her name, Dad, say it right.'

'Does he?'

'A couple of times. He and Olivia go after school. Mum goes at night. She's there now.'

Doing what? Talking to Ulla's head? Stroking with her live hand on the dead one. He felt a flash of revulsion. Gwen would always be where there were feelings to be felt. He could not see her hand without its wedding ring.

He went upstairs, knocked, opened the door. Damon was watching television on a little set on a shelf at the end of his bed.

'Can I come in?'

'Sure.' Damon lowered the sound but kept the picture on. It showed Americans on a beach, laughing, while, as far as Howie could make out, someone was drowning in the sea behind their backs.

117

'What is it?'

'*Baywatch*.'

'Any good?'

'It's all right.'

'They'd better get that bloke out of there.'

'They will.'

'How are you, Damon. Can I sit down?'

'Sure.'

He sat on the bed. The boy shifted so he could see the screen.

'Have you thought any more about coming up to Auckland to stay with me?'

Damon looked at him and looked away. 'A bit.'

'Made any decision?'

'No.'

'You'd have a good time. There's plenty of room in the house. You'd have your own room. Your own TV. There's sets everywhere.'

'That's good.'

'A snooker table. I'll teach you to play snooker. Do you watch *Pot Black*?'

'No.'

'I made an eighty-seven break once. Then I missed on a red. I didn't have my custom-built cue.'

The boy smiled politely and leaned to see the figures on the beach.

'There's a swimming pool. Tennis court. We can go for rides in my launch.'

'What about school?'

'You finish here. Get the year done. Then come on up. Darlene makes a pretty mean pavlova. You like pavlova?'

'Who's Darlene?'

'She's my wife. Your – well, she's not your grandmother, I suppose, but I reckon you'll like her. She's easy come, no fancy stuff.'

'What about . . . ?' Howie thought 'my mother?' He didn't have an answer to that. ' . . . my trampoline? I have to practise.' It had been, but he'd changed it, 'my mother?' Howie felt his throat grow thick with pity for the boy.

118

'What's the best make?'

'I don't know.'

'You find out the best make. Doesn't matter how much. There'll be one sitting on the lawn when you arrive.'

He went downstairs and said to Athol, 'Yeah, he'll come. When the year's finished at school. He can stay as long as he likes. He can go to school in Auckland, that's easy. Any school.' As long as it's not King's bloody College, he thought. He had no time for poncy schools.

Athol had papers spread on the coffee table. 'Let him decide.' He looked up and seemed to remember sounds that he should make. 'I know you think I'm letting my responsibilities go. But I've never been able . . . I love my kids but I'm no good for them.'

What are you good for? Howie wanted to ask. Good at football once, a Colts rep on the wing, good with girls, easy with people. Howie had loved him as a boy, exulted in him. Then somehow Athol had soured and turned away and lost his easiness and speed. He was like a spinning top that slowed and got the wobbles and ended up lying on its side. He lost his hair and grew a beaky nose and seemed to be calculating all the time, in his job, in his daily life. Landlord was the proper job for him – screwing bits of rent from run-down houses. He had lasted just long enough to get his Swedish blonde. And that was a disaster too – that was maybe the cause of it all.

'Go and see Olivia. Say hallo to her,' Athol said.

'What, next door?'

'Mum's not home.'

'I'm not scared of her.' He did not want to go. Olivia was like Ulla, she had no ease with him. And he did not want to go into Gwen's house, it would make him angry. 'Buying more places?' he said, nodding at the papers on the table.

'Improvements. Nothing much. Plumbing's the worst.'

'I thought you'd know your way around the regulations by now.'

A spot of colour rose in Athol's cheeks. 'I'm not into that. I keep my houses decently. There's not a dripping tap I don't know about. And get fixed up. Ask my tenants if you don't believe me.'

119

'Sure, sure.'

'You do your thing, Dad, and I'll do mine.'

'Sure, okay. It looks like Gilbert Fox is down the tubes.'

'Fox is getting what he deserves. She'll be in bed soon if you don't go.'

'You and your mother,' Howie said.

He went through the hedge and tried Gwen's door, and called, 'Olivia', not to frighten her.

Silence, then a voice. 'Who's there?'

'It's me, your grandfather.'

She came down the stairs and opened the door. 'We keep it locked. Grandma said . . . '

'Sure, that's sensible.' He kissed her cheek. 'How's it going? Do you like it here?' She smelled of dog. 'Gwen treating you right?'

'Yes. Do you want to come in?'

'Just for a minute.' He did not know what to say to her. 'Who does the cooking?'

'We take turns.'

'And she does lentils, eh?'

Olivia smiled briefly. 'And chick peas. And brown beans. I like them though,' she said loyally.

The dog appeared at the top of the stairs and yapped at him, then waddled away.

'I'm surprised she lets you have that thing in the house.'

'He's in my room. He stays outside in the daytime.'

'Sure,' Howie said. He could hear Gwen saying, 'Let's compromise.'

'Shall we go in the lounge? Shall I make a cup of tea?'

I'm your grandfather, he wanted to say. Give me a hug, stop doing the Swede. 'I can only stay a minute. I just looked in to say hallo.'

'Well . . . '

'Okay, we'll go in the lounge.'

He followed her there and sat opposite. She would be good looking when some of her fat had melted off. Beautiful maybe, but not pretty. He was easier with pretty; it was fun. This one would be Swedish and cool when she learned how. At this age, though, she was a mess: fat and awkward, and off-centre in

120

her dressing gown. There was toothpaste in the corner of her mouth.

'I'm sorry if I stopped you going to bed.'

'That's all right.'

'It's not really late.'

'No.'

Shit, Howie thought, where do we go? 'Tell me how Ulla is. Did you go today?'

'Yes, I went.'

'How is she?'

Olivia turned her face away. 'She lies in bed with a thing screwed on her head.'

'Does she talk to you?'

'Not much.'

'Why?'

Olivia turned back. She had controlled the tears in her eyes. 'She can't talk.'

'Because of her neck?'

'And her face. Where it's cut. And her broken cheekbone.'

'She knows you though? And Damon?'

'We hold her hand.'

Pretending that it's a part of her. He wondered if Ulla could see what she could not feel.

'They don't think she'll ever walk again.' Her tongue found the toothpaste and licked it away.

'We'll help her. We'll all help,' Howie said.

Olivia shrugged. 'I want them to catch the man and hang him.'

'They'll catch him.' He was shocked. He wondered if anyone had understood her pain, and he reached out and touched her hand. 'Have you got everything? Everything you want?'

'Yes, I'm all right.'

'Plenty of clothes? Money to spend?'

'Yes.'

'How would you like an allowance from me?'

'Dad gives me money.'

'From your grandpa though? So we can be a family.' Tears were in his own eyes, and like her he turned his face.

121

'Dad's not part of any family. Nor is Grandma.'

'Well, you and me and Damon . . . '

'And Mum's not part of anything now.' She got up and filled the kettle and plugged it in. 'Do you take milk and sugar in your tea?'

Gwen came before the water boiled. He heard her feet patter on the boards – quick-stepper Gwen. Olivia called, 'It's open, Grandma.'

She leaned in, stepped in, looking sharp. 'Howie, where'd you come from?'

'I thought I'd say hallo to Olivia.'

'I've got the kettle on,' Olivia said. 'I'll go to bed now if it's all right. Goodnight, Grandpa.'

'Goodnight,' he said, and watched her go up the stairs. Nice legs, he thought, she'll be all right.

'I don't want tea, Howie, and I don't suppose you do,' Gwen said.

'I'm not into tea. I'll have a whisky.'

'I don't keep whisky any more.'

'Okay, so I'll go. Goodnight.'

Gwen laughed. 'Relax. Sit down. I've got some sherry.'

'You know how I feel about that.'

'It's all there is. Yes or no?'

'Yes. Pour the stuff.' He watched her, and felt no break between them, just time pulled thin; and now they stood on angles, touching but apart.

'That girl's not happy,' he said.

'God, what a thing to say. Do you think I don't know?'

'She's got no one. I think she's – lost.'

'I know, I know. Worry about Damon. I'll look after her.'

'What's wrong with Athol? Where's he think he's at?'

'Nowhere new. We should have been Catholics, Howie. Then Athol could have been a monk in a monastery.'

'Talk sense.' As usual she was going off at tangents, crazy places, and pushing him where he would not go. 'He's bloody selfish, that's what he is. And he's got no life.'

She sipped her drink and suddenly looked bored. 'Howie, it's years too late for this. Athol and Gordon – it's all done.'

'Yeah, no-hopers.'

122

She laughed. 'How nice it must be.'

'What?'

'To have a set of words. Has-beens. No-hopers. What else? Paper-shufflers. I forget.'

'Why do you always have to get at me?'

'There's no always, old boy, not for us.'

'Jesus, can't you say anything straight?'

Gwen sighed. 'Well Howie, here we are quarrelling again.'

'I didn't come to see you anyhow.'

'Let's not talk. Just have your drink and go.'

'Damon's coming to Auckland. Why don't you spend more time with her' – stabbing his finger upstairs – 'instead of going to Ulla all the time?'

'It's not your business.'

'Ulla can't talk, Olivia said.'

'Be quiet, Howie. Just be quiet.'

'No, you listen – '

'You can't come into my house and talk like this.'

There was such a fierceness in her that he stopped. He felt that she would spring at him, she was nails and teeth.

'You and me, we're finished,' he said.

'Are you only just finding that out?'

Whatever he said she would be a step ahead, moving away. He said, 'I'm not coming here again.'

'You were never here, Howie, in the first place.'

See? He laughed. He had to laugh. It grated in his throat. 'This bloody house is falling down. You'll be some mad old dame with a string bag.'

'Possibly. But it will be my choice.'

'You'll be there before you know. That's how it happens. Don't come to me.'

'Howie, I promise you I won't.'

'Can't we say goodbye decently?'

'I didn't think sherry would do it.'

'What?'

'I thought it was only whisky. Made you teary-eyed.'

'Shit!' He slammed down his glass and stood up. Tried to think of something to say; but she was watching him upwards, ready for it, and he walked out into the night. Never, he thought, never going back. She's on her own, the silly bitch, she can do without me. He crashed the gate, heard the iron catch rattle. He walked down the middle of the road. Lights struck him in the face and he angled to the footpath – found some steps, went down through houses to another road. A man lectured a woman, hands on her shoulders, holding her off. Her face was down. He thought she smiled privately but he could not be sure. Another bloody Gwen. Always that secret knowledge they claimed to have. 'Thank God for Darlene,' he said.

He walked down The Terrace and up Lambton Quay to his hotel, passing Kitchener on the way. Mine, he thought, and pictured the wreckers going in. He would put a building up, a mile into the sky.

'See if you can beat that,' he said.

Eight

Gwen made tea when he had gone. She wiped the table where his sherry had slopped. And now, she thought, I've cleaned him out and that's the end of Howie for good. They had needed this little scene, it marked full stop. You believe that, she told herself.

She carried a cup upstairs to Olivia. 'He's gone.'

'I heard him. He banged the gate.'

'That's Howie's style. What did he say to you? Anything?'

'Is Damon going up?'

The dog snored on the end of her bed. Olivia stirred it with her foot.

'Yes,' Gwen said.

'How was Mum?'

'No change. She sends her love. She really does, Olivia, you've got to believe in it.'

'I do. But what's . . . ' She shrugged.

'What's the good?'

'I can't get used to . . . '

The part that's lying there and not a part? And her not being Ulla in her head any more?

'Things will change. Wait until she's had a bit more time.'

'It can't make any difference, can it, though?'

'Not to walking, I'm afraid. But there's other things.' Could not think of any. 'What are you reading?'

Olivia angled the book.

'It's a wonderful title. Do you like them?'

'They're all right. I just get – I'm tired of people hurting all the time.'

'I know. I know.'

She went downstairs and drank her tea. She locked the house and went to bed, to sleep. There was too much feeling in her – an overload – for wakefulness. It whacked her like a club and she went out. When she woke at two o'clock she thought, I'm not torn apart by this the way the others are. Was that because she had a place to stand and see it from? She could be still, and understand, perhaps, although she was surprised and rebellious and unhappy. Stillness was a gift of age. And the busyness that followed it allowed her to forget. Busyness too was a gift. But how little time it would take up, out of all the time that lay ahead. Her feelings filled her again and she wept into her pillow.

In the morning she waited until Olivia had gone to school, and Damon had gone, and Athol had driven off in his car. She went next door and opened the house. Butch walked after her, keen, she supposed, to get inside his old home, but she blocked him with her foot and closed the door, ignored his whining. She wanted the place to herself. It was silent and dusty and Athol's efforts to tidy it left the same impression as clothes wrongly buttoned and hair half brushed. Ulla's untidiness had been by overflow. One lived in it. Here there was an absence. Athol was absent from it all.

She went up to the bedroom and drew the curtains back to make some light. Wellington lay in its bowl, with its buildings shining; roofs red and green and cladding polished. The cranes stood long-legged over pits of clay where spikes and webs held the workmen tight. The mountains were unpretentious, lower in the morning than at night; the harbour grey. I like it however it is, Gwen thought. For Ulla though it had never stood facing the right way, or making the right colours – with her sky. 'I wait for my life to start up, Gwen.'

She turned away from it and saw the waterbed. Whose idea had that been? Athol's? Ulla's? One of them had mentioned it or joked about it perhaps, and neither could get out of it then. But Ulla's life would not be started up again in there. Sex had been by timetable and was itemised. No wave-motion could alter that – so Ulla had said, working at language. There was nothing Ulla would not say to Gwen, who was her country in a way. Hang on to me, Ulla. Hang on with your eye and tongue, hang on.

She saw how Athol slept on one side still – on his sea, riding his own waves. Athol would make do without a woman now. It would be, in fact, not making do but finding his shape. In a way he had been without his country too. How impossible, how crippled, how ugly it had been. And how changed now, and turned about – but not to the right place, or even close to it.

Where was Ulla?

Oh be still, Gwen told herself.

She opened the wardrobe and looked at Ulla's clothes. There was nothing there she would wear again. Shoes? Never again. Ulla's big boat shoes, her long-boat shoes, and those sandals moulded for her soles, to ease the strain and ease her pain – and take her walking on their German consonants and vowels. Birkenstock. 'You must try them, Gwen, they are magical.' But Gwen never had; she kept on with her English walkers, and slip-ons for the section and slippers for the house. She held herself tight, not to be guilty about it now. Closed the wardrobe. Did not try the drawers. What was she here for? Photographs.

She found them in the window seat, under blankets from pre-duvet days. They were in a box named Mushroom Soup, the little album, satin covered, jammed into the bottom. She forced her fingers in, scraping them, and jerked it out. Blood on her nail, blood on the satin – never mind, no injury or spoiling mattered now.

The baby lay on a rug, dressed all in white. Was that Ulla, that little vegetable with arms and legs? And the child frowning, was that her? Destinies were unimaginable. Ulla, she thought, looking at the pigtails and bony knees and turned-in feet, someone's going to come and break your neck. Run and hide. Don't come here. Stay away from here. There's a man who will marry you and keep you from your place. See him starting to lean, starting his lean away from you, and drawing you after, so you can't go home.

She looked at them on beaches, standing beside cars, and on the steps of their first house. Ulla and Athol, equal in height;

127

so they could look, Ulla said, straight in each other's eyes. Why did she not see the absence in him? Why didn't she shoulder her pack, get her big boots working, hitch on home? Where was home? Gwen turned back. Snowbound farms and cattle in the barns, and wheat and barley fields in the summer. Berries in the woods. Elk on the roads. Little islands of smooth rock standing a yard above the sea, with pines and silver birch, and a girl fishing. That was one home. There were others. People, school, work, cities. Language. Words that did not have to be turned around and looked at, fitted in. Words you met coming out of yourself. Why did you not see, Ulla, where you belonged? Why did you see magic in his strangeness? It was only difference after all. You were so young.

White ink on black paper: the dead mother's hand. 'Ulla som bebis, 3 månades gammal, på Tallkobben.' 'Ulla fishar.' 'Kräft fest, 1964, Ulla och Tomas.' 'Ulla plochar blåbär.' 'Lucia tåg, 1968.' Ulla so grave, with a crown of candles in her hair. How could she come here from around the world and take bush and beaches, sheep on hills, and Gwen's son Athol, seriously? 'Student-examen, 1974.' With a captain's hat on her head, with her class, her family, her teachers, all around. Gwen wanted to stop there, close the album, stop it. But here she was with her backpack leaning on her knees, holding a cardboard sign that read: Hokitika. Tallkobben is your language, go home, you silly girl. It was too late. On the Cook Strait ferry she looked long-sighted at the Wellington hills. Over the page: 'Athol and Ulla, 1976.' English was the language now, and the hand was hers.

Gwen closed the album and put it away. She did not want to see the children coming, the family together, and Ulla staring out with her clear gaze. That was when I started loving her; when I saw she had to live where she couldn't live; when I saw her look away so far, and close up tight inside and not complain. Anyway, there was daily life – we talked and read and walked and laughed and lived the days through and it wasn't too bad, just that there was a base whose absence Ulla knew. Gwen, in her way, had known it too. Absence of home, absence of love. There were compensations – other sorts of love.

But what happens now, Ulla? What happens now?

She put the album in the window seat and closed the lid. Down in the street the postman went by. He left nothing in her box but something that looked like an airmail letter in Athol's. Gwen went out of the bedroom, outside and down the path, leaving the door open, which let Butch in. The letter was for Mrs Ulla Peet, and was from – Gwen turned it over – Tomas, her brother: Zetterstrom. That nice boy; nice man now, probably. Home in Sweden, bringing up his daughter and son, and bewildered more than anything by a sister with a broken neck. What would he say to her? What could he say? Everything must make a pause for translation now.

Yet Gwen was hopeful. She held the letter in her hand and felt the strangeness of it, weight and shape. It was like that white ink on black paper. Like those low islands and silver trees. He might know something that could be said.

He had said – when was it, '82? – 'I do not think he loves her properly.' 'No,' Gwen had said. 'But the children, she says, must grow up here. I do not see why that has to be.' 'I do and I don't,' Gwen said, and tried to explain. He smiled at her. 'We must wait and see.' He went back home and married and had children of his own; and Ulla went back alone when her mother was dying, and said to Gwen, when she returned, 'It will change now that she has gone.' She was afraid. Too many years must go by. Sweden might become empty now.

'Go and stay there when the children are old enough. Go and see.'

'Yes, I will.'

'I'll visit you. I'll bring a bit of Wellington across.' But she had been afraid that Ulla would not find her own land any more.

The dog was sleeping on the carpet where his basket had been. She left him there and went to the storeroom off the laundry. It was dusty-windowed and cobwebbed, with raincoats hanging on nails and worn-out shoes on the floor. Suitcases, a broken ironing board, Ulla's old pack, were piled in a corner. Beside them, leaning on the wall, were several framed pictures. The one Ulla wanted was furthest in, face in. Gwen took it to the living room, wet a cloth, wiped the dust

129

away. She remembered it: women in a sauna. She looked at the back and found – Ulla's hand – *Badande kullor i bastun. Anders Zorn.* A man who had liked his ladies naked. Tomas had brought it to Wellington, a little bit of Sweden, he had said, and she had had it framed and hung it in the bedroom for a while, then in the hall. Athol had objected to it there, so – had she put it in the storeroom, facing the wall?

Gwen could not like it, even though she saw it was alive. All that broad bottom and pendant breast – there was too much health, steamy and warm. And too much pleasure in it. That startled her. She was not against pleasure. Not against warmth, proximity, lack of shame. She was for it, in fact, although not needing it, not in practice, for herself. But there was, wasn't there, a man in this, invisible and feeding off these women in some way? She felt him out of the picture, in a door, taking more than his eye entitled him to. She would have said so to Ulla once; they said these things and argued back and forth and disagreed.

She carried it home between her fingers and thumb, put it on the sideboard, where the shadows dulled it, and propped Tomas Zetterstrom's letter against the mirror. The letter was more important, she believed, even though Ulla had said, 'I want to see the women in the sauna again' – her first request. Gwen made a cup of tea and sat down at the table to write to Tomas: a bulletin. 'The cut on her face is healing and the bone is knitting, her doctors say.' Was his English good enough for 'knitting'? Well, he'd have to use a dictionary. 'They can't say much about her spinal column except that, in their language, the lesion is complete. Tomas, it's certain that she'll never walk again. New Zealand isn't kind to Swedes.' By that she meant the two who had been murdered in the bush – he would understand. 'We're not a safe country any longer, it seems – but were we ever? The human story is our story too.' Stop that, she thought, don't confuse the boy, just tell him how his sister is. 'She understands what has happened, I think, and what the future will be like for her. What she doesn't understand – none of us do – is how one lives through it, from day to day. She asked to see the Anders Zorn picture again, the one you brought out all those years ago, remember it? Women in the sauna, one kneeling in the tub and the other with a dipper full of water. I don't know why. There's all that skin, coloured like a peach, and backs and arms and hips – does she want to start her new lesson the hardest way? I don't want to take it to her.' Why? she asked. If Ulla wants to know bodies again, by looking at them, before she starts to know there's nothing there, perhaps she's right, perhaps her instincts are working for her. Can instincts work in a thing as out of the common way as this?

Gwen wrote no more. She went upstairs and straightened her bed and shook the dog hairs off Olivia's duvet. Butch, she remembered. Let him sleep. Let burglars come into that open house, there was nothing there. She put clothes in the machine – Olivia's as well as her own – and hung them out when they were spun; then she went back to Athol's house and did the wash there too, why not? Damon, at least, was in her care, until Howie claimed him. How would he enjoy his taste of luxury? Would it wipe Ulla from his mind? In the meantime his underpants – masculine, although surely he had not much yet to fill the pouch. Strange how men's underpants made you think of cruelty and thickheadedness.

That was the sort of thing she might have said to Ulla once – and Ulla, clearheaded, would have replied, 'Can it be both?'

And this, Gwen thought, is how I'll get through the days. I'll fill one half hour, then fill another. What's the time now?

In the afternoon she took Butch for his walk. She remembered – with a shock, always a shock – that sharp-faced boy coming up the road, and she turned away her face as she had done on that day. She tried not to see him and wonder who he was. Was he vicious or had he just been frightened? Was he greedy? Had he been in need? Did he enjoy it, kicking Ulla? Stop, she said. He was out of it, and gone. Had no substance, was not permanent. Why should he have a life? she thought.

Butch pulled her down the road. He stopped to poop and she watched the clouds in the sky; rolled his pellets into the gutter; climbed the steps.

'How is . . . Is she . . . ?'

'Oh, she's improving. It's early days.'

'Tell her I . . . that I send . . . '

'Yes, I will. Goodbye.'

Keep on moving. Butch was good for that. Clever dog. She took him into the village and tied him to the bus-stop seat. A bus went by on the other side, and there was Olivia, hair untidy, tie askew, reading something on her lap – *You Are Now Entering the Human Heart* – and riding patiently to see her mother. Olivia learning to be patient with hurt. I must, Gwen thought – and stopped. Too much 'I must', which put her at the front of things. I must – there again – find another way of saying it. What about 'behoves'? It behoves me to be calm and still and move myself only as it's useful to them. What could she do and say that might be useful to Olivia? I'll do it and say it, she thought. But until she knew she must be silent, must be still. And look after the dog. Olivia appreciated that.

It behoves me . . .

The bus let Gwen down at the hospital and she carried the picture, wrapped in newspaper, up the steps and through brown corridors with dog-leg turns to Ulla's room. Ulla lay on the high bed, in her halo brace, with her tubes. Her eyes were closed but there was a throbbing in the lids when Gwen looked close.

'Ulla, it's Gwen.'

'Gwen.' So slow. 'Hej, Gwen.' Eyes half open. 'Is it night?'

'Yes. Eight o'clock. You've had your tea.'

'I don't remember.'

'Well, hospital teas . . . '

'Yes, I do. I must try not to.'

Was that a joke? Had Ulla made a joke?

'Were you sleeping?'

'Day dreaming.'

'What about?'

'Oh, it goes. I can't remember.' A whisper for a voice, with lovely cadences.

'Olivia came.'

'Did she? Yes. She read to me.'

'What?'

'Her school report.'

'Was it good?'

132

'Oh, middling. Is that . . . ? Is medium . . . ?'

'Middling is right. She didn't show me.' Meaning, you're her mother. How to tell if Ulla heard meanings of that sort?

'And Damon came?'

'Yes.'

'How was he?'

'He sits so still. With folded arms.'

'Like . . . ?'

'Sit up straight.'

'Sit up straight at school?'

'He told me a new jump. The barani. He practised it.'

'He goes so high.' Then understood – not practised the jump, but practised telling Ulla about it. She moved a wisp of hair on Ulla's brow, left to right; saw it creep back.

'Do you mind me touching your face?'

'No.'

'Damon's very young.'

'Yes, he's young.'

'Has he told you he might be going up to stay with Howie?'

'When?'

'Soon. If that's all right?'

Ulla closed her eyes. Everything was slowed down. I'd give her my opinion now, in normal times, Gwen thought. She waited.

'It's all right.' Ulla did not open her eyes, but spoke in more than a whisper.

'You'll be going up there too. Auckland. One day.'

'Will I?'

'Yes. That's where the spinal unit is.'

'How will I go?'

'By aeroplane.' She moved the wisp of hair again. Touch her face, the doctor had said. They need reassurance, they want to feel some contact with the people they love. She had not liked his 'they' and did not trust him to know anything about it.

'There's a letter from Tomas.'

'How is he?'

'I haven't opened it. Would you like me to? I can do the Swedish, I think.'

133

'He'll be upset.'

'I suppose he will. Would you like to save it for a while?'

'No.'

'Stop me when you've had enough.'

She tore the letter open – slowing time, keeping Ulla's time. 'Kära syster Ulla,' she read. Ulla opened her eyes. She listened, seemed to listen with the whole of her face, as Gwen laid each word down carefully. 'Jag vet inte vad jag ska skriva . . . '

'Always will,' Ulla said in a moment.

'What?'

'He says he will always love me.' She smiled. 'Tomas is a little boy too.'

Gwen read on. She heard her vowels too flat and could not round them. Ulla smiled again – at her or at something Tomas said?

'He tells me winter starts and he will buy his little Per some skates.'

'For on the lake?'

'Yes, on the lake. He tells me the snow is on the hills.'

'Long nights soon,' Gwen said.

'Long nights.'

'Shall I keep on reading?'

'Please.'

She tried to make her voice lilt as Ulla's would have done. Lovely language; language for the cold lakes and the sky. She did not need to know the meaning of it. Ulla closed her eyes again. The scar on her cheek made a shiny ridge and made her strange and wounded and cold; but the wound had healed, which made Gwen think of life for her and recovery. She finished the letter. Folded it.

'Tomas,' she said.

'Yes, Tomas.'

'Perhaps one day you'll go and see him again – or he'll come here.'

'Ah, Gwen.'

'People who can't walk do travel. It isn't impossible, you know.'

'I will not travel.'

'We can't say . . . '

134

'You must help me to know what is real and what is not.'

'I'm not sure I know.'

'You must not ask me to help you.' She seemed to sleep then, for a while, as though she had said huge amounts and exhausted herself. And oh how much she has said, Gwen thought.

A nurse came in. 'Sleeping?'

'Yes. Day dreaming.'

'Half an hour. Then we'll have to move her.'

'Why?'

'Shift her on the bed. For pressure points.'

'Bed sores?'

'Yes. We're very pleased with her, you know.'

'The infection's gone?'

'Practically.'

'But all sorts of other things . . . ?'

'It's a long haul, Mrs Peet.'

Where to? Gwen wanted to ask, but felt that as an extension of Ulla she must say nothing to offend; she must make them pleased with her too.

'I brought a picture from her house. I'd like to show it to her before I go.'

'I'm awake,' Ulla said.

The nurse smiled and went away.

'People keep on coming at my face,' Ulla said.

'They're trying to help.'

'The world is right up against my face.'

'It must be hard – '

'I feel as if they've put my body somewhere and now they keep on talking to my head.'

Like that punishment, Gwen thought, where – was it the Redskins? – they buried you up to your neck and your head lay like a ball on the sand and anyone could come along and do anything – play with it, poke out the eyes. 'I brought the picture for you. Would you like to see?'

'A picture?'

'Anders Zorn. The sauna bath.'

'Anders,' Ulla said, properly.

'I can never get it right. Anders?'

135

'Right.'

She unwrapped the paper. 'I'll hold it where you can see.' Which she did: angled down at Ulla, where her own hands would have held it if she had been able to raise them.

Ulla looked at it a while. Gwen watched her eyes move.

'We had wooden tubs,' she said.

'And real stones?'

'Oh yes. Now it is all electrics.'

'See how they gleam. Gleaming flanks.'

'Women are not so fat any more.'

'Does it remind you?'

'Of course. See her back. The water in the dipper is for the stones, to make them steam. But her friend will pour some on to her as well and it will run like in a gutter down her spine, and down between her buttocks there.'

'Tickling.'

'Sliding like a snake.'

'Is it cold or hot?'

'Oh, just warm. Everything heats up. You run out and jump in the lake – that is the cold.'

'Past Anders Zorn watching in the door.'

Ulla laughed. It was like two little coughs, surprising her. She closed her mouth, not liking it.

'Did that hurt?'

'I could not tell where it started from.'

Gwen's arms were aching. 'Can I take it down now?'

'Yes.'

'I'll leave it. One of the nurses can hang it up.'

'No. Take it home.'

'But they can easily do it. They can put it on the end of your bed.'

'I've seen it now. I do not want fat ladies. A little bit of water, Gwen. A sip.'

Gwen helped her. She said, 'I can bring it again, whenever you want.'

'Yes, that will do. Leave Tomas's letter. Put it somewhere I can see.'

Gwen made a tent of it and hung it on the rail at the foot of the bed. 'Do you want to write to him?'

'Soon. Will you scratch my eyebrow? The left one, by my nose.'

'There?'

'Yes, there.'

'You'll have to learn to think scratch. Like in science fiction.'

Ulla closed her eyes. A small tightening showed in her mouth: anger, Gwen was appalled to see.

'You must let other people make the jokes,' Ulla said.

'Yes, I'm sorry.'

'I cannot try very much now.'

'You'd like me to go?'

'Yes, go. You'll come tomorrow?'

'I'll come.'

Gwen kissed her quickly. She carried the picture home unwrapped and people put their heads on one side to look at it. She turned it round and held the naked women to her chest.

How can I learn to help her? I don't want her ever to let me go. But how can I stand it? she said.

Nine

Danny did not mind Sam as long as he was quiet. Leeanne fed him and changed him in her bedroom, and cuddled him as often as she could. She did not talk to him when Danny was around; he did not like it.

'The kid can't fucken understand.'

'It's how they learn to talk.'

'He doesn't need to talk. All he needs is keep his fucken mouth shut.'

She whispered as she fed him in the night. 'We're getting out of here, Sam. We're not staying here. You wait, my baby, we'll go soon.' But she still hoped that Danny would go. He left for work early and came in late, sometimes with a mate or two and sometimes with a woman. 'Hey, Leeanne, come in here.' She did not hear it now more than once or twice a week and he was lazy and did not hurt her deliberately. He did not ask to see her feed Sam. It frightened her that her boniness and whiteness put him off fucking her sometimes. She kept herself out of his way, believing he might hurt her badly then.

She cooked his meals and washed his clothes. She washed his smell off herself as soon as he had gone to work, but it followed as she pushed Sam through the streets. People stepped back from her in shops. They looked at the yellow bruises on her arms and turned away.

'There y'are,' Danny said, slapping money down on the table. He was proud of himself, and liked her best, when he was providing. It allowed her to save a small part of her benefit.

'Good feed, Leeanne. Kid's asleep, eh? Leave the fucken

dishes.' The nights when he was friendly often ended as the worst.

She put Sam in his pushchair and she walked up the hill. She thought that she was bleeding down the inside of her thighs. 'No more,' she said, 'no more, no more.' She sat on a bench in a playground and let Sam crawl on the grass.

How can he be happy? Is it only children who know how? She did not want him ever to know about Danny, and there was only one way – never to go back.

I can keep on walking, Leeanne thought. She looked at the houses all around – up the hill, down the hill, stretching to the sea. Thousands of houses and not one where she could knock and say, Help me please. I keep on walking and where do I go? A man slept on another bench. He had an arm across his eyes to keep out the light and one yellow foot wrapped round the other. He's like me, Leeanne thought, there's nowhere he can go. She faced the other way so she wouldn't see him.

Sam had got to a path and was chewing an empty cigarette packet. She took it away from him and fetched him back. She did not want him ever to grow up; in broken jeans, with tattooed hands and bare yellow feet. How do I stop him? She saw the chances for him narrowed down – a crack in a wall and no way through. Brown for a start. And a mum like me. And someone like Danny standing in for dad. Be happy now, Sam, because it's stacked against you later on. She turned one way, then turned the other, as though by this she might break out and find a place and give Sam his chance. But it was like a blowfly rattling on a window pane. She did not understand the wall between her and other people, who drove cars and owned houses and took trips round the world. How did you get from where she was to where they were? How did you even get a decent couple of rooms and a decent table and chairs? All she had – a seat in a crummy playground, a prickling like blood on the inside of her thighs. And Sam there, on the grass, behaving like things were just okay. Where could she take him before he found out?

She put him in the baby swing and pushed him back and forth. The squeaking of the hinges went through her sharp as wire. You'd think they'd oil it, she thought, but they only oiled the mayor's chair, or whoever. And that rich tart, that MP, who was going to live on the benefit for a month to prove to people like her that it could be done. Jesus, Leeanne thought, I'd like to put her in with Danny for a night. She pushed Sam higher, too high, but it delighted him and she kept on. He needed all the fun he could get because there wasn't going to be any later on. If Danny ever touches Sam I'll kill him, Leeanne thought.

She stopped the swing and listened. 'A helicopter, Sam.' It was somewhere round the hill, behind the pines. Then the noise changed to a clatter like wooden trays. A big white tadpole, Leeanne thought, as the machine leaned towards her on the hill. It came too close and she thought, There's going to be a crash. Men's faces looked out the windows. They were white but did not seem afraid. Tourists, she thought. Stuff the sods. Looking at me.

The helicopter paused and hovered, edging closer to the piece of waste land by the swings. Leeanne covered her ears, then took her hands away and covered Sam's. She could not believe it was going to land. It lurched and found its balance and swung its tail round. The noise was like the inside of a washing machine.

Bastards, Leeanne thought. She tried to keep Sam's ears covered and lift him out of the swing at the same time. The helicopter settled and stood still, but a storm of dust rose from the down-draught of the blades and raced across the waste ground and through the thistles by the wire fence and swept around Leeanne and Sam. Grit stung her face as she covered him. He screamed against her chest. The sound behind fell away to a chuk-chuk and the blast of wind was gone as quickly as it had come. She got Sam free of the swing and looked at his face. Dust in his eyes, that was all; but it enraged her. Men in suits were stepping down from the helicopter and walking bent underneath the down-slanting blades. They smoothed their hair and stood straight, looking round. Leeanne screamed at them. She held Sam in front of her and ran past the broken slide and leaned across the fence, holding him out. 'Look what you done to my baby, you bastards.' Sam howled. She pulled him back and cradled him, and kept on screaming, 'Stupid bastards, stupid cunts, look what you done to my baby's eyes.'

They were still; then three of them turned their backs on her. The fourth, an older man, came across the waste ground, red-faced and slant-eyed.

'Is he hurt?'

'Of course he's fucken hurt. Listen to him.'

'Dust in his eyes?'

'And fucken grit. You got no right to land that thing. This is a kids' playground here.'

The man turned and shouted at the pilot, who was climbing down from his machine, 'You got a landing permit for here?'

'You bet I have.'

'There you are, so it's iegal.' He looked at Sam, who cried still, with a glue of dust and snot on his upper lip. 'I don't think he's hurt too bad. You buy him something, eh? Buy an ice cream.'

She saw his wallet bursting with money and she swung her arm and knocked it into the thistles. 'Keep your fucken money. I don't want your money. All I want is treat my kid decently, that's all.'

'Come on, Howie, you can't do anything there,' a man called out.

'I've got your number,' Leeanne said, looking at the helicopter, seeing blurred letters as her own eyes ran with tears. 'I'm going to lay a complaint.'

'Hey,' said the man, 'I'm sorry. I really am.'

'Yeah,' she said, 'big deal.' She turned round and went back to the seat. She wet a napkin corner with spit and wiped Sam's face and calmed him down. 'Fucken bastards.' She wiped her own. When she looked again the men had walked beyond the helicopter and one was pointing down the slope and tapping a paper in his hand. She could not hear what they were saying. The man who had offered her money stood with his hands in his pockets, looking the other way, towards the hilltop. She found a bit of his skin under her nail and scraped it out. At least I put my mark on the bastard. She strapped Sam in his pushchair and walked out of the playground. The guy on the bench had rolled on to his other side.

'Sleep, you lucky sod,' Leeanne said. She pushed Sam

along streets and up and down hills in the direction of home, but not going there; she was going nowhere. The towers of the city, rising in front, were as far away and strange as cities over the sea. She passed the Indian dairy where Jody had bought her cigarettes. The helicopter swept over, heading for the harbour. She did not look up. Complaining would be useless, a joke. Where? Who to? They'd show her out and laugh when she had gone. She felt tears start in her eyes again, but wiped them away angrily. Fat pricks, useless pricks, they weren't going to make her cry. Sam would get even for her, Sam would get them one day. Up an alley, kick their faces off.

Leeanne made a wail of anguish when she found herself thinking that. She seemed to be joining them, and helping them beat Sam, and she ran around to the front of the pushchair and hugged him and felt his pulses warm on her throat. 'I'm sorry Sam, we're not going to play their game, eh Sam?' He cried as the straps cut into him. She let him go and soothed him and went back to the dairy and bought him a Buzzbar. If he got chocolate on him too bad. She had to give him good times right now. 'We'll go and visit someone, Sam. We'll go and see your uncle. He might give us some money for an ice cream, eh?'

She did not know the name of Brent's street but had called to see him once and knew the way. The house was old but done up, a quarter way along, with verandahs glassed in to make sunrooms. She wanted to live in a house like that, but the rent would be way too much and they wouldn't take solos anyway, nothing surer. Solos were like cockroaches, they sent a pest eradicator round. Leeanne laughed. She began to feel better. Sam had chocolate all over himself. So bloody what? She wasn't going to be a Plunket mother, running round with rusks and nice warm flannels and cotton buds. Sam was going to grow up to enjoy himself. Imagine sticking cotton buds up your kid's nose.

'Hey, look at you. Chocolate-coated baby.'

She climbed the pushchair backwards up the steps and looked down the hall. It was dark, like in a cave, and Brent's door, painted brown, with a shiny knob, looked as if it led straight out the back. She felt her happiness jolt away as though someone had knocked it out of her with a slap. He wouldn't be home. Why should she expect him to be home at this time of day?

She knocked on the door and waited. 'Hey, Brent.' There was a noise inside, a shuffling and a creaking. 'Come on, Brent, it's me, Leeanne.' She tried the knob. 'Open up.'

A woman looked into the hall from another door.

'I'm after Brent Rosser,' Leeanne said.

'I haven't heard him today. Are you . . . ?'

'I'm his sister.' She knocked again. 'Open up, Brent. Come on. It's Leeanne, your little sister.'

'We don't see much of him,' the woman whispered. 'Last night he was in though, because he took a call. I'm not trying to stick my nose in, but . . . '

'Yeah, but?'

'He's acting kind of weird. We hear him moving round, but then he kind of hides. Des and me were wondering if he's sick.'

'I'll find out. Thanks,' she said. 'Brent, open the door or I'll bust it down.'

A key turned in the lock. The door opened several inches. She saw crooked teeth and half an eye.

'Brent?'

'What do you want?'

The woman closed her door with a click. Good manners, Leeanne thought. She was angry with Brent.

'Have you gone bonkers? Let me in.'

'I don't want to see anyone.'

'Too fucken bad, you're seeing me.' She pushed with her shoulder and felt how weakly he leaned to keep her out. 'Shift, Brent. You're not stopping me.' She moved him until he stepped away suddenly. He crossed the room and lay down on his bed. Leeanne pulled Sam in and closed the door. 'Okay, what's up?'

He made no answer but turned his back and drew up his knees.

'You sick or something? Got the bot?'

'Leave me alone.'

'Jesus, I'm your sister, that's who I am.'

He made a little grunt and hunched his shoulders.

'You want to see your sister or not?'

143

'I don't want to see anyone.'

'I should put bloody Mum on you, that's what.'

The curtains were closed and she turned on the light, which made Brent curl up on the bed. She took Sam out of his pushchair and sat him on the floor. 'I'm going to make a cup of tea, that all right with you?'

'Turn off the light.'

'Sure, okay.'

She turned it off, but crossed to the window and pulled the curtains back. 'It's daytime out there, Brent. There's helicopters and things flying round.'

She saw a little movement of interest in his back. 'What time is it?'

'I dunno. About twelve o'clock. You want some lunch?'

'No.'

'I'll make some lunch. You got anything? Jesus, Brent, you used to be clean. Jesus, there's maggots on this plate.'

She ran hot water on them and pushed them down the plughole with a fork, then crossed to him and sat on the bed. 'Hey, come on, what's the matter? Maybe I can help.'

'I'm minding my own business, that's all.'

'Sure, lying on your bed in the middle of the day. You got some *Playboy*s down there, eh? You tossing yourself off?'

'Shut up.'

'Nothing wrong with that, but girls are better.'

'Shut up, Leeanne.'

'Okay.' She sighed. She thought that sex was really half his trouble – thinking about it, never getting someone to do it with. She had tried to get some of her friends at school to take him on but they all said he was weird. 'Hey look,' she said, 'I brought Sam to see you. He's even got chocolate in his ears.'

Brent closed his eyes. His hands crossed on his chest. God, she thought, he's turning into a baby too. She went back to his kitchen and put the kettle on and looked in the fridge for something to eat. There were two eggs in a packet and milk that smelled okay and butter frozen as hard as bricks, but okay too. A lump of cheese, dried up. Fair enough, an omelette. If he didn't eat it she and Sam would, they'd polish it off. She mixed it and put it in a pan on the stove, looking through the

144

door at Brent from time to time. 'Hey Brent, you got a radio?'
Sam crawled in. She wet the nappie again and washed his face,
then carried him back to the main room and sat him in front of
the TV set. She turned it on but kept the sound off. Keep him
happy, that was it, he hadn't seen TV for a while. She found a
little radio and listened to Windy as the omelette cooked. Brent
hadn't moved again. Like a bloody lion at the zoo –
remembering the one she'd seen lying there depressed.

She made tea and put it on the table. Cut the omelette in
half. Knives and forks, pepper, salt.

'Come and get it, Brent. Come on. I'm going to eat your
share.' She took the plate across to him and wafted it by his
face. 'Smell it, eh. Omelettes is one thing I can cook.'

Brent swung his arm up under the plate. He sent it flying
across the room. The omelette slid down the wall and folded
over on the skirting board.

'Piss off, Leeanne. Leave me alone.'

'For Christ's sake, Brent – '

'I don't need you or anyone.'

'I'm only trying – '

'Do you want some money? Is that why you came?' He
swung off the bed. He was thin and white and bent and, she
thought, poisonous. He crossed the room, stepping over Sam,
who had turned round and was getting ready to cry. 'Here you
are. I got money.' He pulled a drawer open and she saw notes
inside, lying loose. He snatched some and held them out to her.
'Take the stuff.'

'Brent, where'd you get all that?' she whispered.

'I work, that's all. For God's sake,' he stuffed the money in
her nappy bag, 'take it and get out. And don't come back. I
don't want you or your nigger baby.'

'You call him that, you bastard – '

'Get out, Leeanne. Get out.'

He grabbed a knife from the table and pointed it at her. She
jammed Sam in the pushchair and ran it at the door, opened it
one-handed; left him bent and bare-armed, venomous. The
door crashed shut behind her and the key rattled in the lock.

'Oh Christ,' she said, 'oh Christ, oh Christ.'

'Are you all right?' the neighbour said, from her open door.

'He's mad. He needs a doctor.'

She ran along the footpath, pushing Sam in a wobbly line.
If she had stayed he would have taken to her with the knife.
And all that money. He had to be mixed up in something
criminal.

I've got to stay away from him. I can't take Sam there any
more.

She stopped around the corner. She regained her breath.
Sam had enjoyed his wobbly ride and was jerking the chair to
make it go. She pulled out the money Brent had stuffed in the
nappy bag. Five-dollar notes and tens, and not as much as she
had thought: only sixty-five dollars. But there must have been
a couple of thousand in the drawer. She was sure she had seen
red notes in a wad at the bottom.

Stay away, she thought, it's dangerous there.

'Calling you a nigger,' she said to Sam. 'You're not a nigger,
are you? You're my little coconut, eh?'

She stopped at a dairy and bought a pie with one of the
five dollar notes, then went back and bought some cigarettes.
She found another park and sat under the trees. She ate and
fed Sam from her breast, then with meat from the pie, and
changed him on the grass and let him sleep. She smoked half
the packet. Cigarettes for a while, for a day or two. Poor bloody
Brent. All he'd really needed was a girl. And a mother. And
some luck. Luck like hers. Leeanne laughed.

Sure I've got luck, she thought, I've got my baby boy. And
half the day left before Danny comes home. Maybe he'll drop
dead on the way. Who needs better luck than that? Drop dead,
Danny.

She found an old newspaper and folded it into a little tent
and put it over Sam's face to shade him from the sun.

He had gone that Friday night, as she had told him. All day
he'd waited in his room. A light seemed to shine in his face
and he could not get away no matter how he turned. People
stared at him, their faces slanting forward on their necks. Brent
Rosser, that's Brent Rosser, they seemed to say. It was like
shitting by yourself in the trees and finding people standing

146

in the trunks all around. Who were they? He did not know. Ponder was over them like a big papier-mâché head with a light inside.

'Ponder,' he said, 'how did you know?' She seemed to swell until her red cheeks cracked and little croaks and wheezes came from her mouth. That was Ponder laughing. She laughed because she had him; she could see.

He put the money in an envelope. Ten one hundred-dollar notes, and they were fat in there and made it like a sandwich he could bite. He put it on the table and waited. He did not want to go out in the streets, which he imagined full of light, and the cars coloured and the people pink and white. He could not go among them, the envelope would shine. He crossed the room and put it in the wardrobe with his shoes.

She'll always know, he thought. Even when I pay her she'll still know.

He heated baked beans and ate them from the pot. He drank water, feeling it go cold into his chest. The sun was gone behind the Brooklyn hills but the sky had turned almost white and shone like a dinner plate. It lit the dog at his kennel and showed his tongue like bacon and flies on his white water bowl. Brent could not leave until the light was gone. He would put the envelope in his shirt and zip the jacket up. Not take his car. Starting it would make too much noise.

The clock went round again. He did not like its face so he put it in a drawer, under his clothes. His watch, black, showed half-past eight. He took the envelope and shut it tight against his skin. The floor creaked as he walked, the door made a sighing: open; shut. In the street the cars were parked up tight. He could not tell, until he passed, which had people in them. Back ways, empty ways – he kept them in his head. Each narrowed to a crossway, into light. Brent Rosser, men in upstairs windows seemed to say.

He crossed a vacant section by a corrugated wall and came into the sidestreet beside Ponder's yard. No people, no cars. Rosser ran. He came to the door in the fence; slid through the opening, stood in the yard; and felt that here, in Ponder's, he was invisible. The timber stacks, the mowers, the circus horse – there was only Ponder here and he was safe from people.

Her light shone in the shop, past the whiteware under the lean-to roof. Rich in there, with brass and polished wood. Ponder was at the front, locking the door. She wore a red dress and a yellow cardigan – and Brent felt easier, watching her. He felt as if he'd woken up and the day had started.

Ponder came back down the shop. She stopped and wiped her nose and patted the handkerchief into shape in her cardigan pocket.

'Brent, come in, don't stand out there,' she said.

He walked past the mattresses and chairs, hunched a little, trying to look as if he was coming in his own time.

'You're late,' she said. 'I'd just about given you up.'

'Yeah, sorry, Mrs Ponder, I kind of got delayed.'

'Now what would delay you, Brent? A girl?' She scraped the rim of a blue glass vase with her fingernail.

'I walked, that's all. It's further than I thought.'

'Did you sell your car?'

'No, not yet.'

'You'd better hurry, Brent. You haven't got much time.'

He did not like that. He wanted Ponder to be friendly. The shop seemed like a boat they were on, all alone in a creek somewhere. She took her handkerchief out and wet a corner with spit and wiped the vase and looked at it with her head drawn back. 'Did you bring what I asked you for?'

'Yes, Mrs Ponder.'

He unzipped his jacket, but she said, 'Not here, Brent. In the office, dear', and led the way and turned on a light on her desk. 'Flick that switch, love,' – showing him where – 'that's right.' The lights in the shop went out. 'Now, Brent, no one can see us.'

He liked that. He smiled at her. 'Now?'

'In your own time, dear.'

He liked her politeness too. He unbuttoned his shirt and took the envelope out. It had stuck to his skin and it came away like a plaster. He smiled at her and said, 'Sorry, Mrs Ponder, I been sweating.'

'A new envelope, dear? No names or anything?'

'Window one, see. My rent bill came in it. You can see the money, it's all there.'

148

'I'm sure it is. Thank you, Brent.' She put it in a bag resting on her chair.

'Aren't you going to count it?'

'Is there any need?'

He felt it would be businesslike and somehow fit him more into her life. He knew what he was going to ask her now.

'You know all about me, don't you?'

'I know you're not bad, Brent, if it's any consolation.'

'What happened up in Kelburn, that was an accident.'

'I don't know what you're talking about there.'

'Yeah you do.' He grinned at her.

'And I think you'd better go now. I have to lock up.'

'You know everything,' he said. 'That's why I want to stay here and work for you.'

'Brent – '

'This is like . . . ' He could not find words for what he felt. 'It's like the inside of a cave.'

'I think you're a wee bit over-excited, dear.'

'What I could do, I could work in the yard and shift the furniture round and stuff like that. You wouldn't have to pay me much. What do you say, Mrs Ponder?'

'No, Brent.'

'I could clean up all that stuff out there. I'll patch that canoe. I'll do all that for nothing if you like.'

'Brent – '

'And no one has to see me, Mrs Ponder. You'll be the only one who knows.'

'Brent. You zip your jacket up. Go on.' He obeyed. 'Now, you go. The way you came. Out the back. And don't you ever come here again.'

'Mrs Ponder . . . ' It was like a pocket turning inside out. He was in the light again, with faces all around.

'If I ever see you, Brent, I'll say a word to you know who. Just one word is all they need from me.'

'Can I – can I – '

'What?'

'Just stay in my room? And not go out?'

'No.'

'You don't know what it's like, Mrs Ponder.'

149

'You're a very dangerous boy, Brent, and I want you out of here. Australia is where you're going to.'

'I don't want – '

'Listen to me. I don't know you. Never ever come back here again. You sell your car. Quickly now. Whatever you can get. And you buy a ticket and you don't ever come back. I'm doing you a favour, but this is the last one. If you aren't gone in a week – and I'll hear, don't you think you can hide from me.' She put her face lower so the light coloured her eyes. 'A week, Brent. Next Friday. You be gone from Wellington. Now quick march, out of here. And don't make any noise.'

'Mrs Ponder – '

'Not a single word to me. Not one.'

'Ah, Mrs Ponder.'

'And don't you start crying because tears don't work with me. I'm going to count to three, Brent, then I'll pick up the phone.'

'I thought . . .'

'One.'

'You told me once you'd like to be a stand-in for my mother.'

'Two.'

'I'm going. I'm going.'

'Australia by next Friday. Don't you play any smart tricks, Brent.'

He turned and ran. An edge of mattress tripped him and he dived into the doorway, striking his shoulder on the jamb. A stove grazed his face; he heard his jaw squeak on the enamel. Head down, he ran – past the grey timber stacks and the star-spangled horse. Iron boomed under his feet. When he looked back from the gap in the wall only the door showed, half hidden by washing machines that had the pale gleam of night clouds in the sky. Ponder was invisible.

Shit on you, he cried silently. Shit on you, bitch. She'd put him out where everyone could see him again.

He ran home, close to walls, head down through fuzzy domes of light. In his room he pulled everything shut – doors and curtains – huddled in his bed, but could not close the blankets round himself tightly enough.

150

Through the weekend and the next week he stayed in his room, except for forays late at night to the dairy up the hill for bread and eggs and milk and cake and tins of spaghetti and beans. He boiled two eggs and peeled them and felt that he was stripping the skin off himself. He could not bear to touch them again when they were naked, and rolled them off the plate into the rubbish. He fried eggs then, and ate them with beans. And once he pulled his shoes out of the wardrobe and sat among his clothes for several hours in the dark until a cramp in his leg made him burst out, rolling and crying on the floor.

He was not going to Australia. He was not going out of his room again. Ponder could do what she liked.

On Thursday night she rang him. Mrs Casey took the call. 'I'll see,' she said, and knocked on his door. 'Brent, there's a telephone call for you.'

He stood with his back and hands flat against the wall beside the door.

'She says it's important.'

'Tell her . . . '

'What?'

'Tell her I'm coming.'

He waited until he heard her go into her flat. Then he opened the door and looked out. The phone was revolving on the end of its cord. He went to the front door and closed it.

'Hello,' he said.

'Brent?'

'Yes.'

'So you're still here?'

'Friday, you said, Mrs Ponder.'

'Don't say my name. Friday's tomorrow.'

'I'll go.'

'Have you bought a ticket?'

'Yes, I got one,' he lied.

'Who with?'

'What?'

'What company?'

'Ah, Air New Zealand.'

'Go and get it, Brent. Read me the number of the flight.'

151

He was silent. The hall seemed to tick and sigh and swing like a boat.

'I'm disappointed in you, Brent.'

'I got one. I did. But I've got to pick it up out at the airport.'

'Brent, you'd better be gone by tomorrow night.' She hung up.

He went back to his room and locked the door. She seemed to be pressing against him. He felt her belly, hard, like sacks of wheat. She did not leave him any air to breathe. Panting, he sat on the bed. 'Stop it, Mrs Ponder,' he said.

He lay on his back. He rolled to face the wall. 'Why don't you let me live with you? Why don't you?'

Then it was day again, with light coming through the curtains. The doberman whined and barked in the yard. Casey thumped down the hall to work and Mrs Casey sang, making high notes like a radio. The plumbing surrounded him. 'Go away,' he wept. He pulled the blankets up and covered his head. Brent, Mrs Ponder said, I'm disappointed in you. She had a platoon of policemen behind her. They wore white helmets and blue shirts. All of them had radios in their hands and they talked messages back and forth: Brent Rosser – Caucasian – fair hair. She seemed to have made him, and dressed him, and stood him up where everyone could see – but she stood, herself, in the mouth of a cave, and she went backwards into it and hid, and only little bits, gleams and eyes, could be seen. 'Let me come with you, Mrs Ponder,' he wept.

No, Brent. You fly away to Australia.

It would kill him, he knew, to climb into that bright tube with all those other people.

Leeanne came. She pushed him backwards at the door. She squeaked a pushchair into his room and sat her baby on the floor. He smelled her. He saw lights flashing on a screen. Heard scraping plates. The baby puffed his brown cheeks out and there were smells of shit and butter in the room. Voices on a radio, and something by his head that wrapped him round with kitchen and his mother. He swung his arm and punched it, belted it away.

Money smelled. It had a sour smell and scraped his hands. He stuffed it into her and looked for a knife to cut her off and free himself; saw her wobble out into the hall, saw the brown door wipe her away. He lay on his bed again but too much light came in. He closed the curtains. Still it came. He rolled off the bed and knelt on the floor. The lino was cold on his palms. He laid his cheek on it, and saw a dark space open on his level. It was like the bottom shelf in a cupboard. He slid in until he felt his hip bang on the wall. He put his arms across his chest and held himself tight, with little pads of mattress pressing down. Over the room the television screen danced and played, but only feet were there and no faces. Faces could not see him any more. He reached out and hooked his pillow down. He went to sleep and when he woke the room had turned dark. He slid out and crept across and switched the set off. The last bit of light, the talking face, went away. No one now. No anyone.

He wanted to tell Ponder about this. He wanted to ask if he could stay under the bed now that he had found a place where no one would find him.

Ten

He looked down from the helicopter and saw the woman pushing her baby through the streets. She was fixed to the pavement, pasted flat: red trousers, white sweatshirt, yellow hair. She slid back under the fuselage and was gone.

'What do you think, Howie?'

'It's not my sort of thing.'

'Bringing good clientele through those streets, that would be the problem,' Sanderson said.

'There's a view,' Dorio said, 'I'll give you that.'

Howie turned from the window. 'You saw how the locals would take it. You can't have people eating, hell, lobster thermidor, with snotty kids howling round outside.'

'Oh Christ, we'd have that playground out of there,' Quested said.

The helicopter landed on the wharf. Howie sat a moment in his seat. He felt a little sick from the sliding up of buildings from the sea. 'I'll walk back,' he said to Dorio.

'Ronnie wants to talk about all this.'

'You talk to him. Just keep him out of Kitchener, that's all.'

'Yeah. Look, Howie, we've got to sort that out. This Councillor Waterhouse is for real. He's on the environment committee, he just about runs it. We rushed that application and it gave him the chance he wanted. You haven't seen this morning's paper, have you? He says he'll stand in front of the bulldozers if he has to.'

'I'd drive right over the bastard.'

'Okay, Howie, but it isn't you in the seat. He's got support and it's building up.'

'They can't vote again. The contract's signed.'

'Sure it is. But a contract can be just a bit of paper. He's talking about a change in the district plan. And getting Kitchener listed as a heritage building.'

'No chance.'

'He can hold us up long enough to get the election over. There'll be a new Council then, it's a new ball game.'

Howie did not want to worry about it. His glass tower was fixed in his mind; it was a fact. This Waterhouse character and his mates, they had to have their bit of – what would Gwen say? – posturing? It did not worry him but it made him angry. Everything was ready and he wanted to *go*. Sitting round made him feel short of air somehow. You had to be moving, doing something, to breathe. Ronnie Quested's restaurant didn't qualify. All right, he had a client and he'd done a lot of work on various sites. But sitting people down to eat was girl stuff; it wasn't the sort of thing Howie could move and push around.

He left Tony Dorio and walked on the waterfront. He lit a cigarette, then threw it away. He still felt sick. A bubble in his chest made him want to belch. All he could get though were little clicks and bad tastes in his mouth. The woman was the trouble. She hadn't just upset him, she had twisted him inside. So ugly, so shrill, and tears like wattle gum sliding from her eyes. He recognised her as though she had stepped over the worn back step and into the kitchen of the house in Henderson where he had grown up. She told him that the past had hold of him, he was still there. Bullshit, Howie thought, but he couldn't get away. She was where he came from; and looking at Ronnie Quested and the rest, she was where he would choose to be. He had wanted to go with her, back into the playground, and sit with her talking on a seat, and hold the baby for her, and not go with Ronnie along the hill and talk about a restaurant that would never be built.

'Ah, bullshit,' he said.

A woman, passing, looked at him, and hurried a few steps.

Sorry, ma'am. But bullshit all the same. He watched an old wooden scow moored to the piles, and Henderson was as gone as that. As gone as tubby freighters loading wool bales at a wharf. Now they had container ships gliding out like apartment blocks. Why not a restaurant then, in place of half a dozen rusty swings? And people driving up to eat, yeah, lobster thermidor, in place of a foul-mouthed tart pushing her half-caste kid in a second-hand pram. Gwen would call her 'one of Roger's children' probably. But that was bullshit too. It was like blaming history. Things always changed and you couldn't blame a finance minister who just went with the times, did what he had to, gave the market the chance it would have taken anyway. There were always people who dropped out the bottom no matter how much you did for them. It wasn't economics, it was nature. But still he saw the woman leaning over the fence, holding out her baby in her hands, and saw her cry and turn away – God, what was wrong with her, he had offered money – and saw his mother too, walking home with groceries in a string bag and wringing out the sheets by hand over the wash-house tubs.

That was who the woman was, his mother. She had stung him on the wrist, stung like a bee.

Howie sat down on a bench. He thought for a moment he would vomit. All that stuff, that old stuff, was turning inside him and was on the point of rushing out. He put his hands on his knees, held on.

'You all right, mate?'

'Yes. Okay.' Even in his distress he enjoyed 'mate'.

'You don't look so hot.'

'Short of breath. Be all right soon.'

He sat there for another half hour. He smoked two more cigarettes and flicked the butts into the sea as straight as marbles. It made him feel better and he stood up and walked through the streets to the Glencoul. Buildings, he thought, that's what I do. The Kitchener is me for the next three years. Then, by God, I'll do another one. He walked on past the Glen and down Lambton Quay, went into the Druids, up two floors, and found Athol in his office in the gloomy backside of the building.

'I'd rip this place down.'

'You probably will one day.'

Howie liked that. 'Come up to the Glen. Come and have lunch.'

156

'I usually just eat something here.'

'Usually ain't a word, it's a bloody yawn. My shout.'

'Hold on. Cancel that sandwich, Jacqueline.' Athol put his jacket on. 'I wanted to talk to you anyway.'

'Save it for lunch.' He did not like talking in the street, he liked to watch people, how they hurried, how they rode escalators and shrank to a pair of shoes and vanished into boutiques and offices up there. That was the modern world, and his work was making it. Kitchener: cracked dirty bricks and broken mouldings. But soon it would make way for his tower in the sky, with lifts of people floating up inside the glass walls. Bubbles in a beakerful of oil. Howie smiled.

'What's amusing you?'

It was more than amusement, but nothing that Athol would understand. He had his houses and his rents, let him stick to that – rotting piles and blocked drains. Not, Howie conceded, that there was anything wrong with a hands-on way of running things, but it was small. His sons were small. Gwen had sewn their seams up tight. She had locked them in their playpens and they couldn't get out. That kid in the park, with his snotty face, had a better chance. At least he had a mother who could throw back her head and scream. She had whacked the wallet clean out of his hand. Howie felt the force of it. She got me there, he thought. He ran his finger on the scratch drawn like a biro mark on his wrist.

'How did you do that?'

'Scratched myself. Ronnie's been showing us some sites.'

'What for?'

'Some bloody thing he's got about restaurants. There's enough eating places in this town.'

'He's got Peter Kleber in with him.'

'Yeah.'

'You want to watch Kleber, he's pretty smart.'

'He's smooth, that's all. He won't stand up and say what he thinks.'

'Fox is gone.'

'No loss.'

'You'll have him in with you next.'

'When Fox gets in,' Howie said, 'I'll take Neil Hopkins too.'

157

They would never understand, his sons, they thought it was all deals and operating, where someone like Gilbert Fox would fit in; where Gordon would fit, the poor little sod.

There's no largeness in them, he thought, and he grieved for them.

They talked about Damon over lunch and agreed that he needn't wait for the school year to end, but would fly to Auckland in a week's time.

'What does he want to do with himself? What's he want to be?'

'At the moment,' Athol said, 'junior champion on the trampoline.'

'Sure. Fair enough. But what's he good at? What does he want to do with his life?'

'It's a bit early for that, isn't it?'

'Thirteen. I knew. I knew I was going to put up buildings. Make 'em big.'

'Damon's not into that,' Athol said drily.

'So what is he into? What's he like at maths?'

'Okay, I guess. I got his report. I'll send it up.'

'Where was he in class?'

'About middle.'

That was not a word Howie liked; it meant going nowhere, it meant being the same as everyone else.

'He's all right at English. Near the top. And French, I think. Or maybe German.'

'Jesus, why those?'

'I don't know. Ulla wanted him to learn languages.'

'And your mother, I'll bet. She'd probably have them doing Latin and Greek.'

'Olivia does Latin.'

'I didn't think they taught it any more.' There was nothing wrong with the stories though, Nero and all that, Julius Caesar, as long as they didn't get mixed up with real life. Gwen wanted to mix them up. Some guy who played his lyre and made rocks move. He'd be good for putting buildings up, Howie thought. But then his head – just his head – went floating on the sea, singing songs. Too bloody morbid. And then there was a

158

woman who killed her children to get back at her husband who had ditched her for someone else; and a father who was tricked into eating his son, in a stew. Give me maths any day, Howie thought. He had been good at maths, always, and at technical drawing, and could have been an engineer if he'd stayed at school. But there was no money. He had done better, though, by coming up the hard way. Money didn't always count.

He remembered the woman, how she'd swung, whacking his wallet into the thistles.

'I've got to go, Dad.'

'What?'

'I've got to get back. My plumber's due.'

'Blocked drains, eh?'

'That's right,' Athol said easily. 'I'm repiling three houses too. I've got to see someone about that.'

Howie looked up at him standing by the chair, with his face smooth and hair smoothed back behind his thin pink ears. He's got his life worked out, he thought. No wife and no kids any more. A sandwich in the office is all he ever wanted. I'm right to get Damon out of there.

He changed his ticket to an earlier flight and was home in Auckland by late afternoon. Swam in the pool with Darlene; did ten easy lengths at her side. He dived into the deep end and lay alongside the stone looking up at her: bubbles like a string of pearls coming from her mouth; eyes like a little girl frightened of the dark. He wrapped an arm around her and carried her up.

'Don't worry, you'll do it. Don't try so hard.'

'It's just when I remember there isn't any air. Then I get kind of paralysed.'

'Leave it now. Tomorrow, eh? Let's go upstairs.' She was always ready for that. And he liked it best, having her, when she hadn't done something right. He seemed to leave his shape pressed into her.

After dinner they made love again, long and slow, and he thought, sixty-six, I should be in *The Guiness Book of Records*. She held his face in two hands, smiling up at him.

'Howie Powie.'

'I reckon I can come soon.'

159

'Don't try so hard,' she said. So he didn't try; and came sweet and easy, like running trills on a harp, and drifted off to sleep with Darlene's long warmth down his side.

In the morning they ate breakfast on the patio. He told her about Damon coming up.

'Next week?'

'Yeah, Friday.'

'That'll be nice. I'm really looking forward to it, Howie.'

He looked across the lawns at the sea. 'This is a good place for a kid.'

'How long will he stay?'

'Dunno. At least till after Christmas.' He did not know why he could not say, He's staying for good.

'You didn't tell me how his mother is.'

'Ulla?'

'If that's her name.'

'Of course it's her name. I don't know how she is.'

'But I thought you said that you had lunch with Athol?'

'The subject didn't come up, okay? All I know is, Damon might as well be a bloody orphan.'

'And Olivia.'

'Yeah, her too. Gwen's looking after her. I'll do the boy.'

Darlene cleared the dishes. 'We'll try to see he has a good time.'

Howie drank a second cup of coffee. Ulla, he thought, long cool Swede. It bothered him that he hadn't asked Athol how she was. There's a space where she used to be, he thought. Long and cool? Not any more. He couldn't work out what she was. Not a person lying in a bed, because you couldn't say she was all there. He pulled a face at the double meaning. In her head she was all there – she was too much there; he had seen her across a room and always thought, what's going on inside her, and had suspected her of judging him. Now, though, she was all brain because the rest of her was cut off. And how could anyone be that, a head on a pillow – like that bloody head floating on the sea?

'Cold, darling?' Darlene said, coming up behind him.

'No.' He wished sometimes she didn't pick up on every sneeze and shiver he made.

160

'I'll get a scarf.'

'I said I'm not cold.'

'Sorry.'

'I was thinking, that's all.'

'What about?'

He could not say Ulla. 'Gordon.'

'Yes, I thought you were. Are you going to go?'

'I haven't decided yet.'

'Poor Gordon.'

'It's his own bloody fault.' Howie could not get his son fixed either: another one with a space where he used to be – except that he was likely to show up and then you were forced to look at him. There was nothing to see. The prosecution should realise it and leave him alone. This morning, though, the judge would say, Guilty. Nothing surer.

'You should go,' Darlene said. 'He'll be looking for you.'

'I thought you didn't like him.'

'I don't very much. But he's so beaten, Howie. And you are his father.'

He looked at her smooth pretty face. She's not there either, he thought. Yet he loved her. She was built into his life.

Maybe I've made her up. Maybe I just invented her.

'I knew it. You are cold.'

'Yeah, get me a scarf.'

I'm the only thing I can be sure of, he thought. The boy too, he's something I invented. But without them he would be alone.

When she came back he pulled her on to his knee. 'Sorry, I'm a bit crabby. Wellington gets to me.'

He let her knot the scarf around his neck. Then she held his face and looked in his eyes. 'I love you, Howie. Don't forget.'

'Love you too.'

'Don't go to the court if you're too tired.'

'I'm not tired.'

'You won't have to visit him in prison, will you, pet?'

'They'll put him in one of those open ones down country, I suppose. And let him out for weekends. He'll visit us.'

If I was put inside, he thought, they'd have to make it top

security and I'd be over the wall on a fucking sheet, trying at least. But Gordon would land a job as tally clerk in the kitchen. He would grow fat in his cheeks and learn to make them tremble even more. I'd see him breaking rocks if it would make a man of him, Howie thought.

He dressed carefully. He knew they would be flashing bulbs at him. Howie Peet come to see his son get sent down would be the biggest part of the story. Tony Dorio and Quested wanted him to stay away, and he should. He hadn't shown his face until now. But that had started making him ashamed. It began to seem like cowardice. He walked a roundabout way from the parking building to the court; enjoyed the gusty wind and the clashing palm fronds in the park. The journalists, the cameras, converged on him as he reached the steps.

'No, it has no connection,' he said. 'PDQ is a different matter. I'm here because one of the defendants is my son, and he, I assure you, has nothing . . . No, excuse me. No comment. Let me through.' He was close to lashing out at the cameras.

'I understand the Kitchener project has hit some snags, Mr Peet.'

'You understand wrong then, sonny.'

'What do you think the verdict will be?'

'No idea.'

'Will you be giving your son a job?'

'I'd give him one before I'd give you one.'

'You had business dealings with Neil Hopkins, didn't you?'

Howie lunged through. He got inside the door and could not see which way to go. Coming here was a bad mistake. He found a toilet and was alarmed at the blotchy redness of his face. He splashed water on his forehead and cheeks and straightened his tie, straightened his hair. Now, how do I get out of here? Then no, he thought, fuck it, no. I'm not going to be driven out by a bunch of snot-noses. I came here for Gordon and I'm staying, by God. Where do I go?

He found his way into the courtroom and sat in a seat near the back, on the aisle. Another mistake. Neil Hopkins, coming in with his lawyer, stopped to shake hands.

'Good to see you, Howie,' as though they were equals.

162

'Neil.' Nothing more. He wasn't going to wish the bastard luck.

The court was filling up. Broadhead and Rope came in with their lawyers – lawyers like barracuda cruising the reef. That's the game, Howie thought, that's where the pickings are; but no place for someone wanting to keep his self-respect. Give me bricks and mortar any day.

'Dad. I didn't think you'd be here.'

'Good luck, Gordon. See me after.'

He was afraid Gordon was going to cry. He's like Fatty Lupton at school, Howie thought. Everybody picks on him and he wobbles like a jelly and starts to cry. Leave him alone, the poor little sod. He could not identify the feeling that made him reach out and touch Gordon's hand. And when, a dozen rows forward, a woman in a brown skirt and flat shoes, with a bag made of canvas and bamboo, darted into the aisle at Gordon, he did not for a moment recognise her; thought it was some crazy woman who had lost her money in Lupercal; but no, it was Gwen, only Gwen, clutching Gordon's sleeve and kissing him. Howie had not thought she would travel up. He turned his face away, not to know her.

The judge came in and everyone stood up: the lawyers in their fancy dress; Gwen in her browns and greys, con-temptuous of the ritual, he could tell from her back. For half an hour he listened as the setting-out was done – lawyers mouthing formulae and doing their steps. Then Mr Justice Paviour was away, and Howie knew from his tone that no one was getting off. The guy was a marathon talker and he left nothing out, but kept an edge on his voice and made cuts and jabs. 'The conditions in which commercial enterprises and their senior executives operated in 1986 and most of 1987 were dramatically different from those existing today. This undoubtedly influenced the nature of decisions that were made and actions taken. But while conditions may change, in the very nature of things, standards of honesty never vary. What is dishonest now was dishonest then and no argument of pressures and influences is able to change that.' He talked about the 'loop' the money went through and the 'wiring diagrams' the lawyers had used to work the payments out. 'We have here,' he said, 'a clear case of theft and, in several counts, of conspiracy to defraud. Hopkins' dishonesty hardly needs elaboration . . . ' All the same he elaborated, and did it too for Dingle and the rest, even for Gordon. They might not be culpable on all counts, he said, but on this and this . . .

You're going down, son, Howie thought.

Paviour made his judgments: guilty here, not guilty there, and Gordon came out even, one of each. That was better than Howie had expected. But he could not help shrinking inside – his son Gordon guilty of theft. He wished it had been some longer and less ugly word.

Sentencing was deferred for a week. Howie waited while bail was allowed, then he went out quickly and waited in the foyer with his back against the wall.

Gwen came out with Gordon and Parfitt, his lawyer. They nudged her along and she turned to speak; you couldn't stop Gwen, she'd have her say – how it had been, how it should have been. They kept away from the others; all of them kept away from each other, Hopkins, Dingle, Broadhead, Rope, as though they musn't be seen to associate, these pirates who had sailed together on the same ship. Now they washed their hands of each other. Howie couldn't believe their uprightness, their frowns and perfect ties and perfect suits, and he saw that Gordon, ruffled and plump and uncoordinated, had a dignity that they lacked. He had been a thief and he knew it. The others seemed to say, All this has nothing to do with me.

Howie waited until Parfitt left, then went across to Gordon and Gwen. There was nothing to say to Gordon, so he patted his arm and said to Gwen, 'When did you come up?'

'This morning, on the plane. I didn't expect to see you here.'

'Why not?'

'Oh, guilt by association. I thought you'd be far away.'

'Lay off, Gwen. Take a break from it. How are you, Gordy? Think you can get by?'

'Of course he'll get by.'

'I asked him. Parfitt will get you to appeal, I suppose?'

'He thinks I'm going to get two years,' Gordon said. He had a wobble in his voice.

164

'That's about what I thought,' Howie said.

'Oh thank you, Howie. Thank you very much,' Gwen said.

'He might as well be realistic. It's no use thinking an appeal is going to work.'

'Look Howie, you can see Gordon any time. How about letting him and me have some time together?'

'Okay.' He kept his temper. 'How's Ulla?'

'Ulla, Howie, it's Ulla.'

'How is she?'

'She lies in bed. She tries to get used to it.'

'Give her my love.'

'Really?'

'Just do it, eh? Come and see me, Gordon, before next week.' He patted him again and went outside.

The journalists were busy round Hopkins and Dingle. He walked along Princes Street and went down through the park. Gordon he began to feel comfortable about, Gordon was human somehow, and Gwen was Gwen and could not touch him now, although he would wear her, he supposed, like a wart in his armpit until he died. But the others, Hopkins and his gang, made an ugly feeling in his head, as though a surface there had been disturbed and underneath was a whorling and sucking. The guys who shift the money here and hide it there and find it secretly in some other place, they went with deregulation, he supposed, the bad side of it. You had to have them if you were going to have the freedom to do things. But by God they were shifty and dirty little sods. They bloody rob everyone, Howie thought. They rob that woman I saw in Wellington.

A name came to him: Gaston Means. It came from way back – sixty years. Some sort of gangster, wasn't he? Some little guy from when the gangsters were big, Al Capone and the rest, and he robbed poor boxes – was that it? – when he was a boy, or robbed his poor old grandma, something like that? His mother had used Gaston Means as an example – when I pinched something, Howie remembered. Gaston Means started that way, robbing his grandma, so you'd better be careful, son . . . Gaston and Means, what a pair of names, and maybe he grew up to be pretty big, though never in the Al

Capone class. But these guys – Hopkins, Dingle – were Gaston Means grown up. Roger's real children, he thought; although they've always been there, doing their bloody thing. He was glad Gordon had got caught and was out of it now.

Howie drove home. He found Darlene out with the flymo, cutting grass, and he stood in the french doors and admired her as she went back and forth, trailing the cord. He turned the power off and laughed at her silently as she flicked the controls.

'Howie. Oh Howie, that was you. You bastard, Howie.'

'Get your togs. We'll have another go at that stone.'

She still could not reach it but that was okay. He lay in the sun with her, on the new-mown grass, and knew that he was lucky; lucky to have her, lucky to be here.

'Guilty,' he said, 'the lot of them. They're going to sentence them next week.'

'How did Gordon take it?'

'He's all right. He's got his mother there.'

'Gwen?'

'Yeah, Gwen.'

'How was she?'

'Shooting from the hip still. Thank God I went in to buy some shoes.'

'Just imagine if you hadn't, Howie.'

'Don't imagine.' He lay on his elbows and looked around. 'I've earned all this. I worked for it.'

'Of course you did.'

'So hold my hand. And let's have fillet steak for tea.'

'Lunch too if you want it, Howie.'

'Okay, lunch. And we'll go out for tea. Somewhere flash.' A restaurant with a view somewhere. Where I don't have to think about Ronnie and his mates. And Neil Hopkins and the rest. For tonight. 'That okay?'

'That's great, Howie,' she said, and held his hand.

Gordon was waiting outside in his car when they came home. They took him to the living room and Howie said, 'You go up to bed, love, I won't be long.'

He poured two drinks. 'Now, what's up?'

166

'I don't know. I just couldn't – be alone,' Gordon said.

'Where's your mother?'

'She went back this afternoon. She had to visit Ulla. I didn't think she'd come up. She never writes to me or telephones.'

For God's sake, Howie wanted to say, you're grown up now, you're forty-one, you don't need letters from your mother.

'Where did you go?'

'We bought some rolls and ate them in the Domain.'

Typical, he thought. She comes to Auckland to see her son and instead of having a decent lunch they end up with rolls in the Domain. She probably had him feeding the ducks. And told him to get an honest job – social work or gardening or delivering Meals on Wheels. And stay away from the bad boys when you go to prison. You don't have to swear, Gordon, just because they do.

'She give you any good advice?'

'No.'

'Bad advice?'

'We talked, that's all.'

'What about?'

'Growing up. What we did and all that stuff. And you and her, when you were poor.'

'Why, for God's sake?'

'I don't know. I never know why Mum says all the stuff she does.'

She's trying to make him soft, Howie thought, instead of hard, which is what he has to be. He had never seen so clearly the difference between Gwen and himself. She would make those days of being poor some sort of magic time and make it seem that that's where they should be today, because of . . . because of 'happiness' and 'being close' . . . instead of seeing that it was a place they had to climb out of. She flew to Auckland to offer a few tarted-up memories to Gordon, like some lolly he could suck while he was inside . . .

'Then she had to catch her plane. I drove her to the airport. Listen, Dad . . . '

'Yeah? What?'

'I know you don't want me here . . . but if I can just . . .

167

while I get myself sorted out. I'll go crazy if I'm alone.'

'You got a bag?'

'Yes. In the car.'

'Go and get it.'

Gwen had made her throw – domains and ducks and memories – but Gordon had come to Howie, and come for real things: a bed, a drink, a place to sit himself down and 'sort himself out'. Okay, Howie thought, I'll give him that; and then he goes to prison because he made a damn fool mistake and got too greedy; and he does his time, and I'm buggered if I'll try to talk some fancy path through all that for him. A bed. A drink. Then he goes.

'I've got Damon coming next Friday' – when Gordon came back – 'so you couldn't have stayed any longer than that.' There were plenty of rooms, but he didn't want to mix Damon up with a failure. No, he thought, not a failure, Gordon's still got his chance if he does it right. But mix him up with a man who gets tears in his eyes.

Gordon blinked. 'Damon?'

'Yeah.'

'What's he coming for?'

'A holiday. Get him away from all that emotional stuff down there.'

'How long will he stay?'

'As long as he likes.' He saw that Gordon was jealous, and he gulped his drink and said roughly, 'He's a kid, Gordon. You're grown up. Come on, I'll show you a bedroom. I want to get my head down for the night.'

Thank God it's noise insulated or I'd hear him crying through the wall. He was, he realised with shame, close to crying himself.

Howie did not sleep well that night. He felt that his house – more than his house, the inside of his head – had been invaded. Bits of time, bits broken off past events, and people who were younger and simpler than they should be, moved in the space behind his eyes. Gwen, Gordon, Athol, Damon, Ulla. Himself. Gwen with Athol sucking at her breast: why should that come back? It disgusted him, not because of what was happening there but because it was old and gone. Ulla with

Damon on her back like a papoose, striding through the wind and sleet in Central Terrace. And Gordon behind a door, where he thought no one could see him, picking his nose. Why that? Why should that appear? And himself in the garden in the house in Miramar, digging potatoes, while sweat trickled into his belly hair and the radio played a rugby match through the open window and Gwen pegged napkins on the line. He could not tell if he was dreaming or remembering.

He got out of bed. There's someone broken in, he thought. It was a house that did not creak or whisper, but somewhere there had been a click and a change of air. He pulled on his dressing gown and went downstairs. The french doors were open and the curtains moved in a breeze. He went to the door and looked across the moonlit lawn. Gordon was walking past the naiad towards the tennis court. His striped pyjamas looked like a prison suit. Escaping, Howie thought, and was pleased at his son's cleverness in switching off the alarm. The grass slopes gleamed. Gordon slid down them like ice. His scalp was as yellow as a lemon. The Rangitoto channel shone and the islands lay flattened out, spreading into the night. Gordon seemed to be walking there.

Don't do that, Howie thought. It was an easy step off the cliff. His spine tingled at the thought of falling. He saw the rocks and sea rushing up, and saw how Gordon would be free. Don't, he thought. Don't be a coward, son.

He lost Gordon in the shade of a tree, then saw him come out shining – like a bloody angel, he thought – and walk straighter, taller than he managed in the day, to a gap in the flax bushes planted to keep the cliff from crumbling away.

Howie did not want him to start back; stumble and run. He wanted him to look down, consider everything, and only then choose to turn away. I'm not going to interfere, he thought. If he jumps he jumps. Gordon, if I save you you'll be a fucking no-no for the rest of your life. Save yourself. I don't care how much you cry afterwards.

He could feel himself sweating, yet he was cold.

Gordon put his hands on his hips. All I need to do is call his name, Howie thought. But he has to call his own. Say it, Gordy, say Gordon Peet. The things you've done are here, not

169

there, you can't work them out by getting in behind the door.

Howie found himself on the lawn. He felt grass pricking the soles of his feet. I'm not going any further, he said, and he stood in company with the cold statue; held her ankle hard to keep in place. He was overwhelmed by love for his son, but would not move, would not let his voice lassoo out. He's got to get himself back from there, it's not my job. Gordon had squatted and put his hands on his knees. It's either a way of jumping or of holding on, Howie thought. He squatted too, keeping the naiad's ankle in his grip. Gwen would do the wrong thing. She'd run and fight with him and scream and hold him by the ankles. They'd fall off together, the pair of them. But I'm fighting for him, I'm fighting too.

Gordon stood up. He put his hands over his head and seemed to yawn. Then he turned away from the cliff and walked up the lawn – saw Howie standing by the statue.

'Hello, Dad.'

'Gordon,' Howie said, naming him.

'You lock up. I've got to get some sleep.' He went into the house.

Howie followed. He closed the french doors and reset the alarm. I should wash this sweat off me, he thought. But he was tired. He lay down by Darlene, who murmured in her sleep.

Good boy, Gordon, you made it. He pulled the duvet over himself, fitted it round his chin. I'll tell you what, though, he smiled as he went to sleep, you would have changed your mind falling down there. It's too late then. You chose real good. You'll get through prison okay now.

Good on you, son.

Eleven

The yard had clouds pressing down on it. Ponder, in her office, felt their weight. She looked up through the ceiling, through the roof; she combed her orange hair with her fingertips. Then she coughed and rolled phlegm on her tongue and spat it neatly into a paper tissue.

Brent squatted in the yard, sending messages to her. I'm here, Mrs Ponder. I've got something for you, wait and see. The bellies of the clouds softened into misty rain. It wet his face and made his cheekbones cold. He did not mind waiting until Ponder came out. She would have to come to padlock the gate. Then he would tell her he had stayed in Wellington, and that he had found a place where no one would find him. He would show her his present and let it shine.

One Friday had passed and here was another. It had to be Friday for Ponder to be working after dark. When he went out on other nights, after the house had gone to sleep, he climbed into her yard and lay between the timber stacks where the eyes of the circus horse could not see. He prowled among the whiteware on his knees, turning narrow corners like a centipede. He pulled the fridges open and felt their inner walls, and opened ovens in the stoves, smelling legs of lamb that had been roasted inside. Then he went home through the empty streets and crawled into his bed under the bed. He kept his blankets there and had learned a way of covering himself from head to toe, rolling one way and then the other until he was done up all round. His pillow enclosed his face along each side. He felt sometimes that he was in a coffin in the ground, with one side open so he could slide out. He lay there in the daytime and the house went on outside: Caseys, Laverys, the meter reader in the hall, the glazier for the broken window out the back. Visitors too, but none for him. He heard the doberman sniffing at the crack under his door and heard Mrs Lavery say, 'Come away, Sting.' When everyone was out he crept around. He used the toilet and ate food. He knew the places where the floorboards creaked and he side-stepped them. He did not want even the dog to know he was at home.

Once Mrs Casey knocked on his door. She tried the handle. 'Are you in there, Brent?' The next day she pushed a letter under. He left it lying. It must have been Wednesday when Ponder phoned. He heard Mrs Casey say, 'Hold on, I'll see.' She knocked on the door and tried the handle again. 'It looks as if he might have shot through . . . No, I haven't seen him since last Friday.' It had to be Ponder. He felt sorry for her. I guess she could have told the cops on me, he thought. Ponder began to take his mother's place. When he crept into her yard late the next night he smelt cooking smells and washing smells and heard her humming tunes although she wasn't there, and heard her slippers smack on the lino with their soles. He seemed to sit between the table and the stove while she did her cooking and her washing up around him.

Friday night. The Caseys were visiting Napier for the weekend. He heard their cracked muffler boom as they took off. The Laverys had gone again to *Terminator 2*. ('Arnie, I'm coming,' Mrs Lavery cried. 'Hasta la vista, baby,' Lavery growled in a German voice.) Brent unsheathed his arms. He put one hand against the skirting board to slide out. His fingers went into the gap between the foot of the bedpost and the wall. Dust had gathered in a ball as thick as cotton wool. Something hard lay under it. He hooked with his forefinger and brought it into his palm. Round and skinny, like his mother's wedding ring. He slid out and pushed the blankets back and went, stepping carefully, to the window. Through the crack in the curtains he saw the doberman lying in the yard. His head was up and his ears pricked. Brent waited till he laid his jaw on the ground. Then he held the ring in the light: a wedding ring, no mistake. It had been used most of someone's life, it was so worn. But he liked it – liked the roundness. Something was

172

engraved inside in letters so rubbed off he could not read. So it's mine, he thought. They lost it and it's mine. I'll give it to her. He held it on his palm, then put it on his little finger, where it fitted tight.

It's for Ponder, she's my mum.

There was still too much light outside for him to go out. He went to the toilet and pissed quietly, then flushed away his morning shit. The dog could not tell his toilet from the Caseys'. He ate a can of beans and a can of peaches. The light had gone from the sky when he looked again. At half-past ten the Laverys would be back. And he had to get to Ponder before nine o'clock in case she left right on closing time.

He locked his door; no click. He unlocked and locked the front door. His way between the lamps was practised now but he did not like the people in the streets. He went across, went back, moving quickly, keeping his hand in his pocket to hide the ring. Headlamps struck him in the face. He turned into a doorway and looked at a display of Indian pickles. The writing on the jars made no sense. But he pulled out his hand and saw the wedding ring and got himself back in place again.

Across the vacant section, where the weeds came to his waist. He could duck down and be in a walkway like a cat, and slide between the grass and broken concrete to the shelter of a rubbish skip. Ponder's iron fence leaned into the street, then warped back and leaned into the yard. No need to climb, the gate was unchained. It left a space wide enough to ease his body through.

Ponder, with her orange hair, sat in the light. He saw what an old lady she was. The glass walls of her office reflected her, and mirrors picked her up as she walked along the shop and locked the entrance doors. She must be sixty. That was three times as old as him. He was overcome with love and he wanted, more than anything, to please her. He sank on to his knees and walked his hand along the ground into the light. His little finger stuck up like the back leg of a weta. The ring gleamed, thin and white. This is for you, Mrs Ponder. I've found a place where no one knows. I'll come round here and help you in the night. Please, Mrs Ponder.

She turned out the shop lights. The ring switched off its

173

gleam. He drew his hand back and hid it in his pocket. Ponder sat in her office; she finger-combed her hair, and sighed. She took a candy bar from her drawer, unwrapped the paper, bit; wrapped the bar again and put it away.

'I'm here, Mrs Ponder,' Brent whispered.

She chewed and swallowed. Opened the drawer again, had another bite. Then she put the bar away and smacked the back of her hand. 'Bad girl,' she said, locking the drawer with a key.

Brent smiled. 'I'll bring you some candy bars,' he said.

'Hey? What?'

'I'll get you some candy. What sort do you like?'

'Who's there? Is someone there?'

He was quiet then. Decided to surprise her with the ring. He backed into the shadows and went on his hands and knees between electric stoves until he was under the lean-to roof. He put his head out and saw Ponder standing side-on, down an alleyway between the freezers. She had armed herself with a walking stick from the office. A black one, with a swan's head: beads for eyes and a piece of ivory for a beak.

Hey now, Mrs Ponder, you don't need that, it's only me. Wait until you see what I've got.

She went from sight, deeper into the yard. 'Is that you, Brent? If you're playing games with me . . . '

He crept along the alley. It's no game, Mrs Ponder. Look't I got for you. I didn't have to steal it or anything. It's from a wedding. He stepped out behind her. 'Hey,' he said, and held his hand up in the fine rain, with fingers spread.

Ponder swung round. He heard her teeth click as she shut her mouth. 'Brent,' she said. 'So you thought you could play your tricks on me.'

'No, Mrs Ponder. I brought you a present. It's a surprise.'

She hissed. Her red fingernails came up and the walking stick whistled at him. 'You sneaky little piece of dirt. I'm going to give you the hiding of your life.'

'No, Mrs Ponder. Hey, Mrs Ponder – '

'And then I'm going to call the police.'

The ivory beak bit him on the ear. 'Ow, shit,' he cried.

'You thought you could play smart tricks on Ponder.

Sneaky . . . dirty . . . nasty little . . .

She hit him three more times. His hands went blunt with agony as he tried to ward off the blows. 'No,' he yelled, 'I brought you a ring.' He stopped backing away and jumped inside the circle of her stick. 'See, look, a ring for you', pushing up his hand into her face. She chopped the stick down again, between his raised fingers, and he screamed with pain – but stepped closer, hard against her chest, and tried to hold her.

'Mrs Ponder, don't hit me. I love you, Mrs Ponder.'

'Love?' she cried, ugly with disgust. She tried to move away from him to swing the stick again.

'I want you for my mother, that's what I mean.' He danced inside her arms, and she dropped the stick to beat him with her fists. He tried to hold her still but they fell across the harrow chains. She came down on top of him, knocking out his breath. He felt her blown up, strong, like tractor tyres, pressing with her stomach as she tried to heave away. 'Mrs Ponder, don't hurt me,' he sobbed. She put her knees on him and climbed to her feet. The roll in her hair had come undone; a piece of plastic dangled on her cheek.

'I should kill you, I should squash you,' she panted.

'Please,' he wept.

'You wait there. You wait right there. Don't you move one inch.' She turned and went towards the door, between the timber stacks.

'No, Mrs Ponder.' He scrambled off the chains and crawled after her. He threw his arms around her knees and held on tight. She tried to turn, one way, then the other. Her bottom rolled across his face as she struck him backwards with her fists but he kept hold, digging his fingers in her thighs.

'Don't get the police, please, Mrs Ponder.'

She lunged to break away, then crashed down on her face and bounced like rubber. He scrambled on her back and lay on her. 'Just stay there. You're not getting them.'

She began to make little cries for help, then set up a screaming, high and thin – dog-scream sounds. She tried to buck him off but he straddled her and put his face inside her hair. He slid his hands around her jaw to block her mouth. Something came out and filled his palm and he looked at it

with disbelief: teeth, slimy, fixed in gums. He flung them back-
handed over the stoves and tried to stop her mouth again, but
this time his fingers went inside. Her back teeth bit him. He
screamed and pulled, and ripped away, leaving a finger pad.
He pushed himself off her back, and turned around, went in a
circle, doubled up; then saw her again, crawling at the door.
The walking stick tangled in his feet. He picked it up and
struck her on the back, but the stick whistled like bamboo and
made a splitting sound. He looked for something heavier,
something to stop her crawling. She went along slowly at the
door, on bent arms, with her hair trailing on the ground.

'I told you not to, Mrs Ponder.'

He reached into the timber stack and jerked a short piece
free. His left hand scalded him but he held on and raised it and
brought it down on the middle of her back. Her arms shot out
in front of her, she looked like an Arab praying, and he raised
the piece of timber again and hit her on the hump of her spine.
It jerked out of his hands. There must have been a nail in it
and it stayed fixed in her bones, pointing forward like a
monkey's tail. Brent made a whimper. He kicked it but it
swung round to point the other way.

Ponder still moved. Her hands tried to pull her at the door.
She would not stop. He ran to the gardening tools leaning by
the harrow and grabbed a spade and ran back to her. She was
turning over slowly, she seemed to grin at him with her empty
mouth. He brought the spade down flat-bladed on the side of
her head. It made a cracking sound, but when he hit again it
sounded wet.

'I told you not to,' he said, and was filled with rage at her
as she lay there on her back with her mouth open wide and
her eyes looking over her head as though she was trying to see
something in the shop.

'You could have been my mother,' he said.

She made a sound of emptying, and blood ran from her
nose and down her cheeks into her hair. He struck her again,
on the eyes. Then he dug at her. He tried to chop her into bits
that he would not know.

'It serves you right,' he said as he worked. He chopped
hard at her neck but the blade would not go through. He

smashed her face until there was nothing left. Then he leaned panting on the spade. When he turned, the horse was watching him. He ran at it and broke its head in pieces. He flung the spade away and saw it cartwheel through the open door into the shop.

'I'm finished with you, Ponder,' he cried, and he trampled on her hair and turned it into mud, until no red was left in it, and nothing left of her to recognise.

Then he ran out of the yard and past the skip into the vacant section. He burrowed in the grass and hid himself, nursing his hand and waiting for the city to close down. Heavy rain fell. It splashed on his face. 'Good,' he whispered, 'that's good.' He opened his mouth and let drops fall inside. He held his hands palm up in the air, almost as high as the top of the grass. The water washed and stung him. It ran down his sleeves into his armpits. Ponder was gone. He had got rid of her and hidden her. There was no one to love any more.

That's real good. Soon I can go home, Brent thought.

The wet cars shone. Lights were on in some of the front rooms and TV sets flickered with horses, faces, cars, fire, but outside everything was still. Drops fell from the wires and hit the pavement with a finger-snapping sound.

Brent crossed the road and turned sharply, close to brick fences. The noise of his shoes was like dishrags. He was drawn along, drawn home, as though each length of street and pavement shortened like elastic, pulling him. Puddles doused their yellow light as he stepped in them. He walked on a black path in a gorge. The way closed up behind him; he seemed to hear the locking of the walls.

'Sting, Sting,' Mrs Lavery cried. She leaned back on the leash, lifting the dog's forelegs off the ground. He saw it standing level with his face, its red tongue out and hungry noises coming from its mouth. 'Sting,' she cried. 'Oh God, Brent, I'm sorry, he's not like this.'

He lay panting on the side of a car as she dragged Sting up the street. Out of the house they'd come, without any warning, and there had been nowhere to hide. And the dog – the dog

177

had wanted his shoes. Crazy for them. Blood, he thought, blood in my shoes. He ran into the house and down the hall; opened his door; closed it hard and quiet and leaned on it. When he had his breath back he turned his key in the lock; locked himself in. Blood on me, he thought. He went into the bathroom, pulled his sneakers undone and levered them off, each one with the toe of his other foot. He did not want to touch them but lifted them by the laces and put them in the shower and turned it on. He used only his right hand, the left one hurt too much. It made him cry out as he slid his jacket off. He put that in the shower too, alongside the sneakers, and angled the shower head so water drummed on it. He took off his socks, his jeans, his shirt, and put them in. Then he ran some water in the basin and tried to wash his hands but could not get the left one in. The pad was bitten off the second finger and the little finger was swollen to twice its size. Broken, he thought, she broke my finger. The wedding ring cut into it. He looked at his face in the mirror. Blood from his ear was caked down the side of his neck. Jesus, he thought, I'm all cut up. Water overflowed from the shower tray on to the floor. He slid in it and almost fell as he turned the mixer off. His clothes had blocked the drain and he pushed them aside with his foot. The water looked almost clean. He had thought it would be red. I'm chopped to bits, he thought, and he stumbled out of the bathroom to his bed, pulled out the blankets, tried to wrap himself and slide underneath. He could not do it. His hand and his ear hurt too much. He moaned and lay on top of the bed and pulled the blankets over his head.

I've got to stay in here, he thought, I've got to stay quiet. I never want anyone to see me again.

Time went by in pieces, which he knew when their edges were closed off. Streaks of light showed small parts he could recognise. In his hand a hammer beat, falling with no weight, then thumping on his bones and making him cry out. He bit into the mattress to shift his pain away.

He found himself in the kitchen, drinking water from a cup. His hand floated ahead of him like a seagull. Then he was

178

drinking from a packet. Cornflakes scratched his cheeks and gathered in his lap. The fridge door opened wide. He put his hand on a shelf, then sat down with his arm inside and went to sleep. Found himself later, and carried it across the room and lay on the bed with the cold bar resting on his stomach. He took the bread knife to saw it off. His arm was a loaf of bread and must be cut in slices. He thought he had done it, but discovered he had not and the knife was gone. He was in a new place – in the corner, by the TV set, which said, Germany, thunder storms, one hundred runs; and savage crime and shocked the nation; not his name. Showed a face he knew was his but no one else would know.

'Brent,' a voice said, banging on the door. 'Answer me, Brent. Brent, are you sick?'

It went away and came back nights later or straight away. 'What's your sister's address? Where does she live? I'm getting her, Brent.'

He grinned until his teeth hurt. He felt them chip and grind. There might have been a sister once but she had no name.

The woman turned into a man. 'Come on, you fucken idiot, answer the door.' He grinned and hid. 'I'm telling you, mate, we're not sharing a house with a fucken nutter, so open up.'

'Don't, Des, he's sick.'

'Stuff him. I want him out. Hey you in there, you don't open up I'm calling the cops to bust the door.'

When they were gone and the sounds were dead he knew what to do and where to go. Ponder had kept a place for him. He had put her where no one would find her and now it was the time to be with her. His arm floated ahead of him and carried him along.

Out of the room, out of the house. He turned in the dark streets; he crept along and did not feel his feet touch the ground. A white cat went with him, rubbing his legs. He crossed the road and it curled away. He smiled at the way things left no trace. Yellow eyes: gone. Walls, doors: gone. Only him, invisible. He made no connections and felt no pain. When he climbed her wall and fell into the timber there was only the far-off rattle of planks. He walked over the place where Ponder had soaked into the ground. It was as cold as footpaths. He smiled and sank his shoulders to the height of stoves. Red hair, he remembered. Candy bars. The line of freezers gleamed in light that seemed to come from nowhere. He laid his face on them, one by one, and opened a long door lying on its side. It had a lovely silence, oil and air and water, and waited like an eyelid to come down. Brent stepped inside.

'Now I'm all right.'

He slid along the cold floor until he was stretched out; then he eased the roof down, bending his arm, and heard at last its soft excluding click.

He let his breath out. He breathed in deep again. He was safe.

'Ponder,' he said, and went to sleep.

Twelve

It would progress to spiritual guidance before long. Gwen would drop out at that point. Abandon the proposed still centre for the flux of experience, for the uncoordinated, the multitudinous, where she must pass her useful life. In the meantime she would lie between the acned boy and the man with the whispering thighs and concentrate on her pelvic tilt. 'This is a t'riffic exercise for the stomach muscles,' the instructor said. 'It also helps with bowel and bladder control and you mustn't be embarrassed if you break wind downwards while you're doing it.'

Howie would like that, 'break wind downwards'. I should save it for him, Gwen thought, even though I don't want to know about such things and never have. I'm here as a penance for too much intellectual pride and puritan withdrawal, stuck between a boy with bad teeth, and bad face too, poor dear, and a man who arrives in leather trousers and combs his locks in every window he can find, listening to a woman, a Kilbirnie housewife, surely, who says 'reely' and 't'riffic' and even 'reely t'riffic', and hurting my spine on this hard floor. I want to go. Before she moves on to 'inner peece'. I don't believe in it, no matter how pronounced. I don't believe I'll ever cure my pride.

Olivia had decided not to come. It made her feel silly, she said after attending once. Gwen excused her. This was a course for lame ducks, not the healthy young. Grief and shock would not be cured by the pelvic tilt, or sleeping on a mat at the end of it. Time would cure, days would cure. Breakfast lunch and tea and school and friends and riding on the bus and walking on the footpath, buying milk shakes and fish and chips, as far

181

as it was possible would cure. Inner peace would be attained through living. That, at least, Gwen told herself, is how it seems to me, although I'm sixty-four and waiting still.

She relaxed her toes, her feet, her ankles, obeyed the Kilbirnie voice up through her body into her head, where it instructed no activity: she slept a while. Then rolled her mat and set off into the night, feeling – it made her smile – peaceful all through. Organic peace. How long would it last? How long before that sort of questioning destroyed it? She walked by the cable car, which peered at her over the top of the hill.

With no way of working from her toes up to her head, would Ulla be able to achieve this sort of peace?

So it was gone. Ulla became a destroying angel; Ulla swooped. This is my life now, Gwen thought – but it mustn't be Olivia's.

Her son Athol ran towards her, gleaming in the half light. She recognised his thinker's head. It was still hard for her to accept that he kept only figures there. Arthur Miller head. Stead head. He should have been turning artistic or at least contentious thoughts. And he should have Ulla there as a fellow human, even if she had ceased to be his wife.

He made his clockwork approach. His glasses showed the emptiness of his head. No, be fair, she said, why should he be what you couldn't be? Poet, scientist, politician, shaker of the world, however small the movement, into some new and better shape. Light had failed to strike in her womb or in her kitchen and she had bred ordinary men. Smaller even than their father, who had large ambitions and energy to match and an inventiveness that operated like a heart or lung. Gordon and Athol, it seemed to her, were equipped with aptitudes, no more than that.

'Hallo, Mum. Where've you been?'

'Yoga class.'

'Huh.'

'Yes, huh. What do you think about, Athol, when you're running?'

'All sorts of things.'

'Really? Tell me.'

'Ah, lay off. I've got to go.'

182

'I'm serious. I want to know what goes on inside you. Don't you think I've got the right?'

He looked at his watch. He cancelled her. Ran off down the footpath on his new expensive soles. His heels bounced up and down, left and right, like rubber balls. What a mother I've turned into, Gwen thought. I drive my sons away into the night. Once I wanted to hug them against me so tight . . . She walked on. The wind was damp and the clouds were low. Will I get my calmness back if I unroll my mat and work upwards from my toes again? I'll lie in the middle of the road and the cars will drive around me carefully and the drivers will look down and say, There's someone who has found inner peace, let's all try that. I'll do it one day, right here on the crossing. I'll change the world.

Then she grinned hard, to free herself. Games. Worse than games: a form of self-abuse that made her shiver with disgust. She walked home, stepping sharp, making a clatter, and called from the back porch, 'Olivia? You there? I'm going next door to have a word with Damon.'

Through the hedge. Tackle things. Keep on facing up.

'Damon. So you're off tomorrow. How do you feel about that?'

'All right.'

'Those things I washed for you got dry. You need some new underpants, tell Howie.'

She could not decide if he had been crying. She touched his head, then touched his face and put her arms around him. He let himself be held but would not soften, and broke away with a sudden flexing of his arms. 'I'm all right.'

'I know you are.'

'I just want to know if Mum's all right.'

'Well, she's not, you know that – '

'I know – '

' – but inside her head I think she's getting it sorted out. She wants you to be where you'll be happy. You can help her by being happy, Damon.' She heard how stupid it sounded, but could not think of anything else that she might have said. 'I bet you'll find a trampoline up there. Probably the best, if I know Howie.' But didn't she insult the boy with this? Say that bouncing up and down was the important thing? He wanted forward movement: what to do? and possibly even: what's the meaning of it? What is love?

'She hasn't forgotten you, Damon. It's just that this is just about the worst shock a person can ever have and she's got to find a place to go, inside her head, where she can be safe for a while. And sure of things until she learns how to carry on. It doesn't leave room for anything else. She's gone back to where she grew up. To Sweden, I mean. Further than that, in a way. She's kind of mixing herself into it. I think it's necessary, for a time. But it doesn't leave a place for you and Olivia much. When she comes out the other side . . . ' She touched the boy again. He drew away.

'She'll never walk though.'

'It doesn't seem so. Unless a miracle . . . '

He made an angry movement, rejecting miracles. 'So she'll never be the same.'

'Her mind will be the same.'

'No it won't.' He was instructing her. 'You know things with your spine, your spine comes first.'

'Who told you that?'

'No one told me. I just know.'

'Well, someone said' – no good naming foreign names just now – 'that the seat of artistic delight is between the shoulder blades and we should worship the spine and the way it tingles, but no one's ever proved you can't do it all in your head. The spine's a kind of fossil, I think, and sensation isn't anything until it's known up here.' She touched her head. 'Anyway, artistic delight is only part of it.'

'I wasn't talking about that,' Damon said. He could not say what he was talking about. 'It's like she's been turned into something else.'

'And you want her back?'

'Yes.' He might cry now. 'But she's not coming. So I want to know, is she all right where she is?'

She watched him with a kind of astonishment, a huge respect. She had thought his physical life left no room for other movement, but he had understood more quickly than anyone else.

'Yes, she's all right. But she needs time, and quietness, and space for all the things that are going on. That's why she's glad you're going somewhere you'll be happy. You like your grandpa, don't you?'

'He's all right.'

'It's not that Ulla doesn't want you with her – '

'The doctor said I should go and sit with her all the time – me and Liv – and talk to her and touch her face.'

'I think he's wrong.'

'Yeah, he's wrong. I don't mind going up to Auckland. It's no hassle.'

'Your father – '

'I don't care about him. He's a jerk.'

'Oh, Damon.'

'All I want from him is his money.'

'Damon, don't.'

He looked at her fiercely. 'You better look after Liv. She's got to be all right.'

'I will. Yes. I will.'

'That's good then.' He turned to the suitcase on his bed. 'Thanks for the washing.'

'I'll write to you, Damon. I'll tell you how she is. Olivia too. We must all keep in touch – and not be broken up.' But she seemed to be twittering. She kissed him. She hugged him for a moment. She went home. Her house that had given her enormous pleasure once was now a shell. She could not feel its spaces any more but felt Olivia, upstairs in her room, like a soft kernel that would grow or die. Damon, it seemed to her, was doing both. He would become hugely strong, and misshapen, and terrible. Olivia was different. She would not toughen and deform, but would stop where she was and go nowhere, or would step across the thing that blocked her path and carry on in some ordinary way. She waited for a sign, but it might never come.

Whatever I say, it can be wrong, Gwen thought. Perhaps, though, it isn't up to me. And Damon too – perhaps one day there'll be a sign for him. Why can't Athol make a sign?

She put the kettle on and called upstairs to Olivia, then went up for an answer and found the girl sitting on her bed

185

with her headset on, listening to music. The sound came distantly, as though from a dancehall half a suburb away. The awful nostalgia in far-off music, the instant stinging in the eyes; she blinked her way past. Mimed tea-drinking in the door. Olivia smiled, from a distance even greater than the music, it seemed, and shook her head. Butch, warming her feet like a rug, showed a canine accidentally. The smell of him! She must be deadened to it, smell-deaf. Her immaturity made Gwen shiver with fright. She closed the door softly and went downstairs and drank her tea in the darkened living room, looking at the city in its unconvincing light. They circled like a family of planets, never touched – she, Athol, Damon, Olivia. What was it they turned about? Ulla? Was it Ulla? And what was she? Shall we fall into Ulla and be consumed; is that the only way to touch?

Olivia came downstairs and took the dog outside to pee. She looked in on her way back. 'Goodnight, Grandma.' Observing forms, they kept proximity – and needed it, if they were ever to put a head on each other's shoulder again.

'Goodnight, love. Sleep well.'

'You too.'

The dog clicked up behind her. Mounted step by step like an old man. The pipes hummed, the toilet flushed. She was in bed – and did sleep well. Whenever Gwen looked in, she and her dog were spread out on their backs like two exhausted runners. There was nothing to exhaust her in her day – nothing physical, but there must be constant movement, pushing and pulling, in her head.

Gwen went to bed and lay awake. She heard Athol climb on to his porch and turn the key in his front door. She heard him pull his bedroom window shut; lock himself in his room alone. The newspapers had lost interest in him. They were full of Gilbert Fox and his resignation, but Athol had no place any more, which must satisfy him. Man in the shadows – no, that implied invisible pressures put on, and Athol would have none of it, of influence and the pulling of strings. Man in the crowd was better, taking his satisfactions in his head. How he must dislike 'Peet', which Howie had in the papers half a dozen times a week, and Gordon would tomorrow when they locked him away. 'Peet' was currency for buying and selling: it was true coin or false. Gwen herself spent the name each day, many times. It would not surprise her if Athol changed it one day to Smith or Brown and stepped outside the world of daily exchange. He would move with the crowd, in perfect isolation, for the rest of his life.

She wanted, in her narrow bed, to talk about this, and she almost wept with loneliness. 'Howie, oh Howie.' It was not love, it was a need for closeness, and he was the only one she knew. No matter if she despised him. All those things she despised were familiar and she was able to hold them intimately. It was a kind of love – yes it was, she was able to see. She did not want him back – would not have him in the same city if she could help – except for moments like this. She felt it pass, and was relieved. She played with Howie cruelly for a while, then thought about him sensibly. His love for Damon was selfish, but useful for all that; it need not be dangerous.

How would the new wife feel? That was the question. This Darlene – a 'reely'-sayer, too, given her background – how would Damon fit in with her?

She went out to the airport and kissed Damon goodbye, then rode back to town in her son's car.

'He'll be all right. He's one tough kid,' Athol said.

'You know he's gone up there for good? Howie won't let him come back.'

'I know.'

'Who do you think you are, Athol? I mean in relation to him?'

He did not reply and she let it go. She said, 'Ulla will come and live with me when she comes home. It has to be downstairs so I'm going to convert the dining room. You'll have to pay for that.'

'All right.'

'It's going to cost a lot.'

'I said all right.'

'I want to spend some money too on Olivia's room.'

187

'Whatever you say, Mum.'

'And when Ulla comes home we'll need a nurse.'

'You think I only care about money, but I don't. Money doesn't bother me at all.'

'Do you know how much a nurse will cost?'

'A lot, I suppose. I want to pay for Ulla.'

'You do?'

'Because there's nothing else I can do for her.'

'Or the children?'

'Yes, them too.'

It was a confession. She glimpsed something in it that might be courage, then it was gone and all she could see was lack and failure and selfishness.

'Put me down here, Athol. There's no need to take me all the way home.'

'I don't mind.'

'You'll want to get to work. I need a walk.'

She climbed The Terrace and went through the university, and cleaned her house and worked in the garden under clouds that brushed her on the cheeks as they went by. In the afternoon she took Butch for his walk, and bought an early *Post* and saw that her son Gordon was sentenced to eighteen months in jail. It was a shorter time than he had expected, but he had shown 'no emotion' on hearing it. The others had got longer. Gordon's failure to run with the big boys brought him a benefit at last. She was pleased, although if she let herself go onwards a little way she would cry for him and wring her hands here in the street. She bullied the dog home and locked him on the section and set off on her daily visit to the hospital. Afternoons were the time when Ulla seemed at her best – if that phrase were permissible. She talked more and smiled now and then in the afternoon.

'How are you, dear?'

'Don't call me dear. Call me Ulla, please.'

'I usually do. You're lucky to have such a lovely name.' Although sometimes she could not say it because it was so strange. But perhaps that was just the long walk through the corridors and the bed that was a machine. Naming should bring her back and into touch.

'Did Damon go?'

'Yes, he's off. On the plane.' Another danger: to baby-talk her. She had almost said 'on the hairy-buzzer'. 'I'll write to him when I get home so he'll get a letter nice and quick.' She hesitated. 'Would you like to write? I can copy it down.'

'Not today.'

'Can I read to you?'

'No. Just sit.'

Gwen leaned over Ulla and looked at her face. She touched her lightly – butterfly touch. 'Your scar is healing. It's not going to show very much.'

'It was a clean cut,' Ulla said.

'Have they done any more tests? On your spine, I mean?'

'They do things all the time. There is a great science of it, it seems.'

'And?'

'What do they find out, you mean? Behind all their smiles is long faces. There is nothing good.'

'Do they say anything about how long you'll stay?'

'Not to me. It's you they'll tell. You are next of kin.'

'Do you want to go to Auckland? To the spinal unit? It's early, I know.'

Ulla smiled. 'Only my head can travel. It does not need aeroplanes.'

Does your head, Gwen wanted to ask, know your body still? Can it shape all those parts down there? And is that sort of life any good to you?

'Where does it go?'

'Here and there.'

'I hung the Anders Zorn in Olivia's room. I thought she might like it.'

'Does she?'

'She hasn't said.'

What short sentences we speak – your turn, my turn, clip clop. Once it had been clever opinions flying back and forth; flicks and twists and dabs of extra meaning. How quick they'd been, modifiers, qualifiers always at the ready. Now they were bare. Nothing was said. There was really nothing to say. Unless we get down, she thought, to the real bareness, to the bone.

189

I'm not sure we'll ever be ready for that, not as a pair. And won't it have to be in Swedish too?

'Would you like me to try and find a book on him?' But how can she appreciate now that her spine can't tingle? That's what I should ask, and then propose a scientific test. Ulla would have liked it once, I could have set it up. But everything is changed now; the world is shrunken to this room and bed, and little services are all that's left. 'The public library will have something, I'm sure.'

'No,' Ulla said.

'Well, all those painters you used to tell me about, who were obsessed with light, and dark nights, and lakes that gleam. Would you like . . . Tell me their names.'

'No.'

'There's a table on a balcony, and glasses and a jug but no one there. I've seen that. With a blue night and a hollow lake and black pine trees.'

'Gwen, be quiet, now. I know how hard it is.'

'It's not hard – '

'Just sit with me, you don't have to talk.'

'Can't you talk then? Can't you tell me what it's like?'

Ulla closed her eyes. She said, 'I don't have any words. My words are all cut off, down there.'

'They can't be. We live in our heads.'

'No we don't. There aren't two places with a bridge between. There's just one place.'

'But people leave their bodies. There's a whole literature – '

'Shsh, Gwen. I don't want you crying or I'll cry too. Then you'll have to wipe my cheeks.'

'I want to wipe them. I want to do that.'

'And my bottom too?'

'Yes. If I have to. I'll try.'

Ulla smiled. 'I like it best when you tell the truth. So much that happens now is lying to me.'

'I won't lie.'

'Then tell me how you think it is for me, to be like this.'

'I think it's hard. It's – impossible.'

'I am not the only one. Other people lie in beds.'

'But you . . . '

'Everything I feel, these people recognise. I can't surprise them. Yesterday I started talking Swedish just to have a place they couldn't follow. The nurse said, "Where did you learn that, in Germany?"'

'Silly.'

'Oh no. A small language. Why should people know what it is?'

'What did you say in it?'

'I said, "I don't want that part down there. Please take it away." Then she said about Germany, and I said, "After that you can take my head." But in English it would not surprise them. They know all the little steps.'

'What comes next?'

'Acceptance, at the end. I learn how to live with it. That is where they will take me to.'

'Will you go?'

'I'll let them try. I must be fair, they work so hard.'

'After Auckland I want you to come and live with me. Will you do that? I want to start converting the room – my dining room it will be.'

'You turn it into my gymnasium?'

'Yes, if you like.'

'You will wash me, Gwen, and turn me and wipe me?'

'We'll get a nurse. Athol's going to pay.'

'Is he?'

'And Olivia will live there too. Upstairs. I'm going to turn the other bedroom into her sitting room.'

'And we will be three girls and share our clothes and go to dances?'

'Ulla, don't. I can't think of any other ways.'

'I can.'

Through that hollow lake, Gwen thought, and down below the edge of the world. She wants to die and she's not going to change. The first part is a step they'll recognise, but not the second. No one knows Ulla. She'll go where she has to go.

Gwen stayed another half hour, then went home through the drizzle. She wrote Damon a letter full of cheerful things, and cooked a meal for Olivia.

'What's wrong with Butch?'

'I don't know. I think he's sick. I had to carry him down-stairs.'

'His breathing sounds funny.'

'Then he couldn't get in his basket. I had to help him.'

'Well, he's an old man. He must be in his eighties. Would you like to take him to the vet?'

'He hates it so much. He tries to bite him.'

'Let's see how he is in the morning. You'd better leave him down here tonight.'

'He'd be upset. He wouldn't understand.'

And he'd probably try to get upstairs in the night and die near the top. And one of us would trip over him and then there'd be another broken neck. Gwen shivered; she felt the fear of breaking travel down her spine. What a long train it was, what a series of couplings, and such a neat arrangement; so vital and tender and alert, the busy thread. She understood how Ulla was reduced, and the burden she must carry; the insult of her unfeeling parts. Physical living was denied, yet she was not excused from it. So if she said, Please may I leave the room, did anyone have the right to answer no?

'Can I try him with a bit of pudding?' Olivia said.

'If you like.'

'No. He won't. Not even custard.'

'Leave him. He probably just wants a good long sleep.'

'I think he's going to die.'

Gwen went across the room and knelt by the basket. The dog lay on his side with his grey muzzle pointing up and his eyes half closed. A mucky eye, Gwen thought; it needed wiping. Olivia cleaned it with her handkerchief.

'I don't think he's in pain,' she said.

'I think it's just old age. His heart wants to give up, probably.'

'Will you help me carry him up?'

They lifted the basket between them and carried it upstairs and put it on the floor by Olivia's bed.

'I'll do the rest.'

'I don't think you should have him on the bed.'

'But he likes it.'

'Olivia, he might make a mess.'

'I'll clean it up. Please. It might be the last time.'

'All right,' Gwen said. 'Call me if you need a hand with him.' She washed the dishes, read a book, listening for sounds of dying and distress. Olivia called goodnight down the stairs.

'Goodnight, love. Is he all right?'

'I think he likes the sound of rain on the roof. He's perking up.'

'That's good.'

'I couldn't take him out tonight so I let him do it in the shower. I'll clean it tomorrow.'

Gwen managed to say 'All right' to that. She listened to the rain herself as she lay in bed. The dog infiltrated more and more, but paid by dying. Nothing was for ever.

I do want meaning so much, but Ulla keeps on telling me no.

Butch was still alive in the morning.

'I think we should take him to the vet,' Gwen said.

'No, I want to have him here.'

They carried him in his basket downstairs and put him on the porch. Weak sunshine came through the glass and made a gleam in his half-closed eyes. He's dying, Gwen thought, as locked up in himself as he's ever been. There would be no final wag of the tail or lick of the hand. Butch would make Olivia no sign.

She found a little sunshine for herself on the steps and sat there reading the *Dominion*. Neil Hopkins smiled out but Gordon was only named. There would be appeals of course and the thing would drag on, but they were marked as jailbirds and would never be clean again. Gordon, she wrote in her head, you must discover what the important things are. When it came to paper she would write something else. How strange that simple good advice was unacceptable. And love was so quickly brushed aside. She must write that she loved him, all the same.

Butch died then. She heard him sigh. It brushed by her and seemed to go somewhere; and it was a final sound, she knew. So, she thought, something goes away. She went to the basket and looked at the odd little dog-shape lying there. Poor thing, she thought, and called Olivia.

'Oh,' said Olivia, 'I thought he'd wait a bit.' She knelt and touched Butch on the head. 'Should I close his eyes?'

'I don't think so.'

'Will you go away for a little while, please?'

'Of course, love. Call me if you want me.'

She sat in the living room with her paper. It escapes, she thought, whatever it is. And with Butch too, only a dog. Her easiness seemed part of her understanding. But she worried that Olivia would grieve in some dangerous way. The dog had seemed the only thing she was sure about.

Later she saw the girl in the garden digging a grave. She used the spade neatly, chopping down, levering out, and made a hole almost as deep as the handle. Gwen watched from the kitchen. Olivia had put her gumboots on and wore her parka for the drizzle that was starting from the north again. She scraped mud from her soles before coming on to the porch for Butch. Gwen did not go out. She wanted to be called, to play a part. She had walked the dog each day after all. But Olivia wrapped him in his sheepskin, folding the ends like a parcel, and carried him down the steps and into the garden as though it were some ritual she must carry out alone. She knelt and lowered him into the hole, then spaded earth over him like sugar from a spoon – mounded the top of the grave and beat it flat with the back of the spade. No words, no tears. She washed the spade under the garden tap and hung it on its nail in the shed. Gwen went on to the porch.

'So that's Butch gone.'

'Yes.'

'He was a nice little dog.' Something had to be said, but surely more adequate than that. Olivia looked at her blankly and picked up the basket with its blanket scraps inside. 'What are you doing now?'

'I'm going to burn it. It smells.'

'Olivia . . . ' The drizzle had wet her cheeks and made them shine.

'I'm all right. Don't worry about me.'

How it made you worry when someone said that.

194

'Leave it till the rain stops.'

'I want to do everything straight away. Will you get me a box of matches?' Gwen went to the kitchen. 'And some old newspaper,' Olivia called.

Gwen brought the morning paper, with its robberies and murders, and Olivia went off, holding it over her head against the rain, down past the new grave to the incinerator. She crumpled paper and stuffed it in, lit it, pushed the basket down on top, and put her parka hood up while it burned.

Athol came through the hedge, bending to avoid wet leaves. He mounted the steps two at a time.

'What's that smell?'

'Burning blankets.'

'What's she doing?'

'Butch died. Olivia is burning all his stuff.'

'What a stink. The neighbours won't like that.'

'Too bad.'

'What happened to him?'

'Nothing. He just died. Old age.'

'Will she get a new one?'

'A new model?'

'I'm only asking. I suppose you saw about Gordon?'

'Yes.'

'He's lucky.'

'I suppose he is.'

'Well, I just thought I'd check.' He went down the steps, then turned back sharply. 'She's not burning the dog?'

'No, Athol. She buried that.'

'Ah, good. I'll see you all later.'

He went back home, and Gwen thought, What a nice little visit. What a nice family we are, looking out for each other.

In the early afternoon she said, 'I'm going to see your mother. Will you come?'

'I've got some things I want to do,' Olivia said. 'Tell her I'll come tomorrow.'

'She'd like it, you know.'

'I want to come. I really do. Tomorrow. Give her my love.'

Gwen stopped at the library and asked for books about Swedish painting. The assistant found two and she sat at a table, turning the pages, saying the names, Lillefors, Fjaestad, Prins Eugene, and looking at the water and the melting snow and the lakes and skies. They really knew about cold and light and emptiness. Why did she suppose that Ulla had gone there? She had had these same books home herself several months ago – studied them silently, not shared. Not sharing meant that she was going deep down; so Gwen had thought, and had waited for the time when Ulla would want to talk about it. What would she say? What had she been looking for there? Was she trying to make a path back home to travel on when she died? Did she have a premonition? And do these men tell her now, Come home, here is your place? Ulla, I won't stop you if you really have to go. But, my dear, there are other ways that you should try. We have blue empty nights as well, and black hills and cold sea, just look out there, past the buildings and across the harbour. Yours, I know, are the ones that you understand. But see some people before you go. Make them know you love them. Make them know you don't despair.

Could she say all that? Would Ulla listen?

She borrowed the books and put them in her bag, thinking she probably wouldn't take them out at the hospital. There was an equilibrium that should not be upset, and all sorts of dangers she did not know. Keeping Ulla calm was what she should aim for, even if it denied her the sharp parts of herself. Strange, Gwen thought, that I can think of her 'self' as though she still has the whole of it.

She walked through the corridors and sat by the bed. Kissed Ulla on the mouth. It was not a nice mouth any more, it tasted stale.

'Hallo, love.'

'Your sleeve is wet.'

'It's raining out there. Wellington weather. Weather and news. Do you want news?'

'Is there some?'

'Gordon's gone to jail for eighteen months. The paper said he didn't show any emotion. I meant to tell you yesterday.'

'Poor Gordon.'

'He was a roly-poly little boy and you thought he'd be happy but somehow he never was. You found him in corners all the time and under beds. He was slower than Athol. Athol you found up trees. Or on the roof. He stood on top of the chimney once, on one leg, with his arms held out.'

'Why?'

'To be the highest thing, I suppose. And the most dangerous.'

'He's not like that now.'

'No.'

'What frightened him?' She said it without interest. There was a dead place where her interest should have sounded.

Before Gwen could answer, a nurse came in, bringing the detective whose lower jaw opened like a drawer.

'Mrs Peet. Mrs Peet' – giving equal nods.

'Mr Hopgood wants to ask you some questions, Ulla. Just a few,' the nurse said. 'Is that all right?'

'Only one,' the detective said. 'It won't take long.'

He drew a cloth out of his pocket, unfolded it, dangled an amber necklace in front of Ulla. 'Are these your beads, Mrs Peet?'

Gwen saw them reflected in Ulla's eyes. They were lovely beads, full of light.

'No,' Ulla said.

'You're sure about that?' His red tongue in his open mouth shrank in disappointment.

'Yes. Mine were rough. And yellower.'

'All right.' He folded the necklace in the cloth, but seemed not to want to let his opportunity go. 'Anything you can add, Mrs Peet, to what you told us a few weeks ago?'

'No.'

'You've had time to think. You got a look at him.'

'Nothing. He was quick. He was like a squirrel.'

'More dangerous than that, I'm afraid.'

'Have you found out something more?' Gwen said. 'Where did you get those beads?'

Hopgood looked at her but had a clever way of seeming not to see. He doesn't like me, she thought. Why is that?

'From a known fence,' he said. 'There's a possible

197

connection. Sorry to have troubled you, Mrs Peet.' Mrs Peet was Ulla. He went away.

'That was a short visit. You should have said they were yours. I like amber.'

Ulla said nothing.

'I never saw you wearing yours.'

'No.'

'Were they valuable?'

'Not very. I got them from my grandmother. My grandfather bought them in Danzig.'

'Is that an amber place?'

'Yes. I never went there.'

'Across the Baltic,' Gwen said. She felt she had to keep talking. 'It's a sea with so much history. What do you call it again?'

'Ostsjon.'

'Erstshern,' Gwen said. Nothing had ever sounded so foreign. 'You're so like us, you Swedes. And yet your language sounds like nothing on earth.'

'You should hear Finnish,' Ulla said. 'What frightened him? Athol?'

Gwen was quiet. The question was alive now. She wanted to be honest, and fair to them both. 'He seemed to reach the end of the things he could do. I don't know. The things within himself. I suppose the word is potentialities. That's the jargon. But he had the imagination to see there was so much more. He could see up ahead somehow. Does this make sense? And it was dangerous. You were there. He took that risk.' Gwen was not satisfied. She missed the mark. But she could not find a way to be accurate. 'I think with you he proved himself, in his own mind. And then he settled back. But nothing stays still. Things started to shrink – and his boundaries came back, and you were outside again. You and the children too. Love was too much. Too dangerous.'

'But inside were things that pleased him very much,' Ulla said.

'Oh yes. Very satisfying. Athol's happy, in his way. Don't feel sorry for him.' She waited for a moment. 'What made you . . . why did you marry him?'

198

'Surely, Gwen, I am allowed to be in love.'

'Yes.'

'But as you know there are other things. One of them – I saw him on the ferry the first time. In the wet. The big waves. Standing in the bow, crossing the strait.'

'Like a Viking,' Gwen said. 'He had that sort of head, when he had his hair.'

'So I went and stood with him and we talked. Yes, enough.'

'What did he say?'

'Nothing that I remember. And I said silly things. But the occasion . . . '

'It got you started?'

'It took us long ways. Past many things. Me at least. Very foolish.'

'Foolish things have to be said.'

'Athol did not make love very well. I had to teach him. Yes, on that same night, straight off the ferry. With me he thought it was Christmas and New Year rolled into one.'

'You probably terrified him.' It was Ulla who bought the water bed, to try and bring him back. What a foolish thing. Gwen felt like weeping for them. 'Tell me about Sweden. When you were a girl.'

'I am Stockholm. From Stockholm. A city girl.'

'No you're not.'

'Yes, Gwen, I am. We came in from the country when I was eleven. I am Södermannagatan. On Södermalm. I lived there all the time I was in my teens, in an apartment that looked at other apartments across the street. Yellow walls, red walls, green window frames. That sounds romantic to you? You must punch your code at the door and walk up many steps. And then live in little rooms with the windows closed.'

'But you went out into the country?'

'We went to my grandmother's summer house in the skärgård.'

'That's the islands you've told me about?'

'When I came back to town I would walk up to Mosebacke and stand on the cliff where the ferries come in. Where Strindberg stood. He has some famous lines in the start of *Röda Rummet*. Every Swedish child reads them, they are compulsory

– about the wind in May blowing from the islands and the lilac trees breaking into bloom and snowdrops coming up through last year's leaves.'

'Did you feel that wind?'

'I felt it, and smelled the flowers in it – or I imagined that I did. And I went there again when summer was over and felt the cold wind coming from the north. I liked that just as well.'

'You must have been a strange girl.'

'I believed in both of them. Winter and spring.'

'Yes.'

'Now it is all winter for me.'

'Why didn't you go back? Just take the children and go?'

Ulla ran her tongue along her lip. 'I would like a drink, please.'

Gwen held the container and watched her sip from the straw. 'Too sweet,' Ulla said.

'I'll tell them.'

'And with the straw you cannot wet your lips. My lips are dry.'

Gwen poured some water in a glass. She dipped her finger in and wet Ulla's mouth.

'Thank you. Water is best. A little sip.' She swallowed. 'When I lived in Södermannagatan,' she said, 'there was a man living over the street; he used to watch me. His window was on the same level as mine. He was the father of my best friend.'

'Did he . . . ?'

'No, Gwen, nothing bad. He did not show himself or do anything nasty. He just turned his light off and stood in the back of the room where he thought I could not see him, and watched. But I could see him standing in the shadows.'

'What did you do?'

'Nothing. It was like he was waiting for something to happen to me. It was like he was watching my life.'

'How long did it go on?'

'Oh, not long. Two or three months. I would not let it change me. I would do nothing. I said to myself "He is not there."'

'But he was there.'

'Oh yes. So, I was nineteen. I came to see the world. I came to New Zealand.'

'And met Athol on the ferry.'

'He, the man, Mr Gullberg, is why I did not take the children back. Athol said I could go, did you know that?'

'I didn't know.'

'But I said no, they will grow up here, and one day I will go home by myself and see if home is still there.'

'Mr Gullberg would be gone.'

'Perhaps. He was a nice man when I met him in the daytime. But he just wanted to have my life.'

'No one can.'

'No.'

'The rest of it, all the rest, you would still find that. The islands . . . ' She took the books out of her bag and held them in front of Ulla.

'That one,' Ulla said. 'Hold it still.'

The jacket showed a night, blue, a lake, a sky, a balcony with a table and a jug – no one there.

'Yes,' Ulla said, 'it is beautiful. It is Norwegian, you know? But a little bit kitsch, don't you think? So much that little countries do is good, but then not quite good enough. It is sad.'

'Shall I leave them?'

'No, Gwen, take them away.'

'Will you let the children come one day. Properly, I mean.'

'Yes, I will. When I know what I have become.' Her eyes made the gesture that her hands would once have made – indicated her body.

'They love you,' Gwen said.

'Of course. And I love them. One day I will know what to do. But not soon, I think. Now read to me. Read something that makes me laugh.'

'Not Strindberg?'

'Oh no, not him.'

Gwen read from *The Vacillations of Poppy Carew*, and made Ulla smile, if not laugh. Then she went home, and met Athol standing by his gate.

'Did the police come to the hospital?'

'Yes. How did you know?'

'They showed me some beads. Were they hers?'

'No, they weren't. What's it all about?' Athol seemed hollower, and grey, like a pencil sketch.

'They took them from an old woman who was murdered last night. She was the one – did you read the paper?'

'The woman in Cuba Street? In the second-hand shop?'

'He chopped her – tried to – chopped her with a spade. I don't want – any connection with that.' He started up the path.

'Athol!' She stopped him with her voice, a slap. 'Have they caught him? Was he the man who came here?'

He stepped up the path again, sideways. 'No, they haven't. They found some fingerprints that matched. I don't want to have any – '

'Athol.'

'What?'

'Does Olivia know about the murder?'

'They showed her the beads. I don't think they told her why. How did we – get into this?'

'We're not in it, Athol. It happened to us. Don't tell Olivia if she doesn't know.'

She watched him disbelievingly as he went up the steps on to the porch. Not a question about his wife – or his daughter, or his mother – just shock, or was it grief, about this new incursion of violence into his world. Oh Athol, she wanted to cry, where have you gone? Before he went from sight she called, 'I'm taking your *Post*.'

'Yes, have it, I don't want it,' he answered, and went inside.

She pulled it from the box and read it before going into her own house. The man was not named but the identikit picture that Olivia had made was published again in a special box. Ulla's attacker was wanted for questioning about 'the spade murder in Cuba Street'. Spade murder. It made her sick and dizzy. Spades were for gardens and for making things grow. And for burying the family pet. She read how he had chopped the woman – Amy Louise Ponder, sixty-six – tried to take her head off, and sliced all the fingers off one hand. That boy, that squirrel boy, had done all this? That boy walking up the road with his bag on his shoulder? She could not connect him with the act.

202

Gwen put the paper under her cushion, hoping Olivia would not find it there. She locked both the doors and checked the windows, then called upstairs, 'Olivia, I'm home.'

'Yes, coming.'

Gwen waited. She heard the girl moving about, jumping down from something, hammering. Worry was her mode of relating now – what worry should be taken from this activity?

Olivia came down the stairs, stepping light and fast, and took the last half dozen two at a time. Gwen had thought she would never see carelessness on stairs in this family again.

She smiled and said, 'Olivia?'

'I vacuumed my room,' Olivia said. 'And I washed my blankets. I didn't realise how much they stank. Poor old Butch.'

'He's safe underground. Lucky fellow.'

'Why lucky?'

'No, sorry, I was just being smart. Ulla seems happier today.'

'Good. Tell her – no, I'll tell her tomorrow. About that picture. Thanks for that. All that shiny skin and soap and lovely round boobs. We should have a sauna.'

'We can get one.'

'I've never really looked at it before. It's real neat, Gwen.'

'What?'

'You said once I should call you Gwen instead of Grandma.'

'Yes, do.'

'But what I did, I changed it to the other wall, where the windows don't make the glass all shiny. There's some new holes. I hope that's no problem.'

'No problem,' Gwen said, using a phrase she had despised but found attractive now. She made a wish of it. No problem for Olivia. Let it be solved by an assertion of youth; by a change of attention. And keep the spade murder away from her. Let her go and smile like this, with that brand new curve on her mouth – smile at Ulla. And save me from standing at the back of the room, in the shadows, in the dark, like Mr Gullberg, watching her life.

Save her. Save us all, please.

Thirteen

Jasmine wore leopardskin tights and a green jacket of nylon fur. Her hair was the colour of tomatoes.

'Jasmine's gunna live here,' Danny said.

She had shoulders like Hulk Hogan on TV, and grunted as she lowered herself into a kitchen chair. 'I don't do any cooking, tell her that.'

'She doesn't cook. You cook. And make the beds, all that shit.'

'What about the rent? That goes up,' Leeanne said.

'No way. I'm paying what Jody paid, same rent.'

'But that's not fair. There's two of you.'

'Shut up, Leeanne. Just make with the cooking. And keep the kid away from her. She don't like kids.'

'They irk me,' Jasmine said.

'Hey, irk, I like. You put 'im in the bedroom. Keep 'im out of the kitchen, okay?'

'He's got to be here. I can't cook and look after him too.'

'So you better learn. Go to school and learn.'

'Tell her not to let him howl. That irks me too.'

'Hee,' Danny said. 'So keep 'im quiet. Stuff a fucken rag in his mouth.'

'Steak remember,' Jasmine said.

'Steak, Leeanne, that's what she likes. You buy porterhouse and rump.'

'T-bone.'

'T-bone too. You got it?'

'I can't buy steak, there's not enough money.'

'Argue and you'll get fucken done. What's tonight?'

204

'Stew.'

'Last time, eh. No more stew.'

Leeanne took Sam to the bedroom and went back and forth to keep him quiet. She served the meal, then sat with him and talked to him in his cot. 'You and me are getting out of here. We're going to run away like Molly Whuppie. I spat in the stew, Sam, they're eating my spit. Let's see how they like that, eh?'

When he was asleep she washed the dishes.

'Jasmine don't wash dishes.' Danny picked up one of her hands, fat and white, with nails the same colour as her hair. 'See that? Look, you bitch, when I say look. That's the sort of hands you gotta have. Not them fucken things for washing dishes. Fucken bones is all you got. See how skinny her arse is, Jas?'

'Yeah, skinny,' Jasmine yawned. 'We going out?'

'Sure we're going. When I say. She don't dry dishes either.'

'I bet there's other things she's good at though,' Leeanne said.

'No fucken lip,' Danny said, but he was pleased. 'Come on, Jas, shift your arse. We're going up the Herm.'

'That dump?'

'So where you want, the fucken Ecstasy?'

'It'd be a change.'

'No lip from you either. Come on, let's go.'

Leeanne finished the dishes. She wiped the bench. She put Sam's nappies in a bucket to soak. Then she went to bed.

Good things: no more Danny with his slobbering and stinking and his twisting any bits of flesh he could find. Unless, she thought, and went cold, he tried to get her in there for fun, to make it three. But Jasmine wouldn't; she wouldn't stand for that. Leeanne relaxed. No more Danny. She could breathe and get real air into her lungs. But that was all; the rest was bad, and she knew that even more than before she had to get out. There must be a place; and she found herself thinking of a little house somewhere, with carpets for Sam to crawl on and shades on all the lights; and a shower with a glass door, warm water and shampoo, and big fat towels when you came out. There'd be a girl next door to babysit and she could go to the pictures,

205

maybe once a week. And have enough for porterhouse and fillet and, yeah, smokes. And there'd be a man, maybe, to take her to a private bar for a gin and tonic – drive her home afterwards and not try to come inside. Wouldn't that be nice? No noise, no fights . . .

'Sio,' she said. But it wasn't him. In the end what she really wished for was to be alone with Sam, be safe somewhere.

She slept until Danny and Jasmine came in. They slammed around in the kitchen and flushed the toilet – had she taught him to flush? – and ran water and spat and gargled and went to bed, where they creaked and groaned for half an hour. Then toilet again. Then some sleep.

Leeanne made Danny's breakfast and got him away. She would say this for Danny, he kept his job. She left cornflakes and milk on the table for Jasmine and washed the naps and swept the house, with Sam close behind her all the way, and taking two steps between the table and the sink before flopping down on his behind. Hey, brilliant. Hey, choice. His first real steps. She wanted to tell someone, tell even Jasmine, but told Sam instead, hugging him, 'You're on the way, Sammy. You'll be as fast as your dad.'

She walked him out to the front steps, where the sun was shining full bore, and sat down and watched him play in the dry flower bed by the fence. Lovely brown, her Sam, and round as peaches, quick and strong. 'What a boy.' He worked his way along the pickets, hand after hand, and looked at her and walked two steps, and sat down hard and grinned. 'Try again.' And he did. She clapped her hands. She fetched him a biscuit from the kitchen. Then she made a cup of tea and drank it watching him. She wished she had a camera to get photos of this. Sam taking one step, two, with his mouth closed tight and his hands up high for balance and his fingers going in and out. God he tried. It was like a spider climbing out of the bath. 'Hey three, hey three, good boy.'

'Shut up out there,' Jasmine said from the bedroom.

'Shut up yourself. Great, Sam. You're going to be a winger.'

The postman worked up the street, three houses one side, back on an angle, five the other. Leeanne was sixth. Funny how you kept on saying postman even when a woman did the job.

Maybe, she thought, I could be a postman and get Sam minded half the day. You could finish by twelve o'clock when you got the hang of it, the last one said.

'None for me, I bet.'

'Yes, one,' and handed her a letter in a window envelope.

More trouble, Leeanne thought. Department of Social Welfare. She sat down and warmed her hands on the wood, leaving the letter in her lap.

'Hey, you got some tea?' Jasmine called.

'Make it yourself.' She heard Jasmine get out of bed and rustle and grunt into her clothes. The hall door opened.

'You gotta make me tea. Danny said.'

'The kettle's hot. Make it yourself.' She did not look round even though the woman, with shoulders like that, could come up behind and strangle her.

'I'm telling him.'

Leeanne said nothing. Jasmine slapped away, bare feet, into the kitchen. Poor bitch, getting Danny. But I suppose you might just take him on if you got a servant too. She picked up the letter, opened it.

' . . . received information that you are living in a de facto relationship . . . changes in domestic status must be notified . . . benefit discontinued from this date . . . '

It knocked all the sense of where she was out of her.

'Jesus. Jesus.'

She sat on the step, rocking back and forth. Sam climbed up and held her knee.

'Jesus, Sam, they want us dead.'

Biscuit on his face. He grinned at her.

'I'm supposed to be living with Danny.'

He wiped his face on her. Spit and biscuit on her thigh.

'Someone's potted us. God, what date?' Yesterday. And the benefit was due next week. 'We got no money.'

' . . . if you wish to discuss . . . '

'Fucken right I wish to discuss.' She lifted him away and sat him down. Went to the bathroom, washed her face and wiped her thigh. She took the flannel out to the porch and cleaned up Sam. 'You wait, my baby.' Anger, like a headache, throbbed in her. 'We'll have some lunch, eh. Early lunch. Then we'll go down there and towel those bastards up.' She went to the kitchen.

'This what you call breakfast?' Jasmine said.

'Eat it or stuff it up your arse, I don't care.' She ran hot water in a pot and put an egg in for Sam's lunch. Mashed egg he loved. 'I eat it. Danny eats it. You can eat it too.'

'He said bacon and eggs. I got a right.' She was in her leopard tights again, with a black T-shirt that showed her shoulders bulging with muscle and fat. Forty, Leeanne thought. Forty-five, and getting Danny. But I'm stuffed if I'll cook for her, not now.

The water boiled. Co-habiting, she thought. Maybe it's co-habiting for her, but Jesus Christ, getting screwed for a T-bone steak. Then she thought of someone dobbing her in and she made a cry, half scream, half growl.

'You're not right in the head,' Jasmine said. 'Danny told me.'

'Piss off, why don't you? Go and stand in a door up Vivian Street, they're missing you.'

'Huh!' Jasmine banged her cup down on the table.

'Try anything with me I'll fucken kill you,' Leeanne said.

'You are. You're mad.'

'Yeah, I'm mad. Just drink your tea and keep quiet, then you'll be all right.' Poor old bag – thought she had a soft place for a while. 'It isn't you.'

'Well thanks for that.'

Sam was coming up the passage. She heard him walk and fall on his behind and pull himself up against the wall. He crab-walked into the doorway, round the jamb.

'Pooh,' Jasmine said, 'what a stink.'

'What did you say?'

Sam walked his two steps and plopped down. He smiled at Jasmine.

'Shitty kids. I hate shitty kids. Why don't you change him?'

'Strip those fancy drawers off you, I bet you stink worse. Jesus, screwing Danny and you haven't even washed.'

'What?' Jasmine could not speak – she stuttered for words. Then she put her foot out sharp and lifted Sam, like on a spade, and tumbled him away.

208

Leeanne threw the water, egg and all. It hissed into a sheet and wrapped round Jasmine's breast. She screamed and fell off her chair, rolling on the floor.

'You touch my kid . . . ' Leeanne stood over her. The smashed egg crunched as Jasmine rolled on it. 'I'll kill you, you touch him.'

'Shit. Shit. I'm burned,' Jasmine cried.

'You asked for it.'

'Help me. I'm burned.'

'Go in the bathroom. Run some water on it.' She helped the woman up, propelled her into the hall and at the bath, turned on the tap. 'Get in there. Take that off.' She pulled the T-shirt over Jasmine's head and helped her into the bath. Splashed water on her reddened breast. 'Do that. Go on, you do it. I'm not going to be your fucken nurse.'

'I'm hurting.'

'Yeah, well, you shouldn't have kicked Sam. Stay in there, keep the water running.' She was sorry for the fat cow, blubbering in the bath, with her dyed hair hanging down in rags.

Sam had stopped crying. She went back to the kitchen and found him poking at the crushed egg. 'Come on, Sam, we're getting out of here.' Carried him to the bedroom, packed the nappy bag, folded her own clothes into the roll bag, with as much bedding as would fit. She took off Sam's napkin and went back to the bathroom, wet the flannel under Jasmine's tap and washed him clean. Put a fresh nap on and left the dirty one on the floor: who cares? She strapped him into the pushchair. 'Okay, let's go.' But she left him inside the gate and went back to Jasmine, a last look.

'There's a doctor down the road and round the corner. I reckon you better get down there.'

'I can't.' She was lying in the water, with her leopard pants still on, a splash of red on her breast as big as Danny's hand.

It's going to hurt like hell, Leeanne thought.

'Sure you can.' She went to Danny's bedroom and got a blouse and skirt from Jasmine's bag. 'There you are, put those on. You better try.'

'Danny's going to kill you for this,' Jasmine whimpered.

'No he's not, 'cause I won't be here.' She handed her a towel. 'Here, wipe your nose.'

She went outside, opened the gate and set off down the road. She pushed Sam with one hand, humping the roll bag with the other. Where to now? Five dollars in her pocket and no place to go.

She left Sam at the foot of the steps and went, listening, slow, along the passage. His door was closed, the same as before, with the brown wood shining and the knob like a crayfish eye. Locked, she bet, and him still in there rotting on his bed. But when she turned the knob and pushed, it opened with a groan and let out a stink that knocked her backwards down the hall.

'Jesus, Brent, what a pong.'

A door opened behind her and there was the nosy bitch from next door again.

'Thank God you've come.'

'Yeah, what's wrong?'

'He's gone. He went last night it must have been. His room's in a shambles. You can smell. Des and me went in this morning and we had to get out, it's so bad. We were going to phone the landlord if he's not back tonight.'

'Don't do that, he's sick. He's at my parents' out Wainui,' Leeanne lied. 'They phoned me to come round and clean the place up.' She lied fast. 'I'm going to stay and look after it until he's okay. That's why I brought my stuff. You don't have to worry.'

'I'm glad someone's doing something at last,' the woman said.

'Sure we are.' She did not know what she would do if Brent came back. 'Well, I'd better get my baby in.'

'Let me give you a hand with your bag.'

'I'm okay.' And she was. Then she had a look around and wasn't so sure. The kitchenette: dirty plates, maggots again. Dishrag stinking so high she picked it up in two fingers; uncovered the rubbish to put it in but found that full, and crawling too. The omelette she had made was rotting on the floor. And clothes in the shower, in a pool and growing mould. Sneakers as well. She opened the drawer: the money was still there. She was frightened and knew that she should take Sam away. Instead she said, 'We're gunna stay here, Sam. We'll clean this up.' She closed the drawer so that she would not see the money. She tried not to think about Brent. She tried to believe he was never coming back.

It took her two days of hard work. She carried all the rubbish out – Mrs Casey showed her where – and washed the sheets and blankets, and washed the curtains too. She threw out the sneakers, and the leather jacket, which had slime all over it – what a waste. She washed the jeans. Scrubbed the floors, borrowing Mrs Casey's scrubbing brush and disinfectant.

'It's nice to see that sort of thing being done again.'

'Yeah, isn't it.'

She bought what she needed from the money in the drawer.

'He wants me to pay the rent. Where do I go?'

Mrs Casey told her and she went to a little office down on Lambton Quay and got the rent paid up a month ahead. Came home and said, 'It's okay, Sam. I think we've made it.'

She stopped thinking about Brent. She did not believe in him. Mrs Casey said he had mentioned Australia; so he was in Oz, okay, goodbye. She put off going to Social Welfare. Next week. Next month. She would go one day.

'We're okay, Sammy boy, isn't this great?'

He could walk across the room now, flopping down only once or twice. He held his hands high, with his fingers going in and out like sea anemones. She loved to watch. She backed away, half a step in front, and coaxed him on. At night they slept in the same bed. She shifted him over and lay on the place he had warmed up. Then he rolled against her and his hands gripped her neck and sometimes his fingernails dug in. She thought he was having bad dreams and she whispered to him that the world was great and they had it made, the two of them; no one could touch them any more. 'It's only me, Sam, it's your mum. As long as you and me, eh, as long as you and me.' She listened to him breathing when she woke. She shifted so his breath made her throat warm and wet. It smelled like toast and jam. In the morning, in the dawn, when he sucked her breasts,

211

he was getting her tastes, it delighted her. 'I'm gunna have to wean you soon, boy, that's gunna be tough.' But not yet. Why should they? Both of them could keep on for a while.

Mrs Casey had shown her the wash-house. She did her wash there every day, keeping it small, and pegged it on the revolving line in the yard, calling Sam, calling him sharp, away from the doberman and his bones. She went to Mrs Casey's flat for morning tea and told her Brent was okay but he'd be out in Wainuiomata for a while; they wanted to keep him and she was going to stay until he came back. She did not touch his car in the street. Mrs Casey pointed it out, but Leeanne thought she wouldn't try to push her luck that far. Besides, she had no key, and a tyre was flat. She said Brent would come for it one day. She didn't have a licence, she said. So she and Sam walked out for the shopping; walked as far as the new park on the waterfront and watched the tugs and ferries, and the rowers in their skinny boats, and Sam played on the swings, where there were no helicopters coming in to scare him, although they sometimes landed on the wharf over the water and sent a dust of ripples running on the surface. The days were fine, the Glencoul gleamed in the sun as though it was covered in gold, but she didn't envy the people in there. She and Sam had their own place now.

The money still made her nervous. She left it in the drawer and took only as much as she needed each time. She put the change back beside the notes when she came home. It wasn't Brent she was scared of but some heavy like Danny coming for it. One day she counted it and found there was $2308 left; she tried to work out how long it would last but came up with all different times. She did not waste it, did not go on splurges, but could not resist smokes, and disposable nappies, which she had never tried and thought were great, and deodorant and eye make-up. No lipstick. She had never used much of that; her mouth, Sione had told her, tasted good the way it was. She bought a cuddly toy, a panther, for Sam. That wasn't stealing, that was a present. And anyway, hadn't she cleaned the place up, and wasn't she looking after it until he came back? 'Fair do's, Brent.' But he was not real. He seemed like someone she had known a long time ago.

212

She still put Social Welfare off. One day, when she needed to, she'd go – maybe when whoever had potted her had told them she was gone and that someone new had moved in, although you could hardly call poor old Jasmine new. She didn't even want to say Danny's name. She didn't want the Welfare knowing anything at all.

Once, in her second week, she had a bad fright. It was eight o'clock, she was washing her breakfast cup and plate, when she heard the doberman going wild in the yard. She pulled back the curtain and looked out and saw Mr Lavery running out to calm him, and two men squatting to look under the house.

One of them knelt and laid his cheek on the path. 'Jesus,' she thought, 'Brent's under there.' They both stood up and looked at plans. So they were carpenters not cops, although the older one was in a suit. She let the curtain drop in case they noticed her but, looking through the opening, saw them talk with Lavery, who nodded his head. They went round the side of the house, out of sight. She opened the door a crack and watched them by the gate. The carpenter brushed his cheek. He said something quiet and the man in the suit said, 'Sure, I'll see he's kept tied up. No worry there.' He turned to come into the house. His eyes were bright and blue behind little squared-off glasses. They saw Leeanne's face before she got the door closed. She stood close to it, and heard him knock and bring Denise Casey straight out. Denise would have been ready, of course.

'Mrs Casey?'

'Yes.'

'I'm Athol Peet. Athco Properties. I thought you'd like to know that we're repiling the house', and he went on to say there'd be no disturbances and not much noise and the whole thing would only take a week.

'It'll be a squeeze under there,' Mrs Casey said, and the man laughed. It was polite and business, not properly amused. Leeanne knew that her flat was next and she moved back so she could walk from across the room.

She heard his footsteps and heard him knock – one, two, hard. He owned the place and didn't need to behave as though opening the door did him a favour. She picked up her tea towel to seem busy.

'Yes?'

'I'm Athol Peet. Athco Properties.'

'Yes. Hallo.'

'And you'd be . . . ?'

'Leeanne Rosser. The rent's all paid.'

'Oh, there's no problem with the rent.' He explained about the repiling.

'Okay,' she said, and started closing the door.

He put his hand on it. 'If you've got a minute. I've got the tenant down here' – he looked at papers on a clipboard – 'as Rosser, Brent, and he's listed as single.'

'Yeah, he is. Well, you see – ' Leeanne took a breath. She explained, trying not to talk too fast: Brent in Wainui, Brent not well, and her coming to look after his flat until he came back. She was his sister. Brent was single all right, and so was she. 'Like I said, the rent's all paid. I'm looking after the place good. Well,' she said, 'I mean.'

'What's the matter with Mr Rosser? When will he be back?' Athol Peet leaned down and seemed to sniff her. He bent his neck sideways to see into the room. Sam was out of sight in the easy chair, cuddling his panther, but he wouldn't be still for long.

'He's had – ' almost said a breakdown, but remembered that landlords didn't like head cases any more than they liked kids ' – he's got something wrong in his guts, in his stomach, and he needs my mum's cooking for a while. He should be okay soon, he'll be back soon.'

'He's lucky to have a mother who cooks for him.'

'Yeah, she's good.' Leeanne was sweating. 'I'm good at housework too. I'm looking after the place real good.'

'I'm sure you are.' He was looking at the bed, and seemed – she frowned at it – amused. 'So, you're Ms Rosser? How many children are here?'

It was the pack of nappies on the bed. 'One,' she said. 'But not his father. He's in Australia. There's just Sam and me.'

'For a while?'

'Yeah, till Brent . . . '

214

'Do you mind if I have a quick look round, Ms Rosser?'

She hadn't told him to say 'Ms'. It made her think that maybe he was going to move on her. He had that look, and solos were fair game, especially when they weren't supposed to be in a place. Leeanne felt a sinking in her stomach.

He came in and looked around: the bed, the ceiling, Sam, no smile, holding his clipboard in two hands.

'And this is your young chap?'

'Yeah, he's Sam.' And wanted to say, He's not a Maori, he's Samoan.

'How old?'

'He's eleven months. Almost a year.'

'Probably just getting ready to walk?'

'Yeah, he is, he's just started. But I watch him. He doesn't bust things. He's good like that.'

'I'm sure he is.'

Athol Peet looked in the bathroom. 'Mm,' he said. He was holding the clipboard in front of his trousers. When he turned she saw his face – a little smile, a twinkle there, which might be just his glasses – and she knew: this guy's not interested, this guy doesn't want sex. He was satisfied already. She said, 'Do you do it yourself? The repiling?'

'No, I've got a carpenter. He only does piles. Most of the houses this age in Wellington are on wood. On totara. I'm redoing all mine.'

'You sound as if you've got a lot.'

His mouth went prim, a rosebud. 'Rental accommodation is my business.'

'How many, then? How many houses?' She knew she could be cheeky: telling would be like eating or playing with himself.

'Well, at the last count' – he was snooty – 'Athco had title to forty-six. Owning of course is not the accurate term.'

'Jesus, forty-six.'

'Then there's bits of commercial property.'

'I'd settle for just one. I'd settle for a couple of rooms like this.'

Sam climbed backwards off the chair and walked across to her without a fall. She picked him up, then fetched his panther

215

and put it in his arms. 'I don't reckon people should own more than they can use.'

Athol Peet laughed. He seemed to relax. Looked in the kitchenette, touched the sink bench and the stove, a fingertap that seemed to say, This is mine not yours. But maybe he didn't know – they didn't know, sometimes, men, what they really meant. She thought she would stroke him a bit.

'You must be pretty smart to get all that.'

'Well, not smart. It's a question of – there's risk in it – and taking opportunities, and taking care of course.'

'You've got enough houses to start a town.'

'I've never thought of it that way.'

'Do you ever sort of lose one? Not keep track of it?'

He laughed again. 'It hasn't happened yet.'

'So what are you shooting for? One hundred? Two hundred? Do you want to own the whole of Wellington?'

'I like doing what I'm good at. Like you bringing up your little boy.'

Buster, you don't know, she thought. You come down and try it. And suddenly she was tired of him and wanted him out of her place. 'Well, my little boy needs his nappy changed.' The wrong thing to say to a landlord, especially when he had a sniffy nose, but what the hell, you eat, you shit, they know it too – and if they don't they bloody should. I'm staying here.

He said, 'Yes, I'm sorry if I've kept you. I like the way you're keeping it, Ms Rosser. Nice clean curtains. Bathroom's clean.'

What do you expect? I piss in the shower? she wanted to say.

'So . . . I'll put you down as tenant. Caretaker, eh?' He wrote on his clipboard. 'But let me know when Mr Rosser comes back.'

'Yes. I will.'

'And I hope the repiling doesn't upset your little boy.'

'No, he'll like it. Sam's good.'

'What I'm not too keen on,' Athol Peet said, 'is dogs in the yard. We'll see about that.'

'Sting's harmless. He's okay.' She closed the door and went to the chair. She sat down and hugged Sam and said, 'Done it,

216

Sammy. Got him, eh?' What a simple sort of bloke. He was like Danny in a way. But God, how far apart they were – Danny would eat him. Forty-six houses, though. Her dad was forty-six. Her dad would have a house for every year of his life.

She felt that Athol Peet came from a story. She couldn't believe he was out there, moving around, with a wife and kids maybe, and just one house he lived in like everyone else. Hey, I could get him, I could have that bloke, without even screwing or anything. He might be the man who took her to the pub for a drink, then put her in a house, the best one out of his forty-six, gave it to her with no strings.

Leeanne laughed. She kissed Sam and slid her finger under his nap. 'Sorry I lied about you, mate. You're not even wet.'

Sam laughed too.

'Go on, go. It'll do you good,' Denise Casey said.

'I don't know. Sam's never . . . '

'You've got to start. He knows me. He'll be just my little chubby-pie.'

That was almost enough to make Leeanne say no: the woman – Denise she had to be – nuzzling Sam and making him squirm. She hadn't been to the pictures, though, for more than a year and it was like a door she had to go through. Yet she felt it might change their lives. Something would break and Sam would never trust her again.

'It's only two hours.'

'All right. Yes.' But you keep your hands off him, she wanted to say. Don't you try and take my baby, wanted to say. Mrs Casey – Denise – thirty-five and a tyke, with none of her own, and trying every night from the sound of it, and crying in the kitchen while she cooked for two. He's mine, don't you try it, she wanted to say.

'Don't look back. Out the door.'

She went to the first one she came to, *Thelma and Louise.* Forgot Sam and loved it: Louise shooting the slob who tried to rape Thelma in the carpark, and then the two women hitting the road. And the two of them in the car with their backs to all the cops, hundreds of the bastards, saying, Stuff them, let's keep going, and driving straight off the cliff. Flying. Dying. It didn't matter. 'Yeah,' Leeanne said. She clapped her hands, a single clap.

The sunshine, when she came out, almost knocked her down. The cars, the people, dragged her back outside. She couldn't believe the world had been going on, and she felt her shoulders sag. Her eyes stung and watered – but that was just the light. Thelma and Louise, eh, it was like Molly Whuppie again. She stepped out sharp and it became a pleasure, she hadn't moved so fast since Sam was born, taking her place on the footpath and making people step aside. She saw the way men looked at her, she knew she must look good; but she stared back cold and hard, Louise's way, and went blam! blam! Guys in hard hats on a site whistled at her – no one whistled when she had Sam – and she said, 'Stuff you', and did the fingers, which made them cheer. Just moving fast, doing, walking, made her feel good. Okay, Sam, I'm coming, we'll go in the park and have a swing.

Then she knew that something was wrong, and she ran on the footpath, her soles smacking, past Brent's car with its open doors and men with their bums sticking out, and barged her way, shouldered, through the people. 'Sam? Sam?' Up on to the porch, where a cop tried to stop her.

'Hold on, lady.'

'I live here. Where's my baby?'

She got half way past but he held her arm. Her sleeve slid down, the blouse came off her shoulder.

'Who's this?' Out her door, head thrust, showing his teeth.

'Don't know, sir.'

'I want my baby. Where's Sam?'

He straightened up his head. Said her name: 'Leeanne Rosser? That right?'

'Yes. Where is he?'

'He's in there.'

'I want to see.'

'In a minute.'

'Sam,' she called.

'Look,' he said, and opened the Caseys' door. She saw Sam on the sofa, eating a biscuit, with Denise beside him looking happy and pop-eyed. 'There he is.' He closed the door and stood in front of it. 'You can let her go' – to the constable, then, 'Do your buttons up,' – to Leeanne.

She obeyed, with fingers jumping. 'I want to hold him.'

'Not long. Some questions first, eh? Come in here. Come on, Leeanne.' He went into her room and stood in the middle waiting for her. Another man came out of the bathroom.

'So you've been living here, have you?'

'Yes.'

'How long?'

'Three weeks. Nearly three.'

'Comfortable? Nice place?'

'It's all right. Why can't I – '

'Where's Brent, then? Where's he?'

She blinked. So it was Brent, and the money. She looked at the drawer and saw the policeman nod and smile.

'That's all his in there,' she said. 'I just been borrowing some for the groceries and the rent.'

'In the family, eh?'

'Brent's always saved up. He's always saved his money.'

'Did he tell you to use it then, before he went away?'

'No. He wouldn't mind, though. He's my brother.'

'Where is he, Leeanne? Where did he go?'

'Don't know. He was gone before I got here.'

'Sick,' he smiled. 'Out with your mum and dad in Wainui-omata.'

'That was just something I said. So I could stay.'

'Where would he be then? You tell us.'

'What's he supposed to have done?'

'Stop fluffing round, Leeanne.' That was the second man, with the jutting chin. 'Just say where he is.'

'I don't know.'

The other took a chair from the table and put it in the middle of the floor. 'Sit down, Leeanne. It's going to be a long time before you see your baby.'

'Why? You can't – '

'Lots of questions, that's why. All you've got to do is answer them.'

'Start with the last time you saw Brent. When was that?'

But it didn't go on very long. She kept turning in her chair to look at Denise Casey's door. She heard Sam cry in there and she started to get up.

'I've got to feed him.'

'Mrs Casey can feed him.'

'I mean my fucken breast, that's what. Jesus!'

They were pleased to hear her swear. The older man smiled. 'Why do you think he'd go up the hill and rob your landlord's house?'

'I don't know what you're fucken talking about.'

'How much money was in the drawer?'

'I didn't count it.'

'Okay, Leeanne.' He smiled again. 'You can go and feed your baby. Then we'll have to go down to the station.'

'Why?'

'You won't believe how much we want to know,' said the one with the chin.

'If I can take Sam.'

'We'll see. Go on,' the older one said.

She went next door and Sam, with another biscuit, and dry tears on his cheeks, started at her from Denise's knee.

'I tried him with some fish but he didn't like it,' Denise said.

Leeanne picked him up and cleaned his face with her handkerchief. She fed him from her breast only in the morning and at night, not in the daytime any more, but she let him have a suck in case the cops came in.

'How long they been here? What's Brent supposed to have done?'

Denise swallowed. She looked as if something was stuck in her throat.

'What's up? He's robbed old Athol's house, is that what they reckon?'

'Didn't they tell you?' Denise said.

'Tell me what?'

'They want to question him.'

'Well, Jesus, I know that. They're questioning me.'

'About a murder.'

'What?'

'That woman with the spade. In Cuba Street.'

She jerked Sam off her breast, then wrapped him on, squashing his face. She felt she had to get the nipple in and have him part of her again. He twisted sideways and complained.

'Did they say that? Brent did that?'

'They asked me everything he did. Who came and all that. And what he was wearing. Marion Lavery too – they're going down to work to talk to her. She saw him when she took the dog for a walk. On the same night that woman got killed.'

'That doesn't mean . . . Brent wouldn't . . . ' But she was saying words just to somehow know herself, and hold herself against the huge new thing standing there. She put Sam down and he walked across the room – one fall – and got his panther from the back of a chair.

'I gotta go in the bathroom.' She leaned over the basin, waiting to be sick, but nothing came although her stomach heaved. Her heart was beating inside her head. 'Now you've done it, Brent,' she whispered.

The big-jawed policeman looked in. 'Come on, Leeanne.'

'I gotta have a pee.'

'Well make it quick.'

'Jesus, you want to hold my hand?'

'No lip, eh. Just get it done.'

They took her back to her room. She passed Sam, on the sofa again with Denise.

'Tell us about the dirty clothes,' the boss policeman said.

She told them: the shower, the clothes, the slime, the dirty water.

'So where are they now?'

'I chucked them out, the sneakers and the jacket. They were no good any more.'

'In the rubbish?'

'Yes.'

'What sort of sneakers? What make?'

'I don't know, I never looked.'

'Where are the jeans?'

'In the wardrobe.'

'Show us.'

221

They put her in a car and drove her to the police station. She did not ask to take Sam. They sat her in front of a desk and asked all their questions again. She knew it was going down on tape – but she told them everything she knew about Brent, everything he said and she said back, and what he did and what he was like. She told about cleaning the flat and finding the money and living there, and said that Mr Peet had told her it was all right and that he was pleased with how clean she was keeping it.

'Did Brent talk about Mr Peet with you?'

'Did he give you any beads or rings, stuff like that? Come on, Leeanne.'

'No, he didn't. Brent and me weren't good mates, he was just my brother. He gave me five dollars.'

'Did he ever talk about someone called Mrs Ponder?'

'Is she the woman . . . is she the one . . . ?'

'Did he, Leeanne?'

'He didn't tell me what he did. He didn't tell me names.'

She told them about living in Auckland but wouldn't give them Sione's name. She gave them Danny's – too bad about him – but didn't say about Jasmine. Jasmine was gone, with any luck. All the time they said, 'Where is he, Leeanne? Where'd he go?'

'I don't know. He's not out Wainui, I know that.'

'How do you know?'

'Because he can't stand them, Mum and Dad.'

'Why not?'

'How would I know? How's my dad?'

'Do you love him, Leeanne?'

'Course I do. What do you think?'

'Brent, I mean.'

'He's just my brother, that's all.'

It grew dark outside. They left her in front of the desk for an hour. A policewoman brought her a cup of tea. She remembered Thelma robbing the liquor store and she wondered how she had sidestepped there, into that movie.

'Read this, Leeanne.'

'I want to get back and feed my baby.'

'Just read it and sign it, then we'll go.'

222

They drove back to her place and found Athol Peet in the hall. He looked at her and did not recognise her. She brushed past and went into the Caseys'. Sam and she hugged and kissed; his arms were soft and tight around her neck. 'Hungry eh, my baby? Where can I bloody feed him so everybody doesn't get a look?'

Denise took her into the bedroom and Des Casey climbed off the bed and went out fast. She fed Sam, but Denise had filled him up with egg and banana and he wasn't interested much. Anyway, she was nearly dry. It was the shock, and the cops, and Brent, she knew. 'Plenty tomorrow, I promise you,' she whispered. She went with him back to the sitting room (Des Casey left again) and said to Denise, 'Thanks. We'll go home now, he's pretty tired.' She went into the hall and round Athol Peet and the two policemen.

'Hey, where are you going?'

'I'm putting Sam to bed. Any objection?'

'Not in there, you're not. We're sealing that.'

'I live there.'

'Not any more.'

'I've paid the rent.'

'Yeah, too bad. We'll be working for a long time yet, so no one goes in. After that it's up to Mr Peet. You ask him nice he might refund you, eh Mr Peet?'

'Of course,' Athol Peet said. He was white and hollowed out. His eyes didn't twinkle any more.

'So where do I go?' Leeanne said.

'Ring up some friends.'

'I got no friends.'

'Well go to your parents.'

'She can stay here tonight,' Denise said from her door. 'On the flip-flop.'

'There you are then.'

'Let her get her stuff,' the older policeman said.

The room seemed unreal. Everything had moved back as though it couldn't be touched. She felt her fingers slide off things. 'Here,' she said, fighting back, 'hold those', and put a packet of nappies in big-jaw's hands. He did not like it. God, he had a mouth like a barracuda. Where do I go? Leeanne thought, where tomorrow? He let her take Sam's clothes, and her own. She put them in the pushchair and he, quickly, balanced the nappies on top. She looked sideways at the drawer.

'Don't push your luck,' he said.

Outside, Athol Peet tried to smile at her. 'I'm very sorry.'

He was the one whose wife had got kicked down the stairs, the woman who was paralysed now for the rest of her life – but Leeanne's mind slid off that, she could not take it in. Could not see houses with stairs for people to get kicked down, or Brent doing it, or this bent man with a wife. She went by him into the Caseys' and found Denise opening the sofa into a bed.

'He won't cry, will he? It's Des,' Denise said.

But it was more than crying that worried Des, Leeanne knew. She stripped Sam and washed him quickly in the bath, and put him on the flip-flop and lay with him until he went to sleep. Then she looked into the hall. A policeman in uniform sat on a kitchen chair outside her door. Where do I go? In the street big-jaw was watching, hands in pockets, while a tow truck pulled Brent's car on to a trailer. He walked along the footpath and came on to the porch.

'You tell us where you go. You don't sneak out.'

'All right.'

'See those two guys there, by the car? They're reporters. You don't say anything to them. Not even your name.'

She went back into the house. So I haven't even got a name any more. In the Caseys' lounge she found Des wheeling the TV set into the bedroom. He did not look at her.

'Goodnight,' she said. 'Thanks for the bed,' she said.

He closed the door.

She lay down with her clothes on. She tried to think about Brent but he would not come. Not even the murder would come. It was something way back, in the dark, and no faces, just something moving and something on the ground. It was only when she thought of her father that she thought of spades – and they were shiny, they just dug the ground. She thought of him, hard. I'll have to phone tomorrow. I'll have to find out if he's all right.

She slept and woke, and heard the TV set, and later on the

Caseys arguing. Denise cried. God she cried, always, what about? She went to sleep and dreamed about Brent hiding under the house. She and her friends hunted him and when they saw him there they pulled their knickers down and showed . . . Jesus, what a dream. She pulled Sam on to her, half awake, and let him suck. Then, when he went to sleep, she cried a bit herself, quietly, for everything.

Des Casey, in the kitchen, woke her up, making as much noise as he could. Denise, in her nightgown, said, 'I'm sorry, you can't stay.'

'I didn't want to.'

'He's coming back at lunch time to see.'

'Sure, Denise. Thanks, eh. You've been real good. Tell the cops I'll send you my address.'

She set out with her pushchair at half past nine, without even the roll bag which was sealed up in her room. Denise gave her a supermarket bag.

'Now I'm a bag lady, Sam.'

She had change from the pictures and used some of it to buy a *Dominion*. Not much was in the story, not even Brent's name. The police were 'following strong leads'. The identity of a man sought for questioning 'would be revealed later in the day'. She could not think of anywhere Brent might be. Not Australia: Brent was here, he was tied somehow. Then she thought he might be dead. The pushchair jiggled and scraped against a lamp post. He would go into the dark and lie curled up. He'd go where no one could see him and pull the door behind.

'Sam, he's dead.'

She heard his name echoing and spiralling away and she cried for him, silently, standing by the lamp post. A woman stopped to ask if she was all right.

'Yeah. Thanks. I'm okay.'

Sam was twisted in his straps, looking up at her. She said, 'It's okay, Sammy, Mum's okay.' God, she thought, I'm crying like Denise, I've got to stop. She went on until she found a seat in a bus stop and she sat there, with Sam walking along and walking back, excited to be up off the ground. 'Good boy, Sam.'

The teachers said both of them were smart, her and Brent.

They said not to waste it, at school. Now he'd chopped a woman up and he was dead, and she was sitting here with nowhere to go. She managed a fierce grin at that. They'd nod their heads and say, See, I told you. But they couldn't have seen a woman murdered and another one paralysed. God Brent, she thought, what happened to you?

People began arriving for a bus. She strapped Sam in and started off again. Going where? She should have asked Athol Peet for another room – he must have an empty room in forty-six houses. That creepy guy, made of bits of stick with skin stretched over. He had a wife in bed for the rest of her life, and she would be the same in the end, just skin and bones.

She climbed a hill and walked on a clay path in pine trees, and came out by the waste ground where the helicopter had landed.

'Hey, Sam, our swings.'

They stayed for the rest of the morning and the early part of the afternoon. She pushed Sam high; she let him walk around on the grass. She had a swing herself, making the iron couplings shriek. At one o'clock she spent the last of her money on a pie from the Indian dairy. She and Sam shared it in the playground. She took his bottle into a house and asked for some water, and drank half of it herself – tried the teat but couldn't make it work. 'How do you do it, Sam? My God, you're clever.' All the time she pushed down the fear, Where do I go? She would not think of her house, down the hill, where she and Jody and Danny had lived. All she would think was, I'll bet Jasmine's gone.

The sun started angling down the sky. When the shadow gets to that first swing, Leeanne promised. She started down, jolting in the pot holes. Sam was worn out and went to sleep. She walked through a cutting with broken concrete on the sides and new graffiti – Killing Bambi – done in red. Brent's place, her place, was over there, locked up by the cops; and down this way . . . She got to the end of the street; saw the dented cars in the panel beater's yard; saw the broken fence and the letter box. Danny's car was parked outside the house. He shouldn't be home . . . Then Danny came on to the porch with a can of beer. He stretched his arms in the sun and sat

226

down on the step. Leanne heard the click and hiss as he opened the can.

She walked backwards. 'No,' she said. 'No, Sam.' He slept on, whistling through his nose. She got out of sight behind a car, then turned and ran the pushchair to the end of the street. We've got to find a room. We've got to get some money! But we can't say who we are any more. Not Rosser, Sam.

She went up the hill and came to the dairy; climbed the pushchair over the step, left it standing by the door.

'Look,' she said to the Indian, 'I'm broke and I've got to find a room. Can you lend me some money?'

'Broke?' he said, making his eyes go a darker brown.

'Yeah, no money. Can you lend me some?'

'You go away now. Right away.'

She went to the supermarket bag hanging on the pushchair and found her pocketknife – apple-peeling knife – in the bottom. Went back to the counter.

'You've got some in the till. Quick,' she said.

The blade was not even open. He reached out and took it from her hand. Said, sadly, 'I pretend I don't see you.' He put the knife under the counter. He put a bar of candy in her hand. 'For your little boy. Quickly, go.'

Crying again. Tears on her face. 'Can I use your phone? Just one call?'

'One. Then you go. I get cross soon.'

She went behind the counter. 'Dad,' she said, 'is that you, Dad?'

'Leeanne, thank God. Ah, Leeanne.'

'Dad, I've got nowhere to go. Me and Sam.'

'Leeanne, Brent . . . '

'I know, I know.'

'Quickly,' the Indian said.

'I can't talk. I'm borrowing a phone. Can we come, just one night?'

'She's gone, Leeanne. Your mother's gone. She left three days ago, before we knew.'

'Where?'

'She's gone to those people, church people, in the Hutt. Come home, Leeanne. There's only me.'

227

'Dad – '

'Get on the bus.'

'I've got no money. Not even a fare.'

'Wait at the station then. I'll come in. You know which unit?'

'Sure,' she said, 'I been catching it all my life.'

She hung up.

'Thank you,' she said to the Indian.

'I keep the knife.'

'Yes, keep it. Thank you.'

She walked through Mt Cook, down Cuba Street and Willis Street and Lambton Quay. Passed the Beehive and the new building for the court.

Her father got off the Upper Hutt unit. His face was ten years older than it should be.

'Don't cry, Dad. Dad, don't cry.'

'Leeanne, Brent . . . '

'I know, I know.' She hugged him, she held him, while people went by looking the other way. Then she wiped his face with his handkerchief. It was ironed by her mother – her last ironing.

I'll do that, I'll do the housework now.

'Won't she come back, with this thing about Brent?' she said on the unit.

'I don't think so.'

'Won't she want her share of the house?'

'We'll wait and see.'

Yeah, Leeanne thought, let's wait and see.

Along by the harbour, on the earthquake fault. Up the hill, the crash hill, over the top.

'Look, Sam. Wainui.' He stood on her father's knee, holding him by the ear. 'I grew up there.' So did Brent. 'It's a good place, Sam. It's the best.'

They got off at the bus stop and unhooked the pushchair from the bus. Her father pushed along the concrete footpath, by the grass. Leeanne carried the bag. She saw the macrocarpa tree she had climbed as a girl – lopped now, butchered – across the football field, beside the creek. She saw the dry culvert where Brent had hidden with his comics and his stolen cigarettes. And her dad with his belt off, trying to give hidings. That was what fathers had to do. Poor Dad.

I'll look after you, Dad. I'll do the ironing. Me and you and Sam, eh, we'll be okay here.

She opened the gate for them. He pushed Sam up the path.

Fourteen

Howie Peet was pleased with the season and the day. Auckland was turning on its sunshine for Damon. A breeze came up the cliff face and bent across the lawn, bringing a smell of medicine and tar. It rattled the flax leaves and sent a shiver over the swimming pool. Cool air moved on his chest and made his belly hair stir and tickle.

'I'll give you five dollars if you can find a cloud in the sky.'

'There's one over there by Rangitoto.'

'That's smoke from a ship.'

'No it's not. Five dollars please.'

Damon was right. Anyway, ships steamed along smokeless today – and you couldn't say 'steamed'. It made Howie pause and search for other words that had lost their meaning. Fly, he thought; aeroplanes don't fly, they don't flap wings.

'Double or quits,' he said. 'I'll bet that seagull doesn't flap his wings for another minute.'

'Okay, you're on . . . He did. Just once.'

'That wasn't a flap. He moved them to balance himself.'

'There, he flapped. He did it that time. It's only – fifteen seconds.'

'Yeah, he flapped.'

Howie wanted everything to go right for the boy. They had not gone right in the first few days. He had found Damon sitting by the cliff with tears on his face. It had made him want to stroke his hair and hug him by the shoulders.

'Are you thinking about your mother?'

'No.'

'What's wrong then?'

230

'Nothing. I'm all right.'

Later, Howie had been disappointed. Boys shouldn't cry. It disturbed him that Damon made him think of Gordon. He had even, once, called him Gordon by mistake. Gwen didn't help, writing letters all the time. There were three letters in the boy's first week, full of stuff about Ulla, Howie would bet. Damon should be allowed to let her settle in place – not forget, of course, but get her sorted out in his mind so she didn't have him crying behind doors. Damon took his letters to his room and read them shut in. That wasn't healthy. One more letter from Gwen and Howie was going to tell her to leave the boy alone. You concentrate on Olivia, he would say. I'll look after Damon, I know how boys tick.

The trampoline was a big success. Howie hadn't known how good Damon was. He hadn't known the things you could do on a trampoline. You could fly – Damon could fly. Spread out, sinewy, he lay on the air; he banked like an aeroplane and sprang up, rigid, like an African deer, a gazelle. (Darlene clapped as though she was at a concert.) It had to do with timing and balance. Howie liked that, but he would have liked more freedom in there too. He would teach Damon to box soon; he would buy some practice gloves and a punch bag and a speed-ball. In the meantime he taught him snooker shots. The boy was good, he had a good eye.

And he was amazing in the water. He can swim like an eel, Howie's mother had said of him, and Damon was the same, his body seemed to have no joints in the water. He stayed down deep, blowing pearls each side of his face, his hair waving like seaweed, until Howie grew anxious. But he turned away indifferently – you couldn't treat a boy like he was a girl and fuss over him. There were risks a boy had to take. He saw how the trampoline would break your neck if you came down wrong or hit the side, but he didn't say it – didn't even think it after a while. Let Darlene say it: 'be careful' was a woman's job.

'He'll drown, Howie.'

'No he won't, he knows what he's doing.'

On his first swim in the pool Damon had brought up Darlene's stone. Howie said, 'Don't touch that stone down

231

there,' but the boy was gone, as smooth as oil, into the deep end, trailing pearls. He had the stone, found it, innocent, and brought it up, held it high – 'Look't I got.'

'Sorry, love, he didn't know,' Howie said to Darlene, but her mouth had darkened into that O that meant she really was upset and she had turned and gone into the house. Howie took the stone from Damon and explained to him and threw it back, and Darlene tried for it once or twice, half-heartedly, but the fun had gone out of the lesson for Howie. He didn't care whether she got it or not.

'He likes your cooking.'

'I like cooking for him,' she replied.

At first he did not think it was true. Her brightness in the kitchen seemed no more than quickness to him. He had liked watching her with her knives and mixers and ingredients, and enjoyed tasting things before they were done, but she did not seem to welcome him any more. It'll come right, he thought, she just needs time; and slowly Darlene began to change. She made herself easier and happier with the boy. Howie was disturbed by it, for it seemed behaviour she had decided on and was putting into practice. Touch Damon, smile at him, laugh and talk, and clap when he does his tricks on the trampoline. She's making herself fond of him, Howie thought. You can't do that. But it seemed that Darlene could. He watched her nervously and with respect. Making love to her, he became less sure of what he did. 'Maybe we shouldn't do it so much, with the boy in the house.' Soon he used that as an excuse.

'Call her Darlene, don't say Grandma,' he told Damon.

'Sure,' Damon said, and used the name unselfconsciously.

Darlene was old-fashioned enough to be uneasy about it, but Howie said, 'You can't switch things like that on and off. It's better if you're just a kind of friend.'

'I feel more like his mother than his grandma, anyway,' Darlene said. 'Howie, Damon should be at school.'

'It's only one more week. They only go on picnics. He can start again next year.'

'He's staying here next year, is he?'

'Yeah, I guess. Is that okay?'

'I don't mind, Howie. In fact I like it. I just like to be told, that's all.'

'So I'm telling you.'

'It gives me something to do. As long as someone doesn't come and take him away suddenly.'

'Athol won't. And Ulla can't, for sure.'

'That's another thing, Howie. He should be writing to her.'

What were all these 'shoulds' from Darlene now? She jabbed the word at him and he didn't like it. But he found he couldn't bully her any more and was forced to treat her carefully.

'I'm going down to Wellington next week,' he said to Damon. 'Why don't you write a letter and I'll take it to your mother?' He half expected a burst of tears from the boy – and if that happened he would blame Darlene. But Damon only said, 'Sure. What day?'

So Howie took an envelope labelled 'Mum' on his next trip. It lay in his briefcase with his papers and his half of Johnny Walker Black, and it seemed to tick there like a bomb. It might say, I want to come home. It might say, I don't like it here, I want to live with Grandma and Olivia. Howie felt dizzy when he thought of it. He had to leave the meeting for the toilet and splash water on his face. Tony Dorio came in and frowned at him.

'You all right, Howie?'

'Sure. I just can't stand Ronnie rabbiting on.'

'You're the chairman, you can stop him.'

'I can't concentrate today. Look, Tony, I'm not coming back. Fill in for me.'

'There's this thing about our friends over the way I want to bring up.'

'What about them?'

'They're still on about a district scheme change. All they need to do is publicly notify it. Then they can say, No permit mate.'

'They haven't got the nerve,' Howie said. He was the one who had the nerve. There was nothing left to fight about in Kitchener. That battle had been won when he'd out-manoeuvred Cora Dunwoodie.

233

'The environment committee's meeting now,' Dorio said. 'I think we should stay around and hear what they decide.'

'You stay around, Tony. Look, we've got it sewed up tight. They're on an ego trip. Now I'm going. Just sink that bloody restaurant, will you?'

He ordered a taxi for the hospital but half way there he said to the driver, 'Do you know a kids' playground up by the pines, over Newtown?'

'Yeah, maybe.'

'Take me there.' He wanted to put off delivering the letter.

The taxi climbed in narrow streets, through cuttings faced with concrete, and stopped at an iron gate leading into a park. Two swings and a seesaw stood in dusty hollows in the grass. A hurricane wire fence ran up one side. The thistles where the woman had punched his wallet grew up against it like a hedge. He looked for her but the park was empty.

'You getting out?' the driver said.

'No.'

There had been swings at Falls Park. He had been able to turn them almost over the bar. The squeak of swings, the iron shriek – he would never forget. The woman with the baby seemed to be in that place too, standing in the paspalum by the changing shed.

'What do you reckon about a restaurant here?'

'Restaurant? You're joking, mate. A soup kitchen, maybe.'

'Is that someone sleeping in the grass?' He saw two bare soles like white faces looking at him.

'Yeah, some wino. Junkie maybe.'

Or someone with nowhere else to go, Howie thought. He told the driver to take him to the hospital. There he walked through corridors, turning his eyes away from the sickness: men younger than him being wheeled in chairs and breathing oxygen in plastic tents. There was something cowardly about it. The man in the park was braver, lying in the grass. When your health was gone you should keel over and die, not put other people to this trouble. What it meant, when you came to it: Ulla should die. Howie could face things like that.

He sat down to wait until she opened her eyes, and could not help looking at her, looking for Ulla. Her hair seemed darker. It was dry and scurfy inside the brace screwed to her head. One of her eyes showed a streak of eyeball, yellow-white. He could not see her as a woman any more. Her face was fatter, but her body must be wasting away: was that what happened, the muscles lying thin, and no messages getting through to help them stay alive? The collar round her neck marked her live parts from her dead. It looked greasy inside, and the sheepskin in the plastic armour that encased her sides had bare patches, like a moult.

'Howie,' she said. 'What a nice surprise.'

'Hallo, Ulla. I brought you a letter from Damon. He's doing well.'

'Damon?'

Sure, your son, he almost said.

He took the envelope from his briefcase. 'It says "Mum". See?'

'"Mum". That's me?'

I didn't come to play games, Howie thought. 'I'll leave it. One of the nurses can read it to you.'

'No. I'm tired of nurses. You,' she said.

'If that's what you want.'

'First, though, have you got a drink?'

'Water, you want?'

'I want some whisky, Howie. Gwen said you carry it in your bag.'

He moved his leg to hide the briefcase, then realised she could not see down there. 'I'm not sure . . . ' meaning to say 'I've got any left,' but was impatient with the lie. 'Do they let you have that sort of stuff?'

'No.'

'Well, I can't . . . '

'I thought you were the man who broke the rules?'

'That's me, not you.'

'Think how they've got me, Howie. All tied up.'

'Yeah,' he said.

'So I want a drink, to remember what it tastes like, one more time.'

'All right.'

He was afraid. He took the bottle from his bag and poured

half an inch in her water glass. What if she choked? Could she cough? What if he killed her?

'How . . . ?'

'Just a sip. Just wet my lips with it.'

He let some whisky run into her mouth – half a teaspoon, that was all. Ulla gasped.

'It's not like akvavit.'

'Is that what you drank?'

'My father drank. Whisky is not so nice.'

'You asked for it.'

'Yes, I did. But a little bit of water now, please.'

'What'll I do with this?'

'Drink it, Howie. Drink to my health.'

He did not like that. He could not tell what she aimed at him. And he did not want to put her glass to his mouth.

'You must say skål.'

Whisky was a disinfectant – one gulp, he thought. 'Skole! Okay, water.'

He poured some in the glass and put the rim carefully on her lip – saw how dry it was and how dry, bone dry, her teeth. Poor bitch, he thought; tied up is right. She should be allowed to die.

'Now read the letter,' she said.

He tore it open. He had lost his anxiety. Damon would say good things.

'"Dear Mum,"' he read, '"Grandpa's going to take this letter to you. I've been up here for two weeks and it's cool." Cool means – '

'Yes, I know. Go on.'

'"There's a swimming pool and a tennis court and a TV set in my room. Grandpa bought me a new trampoline. I can do the double cat twist now. Darlene's neat. She's cool. She cooks lots of puddings but that's okay. Grandma writes a lot and tells me how you are. When you come to Auckland I'll come and see you."' Then he had written 'I hope', but had crossed it out. 'Love, Damon', he wrote, and put a small X for a kiss.

As a letter it was what Gwen would have called sparse. Howie felt uncomfortable reading it. He wanted more for the

236

woman in the bed and was disappointed in Damon for not trying harder. What had he been about to hope?

'There's a kiss in here if you want it' – and kissed her quickly on the cheek.

'Thank you,' Ulla said. 'It is what Gwen would call a liberty, but thank you, yes.'

Why do we both think about Gwen? She's got a bloody hold on us, he thought. 'Does she come and see you?'

'Like her letters to Damon, a lot. She is very good. She is building a room for me in her house.'

'With all the stuff . . .'

'Special beds?'

'Yeah, all that?'

'Pulleys and slings? Slings and arrows?'

He thought of that head floating on the sea, singing its song. Was Ulla singing? What was her song?

'Everybody is so sure I'm going to Auckland,' she said.

'Don't you have to go there first? The spinal unit's there.'

'I don't have to do anything.'

'Not in that sense – '

'I'm grown up. Would you say I am grown up, Howie?'

'Sure you are – '

'When I came to New Zealand and met your son I was a girl. But I am a woman now. Look at me. I say where I go and what I do – up here, in my head. But nobody listens, because down there is my important part.'

'So,' he said, 'what do you want to do?'

'I don't know yet. Don't be scared.'

'I'm not scared.' But he did not know what she might ask. He said, 'This bed and stuff, I can dub in. I'd like to do that.'

'Athol is paying. My husband pays.'

He asked if Athol came to visit her and she said no, she did not want it, nor did he; and Howie saw they were past the danger of her song. He put it aside – what song? Crazy Gwen's stuff. 'Athol needs a swift kick. What's wrong with him?'

'Leave Athol alone.'

She closed her eyes, and opened them, showing more blue. 'I will not ask him to help. Or you.'

'Help with what?'

'Oh, things I am thinking about. Tell me, Howie, will the police ever catch that boy?'

'They won't say. They're playing it close.'

'And he is the same one who chopped the woman up?'

'They think so. All they can't find is who he is. You don't want to think about it, Ulla.'

'What do I want to think about?'

'Take it easy – '

'My future?'

'I'm sorry, I've upset you. I'll go.'

'Tell Damon Mummy's being brave. Say I won't give up, I'll do the double cat twist soon.'

'Stop whingeing. It happened. This is how it is, okay?'

Whiter blue, a flash. 'Ah, thank you, Howie. Thank you for that.'

'Do you want me to bring more letters when he writes.'

'Don't make him write. Let him enjoy his puddings.'

He picked up his briefcase and went into the corridors. Poor bitch, he thought. I would have helped her once but I can't now. I've got Damon to worry about. *X ray*, said a notice, *Autoclave.* A trolley came along, with a nurse holding a bottle up over a woman who should have been left to finish her life in peace. Why did they try to save them? For what? They had nothing left. It was like the soaps on TV that Darlene liked to watch: the doctors brought some poor sod back to life with those bloody ping-pong bats that jolted the heart, then punched each other on the arm and grinned like chimpanzees. You didn't see the patients after that. All you saw was the doctors screwing their girlfriends.

He stood on the hospital steps and watched the traffic in Riddiford Street. A soup of petrol fumes lapped against the buildings. Mostly, in Wellington, the wind blew fumes away, but today was one of the still days the locals crowed about – half a dozen a year. The Brooklyn hill stood up high, waiting to hide the sun. Ronnie's restaurant was on the wrong side, you wouldn't even see a sunset from it, just Newtown and this – what had Ulla told him once? – hospital in Swedish was 'sick-house'? He started down the steps to find a taxi and get away, but saw Gwen climb down from a bus and walk towards him. He went back up the steps and waited for her.

She walked tiredly, but you still looked at her twice. Darlene was pretty – round in the face, American looks – but Gwen had been a kind of beautiful. Not the sort that he liked best, which was blonde and fresh, open air; but closed in, hidden, private somehow. She had a bend in her face – it went off to the left – but that didn't spoil it; it only made you look again, and made you think that she must be amused, deep inside. He had found a painting once, by an Eyetie whose name he couldn't pronounce – very nude, big hips, black triangle, but the face had been like Gwen's, crooked and faintly amused. She wasn't too amused when he showed it to her – thought it was just the sex had got him; and the centre of the picture was, fair enough, the cunt. But he had been hurt that time, yeah hurt, at being misjudged. It had become an argument about 'the important things in life', which, of course, she was the expert on, and him always trying to catch her with no clothes on. 'What's wrong with that?' 'If you'd just look at my face sometimes. I've got something up here, in my head.' 'Jesus, it was your head I was talking about.' So on, so on, all their married life . . .

'Howie! Have you been seeing Ulla?'

'Yeah, I called. Damon sent a letter down for her.'

'What about?'

He told her, and told her Ulla had asked for a drink of whisky. Gwen would smell it anyway.

'I hope you gave her some.'

That surprised him – her anxiety and gentleness.

'I let her have a sip. She didn't like it much.'

'How did you find her?'

He wet his lips. She seemed to be asking him to soften. 'I've never understood Ulla very well. Ulla, I mean. I guess I'll never say it right.'

'Was she pleased with Damon's letter?'

'It was a bit – sparse. She seemed to like it well enough. Damon's got a lot to get used to.'

'We all have. You look tired, Howie.'

'I'm all right. Never better. How's Olivia?' He could not believe they were having this sort of conversation. Her

239

tiredness was the cause, not his – but when tired she most often wanted to snap.

'Her dog died. Butch, remember?'

'What of?'

'Old age.'

'Shall I buy her a new one? Would she like a puppy?'

'No, don't, please. She's gone past dogs. She seems to be starting to grow up.' She told him that Olivia had buried Butch in the garden and not marked the place but had planted beans on top without seeming to remember. Howie laughed. Gwen smiled at him. 'I thought that would appeal to you. I went to see Gordon yesterday.'

'Yeah?'

'You know he's in Mount Crawford, did you hear?'

'It's a soft place. They'll let him out for weekend leave.'

'Not yet they won't.' Too many scandals, she told him: crooked lawyers pruning their roses on Sunday afternoon when the public thought they were inside breaking stones. 'The people they stole from are living on crusts.'

'Not crusts, Gwen. Come on.'

'They stole from pensioners. At least Gordon wasn't doing that.'

Howie had Gordon in place; he wasn't going to think about him. But he began to see how much Gwen took on, with Ulla and Gordon, and Olivia, and all the 'issues' as well that burned her up. She would not abandon those. He thought of telling her about the woman knocking his wallet out of his hand. That would please her. She'd say, probably, 'You asked for it.' But she – the woman – was private to him; she came to him in secret and troubled him with her face, so ugly in its rage. He felt the jolt of her hand like a shock of electricity. The scratch on his wrist was healed but it had left a scar, raised in a welt, that itched in the night and kept him awake. Gwen would make a great deal of that. He could make nothing himself, but thought her nails had not been clean and he should have had a shot of something against infection – like Tony Dorio in Turkey with his wife (another traveller, like Gwen, wanting crazy places), bitten by a dog and getting a rabies shot, needle in his stomach, hurt like hell. Howie shivered.

'What's wrong, Howie?'

'Ah, nothing. Who was that bloke, the Greek with the lyre, who made rocks move?'

'Orpheus. Why?'

'I was thinking, his head . . . Ulla reminds me . . . '

'How clever of you, Howie. Yes.'

He smiled. 'You can't live forty years with someone, something rubs off. Well, gotta go. Plane to catch.'

'Yes, goodbye. I'm sorry that things aren't going well in your work . . . '

He had gone two steps down, but turned and went back. Her face slanted as she frowned at him. 'On the radio, just before I left. I thought you'd know.'

'What?'

'The council not letting you have a permit. I think it was to pull that building down in Lambton Quay. Howie . . . ?'

He turned from her and went down the steps. That's what comes of being soft, he thought. He had travelled too far from where he was meant to be.

No taxis. Where was a taxi, where was a car? He understood why Ronnie Quested carried a cell phone. Buses went by. He could not work out from their names which way they would take him. I'm building this city and I can't even read the buses, he thought. In the end he got on a station bus and it let him off only a few steps from the office. He rode up in the lift and went in to Dorio.

'Howie,' Dorio said, 'where the hell have you been? I needed you.'

'What's happening? Make it quick.'

'It doesn't matter now if it's quick or slow. The whole thing is finished, understand?'

Howie sat in a chair. His knees would not hold him. The glass tower crashed down; sheets like ice came sliding off the walls.

'Ronnie had a field day. He saw the whole thing coming. Where were you, Howie?'

'Was there anything I could have done?'

'No.'

'So it doesn't matter. No permit, eh?'

241

'Exactly that. They've notified a change.'

'Can they say no on that basis? A committee decision?'

'Lonnie says yeah, if Council gave them delegated power. We can appeal. But look, Howie, this fucking thing can drag on and on. It's costing us.' Tony did not often swear. 'We haven't been thinking clear. None of us have. Especially you. You're supposed to be the boss but you're up in the air these last few weeks.'

He could not object to that; had no strength for it. 'So what do we do?'

'We've still got the rights to the air space. We've got that till 1999. So we hang on and let it ride. Three or four years. Then we'll try again. We'll get it one day, nothing surer. Maybe we can tell them that we'll save the facade, heritage building stuff, maybe that. But for now we let it go.'

'Get our costs back?'

'Sure we do. We're not letting them get away with that. But we do it easy, Howie. If we want the thing to go again we've got to keep them on side. We don't make a big production of it.'

I haven't got three or four years, Howie thought. 'Where do we go then? Restaurants?'

'Restaurants? Ronnie was playing games. It's a shopping mall. Along on the Imperial.'

'Shopping mall?' Howie could not see it. The building would not stand up above the roofs all around.

'Ronnie's had that one brewing too. He had it on the table before Kitchener hit the ground.'

'Has it, Tony? Hit the ground?'

'Sure, it has. For now. Dead as a doornail.'

Doornail, I like that, Howie thought. 'Can we get this shopping mall?'

'Ronnie says maybe. He's got a client. The property's the hard bit. It all rests on Gil Fox.'

'Fox?'

'Ronnie says. I'm not too clear on it. Look, Howie, I know how you feel, but you're outvoted. I'm warning you, you're on your own.'

'Gilbert Fox.'

'He's maybe holding an option, I don't know. Ronnie knows.'

'So you'll go with them? Ronnie and Fox?'

'And Doug Sanderson. And Peter Kleber.'

'Kleber too? He'll work with Fox?'

'It's business, Howie. It makes sense. Who you like doesn't come into it. Do you want to see this thing? I've got it here.'

'No,' he said, 'I don't. Leave me out. I'm going home.'

That's the way it comes to an end. That's the way your life comes crashing down. I cared too much about it, he thought.

He did not want to see anyone; took a room at the Glencoul; said, 'I'm not here. No calls.' He lay on the bed until the hills across the harbour had turned black. Then he ate in the restaurant, picked up an *Evening Post* and went back to his room. Darlene only half expected him – no need to phone. He watched the harbour again, the lights of cars moving in Eastbourne and Days Bay, and the few pin-pricks on the hills. We don't get far up in this town – although a necklace curve went up, the road to Wainuiomata. The road to nowhere, he thought. There's Auckland and Wellington and nowhere else. I should have been born in a bigger country.

He read about himself in the paper: his unavailability for comment. It bored him. Game-playing bored him. It was meat and drink to Ronnie, of course, and Fox and Kleber. Tony Dorio would learn it too. I'll set up something on my own, without them. I'll do it in Auckland, not this town. But Auckland would not come clear – a canyon street, a grey sprawl. Had he lost it too? He saw his tower in Lambton Quay, full of green light, and little streaks of red in it as the lifts went up.

The phone rang. 'Mr Peet, it's your wife calling from Auckland. Shall I put her on?'

'Howie,' Darlene said, 'are you all right?'

He told her not to worry, he'd had to stay the night and was so busy he had forgotten to call. There was nothing down here he couldn't handle. 'Don't say where I am. I don't want reporters hanging round. Just say I'm unavailable. I'll be back tomorrow.'

'Yes, Howie. Kiss, Howie?'

'Yeah, okay, kiss.' Hard to say. She gave a little half-laugh

243

and hung up. He did not seem to make her laugh any more.

He picked the paper up and rattled it as though to shake out something to distract himself with. Starvation. Massacre. He was dismayed. Found a murder – was struck, dizzied, by the name Peet jumping out.

They were seeking – who was seeking? – Brent Nelson Rosser, who might also have information regarding the attack six weeks ago on Mrs Ulla Peet in her home in Kelburn . . . the murder of Mrs Ponder was particularly savage . . .

So, Howie thought, they know who did it. They've taken their time, but now they know.

'A bizzare twist to the case,' he read, 'is that Mr Rosser was, until recently, a tenant in a house owned by Athco Properties, a company registered in the name of Athol Peet, Mrs Peet's husband. The police attach no real significance to this.'

Small towns, Howie thought. We don't have any cities, we have towns. The guy who kills your wife lives down the street. It seemed to make his tower more unreal. Athol's fifty houses were the scale. He folded the paper and left it in the chair; put his jacket on, went into the streets. It was half-past nine and dead: it might as well be Henderson on a Sunday night in 1946. They don't need me, Howie thought. They don't need that Beehive either, or the men inside – all they need is a few clerks to run this country. He went up Bowen Street and climbed the steps round the Commerce building – shaped like a liner, sailing where? The cemetery behind it gave a better idea of the town. He crossed the pedestrian bridge over the motorway, walked on gravel paths through more old graves – leaning headstones, lost half-names, Elizas and Thomases who had thought they were important once. The guy who murdered your wife, who chopped her up, might be sitting on a gravestone, drinking beer. That was how small it was. Why should I build them anything?

He climbed above the rose garden and the begonia house, where glass panels made a chessboard pattern, gleaming or dark; and looking over the city he suddenly found it huge: it shone, it pulsed, it stretched and climbed the hills, with pods pushing out, illuminated. It was like a box spilled; it was a box of jewels. He wanted his tower again, climbing up and shining,

244

with a thousand people inside. He could not understand how they had taken it from him.

The cable car went down, the wires hummed, and the city said it was alive – and that he had no part in it. He refused to let his sadness increase. It would reduce him, Howie Peet, to nothing at all. It was better to be angry, and be stupid. 'Keep your bloody city,' he said. And might have gone through the university and down the long steps to his hotel, but found Central Terrace opening like a mouth and went in there. A man ran by, blind behind his glasses: my son, he thought, Athol Peet. He ran with a shuffle, grown old. But he had had a shock today. The spade murderer had been one of his tenants. That would knock his faith in his houses out of him. Little houses, Howie thought, no safer than what I build. He watched Athol run away into the dark.

The houses on the high side stood half lit. The one he had lived in was no brighter than the rest. It had its gabled windows set too close, like a frown. Gwen had let it run down and lose value, but would say it didn't matter just as long as she was happy there. It was a home, not a house, she would say. But how did she feel, knowing that the murderer had prowled around in there? From the windows, Howie thought, you would have been able to see the top floors of my tower. It would have stood above the hill and been like a lighthouse – but it's gone, and I'm the only one who cares. She doesn't believe in high-rise buildings. How can you 'believe in' and 'not believe'? People can't live their lives like that. He wanted to go up the path, into the house, and argue with her. He had never hit Gwen, but knew that he might hit her tonight. He could have been a murderer coming off the street.

He watched her shadow in her upstairs room – furry, unformed – but he had years of knowledge to find her shape in it: her slanting face, her thin chest, and her schoolgirl arms behind her back, fingers like a typist, doing up her bra. 'All those years and I never saw you,' he said, 'but you kept on asking me to look into your mind.' Through her eyes, back there, was her mind. All it ever gave him were new words – should and shouldn't, is and ought. No one won. But was it, in the end, her victory, if he stood out here in the night and remembered, if he found a word of hers – elegiac – to explain? I don't know, he thought. She can laugh at Olivia growing beans on top of her dog. It evens out. You get tough, Gwen; I'll be sentimental. It'll only happen on the night when I lose Kitchener.

Athol ran out of the dark, like climbing from a pit. 'Dad' – panting, hands on knees – 'have you been at my place?'

'Just walking. Like you run. You didn't go far.'

'Did you see . . . did you see . . . ?'

'Get your breath.'

'Did you see about the police . . . identifying . . . ?'

'Yes, I saw.'

'He's the one who murdered that woman with the spade. And the worst thing – he's been living in one of my houses.'

'So the paper said.'

'They've sealed it. Sealed the room. His sister's been living there. She's a solo mother.'

'There's a lot of them around.'

'I met her.'

'Yeah?'

'They asked if I knew her before. They even thought . . . '

'You had something going?'

'It's crazy. I can't stand any more of this.' He opened the gate and went through.

Another one like Gordon, falling apart. 'You should have come in with me. You lost your chance, Athol,' Howie said.

'You haven't done so well.'

'I'm starting again. Not in this bloody town though. Up in Auckland.' Athol turned his back. He went up the path.

'With Damon when he's old enough. I'm keeping him,' Howie called. He held up his hand with two fingers locked together. 'Me and Damon, we're like that.'

He heard Athol open and close his door.

They're not my sons, he thought. How did I get them? He went past the university and down Allenby Terrace. Over there, a block away, the councillors had changed the rules today. He did not look in that direction, or turn his eyes along Lambton Quay. Went up in the lift, past the bar where maybe Ronnie Quested and Gil Fox, and Tony Dorio too, were talking, with their whiskies, with their malts, about shopping malls and PDQ, and how to ease the old man out. Old man, that's me. But he liked the name. Didn't it stand for toughness and experience? I'll start again in Auckland. And I'll train that boy. He can come in with me. By God I'll make sure that he doesn't grow up soft.

He drank some Johnny Walker.

The trouble is, I love him. That's the trouble, Howie thought.

He flew to Auckland in the morning and drove from the airport to his house on the cliff. The cream-brick fence, mown grass, hibiscus trees coming into flower seemed to be in another country, and Auckland was a new part of the world. The sun shone, the air was warm and still. This is where I'll stay from now on, I'll do it here. I'll show them who Howie Peet is. Howie and Damon, we're a team.

He put his car in the garage and keyed himself through doors into the house. White carpets, yellow mats, glass open wide, with the inside and the outside running together. The lawn sloping to the cliff was another carpet. He heard Damon and Darlene in the pool and walked down; patted the naiad's bottom; picked up a tennis ball and lobbed it into the court. He saw a dance of swimsuits, and bubbles, streaming hair. They were down there in the deep end, the boy turning round her like a shark. I'm home, he told them, come on up.

They rose together. Their faces broke the surface, flat as plates. They flashed their teeth at each other and Damon shouted, 'Hey, you got it.'

They saw Howie. They shone at him.

'Grandpa, she can do it. By herself. She got the stone.'

Darlene raised her hand and showed it fastened in her palm. They sank, and came up laughing.

'Surprise, Howie. Aren't we great?' she cried.

3

Fifteen

Ulla agreed to go to Auckland. She spent five months in the spinal unit, where Gwen visited her every few weeks. Damon went in the weekends, and Howie made a visit before he had his stroke. After that Darlene took to going in his place, but she and Ulla found almost nothing to talk about so Darlene waited in the car, reading a book, while Damon went in.

Ulla was a good patient. Everyone was pleased with her. 'I must not disappoint them,' she said. She talked about 'them', not about herself. With her brace off, her cheek healed, her hair growing longer, her face began to look like Ulla's again. She allowed Gwen to photograph her and send a print to Tomas. 'Ulla learning her wheelchair, Spinal Unit, May '92', Gwen printed on the back. Would Tomas see the stillness at the back of her smile? In the letter she wrote: 'She tries very hard, she's a very good patient, they're all pleased with her', but did not say, I'm afraid, Tomas, of what's going on in her mind. She's doing it for them not for herself.

If Gwen had said that to the head nurse or the doctor it would not have surprised them. Nothing a patient thought was new to them. They had made a science of understanding. She was impressed and appalled by the spinal unit. How valuable it was, what marvellous work – but what a foreign country, how invented it seemed. The language spoken there was like Esperanto. Ulla only pretended to know the words. She smiled, cooperated, but kept her own language in her head and spoke to no one in her proper tongue. Gwen was impressed and appalled by her too.

She had two white scars on her forehead, where the halo

brace had been fixed. They were like the lids trapdoor spiders built over their nests. If you lifted them and nothing came out, you might find your way to Sweden. That, Gwen was sure, was where Ulla spent her time. By the cold lakes. In the frozen city. She could not lift her face to the flower-scented breeze that blew in from the islands in the spring, but she widened her eyes, she opened her mouth and tasted it. Is that what you are doing?, Gwen wanted to ask, but was frightened her invasion, however gently made, might bring some glass structure crashing down. Instead she reported, made remarks, made Ulla laugh; and she watched. There was a busyness in Ulla, but it was invisible, like the busyness in a tree: everything still, but roots holding, nutrients passing, sap flowing through the branches into each leaf, and every leaf busily receiving from the sun. Such incessant taking in, such *function* in each cell. So Ulla's mind was busy with that still busyness, while her body lay in bed and the muscles wasted.

Home in Wellington, Gwen studied Sweden. If she could make a part of it her own then maybe she and Ulla would meet there. She borrowed books of photographs – castles, lakes, wheatfields, forests, Stockholm – and read a history of Sweden, where she found to her surprise that it had been a major power once, with armies laying waste to northern Europe and a king as hungry for conquest as any Alexander or Napoleon. That little land! Those nine million people. She had liked them better in longships, sacking churches. And she read novels – Moberg and Lagerlöf and Wästberg – and poetry, when she could find translations, and thrillers (enjoyed Sjöwall and Wahloo), and looked at *Pippi Longstocking* again. She went to Swedish movies and thought that she might learn the language that way, if there was time.

But most of all she looked at paintings. She climbed the stairs while Olivia was at school and studied the women in the sauna; saw the way their skin glowed, the gold of them, the soapiness of them, their warmth and blandness, one with a dipper, one kneeling in the tub, but felt their spirit too, a contained fierceness, feminine. The man, the painter, had not intended it, he would have had no knowledge of it. Again she resented him, and one day ventured a remark to Olivia, who laughed and said, 'But if no one was looking there wouldn't be a painting at all. I thought there had to be someone standing in the door.' Gwen was confused. She wondered if she were growing old. She had congratulated herself all her adult life on her mental largeness, but now found whole areas pinched and small. The women kept on glowing. They kept their warmth and calmness, they radiated invisibly. (And still the unseen man stood in the door.) She wanted to talk with Ulla about it, but never mentioned painting to her at all; tried simply to put her own knowledge on a plane that might intersect with Ulla's and lie flat with it in the end. She studied the white lakes and blue hills and the night skies filled with summer light – Swedish, Norwegian, Danish, it did not matter. The sea that drank whiteness from the sky, the stream that drank into its depths the brown trees and the snow and drank the viewer into itself too. Aware of the symbolic content – how could she not be? – she yet refused the meaning and asked the paintings simply to work on her as Sweden had worked on Ulla and informed her. If Ulla is going there, she thought, I want to go too.

Meanwhile there was Ulla's physical life. Understanding it was impossible. Physiotherapy, the pool, were pleasant no doubt after bed, although there was something kitcheny about the one and foetal about the other. But putting to work muscles that were unattached by consciousness was outside nature, it seemed to Gwen, and she had to admonish herself: you know nothing about it, you'll never know, so just let the people who do get on with it. Let them manipulate to clear Ulla's bowel and press her ribs to help her cough and check her skin for sores and dress the split in her natal cleft. All that will be yours soon enough, when she comes home. So get ready for it, get your head ready, or else you're going to be no use to her. But 'her', Ulla? Gwen began to see the body in the bed, even the body in the chair, as not having any part in that identity, even though the face was Ulla's all right, eyes and mouth and nose and ears and tongue. Ulla saw and heard, Ulla thought. Must she always drag that other part around?

Turn and lift and lever, rub and roll. 'I do not even have to cooperate,' Ulla said. 'It is like the next stage in evolution.'

253

'Is she really as calm as that or is she pretending?' Olivia said.

'A bit of each. She has to pretend.'

'She looks awful.'

'Well, the muscles waste. You can't hold your stomach in so you get a pot belly. We have to try to . . . ' Gwen shrugged.

'I'm talking about her face,' Olivia said. 'Where has she gone?'

'We'll never know. Places, I think, you and I can't go.'

'She wants to die, doesn't she?'

'In her situation she looks at all ways, I suppose. It's not that she doesn't love everyone still.'

'I'm not talking about love. I can remember that.'

'I can too.'

'If she wants to, I'll help her, if no one else will.'

'Oh no, Olivia, never say that. You're much too young.'

They came down steeply to avoid the wind and sideslipped on to the runway – a Wellington landing – and Gwen thought she would not take Olivia again, there were too many risks. They went home by taxi and lived around the carpenter and the plumber for two more weeks. Gwen had decided to do the painting herself, not to save money but to fill her days. She was quick and clean with brushes and paint, for which she must thank Howie. She had had Ulla's bedroom/living room – Ulla's room – lined with pine, tongue and groove, and she put two coats of clear varnish on, trying for a look that might be Swedish. The carpet had been taken up and the floor sanded. A new wood-burning space heater stood angled on a tile hearth in one corner. Ulla would be able to watch the flames. It would be, a little bit, like a sauna room.

Was all this a mistake? Was it interference?

Gwen tried to keep her life full of activities so she would have no time for brooding about Ulla. She stopped her yoga classes and began a transcendental meditation course, by mail. The mantra she was given disappointed her – it sounded like a deodorant – so she made up her own, monosyllabic, round and smooth, and managed several times to plummet down behind it, trailing bubbles, into a place where not a thought intruded and the mantra itself floated away like a sea creature and was lost. But mostly she found herself as troubled during meditation as before and after, and she gave it up, promising that she would do it properly one day, not by mail. There was too much to think about and no chance of resting yet.

Howie was a worry. She had not expected that he would take a place in her life again. 'It would be a real kindness if you would visit him. Damon would love to see you too,' Darlene wrote. A stroke, Gwen thought. How appropriate for Howie to be struck down instead of pinched and prodded to his death. But why couldn't it have been a clean blow, a knockout punch? Why must he sit in a chair, gargling for words that would not come, with his face enraged and purple? It was cruel. She looked back from the lower lawn, where she had strolled with Darlene. Wrapped in his mohair rug, he was like a child with the mumps. He had a dreadful simplicity. A word was all he wanted, but it never came through. Her name? Some single-syllabled declaration – of love, of regret, of pleasure in their lives? She wanted to know. But all he got out were sounds like the death cries in American comics.

'He's so angry all the time,' Darlene said. 'And yet if he could just say what he thinks, just a word or two, it would be enough. He'd be happy.'

'He's lucky he's got you,' Gwen said. Darlene was what her mother would have called 'a brick'.

'I try to make him happy. But the one he loves is there' – nodding at Damon on his trampoline. 'You'll let him stay, won't you, please, for as long as Howie . . . ?'

'It's up to his parents,' Gwen said. 'But I think you can be reasonably certain . . . ' She walked down to the cliff edge and looked at the gulf, with its yachts leaning over in the breeze and a container ship, made of blocks, turning in from the channel past North Head. She wondered how far Howie saw. Were his eyes affected? He sat, done up in wrappings, in his chair, a king up there above the shaven lawns, until you came close enough to see he was a cripple. Even from this distance his eyes were blue.

'You're standing right where it happened,' Darlene said.

'Here? His stroke?'

'I was playing tennis with Damon and Howie was sitting

255

up there having a whisky. I have to lob a lot, it's my fault I suppose, but if I don't I hardly win any points at all.'

'Yes?'

'I hit one and it went right over the wire and over the cliff. We only had two good balls so Damon said he'd get it and before I knew what he was doing he was out of the court and half way down the cliff.'

'Down there?' Gwen looked with horror at the sea and the rocks.

'I called at him not to go any further but he's so quick and agile and there's no danger, I suppose, with a boy as confident as that. Then Howie came. He'd seen it and he ran down the lawn. Oh Gwen, it was horrible. I could tell something had gone wrong. He couldn't call out or get his breath, he just watched Damon go out of sight – down there, where it bulges out and then cuts underneath. Damon says there's lots of handholds, but it looked as if he'd fallen. We couldn't see where he'd gone. Then Howie just – I don't know – I felt something give way in him and he fell over.'

Struck down by love, Gwen thought. She looked with tenderness at the figure in the chair. She felt as if he'd had a victory.

Darlene went on with her story, which finished with Damon climbing back, the tennis ball tucked in his shirt – Gwen could see him, eyes bright, hair upthrust by the wind – and with the ambulance and the hospital. Howie up there now was extraneous – his going on was a long unnecessary part, it unshaped his life. He should have died and not become a gargoyle in a chair, clawing at words he would never say. Gwen was close to weeping for him.

'What's that scar on his wrist that he rubs all the time?'

'I don't know. I asked him once, when it was all festery, and he just smiled and said a woman scratched him. You know Howie.'

I do, Gwen thought, and I don't. I never knew he could love so hard it would nearly kill him. Although I thought he might die in the act, on top of this nice woman I never thought I'd call Darlene.

She cupped his hot cheek – his Muldoon cheek – in her

palm. She kissed his brow and went away. Howie, she thought, I loved you once. I thought that you were going to set me free. But the thing I wanted to be free of was my own uncertainty. I didn't know it then. If I had, we wouldn't have hurt each other so badly. I would have said no and gone away. You thought I was class and you had to have me. And I thought . . .

What had she thought, in those unhappy times when her life had been all gropings out and shrinkings? Two drinks at a party (she who almost never drank and never went to parties) and she had glimpsed a largeness in the strange and loud young man. Wilfully she had turned after him, expecting that sighting, that near-vision, to return, but it never had. She married, expecting it, hoping to turn her life, that she recognised as cramped, turn it free. What a story! She had not been cramped at all, just turning in the narrow part of ways that would open out, and hurting herself there from impatience.

I might have been anything if I hadn't married him.

Again she flew home to Wellington. She prepared for Ulla – another sort of union and one that might demand from her the rest of her life. She had the room furnished with bed, slings, transfer board and wheelchair. Athol paid the bills without complaint. He came through the hedge from time to time and looked at the new room with puzzlement and distaste, but said nothing. Athol had been left far behind. He would never see Ulla again, although he might look in and say hallo. Might manage that. But look at her with understanding? Gwen believed it impossible.

'Athol,' she said, 'you're looking tired.'

'I don't sleep very well – but I'm all right.'

'Why don't you sleep?'

'My mind won't let me. I lie awake thinking about things.'

'What things?'

'That boy who lived in my house. And his sister. Everything that goes on – down there.'

'It's nothing new, Athol. Why have you just discovered it?'

'We don't have to know about it, do we? Surely we've earned the right. I've worked hard. I haven't touched it, why should it touch me?'

257

'I thought you wanted to help the girl?'

'I did. But *why*? I'm not the one responsible.'

And yet Brent Rosser and his sister, and Ulla too, had knocked all his faith in his houses out of him. The spade-murder was enough to knock one askew. But Athol had been so strong, so *pure*, a monk in his cell. He should have been able to hang on and not be forced out into the world, where he could only be confused. How pale he was, and lined, and hollow-chested, skinny in his wrists and throat; he was like an old man.

'Athol,' she said, and tried to take him in her arms, but he turned side on and sharpened his elbow.

'Don't, Mum. That's not what I need.'

Oh yes it is, Gwen thought, rubbing herself. You need pulling back from far away, though I can't be the one who does it. She wished that he would go away so she could cry for him.

'It's not fair to blame Ulla,' she said.

'I don't blame her. But somehow she connects us all and I can't stand that. I can't stand seeing her or thinking about her, Mum.'

'Then stay away. Just pay the bills.'

'I will, you needn't worry.'

'The children. Do you blame them too?'

'Of course not. I love them. But they seem . . . '

'Tainted?'

' . . . tainted with it.'

All she could do was send him away – through the hedge, back to his empty house – while crying silently, Athol, Athol, as though his name might save him. She did not know where he was or what he might go on to, just that he was lost, he was lost.

'Athol,' she said, the next time they met, 'go and see Gordon. He's only across in Mt Crawford. You can't behave as though he doesn't exist.'

'I went yesterday.'

'That's wonderful. How did he seem?'

'Happier than I thought he'd be. I'm not going again. We've got nothing to talk about.'

'Is he tainted too?'

258

Athol stepped back. 'If I say anything at all you turn it against me.' He walked stooping through the hedge. Whenever he left her now Gwen thought it might be the last time they would meet. They could have talked from window to window if they'd wished, yet he seemed more distant than Gordon, who was locked away on a hill out beyond the airport. Athol lost, Gordon found again: would that be the way it would stay until the end? For so long it had been Gordon lost, in those secret places where boys went – biological swamps, psychic recesses. Athol had seemed neatly to avoid them, through speed and agility and his youthful glowingness. How insufficient they had proved, while Gordon's painful sojourns had prepared him for survival. She was not any longer an expert on her sons but she thought she could identify Gordon as a survivor. Saw it in the way he had become practical. In the way he was present now and not always hoping and lip-chewing and getting his sideways look of bafflement and rage. He was no longer disappointed, not disappointed in himself.

'It's a great school, this' – meaning Mount Crawford. 'You should have sent me here when I was a boy. Look, cut my hand in the workshop. Four stitches' – said with pride. 'I'm going to do something with my hands when I come out. Be a gardener maybe. I'll come and clip your hedges free, how's that?'

That would be good. She would be glad to have him. She might even bring him in to smile at Olivia. There was an innocence in him that must be seen as hard-won after the muddy turnings, the ambitions, of his life. Olivia seemed open to plain ways. (Was even talking of leaving Marsden and going to Wellington High.) She might bring him in to visit Ulla.

'When do you qualify for weekend leave?'

'I'm not sure I want it. What you can do, Mum, is bring me some books. Gardening. I don't mean vegetables though. Trees and shrubs. Get it okayed with the governor.'

'Ulla's coming down next week. I've hired a nurse.'

'Maybe I should train for that. Be a nurse, maybe.'

It did not surprise her that he was self-centred – self-fascinated. It was the likely consequence of so great a turning round in his life. She might smile and laugh with him, even embrace, but she doubted that they would now grow close.

'Poor old Pop, eh. The poor old sod.' That was all he could find to say about Howie. Still, his smile was natural and made her feel warm.

'Goodbye, Gordon. I'll come again soon.'

'Bring those books.'

She went home and mowed her lawns and felt guilty about the dried grass pasted on the blades. Gordon would not be pleased with that. But Ulla's room excited her – its apparatus suggesting there were things that one might *do*, and its varnished brightness, the clean timber, the books – selected books – in shelves low enough for Ulla to read the spines from her chair. If she sat in the window bay a view of the harbour and the mountains would open up.

The nurse, Lorraine Sealy, was businesslike and middle aged. She gave one confidence. Gwen described her so at the spinal unit and was encouraged by the approval everyone felt. Lorraine had nursed 'quads' before and would be happy to train Gwen on the job – Olivia too. 'It's largely a matter of being practical and positive and persistent. I call those my three Ps.'

'Persistent?' Gwen said.

'I mean,' Lorraine said, 'that every part of a routine must be carried through. No matter how uncomfortable it may seem. If you neglect some little thing it will be the patient who suffers in the end. A day has to be very structured. Don't worry, Mrs Peet, it's not as heartless as it sounds. One must never lose sight of the person in there.'

'The fourth P.'

'Exactly.'

She might, Gwen thought, be very good. She might be horrible. In the meantime, one pretended confidence.

'She will not want to be my friend, I hope,' Ulla said.

'I think she's too professional for that.' Another P. And didn't 'persistent' imply that Lorraine Sealy expected Ulla not to cooperate? Things would be done to her for her own good.

By the time Ulla flew down, Gwen was nervous. A crane lowered her from the back door of the plane. The queen might travel so, enthroned. They kissed her on the tarmac, Gwen and Olivia, and the nurse who had travelled with her handed the case notes to Lorraine. An ambulance took Ulla home to the house that might be described now as a sjukhus. Gwen tried to see how it might look to Ulla as her home. How Lorraine Sealy might look, as her nurse. And she, Gwen, as friend. A sense of bleakness fell on her. Ulla's smile, no more than a crooking at the corners of her mouth, said, This will do. It said, I'm not here anyway.

'Now,' Lorraine Sealy said, 'we'll try out this bed.'

They tried it out, using the sling to make the transfer. Then they stood around and looked at Ulla. So this is it, Gwen thought, this is what we do. She wheeled the chair into a corner of the room. 'I'll make a cup of tea. Can you drink tea?' she asked Ulla.

'Oh yes, I do all the usual things.'

Is it really going to be like this for the rest of our lives? She filled the kettle and put it on, wondering where to hide.

But as the days went by she found she was with Ulla more and more, reading to her, wheeling her about the ground floor and down the new ramp into the garden. She did much of her housework with Ulla sitting by. She learned to wash and massage her and search her body for places where pressure sores might start. She helped her on and off the commode. Took her temperature, gave her pills. Fed her. Helped her swallow, helped her cough. Once or twice she cleared her bowel, using a rubber glove. It troubled her not to be troubled by it. She felt that she was losing sight of Ulla. Lorraine, who did most of it – and well and unobtrusively – seemed more alert to Ulla's moods than she. Gwen was glad to see her go at the end of the day. She looked forward to the weekends, when Lorraine was off.

'I'll share the nights,' Olivia said.

'There's nothing to share.' She set her quiet alarm for half-past two and padded down and shifted Ulla – changed the pressure points with a heave. Olivia need not be troubled with it. Fifteen-year-olds needed their sleep. She gave Ulla a sip of water and went back to bed. It was not hard. She wished that Ulla would hold her sometimes, with a demand. Hold her with the turning of an eye. It was too easy. Did Ulla lie awake when she was gone, having a life in her head? This doing all the time, this turning, feeding, easing, made a surface they skated on.

When was Ulla going to look at her and talk to her?

One afternoon she answered the door and found Franklin, the police inspector, standing with his back to her, looking at the view.

'A nice place you've got here, Mrs Peet. An outlook like that can't be bought with money.'

In fact, it can, she wanted to say. 'Do you want to come in?'

'If you don't mind. I won't take much of your time.' He had not been so friendly before.

'Has something happened? Something new?' She led him to the kitchen. He looked out the open door at Ulla's ramp to the garden.

'Changes here.'

'Yes. Ulla's been home from Auckland almost a month. We've turned the front room into her room.'

'How is she?'

'No different. Is it her or me you want to see?'

'I've got something I'd like you to identify, Mrs Peet.' He took an envelope from his pocket and tipped a ring on to his palm. She recognised it at once.

'My wedding ring.' Took it, turned it, slipped it on her finger. 'Where did you find it?'

Franklin made a small forward movement of alarm.

'You don't want me to put it on?' She grew alarmed herself and found the ring easy to pull off. Her fingers had lost flesh, perhaps from work.

'Do I keep it? Do you want it back?'

'You're positive it's yours? No mistake?'

'Oh it's mine all right. You can't wear a ring for forty years. Where did you get it?'

He took it and dropped it back in the envelope. 'From a man. The body of a man.'

'Body?'

'I'm afraid so, Mrs Peet. He was wearing it.'

'My ring? Who was – how did he die?'

'I don't have a report yet. The truth is, he's been dead for a long time.'

'How long?'

'About seven months. I'm sorry this is so unpleasant for you.'

Her sickness was more mental than physical, although she felt a burning in her throat.

'Here, sit down,' Franklin said.

'I'm all right. Was it the man – was it Brent Rosser?'

'Yes.'

'Where?'

'Some movers found him. They were shifting some of the second-hand stuff in Mrs Ponder's yard. One of them opened a freezer and there he was.'

'Freezer?'

'It wasn't switched on. The body was badly decomposed, after so long.'

'Wearing my ring? Did someone put him there?'

'We don't think so, Mrs Peet. He got in by himself.'

'And got locked in? He suffocated?'

'There were no marks as if he was trying to get out. We think he probably just went off to sleep.'

'Why though? Why?'

'He could have been hiding. We were getting close to him in your son's house. Anyway, Mrs Peet, I guess it's all over. We're not looking for anyone now – '

'It's not all over.'

'I can see what you mean – '

'A dead man wearing my ring. How can it be all over for me?'

'Well – '

'And Ulla lying there for the rest of her life?'

'I'm sorry, Mrs Peet.'

'Why would he go there after killing Mrs Ponder? Wouldn't you have had policemen there?'

'Yes, we did. We had a man. But we locked it up and sealed it probably just before he turned up. There wasn't any need any more. And then no one took much notice of the stuff. It was basically a junk shop, Mrs Peet. And the estate took time, it wasn't easy. In fact the business was legitimate. It was in her house out in the Hutt we found the stolen stuff.'

'Was she as rich as everyone says?'

'Yes, she was.'

'All from stolen property?'

'Most of it. But that doesn't mean . . . Rosser doesn't deserve any pity, Mrs Peet. It was the worst murder I've ever seen. As well as that, your daughter-in-law . . . ' he gestured at Ulla's room. 'Anyway, I've got to go. Do you want this ring back when we've finished with it?'

'No. God no. Put it in the police museum or something.'

She showed him to the door. 'My regards to the other Mrs Peet,' Franklin said.

She watched him go down the path through the agapanthus; heard him open her gate and fiddle with the catch to make it shut. He drove away. Cold clouds locked in the city, but he seemed to have gone down into some sort of freedom, leaving her in the house that puffed its air out like a smell of decomposition. Thick air at her back and hot rooms and conversations tangled like wool and yet so simple – lying and simple – and in there now, and in her head, images that might become obsessive.

She stepped on to the porch and closed the door. She went down the steps and up the side path – down, up, angle, turn, as though she might escape by geometry. She took her trowel from the bench in the glasshouse and crossed the lawn and started weeding the garden, although in mid-winter it made no sense. She was wearing her slippers too, how absurd. The damp grass made the soles spongy. She felt her socks grow wet, but she kept on, loosening weeds, knocking the soil from their roots and laying them on the edge of the lawn to pick up later. A fine drizzle wet her hair and shoulders. It would make a bride's cap on her hair and she would be wed perhaps to that boy who had died in the freezer. In the freezer. She made a caw of horror and amazement. And here she was weeding over the dog, dead for the same number of months, and she must dig shallow so as not to disturb his bones. A bracelet of bright hair about the bone. Such lovely words, from where? Such comforting transcendence. They would not rid her of this latest death.

'What are you doing, Gwen?' Olivia cried. She stood on the back path in her Marsden green, looking grown-up. 'You'll get soaked. Come inside at once.'

Gwen did not want such adult language from the girl. How careless of her to provoke it. 'Yes,' she said, 'it is a bit too wet. Another day,' and she ran across the lawn and took her slippers off at the back steps. 'These are ruined.' She dropped them in the rubbish tin. 'I'll have to buy a new pair.' She shook the drizzle from her hair. 'Had a good day, love? Anything sensational at school?'

'What were you doing out in the rain like that?'

'It's not really rain, is it? I got tired of the house. I should have put my gumboots and parka on.'

'Is something wrong with Mum?'

'No, dear, or else I wouldn't be outside, would I? Come on, you need to change too. We can't go getting colds, not with Ulla.'

She showered and put on dry clothes and a pair of soft shoes. When Lorraine had left she said, 'Come in here, Olivia. I've got something to tell Ulla and you.' She did not want them hearing it on the TV news.

'Something new?' Ulla said. 'I don't know if I can stand it.'

'You're as tough as old boots,' Gwen said. But she breathed deep and stilled her face. It was not for joking about.

'Is it Grandpa?' Olivia said.

'No, not him. I had a visit from Inspector Franklin.'

'I thought I heard his voice,' Ulla said.

'He brought my wedding ring for me to identify. Brent Rosser had it.'

'Does that mean they've got him?' Olivia said.

'No, love, it means they found his body. Brent Rosser's dead.'

She told them the facts of it, keeping her feelings under control. Olivia matched her for stillness.

'So,' she breathed, 'all that time . . .'

'Yes.'

'I'm not going to say what I think.'

'Not if you don't want to.'

'Is that the end of it, though?'

It did not end as though it were a happening or event. 'As far as it can be,' Gwen said. Each of them would end it by a death, but it might be unimportant by that time, like a scar on

265

the body, seen only when you twisted your head or looked at some odd angle in the mirror. Unimportant for Olivia. She had the time. It seemed that she had the toughness too. Not for Ulla though. Not for herself.

Ulla had closed her eyes. She did not open them until Olivia had gone.

'He died from suffocation?' she said.

'Inspector Franklin said it looked as if he went to sleep. I don't know. They can't really tell. There mightn't have been any . . . ' Horror? Pain? There were no fingernail scratches on the inside of the lid.

Ulla closed her eyes again. 'What a strange sad life.'

'Do you want to talk about him?'

'No.'

'We can if you like.'

'I want to think about him for a while.'

'Yes. All right.'

Gwen helped Olivia make dinner, and could not understand, could not make her own mind work at all. The thinking that Ulla might do was unknowable – it was like a country locked in behind high mountains, it was Lapland or Tibet. I can never go there, Gwen thought. You need to lose your body, and then . . . The brain had a changing structure, wasn't that the theory, the latest one? It laid down new pathways, neural pathways, in response to its own experience. And Ulla had that, her brain had that: new special private experience, and new mind pathways, along which Brent Rosser, it seemed, might find his way . . . Gwen understood the silliness of her Swedish studies. Mystic landscape, mystic north? Ulla had passed through and gone somewhere else.

She heard Athol arrive home and she gave him five minutes before she rang.

'Athol, I'm not sure if you've heard the thing that's happened – '

'I have,' he said.

'I had a visit from Inspector Franklin – '

'I know all about it. And I've told you, Mum, it's not my business. I'm not having anything to do with it any more.'

'Athol – '

266

'I'm not even going to talk about it. So stop ringing me. Goodnight.' He hung up.

And that, she thought, is how you step backwards out of life. Into your little mock-universe, about which you know everything. But it was spoiled for him; it had been invaded and he would find no safety there. One day he must come into the real world again. Athol, it will be different here by the time you come back. Ulla won't be alive any more.

She ate with Olivia, then fed Ulla. She sat with them both, watching Inspector Wexford on TV. Corpses there too, though none wearing wedding rings on decomposed fingers.

'And always the answer,' Ulla said.

'Yes.'

'How well the British act, though. They never say it wrong.'

Later Gwen read to her. 'What would you like?'

'*Aftonland*. The first ones.'

'You can say those by yourself.'

'I like to hear your voice, Gwen. I like someone with me.'

Gwen read, and stopped. 'These are too sad.'

'No, go on. They are not sad.'

' "Some day you will be one of those who lived long ago." Well, it's a marvellous first line; and last line too. "Your peace shall be as unending as that of the sea." '

'He doesn't quite prove it,' Ulla said. 'But it is nice to think. Read the next.'

' "All is there, only I am no more,
all is still there, the fragrance of rain in the grass
as I remember it, and the sough of wind in the trees,
the flight of the clouds and the disquiet of the human heart.
Only my heart's disquiet is no longer there."

'Now you say it in Swedish.'

And when Ulla had finished: 'Oh, that's good. I believe it in Swedish.'

'That is because the last word is 'längre'. You believe the sound of it.'

They talked, and read, and seemed to be saying things that carried an understanding . . . What was it? Just that they had met each other again? And need not speak, for there was nothing yet that they could put in so many words: This is what I must do, and you must do that?

'Are you saying you forgive him now?' Gwen asked, when they talked of Brent Rosser.

'No,' Ulla said. 'How can I when he was so careless with my life? But there he is, and we can't understand, and so we have to leave him in peace.'

'It's not easy.'

'For our sake, not his. We can't let him say how we go on.'

'But you've thought about him?'

'Let's not talk, Gwen. No more tonight. I think I can sleep now if I try.'

Gwen made her comfortable. 'Ulla love, I want you to know that I'll do whatever you want. I'll be your hands.'

'Yes, I know. It will be hard. Hard for you.'

'I don't mind.' She kissed Ulla on the mouth and went away. She sat on the back porch in the dark, with her fingers folded, and watched the moon, lopsided in the sky, and black clouds rolling up over the northern hills. A cold breeze, not unfriendly, blew about her cheeks and in her hair. She would know peace; a few months, or weeks perhaps, of peace, living with Olivia and Ulla. Then she would do as Ulla asked, and be the hands Ulla did not have. And whether she went on then, or stopped, did not matter. Prison perhaps? It did not matter. In giving herself to Ulla she took possession of her self, which she had been estranged from for so long. Estranged? She had never possessed it at all; had possessed only pieces – an interest here, a passion there, enthusiasm for a theory, a technique, some of which had led her to quietness for a while. Now, it seemed, she had her self; had interest, passion, quietness, all in one.

So, Gwen thought, I'll sit here on my steps and be happy tonight. How lovely it is, surrounded by the darkness, surrounded by the wind: me, Gwen Peet, sitting here alone.

Several weeks later she said to Olivia, 'Does that new licence of yours let you drive with a passenger?'

'If it's an adult.'

'Can you take the afternoon off school and drive me somewhere then?'

Ulla had given Olivia her car. The girl drove with care, nervously, down Glenmore Street and Tinakori Road.

'I still have to look down when I change gear.'

'You'll get the hang of it. Relax.'

'Are we going to Wainuiomata because Brent Rosser lived there?'

'Yes.'

'I'm not going in. I don't want to talk to them.'

'I don't either. I just want to see.'

'How do you know the address?'

'I looked up Rosser in the phone book. It's not a very common name.'

They went along the Hutt Road and over the hill.

'It's like a country town,' Olivia said.

'That's what it is. It doesn't really have much to do with Wellington.' She had a street map open on her knee and directed Olivia left and right. 'That one. Where the woman's going in with the pushchair.'

'Won't she see us?'

'There's a notice on the gate, see? Broccoli. I think I'll buy some.'

The woman had lifted her child out of the pushchair and was following him slowly up the path. Gwen opened the gate.

'Excuse me.'

'Yeah?'

'Do you sell broccoli?'

'Yeah, we do. Dollar-fifty a head.'

'I'll take two, I think. Is it nice?'

'My old man grew it. Sure it's nice.'

She was the woman who had lived in Athol's house: Brent Rosser's sister. Gwen had not expected to find her here. She had a birdy, beady face, pretty in a sharp-boned way: sharp enough to cut.

'I'll have to get it from around the back.'

'Leave your little boy. I can watch him.'

'He opens the catch. He'll be out on the road before you know it.'

'I'll be careful.'

What would she say if I told her my name? Your brother crippled my daughter-in-law, I could say. But she felt that the woman would simply look at her child and find her answer there. The child had probably answered Brent Rosser's death. A Maori child – or Islander perhaps. And out of wedlock, almost certainly. I could ask Inspector Franklin to give her my wedding ring. Legitimise him, wouldn't that be nice?

She lifted the child away from the gate and stood him on the lawn. 'There, run around there.'

The house was white, with green sills and a green door. A rowanberry tree grew on the lawn and borders of impatiens lined the path. Everything was clean and colourful. It was snobbish of her to be surprised.

The child took two handfuls of flowers. He looked at her, a challenge, and pulled them out.

'Good boy. Does your mummy smack? I'll bet she does.'

But the woman only made a face at him when she came back. She gave Gwen the broccoli heads, wrapped in newspaper like giant flowers.

'Nice enough for you?' said with an edge.

'They're beautiful.'

'Three dollars.'

Gwen paid. 'Your little boy is beautiful too.'

'Yeah, he's great. He's really going places.' She smiled with backward-sloping teeth, but looked more sunny than sharkish.

'What is he, I can't tell? Is he . . . ?'

'Samoan.'

'Oh, I see.'

'Any objection?'

'No, of course. It makes him look so – lovely.' Look after him, she wanted to say. Don't let him get like Brent. 'Goodbye. Thank you for these.'

'Thank my old man.'

In the car, Olivia said, 'Was that Brent Rosser's sister?'

'Yes, I think so.'

'She looked all right. Is she the one you wanted to see?'

'I didn't want to see anyone in particular. I just wanted to know . . . ' That people who had been in it, in the crippling, in

270

the deaths, on the other side, were going on. The way Olivia was going on – although it wasn't over for her yet.

'We'll stop in Petone and get some fish and chips.'

They ate them on the waterfront, sitting in the car, then walked to the end of Petone wharf.

'See out there,' Gwen said, 'that little island just off Somes Island. They put a Chinaman on there once, in the early days. They thought he had leprosy so they just left him there.'

'That's cruel!'

'They gave him food. They sent it across from Somes Island on a pulley. He lived in a hut there until he died.'

She looked past the islands to the harbour mouth. White waves were breaking on the rocks of Barretts Reef. Wellington was dangerous to get into – and dangerous once you were inside.

'We'd better get home.'

Olivia made no move. She had her head down. Was she crying? 'Mum can still joke, you know?' she said.

'Yes, she's managed to keep her sense of humour.'

'I was telling her about the new computers at school and she said, "My hardware's gone. All I am is software now."'

'That's very clever.'

Olivia peered down into the water. 'Little fish.'

'See them flash.'

'She wants to die soon, doesn't she?'

'Yes, she does.'

'Do you think it's right? Has she got the right?'

'I think she has.'

'Has she got the right to ask someone to help her?'

'Not you, Olivia. I've given her the right to ask me.'

'Will it be like that man in Christchurch, helping his friend to die?'

'Something like that.'

'Lorraine won't let you. She's a Christian.'

'Lorraine won't know.'

'See the fish again. Millions now. How will you do it? What stuff?'

'We're saving up. It mightn't be for quite a while yet.'

'Could she change her mind?'

271

'She might. But I don't think so. She wants to talk to you first. And Damon.'

'I don't want to go away. I want to be in the house.'

They walked back along the wharf. The winter sun sank towards the hills. Traffic ran in unbroken lines on the waterfront road.

'Can you drive in all these cars?' Gwen said.

'Yes, I've got to learn.'

She waited, and saw a place and slipped into it. They drove back through town and up to Kelburn.

The city hummed around them and the early lights went on.